the perfect life

Erin Noelle

The Perfect Life
© 2016 Erin Noelle

Cover Design by
Hang Le

Editing by
Kayla Robichaux

Proofing by
Jennifer Van Wyk & Jill Sava

Interior Design and Formatting by
Christine Borgford, Perfectly Publishable

For those who think it's greener on the other side . . . it's really just a field full of pretty weeds growing out of cow shit.

prologue

THE YOUNG MAN instructed the taxi driver to pull over at the curb near the intersection of Beacon and Charles, a popular tourist area that encompassed Boston Common, Public Garden, the bar where *Cheers* had been filmed, and a handful of other attractions all within a fifteen minute walk of each other. After paying for the ride, he exited the yellow four-door sedan into the frigid New England night, pulling his dark hoodie over his head to block the wind and any possible lingering glances from passersby.

Slinking away from the busy street and into the shadows of the sidewalk, he hoisted the strap of a small charcoal bag up high onto his shoulder while moving swiftly, north on Charles St. and away from the crowds of sightseers. Despite the fact it was almost midnight on a Sunday, people were still out and about at the pubs and bars celebrating the New England Patriots' win in the AFC Championship game that evening. The man, however, had no interest in post-game festivities. Completely focused on his mission, if he proved successful and the opportunity turned out to be what was promised, he'd not only be collecting a substantial sum of cash, but, most likely, it'd be the opening he needed to do bigger and better things in his career. And for that reason alone, he vowed not to fail.

With long strides in his faded black jeans that matched the rest of his night-camouflaged outfit, he quickly approached Chestnut St., where his assignment was located. Again falling back out of sight, he scanned the area a full three-hundred-and-sixty degrees—twice—before silently declaring the perimeter safe. He made a sharp right turn behind the eight-foot hedges that followed along the back property line of the row of upscale townhomes and then crouched down, advancing with ninja-like stealth against the hard, icy branches and foliage.

Approximately eighty yards deep, he slowed his movements and began searching for the cut-out he was ensured would be there by the anonymous tip he'd received. Fortunately, within a matter of seconds, he found the small, round hole in the bushes that was specifically positioned low to the ground, where most people would never notice it. He pulled a camera body and a Nikon midrange lens out of the bag and fused them together with lightning-fast speed, an action so natural to him he could do it with his eyes closed.

He dropped to his stomach and army-crawled forward through the wet snow as he brought the viewfinder up to his eye. Pointing the expensive lens through the opening in the shrubbery, he twisted the focusing ring back and forth until he could see clearly through the glass French patio doors and into the softly-lit living room of the house.

Timing was always key when he worked; encapsulating transient moments into a single frame in a way that told a thousand-word story was a true art. But this time, it was even more imperative than normal. Not only could he not get caught, but there was no guarantee the subjects would be engaging in the manner that he needed. The old adage 'You can lead a horse to water, but can't make them drink' had never been truer, and it was by sheer luck the image that greeted him was exactly what he'd hoped for. The money shot.

A wicked smile spread across his face as he pressed and held the shutter button, capturing a multitude of photographs one right after another. A familiar, beautiful blonde woman. A rugged, dark-haired man with a grizzly beard. Kissing passionately. Touching sensually. Losing their clothes. Tangling in each other. The scene played out in front of the camera like one of those flip-books coming to life. This one published by *Penthouse*. Even with his unwavering concentration on the job at hand, the man found the carnal acts between the woman he photographed on a regular basis and her unknown partner highly arousing, and he planned to save the pictures for his personal use later.

The high-pitched yap of a dog broke through the silence of the night, and the man cursed under his breath as the zealous couple abruptly stopped their erotic exchange and turned their attention to the small backyard. *Fucking mutt.* He snapped several more rapid shots without even looking through the viewfinder before he inched away from the hole. Then, swiftly shoving the camera and lens back into the bag, he fled the scene without being detected.

Catching a cab back to his apartment, the man wasted no time uploading the memory card to his laptop and shuffling through the images until he found the most incriminating ones, including a perfectly-in-focus shot of their faces, proving their identity. *Maybe I should've been thanking that dog instead of wishing it dead,* he thought. He did some minor touch-ups to the photos, fixing the clarity and adjusting the intensity of the shadows, and once he was satisfied, he emailed the pictures off with a smug grin.

Lives would be destroyed.

Relationships broken.

And he didn't care one bit, as long as he reaped the rewards.

chapter
one

"The purpose of
life is not to
just be happy.
The purpose of life,
my love,
is to feel.
You must understand
that your pain,
is essential."
–Christopher Poindexter

Five months earlier
MONROE

"REMIND ME AGAIN why we're doing this." I sucked in my abdomen and rolled my shoulders back as Colin tugged the zipper of the pale blue designer evening gown over my hips and halfway up my spine to where the silky fabric ended.

My husband chuckled and bent down to brush his lips over the delicate skin just below my ear, our matching emerald gazes locking in the full-length mirror that hung in my spacious walk-in closet. "For the kids, Roe." His proud smile spread so wide that his eyes crinkled at the corners. "You do it, because you love the kids more than anything else."

I blew the held breath out through my painted red lips and

leaned my head back to rest on his tuxedo-clad chest. "You're so right."

My mouth curled up at the edges in a playful grin as I twirled around to face the real him instead of his reflection. Raising up on my tiptoes, I straightened his bowtie then affectionately tapped my finger on the tip of his nose. Even when I was wearing heels, Colin towered over me with his substantial six-foot-six stature. Although he often appeared thin when compared to the colossal offensive linemen who protected him on the football field, his shoulders were quite broad, and when I stood next to him he made me feel petite and very feminine.

"I do love those little monsters like nobody's business," I admitted with a snicker, "but I just wish we could've had a casual afternoon barbeque to gain sponsorship for the house, rather than a fancy-shmancy, high-society gala. I'm sure most of the guys aren't too thrilled to be spending a Saturday night in an uncomfortable tux, making small talk with uptight Boston socialites while having a string quartet for a soundtrack."

"They don't mind at all," he assured me, his expression one-hundred-percent sincere. "Especially since everyone's in a good mood, now that we wrapped up our preseason Thursday night with another win. Plus, I'm not sure a midday picnic at the Common would've brought in the same kind of money that a black-tie affair at The State Room will."

I sighed and looked away, still tense about the evening to come.

"Stop worrying so much, sweetie," he reassured me. "This money is all going toward the kids. Every single penny. Tonight is about you, your dream, and bringing a Mending Hearts house to Boston. My old town. Your new town. Now our *home*town. We wanted to make a difference, and this is our chance."

Colin gently held my arms just above my elbows and leaned down to stare at me straight in the eyes, his brows lifted high into his forehead as he continued talking. "I know these things aren't easy for you, but this isn't about meaningless movie premieres and red-carpet-rich-people rendezvous. This is *real*. These kids need people to fight for them . . ." He trailed off and skimmed both of his hands across my bare shoulders and up the sides of my neck until he cradled my jaw. I heard the unspoken words "just like you needed someone, but didn't have" plain as day, but his tender lips would've never been so harsh when speaking to me. "And we're those people, Roe. You and me. We're a team. To the very end."

"To the very end," I repeated the four words we'd both concluded our handwritten wedding vows with. It had been our mantra ever since. The words that our entire relationship was built around.

His boyish smile returned as he pressed his lips to the top of my head. "The car will be here in ten minutes. I'm gonna make a quick phone call in my office, and then I'll meet you downstairs. I promise I won't leave your side all night, gorgeous. Not even when everyone tries to steal you away from me."

He gave me a final chaste kiss on the cheek before striding out of my closet. Watching him with an overwhelming sense of appreciation and affection, I said a quick *thank you* up to the heavens above for blessing me with such an incredibly understanding man in my life, then pushed back my own personal anxieties and fears to focus my thoughts and energy on the important aspect of the evening. *The kids.* If everything went well, the money that was raised could provide the rest of the funding we needed to get the children's home up and running. I'd been working for over a year to make this dream a reality, and I was eager to finally be able to see it all come to fruition.

And once that happened, every single second in the too-tight strapless bra and toe-pinching stilettos would be worth it. Boring music and all.

THE LIMO DOOR opened and we were immediately greeted by an onslaught of flashes from the multitude of cameras lining the roped-off, red-carpeted walkway. Colin grabbed my hand and helped me gracefully exit the backseat of the car as paparazzi called out our names so we'd pose for their shot. We both smiled and waved, genuine in our regard for those who'd come out to give our important event some runtime in the press. I greeted several of the familiar local photographers and columnists as we stopped to take a few pictures, and I loved how their eyes would light up when I remembered their names. Making other people feel special always made me feel good.

Before I knew it, we were ushered inside the downtown Boston skyscraper and whisked up the elevator to the top floor of the Sixty State Street building, where the First Annual New England Mending Hearts Gala was in full swing. All of the men were dressed similarly to Colin—in black and white tuxes—though none looked quite as dapper as my unbelievably handsome husband, while the women sparkled and glittered in their formal attire, the elegant dresses spanning the entire color spectrum from snowy white to onyx black and every shade in between.

Classical music floated lightly through the air as I scanned the massive, contemporary space, which was tastefully decorated in an array of blues—the color used worldwide to represent child abuse awareness, hence the reason for my own gown's hue. Guests mixed and mingled with easy conversation and sincere smiles. Some chose to find comfort at the tables and chairs expertly positioned around the room, while others opted to stay on their feet, most of them flocking toward the floor-to-ceiling windows that provided a panoramic view of the skyline and harbor. I couldn't blame them much, though. The spectacular backdrop was the main reason I'd selected this venue over the others I'd toured. It was absolutely awe-inspiring.

"Ma'am, can I interest you in a grilled scallop wrapped in prosciutto?" I hadn't even noticed anyone approach while completing my thorough inspection, but the deep voice jolted me from my thoughts as he extended the silver tray filled with delicious-looking hors d'oeuvres.

I replied with a friendly nod and a "Yes, thank you," as he handed me one of the finger foods on a small napkin, and then watched as he repeated the action with Colin. Before I even had a chance to swallow down the savory treat, a cocktail waitress appeared to offer us both a glass of wine, which I gladly accepted, but as usual, Colin declined. In the seven years we'd known each other, the only time I ever saw him drink alcohol was at our wedding reception, and even then, it was only a single glass of champagne during the toasts. My man treated his body and mind like a temple, and with his openness about his spirituality, he never wanted to be seen indulging in any activity that could be construed as damaging or immoral.

"It looks amazing, Roe," Colin murmured in my ear as he laced the fingers of his right hand through my free one, slowly guiding us away from the entrance and toward the heart of the party. "I knew you'd put together something great, but this . . . wow, you've completely outdone yourself."

"Thank you." I beamed up at him, my cheeks lifting so high I could see them in the lower portion of my line of sight. "I've been obsessing about it so long, I was starting to wonder if perhaps I'd overthought the whole thing. But now that I see it all come together . . . I'm really glad we didn't do that picnic."

Laughter rumbled so deep in his chest that the vibrations resonated through our interlocked hands and warmth bloomed inside me. There was nothing better than the sound of Colin Cassidy's unbridled mirth, especially when something I did or said was what caused it. Unfortunately, I wasn't able to try and make him do it again before we were noticed by a small group of partygoers and were swallowed up by enthusiastic greetings and introductions for the next half-hour.

After making our way through the first throng of gracious guests, I finally spotted Allison Northcutt, the one woman I'd been searching for since we arrived, talking to several people close to the area roped off for the silent auction. She was my closest female friend, my life mentor, and my soon-to-be new boss. And other than Colin, she was the person I trusted most in the entire world.

My entire body relaxed the moment her gaze found mine and she smiled brightly, lifting her arm in the air to beckon us over. Squeezing Colin's hand, I tugged him in her direction and made a beeline to where she stood.

"Monroe, love, you're absolutely gorgeous!" she exclaimed as I unwound my fingers from my husband's grip and received her in a tight embrace. After releasing me, she moved her warm, inviting arms to Colin's neck, having to nearly jump up to hug him. "And you, young man, grow more handsome each time I see you. It appears life in Boston is treating you both well."

"It truly is. We love it here. And speaking of gorgeous . . ." I paused to blatantly allow my eyes to drift up and down her classy sapphire gown. "Look at you! That dress is stunning, and you chopped off all your hair since I was in Detroit a couple of months ago. It frames your face perfectly."

I reached up and smoothed my hand over her brunette bob, admiring the sophisticated cut. Allison may have been twenty years my senior, but ever since I met her my freshman year of college, she'd always seemed so youthful and energetic—both in appearance and spirit—that I never thought of her as being that much older than me. From the moment I first walked into the original Mending Hearts house in Detroit that Thanksgiving Day almost seven years ago, introducing myself and expressing my desire to volunteer, she and I had hit it off immediately. Our relationship had always been a well-balanced combination of professional and personal respect.

"Thank you, my dear, but enough about me." She waved her hand in front of her face, humbly passing off my compliment. "Tonight is your night, and I've got some people I'd like you to meet. I know you're familiar with all of the members of the Board of Directors from your undergrad days with me in Michigan, but I don't believe you've met any of the staff from the Chicago house yet since it kicked off right about the time you guys moved here. Have you?"

"No, I haven't." I smiled politely as I glanced over to the trio Allison had been talking to before Colin and I approached, waiting patiently off to the side. She motioned for them to join us and smoothly began the introductions.

"Monroe and Colin Cassidy," her eyes shone with delight as

they bounced back and forth between us and them, "this is Jeff and Tracie Long." She tilted her head in the direction of the friend-ly-looking, middle-aged man and the small, curly-haired woman at his side who were standing directly to her right. "They are the se-nior advisors at the home, with Jeff obviously being in charge of the boys and Tracie looking over the girls."

Colin and I shook their hands and we exchanged cordial pleas-antries. I immediately liked them, knowing from my days working at the Detroit house that the senior advisors were dedicated, devot-ed, and big-hearted people, living in the centers full-time to care for the children in their custody. I could tell Jeff was trying his best to play it cool around Colin, but there was no hiding the awestruck ex-pression in his eyes when the starting New England Patriots' quar-terback laughed at something he said and patted his shoulder.

Allison then sidestepped toward me to make room in our semi-circle for the other man who'd been hanging back to join us. "And this is none other than Dr. Oliver Saxon, who, as you already know, is the Executive Director," twisting to face me, her already brilliant smile grew even bigger, "and now your counterpart, *Dr. Cassidy*."

A girlish-sounding high-pitched giggle bubbled out of me and, instinctively, my cheeks flamed. With the combination of Allison emphasizing and bringing attention to my newly-earned doctor-ate degree and the completely unexpected image of Oliver Saxon, something strange happened inside of me, and that unnatural sound was the embarrassing effect.

I hastily thrust my arm in his direction, hoping to minimize any awkwardness my random laughter may have initiated, and threw on my best charming-the-public smile that I'd been perfecting since I was in diapers. Thankfully, he didn't miss a beat, fitting his strong hand around mine, and when our skin met and an unanticipated tingle ran down my spine, I started talking before I could do any-thing else to mortify myself.

"Allison's told me so much about you, Oliver. It's a pleasure to finally meet you." I left my hand in his just long enough to be cour-teous then pulled back to break the contact; however, I couldn't for the life of me tear my gaze away from the unique color of his eyes. A mix between amber and light brown, they almost looked fake, but I was too well-mannered to ask if they were tinted contacts.

"Likewise, Monroe. I was thrilled when I heard about the Board's decision to grant you this chapter of Mending Hearts," he replied rather formally before tilting his lips up into a shy smile. "We've been able to make big strides in just over two years at the Chicago house, and I've got faith you'll do the same here in Boston."

Breaking our charged stare, he shifted his attention to Colin and they did the whole man-handshake-thing, giving me a few moments to take in the incredibly intriguing Oliver Saxon, while making it look like I was just paying attention to my husband. It wasn't that I was so much as ogling him, because he wasn't really the type of guy you ogled—especially in a ballroom full of professional football players and relatively-famous people from the New England area—but instead, I was simply assessing him. By practice, I was an analytical person, and my job was to evaluate people. So, yep, I was totaling assessing him.

He was much younger than I'd assumed when I heard Allison talk about him before. With a name like Oliver Saxon, I thought he'd be approaching senior citizen status, if not already there. And even though this guy was probably still older than my twenty-five years, my initial guess was he was somewhere in his early-to-mid thirties and was still a good couple of decades from applying for his AARP membership.

Sharp, well-defined bone structure was emphasized in his strong cheeks and precisely-angled nose, and his jaw and chin were covered in a thick, closely-trimmed beard that matched the long, chocolate brown hair pulled back into a knot at the nape of his neck. Ranging somewhere between mine and Colin's height, probably hitting around the six-foot mark, the standard tuxedo option hid both his lean body and fashion personality, but the trendy, thick-framed glasses perched on his nose and the black Puma tennis shoes he wore on his feet gave me a small insight to his nerdy, hipster-vibe.

Just as the two men were wrapping up their cordial

how-do-you-dos, Barry Maxwell, head of public relations for the Patriots and a good friend of mine and Colin's, appeared on the opposite side of my husband with an apologetic smile. "Excuse me for interrupting, but I was wondering if I could steal the big guy away from you all for just a moment. I promise not to keep him long."

Colin's concerned eyes intuitively cut over to me, silently asking if I'd be all right for a few minutes while he took care of whatever it was Barry needed. I nodded confidently with a reassuring smile. "Go ahead, babe. I'll hang out with these guys until you get back, just visiting and preparing for my speech."

A quick peck on the cheek and he was gone, immediately followed by the Longs, who excused themselves to grab a drink from the bar. I turned around to ask Allison when she wanted to schedule visits to the two properties I'd narrowed the search for the center down to, but someone else had pulled her off to the side, leaving Oliver and me alone.

I prepared myself for the usual anxiety I felt when encountering a one-on-one situation with an unfamiliar man, but it never surfaced. And in its place, a profound sense of fascination filled me. I bit my lip, finding myself oddly excited to be in his presence, and *that* was the part that unsettled me. Dr. Oliver Saxon captivated me in the most unusual manner, though I had no idea why. And I wasn't sure I wanted to find out.

chapter
two

"When we met, we knew-
we were kindred souls;
people like us
only came around once
every blue moon
and I could not tell you
enough
how dazzling it was
to know that for that night
the universe wore
a dress
the color of indigo."
–Christopher Poindexter

OLIVER

SHE WAS EXACTLY like I expected her to be. Yet I still wasn't fully prepared for the impact she made when I met her.

Sure, I'd seen pictures and interviews of Colin "Clutch" Cassidy and his Sundance Wife, Monroe Taylor Cassidy, on TV and the internet. Hell, I didn't even follow sports, but I bought the damn *Sports Illustrated* that featured them on the cover the year before, and then read the in-depth article about how their Good Samaritan volunteer work brought them together in college, and later transformed them into one of the most beloved couples in American society. I'd convinced myself it was because the Mending Hearts foundation was highlighted in the piece—the first and only time my name would ever appear in print in any sports-related publication— but even then, I knew my reasoning was only partially true.

You didn't have to watch ESPN regularly to know who they were or to find information about them. In the short time they'd been in the public eye as a couple, Colin and Monroe Cassidy had become household names as the entire country applauded, admired, and adored them for their spiritual strength and selfless acts. Anyone and everyone who'd spent any time around them claimed they were the most genuine and authentically nice people they'd ever met. And now I knew they were right.

I also knew she was drop-dead gorgeous; any man who could see wouldn't argue that fact. A little taller than the average woman, but not towering, runway-model height, Monroe was destined to be beautiful, having been born to childhood-Hollywood-actress Vivian Taylor and the late rock legend Sage Hawthorne. With a combination of her mom's long, blonde hair and flawless, heart-shaped face, as well as her dad's striking green eyes and olive complexion, she'd been blessed with both of her parents' best physical attributes, and the ending result was exquisite. I usually wasn't the type to gawk at another man's wife, but nobody, it seemed—neither man, woman, nor child—was immune to the beauty that radiated from her.

And that was only what they saw through photos and video clips. Seeing her in person, talking to her, shaking her hand . . . it was almost like an out-of-body experience. Yes, I was a hot-blooded male who couldn't help but appreciate her stunning outer appearance, but it was about so much more. *She* was so much more.

The aura around her was warm and bright and overwhelmingly inviting. Her voice was calm and comforting, her touch soft and soothing. And I gathered all that in less than five minutes of being in her presence. Innately, I knew Monroe was one of those people who you could sit down with and spill all of your problems to, and I was positive she was able to console the saddest of hearts and encourage the most despaired of all souls.

"Have you ever been to Boston before?" Her voice broke through the silence between us that had begun to borderline on awkward. I knew I was openly staring, just as she was, and I wondered what she thought of me. Did she have any preconceived notions? How did I measure up? Then, I chastised myself for thinking she'd ever given me a passing thought before that moment. Why would she have?

"No," I finally responded, once I realized she was still waiting for an answer. "The farthest east I'd ever been before yesterday was Indianapolis."

She scrunched her tiny nose up like she smelled something foul, but said nothing.

"What? You don't like Indy?" I asked, praying that was the case and not because the travel deodorant I'd purchased at the airport had chosen that minute to stop working. "It wasn't my favorite place in the world, but I didn't think it was that bad when I visited."

She threw her head back with a deep-rooted belly laugh and my heart skipped a beat at the sound. "No, I have no issue with the city itself," she clarified. "I'm just not a big fan, because that's where the Colts are from."

I blinked hard, thinking perhaps I'd misheard her. "The *who?*"

"The Colts. You know, the football team? They're the ones who knocked the Pats out of the playoffs the last two years, so I'm still a little bitter."

I dropped my chin to my chest as embarrassment heated my face. *Of course she was talking about football, Oliver.* Her husband, after all, was the poster boy of the NFL. "Uh, yeah, I, um . . . I should've figured that out. Sports aren't really my thing, so my brain is a little slow in making the connection."

"Well, what is your thing then?" she probed, pursing her lips in a little smirk as amusement danced in her expressive eyes. "I mean, other than the kids, of course."

I didn't hesitate for a single second before blurting out, "Jazz."

"Jazz?" The surprised look on her face told me I'd caught her off-guard with my answer, but she recovered quickly, keeping the lighthearted tone in her voice. "Jazz what? Jazz hands?" She chuckled at her own words then narrowed her gaze and wagged her index finger at me in a playful manner. "I bet jazz hands are your *thing*. Aren't they, Dr. Saxon?"

"Only when I'm reenacting *Grease* in the shower," I replied deadpan, hoping she'd appreciate my dry sense of humor. I knew it wasn't for everyone.

This time, however, she didn't miss a beat. "'You're the One That I Want' or 'Summer Nights'?"

"Those are for novices, Dr. Cassidy." I shook my head, pretending to be offended. "My favorite is 'Look at Me, I'm Sandra Dee,' but occasionally . . ." I paused to shimmy my widely-spread jazz hands out to the sides as I twisted my hips back and forth in what could only be described as the worst dance move ever performed. "I'll bust out with 'Beauty School Dropout' if the mood hits me just right."

Naturally, Allison chose that exact moment to rejoin us, and if my boss didn't already know I was one peculiar, idiosyncratic dude, she most definitely would've had second thoughts about putting me in charge of one of her children's homes. But, thankfully, she'd figured that out long ago, and realized that for some reason or another, the kids—especially the teenagers—couldn't get enough of my quirky behaviors. From the time I was a young kid, people would comment about my different personality. They'd tell me it was endearing, but I knew they really meant weird. It never bothered me though; my parents had taught me early on to embrace my individuality, so I did.

"Oliver, darling, there's a time designated for dancing later this evening when you'll be able to show-off all those hip moves your kids teach you," Allison teased, unable to keep the ridiculous grin from spreading across her face, "but they've just alerted me it's time to head toward the stage. We're going to do the official greeting and introductions, and we all need to get in place. We can play later; let's go."

Without waiting for either of us to respond, Allison spun

around on her heels and took off toward the grandiose wall of windows, where the makeshift platform had been set up. Before I followed after her, I stole a glance over at Monroe, delighted to find her mouthing the words to "Look at Me, I'm Sandra Dee" as she flashed her not-so-subtle jazz hands at me. We both exploded in a fit of laughter, only to be quickly silenced by our boss's warning glare that she threw over her shoulder, just like my parents used to do at church when my sisters and I would act up.

"Come on. Let's go before we upset Mom," I joked, offering my elbow to her like a gentleman. "And besides, you can't be Sandy. I'm her. You have to be Rizzo."

After a few seconds filled with obvious apprehension on her part and absolute hopefulness on mine, she finally slid her hand inside my arm, very loosely holding onto my lower bicep. I wasn't sure what caused her hesitation, but it stirred an uneasiness inside of me I wasn't accustomed to. Surely she had to know I wouldn't hurt her. My entire life wrapped around helping to heal children who'd been physically and sexually abused, most often by those whom they loved and/or trusted.

"I can't be Rizzo," she said softly as she sidled up next to me and we started to move toward where Allison had stopped. "I never smoke, I hardly drink, and the only reputation I have is that I try to live by the highest moral and ethical standards possible."

"Wow," I replied, slowing my stride so I could look over at her. "That seems awfully boring. Excuse my bluntness. And it's not that you need to smoke or drink to have a good time either, but always trying to live up to some preposterous ideals set by society that are impossible to achieve . . . you're cheating yourself out of a lot of good life moments. Many of my favorite memories came from when I was doing something I shouldn't have been doing."

She peered up at me as we inched along, allowing me to guide her through the slew of bodies, and her happy smile shrunk into a pensive twist of her lips. That was the second time I'd seen her do that with her mouth, and I really fucking liked it when she did. My dick twitched behind my zipper as I waited for her response. *Okay, maybe I liked it too much.*

"I call it being safe." Rolling her shoulders back and lifting her chin as she spoke, her straightened posture was meant to reinforce her statement, which I'm sure she felt didn't require any further explanation. I was afraid she was going to release her grasp on my arm and walk away from me, but thankfully, she didn't until we reached our destination. And even then, the moment she dropped her hand, I could feel the lingering warmth where her fingers had been.

While we waited next to the stage as Allison worked to get everyone in the correct places, I leaned down to where she stood in front of me and whispered, "You know the brilliant Harry B. Gray once said, 'No one ever achieved greatness by playing it safe.'"

The minute the words tumbled from my mouth, I wanted to kick myself for saying them. Why in the hell didn't I just drop it? I was never one of those people who always had to have the last word in a discussion or couldn't accept when I was wrong. I prided myself on my humbleness and modesty, never having any issues with accepting my shortcomings, and constantly working to learn more and keep an open mind.

Yet I said it anyway. Almost as a dare. A challenge. Goading her into continuing the conversation. I barely knew her, but I had an intrinsic urge to ruffle her feathers. Get her a little flustered. Convince myself she wasn't as perfect as she seemed.

Slowly, she turned around to gaze up at me through her thick, long lashes with a steely determination and confidence I was only used to seeing when I looked in the mirror. "I have no idea who Harry B. Gray is, but I can assure you of one thing." She paused to bless me with a breath-stealing smile. "He's never met me."

ALLISON ELOQUENTLY GREETED the several hundred guests and introduced them to the people standing behind her on the stage, which included the Mending Hearts' Board of Directors, myself, and Jeff and Tracie Long. Then she began to tell the story about how she originally got the idea to start up the not-for-profit children's home in Detroit dedicated to providing a refuge for abused children. It was a story I'd heard her recite many times over the years I'd known her. As she painted the picture of the numerous bruised and battered foster kids that her biological parents had taken in while she was growing up, I found myself scanning the crowd filled with people who had deep pockets and spent an obscene amount of time in a gym.

From the massive, musclebound New England Patriots football team and the swimsuit-model eye-candy hanging from their arms, to the beady-eyed, East Coast business moguls and their Botox-brides, I could honestly say I'd never felt more out of place than I did at that moment. It wasn't that I'd never been around rich people before, or that I felt insignificant or unworthy around them, as self-esteem was never an issue of mine. I knew I was a reasonably intelligent, attractive enough guy with a rewarding career who truly enjoyed helping those in need. But those people . . . they were from a different planet. Maybe it was the difference in the mindset of people from the Midwest to those from the Northeast, but whatever it was, the stifling atmosphere surrounding them hung heavy with arrogance and pompousness.

When my gaze landed on the star quarterback, front and center in the mass of the elegantly dressed bodies, I realized everything I'd previously thought about the rest of the guests didn't apply to him. Not a single bit.

Like his wife, Colin Cassidy radiated charisma, and people naturally flocked to him. His pearly-white smile was friendly and unpretentious, and in the few minutes I'd spoken with him, I instantly understood the draw. He made you feel like he was genuinely interested in what you had to say, even if it was menial small-talk, and though I was most definitely a heterosexual, female-loving man, there was no denying his conventional good looks.

My attention shifted to the people directly around him. On his right stood a couple who I guessed was in their fifties, and straight-away, I pegged them as his parents based solely on the physical resemblance between him and the older man. The woman, who reminded me a lot of one of my favorite elementary school teachers, had her arm hooked around Colin's, and her face glowed with pride each time she glanced up at him. That look was most definitely one belonging to a mom.

On the other side of Colin was a guy and a girl who appeared to be around the same age as Colin, in their early-to-mid-twenties, and by his obvious level of comfort and familiarity with them both, they were all clearly close to one another. My initial thought was that they were his siblings, but after a few moments of scrutinizing them, I wasn't so sure. The young woman was petite, maybe five feet and a hundred pounds, and though her tiny nose and brown eyes were a bit mousy, she was undoubtedly attractive. Straight, platinum blonde hair, which I doubted was her natural color, fell down her back, nearly reaching her waist, and despite donning small features everywhere else on her body, the plunging neckline on her ruby red dress proved that her full breasts were the one exception. The guy, on the other hand, was of average height and build, much like myself. He had matching brown hair and eyes and a clean-shaven baby-face, and whereas I would've said he was a decent-looking guy, handsome even, he definitely didn't demand attention like the two people he was standing nearest to.

Just as I began to study the younger couple's body language, attempting to determine whether their relationship was romantic or platonic in nature, the entire room broke out into a deafening applause, yanking my focus away from the people-watching and back up to the podium, where a teary-eyed Allison backed away from the microphone and a poised Monroe approached.

God, she is stunning.

Thankfully, every eye in the room was fixed on her so I could openly stare without it being weird, even if they were all looking at her front and my view was from the back . . . and an unbelievably stimulating view it was. I felt sorry for any of the men she would be hiring to work in the house with her on a daily basis, wondering how any of them would be able to keep their focus on the task at hand for long. Unless, perhaps, they were gay, and even then, I'm not sure they'd be able to resist her allure.

"Thank you all so much for that warm welcome," Monroe addressed the crowd with her melodic voice. Even though I couldn't see her face, I could hear the smile in her tone. "And thank you again to Allison Northcutt for not only having the dream, but the desire and dedication to conceive and create the incredible, life-changing organization, Mending Hearts."

Everyone began to clap again, and once the noise level died off, she picked up where she left off.

"Leading up to this night, I spent more hours than I'd like to admit preparing for this speech. I threw away notecard after notecard, continually failing to find the right combination of words to reach each and every one of you in a way that would properly convey the significance of what all of us on this stage are striving to do, one city at a time. And then one night last week, well after I should've been in bed, my husband Colin," a brief pause as she nods her head in his direction, "walked into my office and asked me what was keeping me up so late. After I explained my dilemma to him, he didn't say a single word, but he walked over to my bookcase and grabbed a photo album off one of the shelves. Dropping the heavy book on my desk, he opened the front cover to reveal pages and pages of the kids I had met and worked with during the four years of my undergrad at the Mending Hearts house in Detroit. Tears sprang to my eyes immediately at the photos of those smart, bright, loving children, and the sense of overwhelming joy that flooded my body reminded me of how I could reach each of you."

As she spoke the final few words of the last sentence, a screen dropped down from the ceiling off to the side of the platform where no one was positioned, and within moments, a giant collage of twenty-five different children's images appeared. Several murmurs could be heard amongst the large group, and at first, I was a little confused, thinking the pictures were the ones she was talking about in her story.

But I was wrong.

And she was a genius.

"All of the photos you see here," she turned her head to face the oversized screen just as the collage disappeared and another one took its place, "are loved by people in this room. Sons, daughters, grandkids, nieces, and nephews. These kids are the lights of your lives, the ones you'd give anything for."

The quiet whispers became a low buzz, numerous people smiling and pointing at pictures as they recognized faces.

Monroe shifted her attention back to the audience as she drove her point home. "Now imagine someone physically or sexually abusing your little loved one, and think about how you would feel. The rage. The disgust. How you'd want to help them. How you'd want to punish whoever was responsible. Think of the lengths you'd go to do whatever you could to help." Waiting for her words to sink in, she waited a couple of seconds before continuing, "That's what we do at Mending Hearts, for the kids who either don't have anyone to stand up for them, or for those who are too afraid of the offender to tell anyone else. We help them heal. We work closely with law enforcement agencies to obtain justice in their name. And we teach them to be survivors. Not victims."

Like a famous orator, she commanded the room with ease. Every person within earshot, event staff included, hung on her every word, utterly enthralled by her message. Hell, I knew everything one could possibly know about the organization—for Christ's sake, I had *lived* at the Chicago house for over eighteen months before Jeff and Tracie came along—and I was spellbound, ready to donate money for the cause.

After Monroe concluded the speech, letting everyone know how they could follow the progress of the new Boston chapter online and announcing the tentative grand opening for the following February, which was only a little over five months away, she stepped off the stage and was instantly swallowed up by a swarm of bodies trying to get near and congratulate her. I wanted to be one of those people to tell her how she'd nailed her presentation and that I knew, without a doubt, she was going to be an amazing inspirational leader for the kids at her house. But instead, I watched from the background, not quite ready to tear my gaze away from her.

A few minutes passed, and I began to worry I was teetering between a random bystander who was just taking in what was going on around him, and a creepy lurker, so I turned around and stepped off the raised platform, moving toward the restrooms for a much-needed break. Thankfully, no one else was in the bathroom and once I emptied my bladder and scrubbed my hands, I splashed a little water on my face, hoping that would help wash away the trance Monroe Cassidy had put me under. And when that didn't work, I pinched my eyebrows together, shaping my forehead into a stern V, and asked aloud, "What in the hell is your problem, Sax? Get a fucking grip."

The door swung open, and two exceptionally large men—who I could only assume were linemen by their lack of necks—entered the washroom, both nodding a silent acknowledgement in my direction before moving to the urinals. Taking that as my cue that my pep-talk was over, I dried my hands with a paper towel and wasn't surprised in the least when I missed the two-foot shot into the trashcan as I walked out. Mortified at my lack of hand-eye coordination, I hastily picked up the wadded paper ball, disposed of it, and barreled through the door, not bothering to look back and see if the other men had witnessed my fail.

As I emerged back into the main space, I avoided the throng of people still gathered around Monroe and Colin, and strode across the room to the less-crowded lounge, sidling up to the bar for a much-needed drink. A strong one. The bartender promptly poured four fingers of his finest scotch into a highball glass and I shoved a ten-dollar bill into the tip jar before blowing out a deep breath. Looking around the secluded area, I noticed the young couple, who I'd been studying while they stood next to Colin earlier, were only a few feet away from me. They appeared to be in a heated argument, based on their body language and the scowl on her face. I twisted my body so it appeared I was looking out at the people in the ballroom, but I could still see them easily off to the side.

Though his back was turned to me and I couldn't see if his

expression matched hers, there was no denying the irritation in his voice when I heard him say, "I can't believe you're leaving! You're so fucking immature and selfish when it comes to this shit, Effie. If you're not the center of attention, you're not interested."

"That's not true, Seth! I've always supported you and Colin! I went to every single one of his games when we were growing up, and all of your . . ." The young blonde huffed, throwing her hands on her hips and pushing her exposed chest out.

"All of my what?" he demanded, matching her combative stance. "My debate club matches when we were in school? Never. My rowing meets? Only when Mom and Dad made you go, and even then, you spent the entire time flirting with the other guys on my team. And God forbid I ever bother you to come to one of my *boring* choir performances. You may be surprised to learn that your *only* sibling is actually pretty damn good at something too, not just the next-door neighbor that you've had a ridiculous crush on since you were in diapers."

She glared at him, but didn't deny his allegation, so he continued, "Shocking, I know, but the world doesn't revolve around you, princess. It's time to wake up and face reality; if *he* wanted to be with you, it would've happened a long time ago. He's married and he's happy. And if you want to continue to be a part of his life, you need to realize what that part is—it's his friend. It's the sweet little sister he never had, though I'm tempted to tell him you suck at that role."

"You wouldn't!" Her dark eyes grew wide with shock and filled with tears. "Seth, please . . ."

The young man fell for her theatrics and stepped toward her and pulled her into a hug, shaking his head. "No, of course, I wouldn't," he replied much softer, "but you've gotta stop this shit, Eff. It's not worth losing him completely. He'll always pick her."

She sniffled and nodded then stepped back out of his embrace, plastering a fake smile on her face. "You're right, smarty pants. I guess that's why you got the big brains and I got the good looks," she teased in a blatant attempt to distract and deter. "I'll stay a little while longer, but I'm still gonna go meet some of my friends at King Street Tavern in a bit."

"Sounds good. Now let's go rejoin everyone before Colin sends out a search party for us."

The two of them sauntered away, so caught up in whatever the hell *that* was all about that neither of them ever once looked in my direction. A little overwhelmed by the entire night, I picked up my glass, took a sip of the chest-warming amber liquid, and moved away from the bar and over to a vacant spot by the floor-to-ceiling windows that spanned across an entire wall.

Peering out into the Boston night skyline, I couldn't help but be impressed, and for a few moments, I forgot all about the scene taking place behind me. The brilliant city lights dimmed gradually until they disappeared altogether into the black water of the Massachusetts Bay. The view from that high up was like nothing I'd ever seen before, and internally, I vowed to myself to begin visiting more places.

Prior to completing graduate school seven years ago, the only state I'd been in, other than Illinois, was Missouri, as I was born and raised miles inside the shared state borders. Even after earning my doctorate, I'd thrown myself into my work and music in Chicago, never taking the time to travel too far away from my adult home. But after spending only two days in Boston, I was ready to see more. More of Boston. More of the country. More of the world.

"So what do you think?" Allison's voice startled me, as I was so lost in my thoughts I didn't even notice her slip up next to me.

I greeted her with a friendly smile then returned my focus to the scenery. "Breathtakingly beautiful."

Snickering under her breath, she nudged my arm with her shoulder. "I know what you thought of Monroe. I was asking your opinion of Boston."

"You think you're a lot funnier than you really are," I teased, pausing to bring the glass of Glenlivet up to my mouth and swallowing back a healthy portion before finishing my thought. "But I've found them both to be quite remarkable, thank you very much.

She's going to do great things here. The people adore her."

"That they do. It's hard not to," she agreed with an emphatic nod. "And you're right, she's got the drive, the determination, and the resources to do whatever she sets her heart and mind to. I just feel blessed that she found her calling with us at Mending Hearts."

I grumbled an "Indeed," not knowing what else to say as I reached up and tugged on the shirt collar that seemed to suddenly shrink. Talking about the woman I'd spent most of the evening gawking at like a teenaged-boy with his first nudie magazine made me uncomfortable. I wanted to change the subject, but before I could think of a different topic, Allison began speaking again. "Can you meet me at the hotel restaurant for lunch tomorrow? Say 12:30? I have an offer to make you that I'm hoping you'll be interested in."

"An offer?" The mystery in her voice piqued my interest and I quirked my eyebrow up with cat-killing curiosity.

"Tomorrow." Then she disappeared as quickly as she'd appeared, and I was left pondering and speculating a million different ideas without having much clue about what I was trying to figure out. I slipped out of the gala shortly after that, forgoing Allison's ridiculous suggestion earlier in the night that I take part in the dancing portion of the event. All I wanted was to get back to my hotel room, take a shower, and go to sleep, so the next morning would arrive as quickly as possible.

Unfortunately, as I tossed and turned for hours upon hours in the dark of the night, held captive by my out-of-control racing thoughts that didn't have an off-switch, I finally turned the television on and began surfing through the channels. Passing over infomercials, news channels, and a rerun of *Law & Order* that I'd previously seen, I landed on the American Movie Classics channel and my entire body froze, the remote control sliding out of my rigid hands onto the mattress. Plain as day, smack dab in front of me, Danny Zuko and Sandy D. were dancing their way across the carnival and my hotel television screen, singing 'You're the One That I Want' as I watched in awe. *What were the fucking odds?*

The last thing I remembered before falling asleep with a

stupid-ass smile on my face was picturing Monroe in a pair of skin-tight, black leather pants with red kitten heels, singing the *Grease* soundtrack to me. It was a good thing I didn't have to face her again before I went back home.

chapter three

"The problem with love
these days is that society
has taught the human
race to stare at people
with their eyes rather
than their souls."
–Christopher Poindexter

MONROE

THE SCREECHING ALARM clock mocked me from across my bedroom. The bright red numbers on the display read 6:30, but I swore it lied. There was no way it could already be time to get up; I'd just laid my head on the pillow five minutes before. At least that's what it felt like.

The night at the gala had run late. Real late. With Colin and Allison by my side, the three of us stayed until the very last guest had left, thanking everyone for coming out and showing their support. Encouraging words accompanied by checks with multiple zeroes made every excruciating moment of balancing in those death-traps called stilettos worth it. The early tally of donations before we left totaled close to twelve million dollars—more than enough to purchase a property for the location of the Mending Hearts' home, as well as cover a couple years of operating expenses. I'd already narrowed down the final selection to two locations, both well within the budget. It was all I'd hoped for and so much more, and I was over-the-moon ecstatic when I'd gotten home, but thoroughly exhausted.

Rolling off of my way-too-comfy, pillow-top mattress, I slugged across the room and slammed my hand down to stop the maddening noise. I'd purposely set the alarm up on the dresser instead of the nightstand so I'd be forced to actually get out of bed to turn it off, preventing me from hitting the snooze button multiple times while staying warm and cozy under the sheets. I'd discovered that method worked best when I was in boarding school, when there was no one else around to ensure I was up and at class on time. There was a switch in my head that flipped when I was up and on my feet, demanding I stay up for good. And although I yawned and stared longingly at the jumbled-up covers calling out to me to re-join them for a few more hours, I slipped on a black sports bra and matching yoga pants, brushed my teeth, put my hair in a ponytail, and then headed downstairs to the state-of-the-art home gym in the basement of our recently-renovated Beacon Hill residence. I was begrudgingly ready to start the day.

My workout proved to be more of a struggle than it usually was. I was panting like a dog on a hot summer day and pouring sweat before I even finished the fifteen-minute warm up on the elliptical. I openly cursed myself for the fourth glass of wine I had the previous night. I knew when I accepted it that I'd pay the price, yet that thought didn't make me feel any better as I could actually smell the Sauvignon Blanc in my perspiration.

Moving to the leg press machine, I attempted to focus on the beat of the song that played loudly through the surround-sound speakers. It was a catchy new release I'd heard frequently on the radio, but my concentration was shot, and no matter how hard I tried, I just couldn't get in the zone. Refusing to give up, I powered through for a little over an hour and a half, and by the time I turned the lights and music off, I felt a little more like myself. A sticky, sweaty, smelly version of myself that desperately needed a shower.

The second I opened the door of the sound-proofed room, I

was assaulted by a mixture of rich, flavorful aromas descending down the stairs from the main floor. Bacon, coffee, and maple syrup. What wasn't to love? My stomach growled ferociously in response, and not wasting any more time, I bounded up the steps two at a time to my master bathroom, rushing to get clean so I could dig into whatever deliciousness that was being prepared in the kitchen.

It was too early to get dressed for the lunch I had scheduled with Allison at her hotel, so I opted for another pair of yoga pants (a staple of my wardrobe since college), gray this time, and a navy Patriots tank top before heading back downstairs. In the three years we lived in this house, I still hadn't gotten used to all of the levels and the maneuvering up-and-down steps. I knew one day my thighs and ass would thank me for the bonus workouts they got each day.

My mom's place in California—the one I'd grown up in until she shipped me off to Brentwood Prep Academy—was close in square footage to ours, but that's where the similarities ended. Where her two-story Mediterranean villa sprawled out over a considerable chunk of land in an exclusive gated community, our five-level home (which included the completed basement and rooftop deck) was nestled in between two other old Colonial-style brick row houses on Chestnut Street, a road traveled daily by thousands upon thousands of locals and tourists alike, smack dab in the heart of Beantown, U.S.A., a name only used by people who weren't originally from there. People like me.

"What in the world is all this?" I asked with a chuckle, hovering under the archway that separated the living room and kitchen. "Did you invite the offensive line over for breakfast or something?"

Colin, still dressed in his pajama pants and a plain white t-shirt, whisked something feverishly at the stove while I gaped at the steaming, mouth-watering spread on the butcher-block kitchen island. Buttery scrambled eggs. Waffles. French toast. Crispy bacon. Sausage. Hash browns. Flaky buttermilk biscuits. And fresh strawberries with homemade whipped cream to top it all off. I'm pretty sure I gained five pounds just looking at it all. So much for that workout.

"I'd need a lot more food than this, if that was the case," he contended as he shot me a teasing smile. Momentarily abandoning the baked beans in the saucepan, he set the wooden spoon down on the counter, turned the heat down to low, and closed the distance between us to kiss my forehead. "Morning, gorgeous. I'd give you a proper hug, but my hands are all greasy. How was your workout?"

I scrunched my nose up and gave a sharp shake of my head. "It sucked."

His chest shook with laughter as he bent down to rub the tip of his nose against mine. An Eskimo kiss, it was called, according to Colin. My mom wasn't big on any kind of kisses, hugs, or demonstrations of love for anyone other than her current boyfriend or husband, and since I'd never had a boyfriend before him, it took me some time after Colin and I started dating to get used to his open displays of affection—both public and private—but soon . . . soon I began to love them. To live for them. They were my drug. He was my drug. All I needed to keep my perfect world balanced and myself grounded.

"You knew better when you took that final glass of wine last night. I saw the hesitation in your eyes," he half-scolded, returning to the food I still contended was not a breakfast food at all, despite his and his parents' claim otherwise. I didn't care that Google backed them up, maintaining beans were common in breakfasts throughout many countries that were once a part of the British Empire. The only way I was eating them at nine in the morning was if I was camping, or it was the apocalypse. Otherwise, they were a lunch or dinner-only menu item.

"Yeah, I did." Sighing, I shuffled inside the gourmet kitchen and plopped down on one of the four bar stools situated around the island, where we ate ninety-nine percent of our meals. It was *my* seat while we were in this room, which was more often than not if we were home. When we originally bought the house after Colin was drafted by his hometown team, the first thing we did was have the entire thing gutted and redesigned to our liking.

The kitchen was my husband's pet project, as he claimed it

would be the heart of our home. He personally selected every-thing from the mahogany cabinets and black-and-tan marble coun-tertops, to the natural wood accessories and the toaster that had more settings than a spaceship. Warm, cheery butterscotch walls. Restaurant-quality stainless steel appliances. Ornate hardware on all of the drawers and cupboards. It didn't make sense to me then, but as we settled into our life together, I soon discovered that if we weren't in our bedrooms, chances were we were in the kitchen—ei-ther comparing our daily schedules over coffee and a healthy break-fast in the mornings or catching up at night over dinner. It was *our* place. Just like this was *my* stool. Unfortunately, our already-busy schedules only seemed to be growing more and more hectic over the previous few months, and we'd been missing each other more frequently than I'd have liked.

"You never told me what this is all for," I reminded him before I snuck a piece of bacon and shoved it in my mouth.

"We're celebrating." Peering over his shoulder, he smirked as he watched me chew the heart-attack inducing deliciousness. "And get your grubby little fingers out of the bacon until it's time to make our plates."

I moaned as I swallowed. I couldn't help it. It was that good. Bacon was my weakness; I could never have a pet pig.

Once I'd finished climaxing with Wilbur's belly, I realized my husband was still staring at me, his expression unreadable. "I hope you don't do that in public, Roe. That sound would give a hundred-year-old man on his deathbed a woody."

My right eyebrow arched high up into my forehead, a combina-tion of confusion over the celebration comment and a where-in-the-hell-did-he-come-up-with-some-of-this-stuff look. I opted to ignore the old-guy-with-a-boner explanation and find out when I could have more bacon. "What are we celebrating?"

He twisted back around to stir the beans, even though I could see the burner was off and they were clearly ready and didn't need stirring. The only time Colin didn't face me when he was talking was when he was nervous. And only one subject made Colin nervous.

"Well, the success of the gala, of course. I know I said it last night, but I was so impressed with everything. You kicked ass, babe." He paused briefly to exhale loudly then continued on. "This is also my last Sunday home before the season starts. After this, we won't get to do our Funday Sundays until after playoffs next February, and I knew you were going to meet with Allison later, so I wanted breakfast to be awesome." Another pause. Longer this time. Two deep breaths. "And after we got home last night—"

"This incredible guy showed up," a familiar male voice that belonged to Colin's childhood next-door neighbor and best friend finished the sentence from behind me.

I quickly spun around to find Seth Andrews closing in on where I sat, wearing only a pair of loose athletic shorts and with his brown hair all a bedhead mess. He scooped me up off the seat and twirled me in the air as he covered both sides of my cheeks with kisses. I squealed with delight.

"Roe, baby girl, you were amazing last night!" he exclaimed as he eventually lowered me back on the cushion then parked himself two stools away from me. *His* spot. "Not only did you look absolutely stunning, your speech was fuckin' killah. Those snooty assholes were eating out of the palms of your hands."

"You do know you're one of those snooty assholes, right?" Colin scoffed from the refrigerator while pulling out the milk and orange juice. "And watch your language in my house, especially around Monroe."

Seth rolled his eyes and snatched two pieces of bacon from the platter, giving one to me and keeping the other for himself. I giggled as Colin flared his nostrils when he caught us. "Roe doesn't care if I curse. She works with teenagers. Kids these days throw *fuck* around like it's an everyday word. I bet Oscar the Grouch teaches them how to spell it on Sesame Street now or some shit."

I wanted to agree that he probably wasn't far off, but instead of riling up Colin even more and forcing him to get out the swear jar, I redirected the conversation. "I was wondering if I was gonna see you here this morning," I said to Seth, "but when you weren't around at the end of the gala, I thought maybe you had to take Effie home and didn't feel like driving back into town."

"Nah," he shook his head as he grabbed a strawberry, "she wanted to go meet some of her friends at a bar, and I didn't want her on the streets by herself, especially considering the fancy shit she was wearing. So I escorted her there and hand-delivered her to a girl I somewhat trust. Then I ran into a guy I knew from school, so I stayed and had a couple beers while I waited for you two to get home."

"You must've been quiet when you got here. Or I was so tired that I just passed out, oblivious to the world around me." I shrugged my shoulders, not surprised.

Colin rounded the island with his hands full of plates and silverware, first arranging a place setting on the mat in front of me then doing the same for the two of them. "It must've been the latter," he chuckled as he looped his arms around Seth's neck from behind, "because somebody was *not* very quiet last night."

Seth craned his neck up and back to meet Colin's gaze, a mischievous gleam in his eyes matching the roguish grin tugging up the corners of his mouth. When their lips met in a tender, but passionate kiss, the electric charge in the room shifted instantly and goose bumps painted my arms. My heart soared for them as I said a prayer that they finally worked out some of their ongoing issues. They loved each other in a way I believed I'd never fully appreciate or experience, but regardless, there was no denying when you were around them—or at least when I was around them and they could be their true selves—that they shared a connection so deep it rooted in the very fiber of their beings.

Colin and I were soulmates, but he and Seth were each other's true love. They both knew if they ever wanted to take their relationship to the next level—outside the confines of our home—I'd happily step aside for that to happen. It wouldn't change things between Colin and me; we'd always be there for each other to the very end, but things weren't that simple for the two of them. Colin was raised a devout Catholic by two extremely intelligent, yet very staunch-in-their-ways, parents. His dad was the football coach and Ethics teacher at St. Thomas More, the high school Colin had graduated from, and his mom was the Associate Dean of the Religion Department at Wellesley College, one of the most revered and respected institutes of higher education in the country. Their family had never missed a Sunday Mass, and up until Colin left home to attend the University of Michigan, he was required to read and discuss Scripture with them weekly. They still invited us to attend church with them regularly, though we rarely went in the fall and winter due to his games always being on a Sunday.

It wasn't until he and Seth—who grew up next door to each other since they were seven—discovered their sexual attraction to each other the summer after their senior year of high school that Colin began to question his spirituality and beliefs. He'd only discussed that time in his life with me once. The day his secret had been revealed.

I smiled at the handwritten note taped to the classroom door in the Social Work building before abruptly spinning around on the heel of my snow boots and heading back in the direction I'd just come from. Even though I thoroughly enjoyed the weekly Community Intervention seminar with my graduate advisor, any time a Friday afternoon class was cancelled, it was a win in my book, and I didn't ask any questions. Plus, I had an awards dinner to get ready for and still needed to shower and blow-dry my hair.

I still couldn't believe the life I'd discovered at the University of Michigan. A life that included fancy awards dinners, random interviews by members of the media, and many Saturdays spent watching the football team play at the Big House. And it was all because of my best friend, my soul mate, my other half—Colin Cassidy, the man who had led the Wolverine football team to their first national championship in over fifteen years.

It all seemed like some sort of fairy tale, and truth be told, there were still some days I wondered if I was going to wake up to find out it was all just a dream. It wasn't how I planned for my college years to go. I wasn't looking for him; that's for damn sure. But he just sort of appeared and implanted himself in my life, and we never looked back. Inseparable from the word go.

He was an exception to my general rule of not letting people get too close. Having been raised in the Hidden Hills of Los Angeles, especially with the mom I had, I'd learned early that most anyone who wanted to get close to me was either using me or trying to manipulate me for their own benefit, so I kept to myself as much as possible. Which was exactly why the day after I graduated high school, I stuffed all of my personal belongings inside my Porsche Cayenne—a sixteenth birthday present from my fourth stepfather—and hastily sped away from the West Coast, never to return. For three long but gloriously peaceful days, I'd driven cross country until I'd reached my final destination of Ann Arbor, Michigan.

Michigan was the college I'd set my sights on early in high school because of its top-rated Social Work program and the fact it was located over twenty-two hundred miles away from my mother. When I was awarded several academic scholarships my senior year—enough to cover my full tuition, as well as room and board—no longer did I have to worry about depending on my mom footing any part of the bill, and I was free to make a clean break. A fresh start to just be me. Monroe Taylor, a wallflower who was one part quiet, four parts nerd, and totally okay with being invisible, as long as she was making a positive difference in the lives of children who needed someone to stand up for them.

No, Colin was never a part of the plan, but he had proven time and time again to be the best thing that ever happened to me. He was my rock.

A gust of frigid air snapped me out of my reminiscent haze as the door swung open and a couple of girls entered the building, both greeting me with a nod and cheery smile as they slipped by. I returned the friendly gesture and wrapped the gray cashmere scarf tighter around my neck before braving the sub-zero temperatures yet again, the grin on my face never faltering as I skipped my way down the front steps and across E. University Avenue to my apartment, which was strategically chosen for its close proximity to the building most of my classes were in and my part-time job at the Ginsberg Center for Community Service.

After a quick elevator ride up to the top floor, I dropped my book bag off in my small one-bedroom studio and took a few minutes to freshen up before heading to Colin's place for the weekend. Even though I knew Colin didn't care if I was wearing makeup or if my hair was done, ever since winning the big game the month before, it seemed like pictures of us continued to end up plastered across social media. And despite the hatred I had for the fake-and-phony life I left behind in L.A., I still didn't want to look like a house troll next to my nationally-worshipped "boyfriend," as had been deemed by the local paper.

Colin Cassidy, the Catholic kid from Boston, who was once only known for his strong religious beliefs and antics both on and off the field, had become a household name after he led our team back from what many thought was an insurmountable thirty point deficit in the second half of the big game. The broadcast announcers had deemed him "Clutch" Cassidy at some point during the fourth quarter, and when the television cameras caught the two of us sharing an emotional embrace on the field after the game, headlines ran pondering if I would be the future "Sundance Wife."

The immediate attention we'd received afterward had thrown us both for a loop, being interviewed together on morning talk shows and invited to all sorts of events and parties, but with the strong bond we shared, the two of us sat down, talked it all out, and decided to play along with it, as the publicity it was providing for Colin was invaluable. NFL teams, as well as a countless number of sponsors, were watching him closely, and the fandom he was creating played a huge part in his worth both in the draft and in the open-market of commercialism. However, Colin knew one of the main reasons I escaped my life in California was to get out of the limelight, but I assured him that as long as he was by my side, I was more than fine playing along for him. Not to mention, it gave me multiple opportunities to raise awareness and bring in donations for the Mending Hearts home I volunteered at.

Growing up as the only child of Hollywood actress, and known party animal, Vivian Taylor, meant I had paparazzi following me around from an early age, all of them waiting for me to follow in my mother's scandalous footsteps. But once most of them figured out I was nothing at all like the woman who gave birth to me, other than our long blonde hair and heart-shaped face, they began to lose interest. I supposed photos of me at

National Honor Society meetings or volunteering at women and children's shelters didn't sell to the tabloids like snapshots of other stars' kids stumbling out of dance clubs, drunk and high, and making out with a new warm body each weekend. Not that I'd minded fading into the background one bit.

I gathered my toiletries and dropped them in my overnight bag, as I was sure I wouldn't be coming back to the apartment until Sunday evening. Though Colin and I had never been sexually intimate, a kiss hello or goodbye every so often and lots of big bear hugs were the extent of our physical relationship—I'd started spending almost every weekend at the off-campus house he rented. We'd often stay up late binge-watching TV shows or movies, and he never wanted me to be out on the roads at three or four in the morning. And it wasn't like I minded being cuddled all night by his big, strong body, feeling safe and secure.

Grabbing my phone off the bed, I shot Colin a quick text to let him know my class had been cancelled and I was headed over early, but I didn't wait for a reply before I threw it in my purse and headed out the door, duffel bag in hand. He was either at the Athletic Center hanging out with his teammates and coaches, or at home playing video games with his childhood best friend, Seth, who had come into town for the weekend to attend the awards dinner with us. But either way, I had my own key to let myself in.

The drive to his place was quick, a trip I usually made on foot when the temperatures were above freezing, and when I pulled up in the driveway of the 1940's Craftsman-style bungalow, I excitedly hopped out of my SUV and bounded up the front walk to the porch. Inserting my key into the lock, I turned it left and pushed the heavy wooden door open, surprised not to see anyone in the living room or kitchen.

"Hello?" I called out as I let myself inside. "Colin, babe? You here? Seth?"

I got no response, but since both of their cars were parked out front, I assumed they were out back. I glanced down the hall, noting that Colin's bedroom door was closed, so I moved toward the sliding glass doors that led to the patio, but stopped when I heard something that sounded a lot like moaning coming from his room. At first, I thought maybe I'd just imagined the noise, but as I stood statue-like in the small dining area and listened to *the moans grow louder and more insistent, I realized it wasn't my mind playing tricks on me. There was no doubt what was going on behind that door.*

Slowly, I tiptoed down the hall as the pleasure-filled groans and the sound of bodies feverishly slapping against each other echoed throughout the house. My heart splintered before cracking in anguish. A steady stream of tears rolled down my cheeks as reflux burned its way up my esophagus, the deceit and deception searing the back of my throat.

"Yes, oh, my God, that feels so good. Don't stop . . . whatever you do, please don't stop."

The throaty voice urging his partner on most definitely belonged to Colin, decimating the tiny sliver of hope my heart was hanging onto, praying it wasn't really him. My anger didn't revolve around my jealousy of wishing it was me in that room with him, but instead, it was the lies that he'd told me of how he had no interest in being with any of the girls that were constantly throwing themselves at him. He'd fed me a heap-load of bullshit, and like an idiot, I'd believed him. Believed he was different.

Suddenly, a surge of rage flooded my veins, and without thinking of the repercussions, my shattered heart and crushed dreams being the sole driving forces, I shoved the door open, ready to go bat-shit crazy on my soon-to-be-ex-whatever-he-was and the shameless, football-groupie bimbo he had with him.

Only, when the door flew open and banged violently against the wall, the scene before me was revealed and I gasped in disbelief, my hands flying up to cover my gaping mouth. Seeing Colin and Seth naked and entwined in each other made my head spin and my heart skip a beat, but it was then that everything suddenly made sense about why Colin and I worked.

I was his cover, protecting his secret.

He provided me with the sense of security that I so desperately needed.

We were the best of friends and loved to be together.

And together, we formed the perfect arrangement.

"Aren't you gonna eat, Roe? You need to feed those muscles you worked out or you'll be drained later." Colin's voice broke through my sappy thoughts and I looked up at him and Seth with a smile. Even though the three of us had talked through everything that night, and we'd all moved on with our mutual understanding, I silently wished for more for the two of them.

"Yeah, I know, bossy pants," I replied as I began to load my plate with a week's worth of calories, making sure not to miss at least a sampling of everything my amazing husband had prepared. After all, we were apparently celebrating. "Do you two have plans, or are you keeping Funday Sunday here today? I've gotta leave around noon to meet Allison, but I should be back around two or three this afternoon."

"Don't forget we've got tickets to the Red Sox-Yankees game tonight. I've already texted Barry, and he got us two more for Seth and Effie. We don't have any plans until that though," Colin threw Seth a sly smile, "but I'm sure we can find something to keep busy with until you get back."

I playfully rolled my eyes and shoved a bite of French toast in my mouth as Seth leaned over and caught Colin's earlobe between his teeth. My inner thighs tingled and my belly fluttered at the suggestive sight of the two them, but I ignored the sensations like I always did. Like I'd trained myself to do for the past eleven years whenever I'd felt those things.

"Has anyone told Effie she's coming with us to the game?" I asked, not skipping a beat.

"Yeah, I texted her a little bit ago," Seth responded when he released the delicate skin from his mouth's grasp. "I told her to be here between 6:00 and 6:30. I think first pitch is at 8:05."

Swallowing a big gulp of juice, I nodded and wiped my mouth with a napkin. "Perfect. I'll be ready then."

Easy conversation flowed between the three of us as we finished off the food on our plates and worked together to clean the kitchen. By the time all the dishes were loaded in the dishwasher and the counters were shiny and sparkly, I only had enough time to briefly check my emails and social media accounts before getting ready for my lunch, which I would not be hungry for.

At precisely 12:30 in the afternoon, on time as I always prided myself on being, I walked through the doors of the Revere Hotel and straight into the Rustic Kitchen Bistro, one of my favorite restaurants in town. Almost instantly, I located Allison who was waiting off to the side of the hostess stand with her usual warm, friendly smile spread across her face . . . next to the one person who had stood out most in my mind from the night before—Oliver Saxon.

chapter four

"Never could
I
breathe love
if I did not
first learn
to inhale
a little bit
of chaos."
–Christopher Poindexter

OLIVER

I SMELLED HER before I saw her. I know . . . fucking weird. But as soon as she stepped into the foyer of the restaurant, where Allison and I were waiting for our table, I was aware of her presence, even though I couldn't see her. She had on the same perfume she'd worn the night before at the gala. Orange blossom with a hint of vanilla. A scent that reminded me of the orange cream sodas my three sisters and I used to get when we were kids at Casey's General Store, the place our parents would pick up pizza every Friday night. As I got older and started partying in high school, my friends and I learned those same drinks were the perfect mixers for cheap vodka, and many of our weekend nights were spent sitting around a campfire on someone's land, sipping on that sweet, fruity concoction that somehow never caused a hangover. Back when life seemed easy and all I was interested in was having a little innocent fun. Back before everything changed.

"Monroe!" Allison's face lit up next to me when she spotted her friend, our colleague, welcoming her with a hug and a kiss on the cheek. "I'm so glad you could make it. Oliver and I just got here."

Still reeling from the primal reaction that Monroe's scent alone had on me, I was thankful the two women acted like they hadn't just seen each other the previous evening, fawning over each other's hairstyles and outfits for several moments. It gave me a few extra seconds to get my shit together and process the fact Monroe was apparently joining us for lunch, a detail I was sure Allison had not-so-accidentally failed to mention. The foyer of the restaurant suddenly heated up, rising to temperatures that rivaled the fiery pits of Hell. The sinfully sensual fantasies I'd had about the married woman standing only a few feet away from me while I'd jacked off in the shower that morning flooded through my mind once again. Had I known I'd be sharing a meal with her mere hours later, forced to hold a conversation and not think about how I'd envisioned her naked body looking and feeling underneath mine, I'd have definitely held out until I was safely back home in Chicago the next day, nearly a thousand miles away and with no chance of a humiliating run-in.

"Hey, Oliver. It's a pleasant surprise to see you again," she greeted me cheerfully, though it was apparent that Allison had also neglected to inform her that our lunch would be a party of three. "And thank you again for coming last night. Having you, Jeff, and Tracie there for support meant so much to me."

The same lyrical voice I'd pretended was moaning my name in sweet release prompted my pulse to spike along with my internal thermostat. As I pivoted around to offer a polite smile and hand-shake, I inconspicuously tried to rub my sweaty palms on the dark denim of my jeans while also ensuring the growing bulge in my pants was hidden behind my fly. Thank God, it was. Lifting my gaze to meet hers, the instant our eyes locked, I sucked in a deep breath and completely lost my train of thought. I froze mid-movement, my arm embarrassingly stuck reaching out between the two of us in no man's land. Every drop of moisture that was in my mouth

evaporated, and then somehow multiplied exponentially and reappeared seconds later in my armpits. Much like it had done the first
time I met her.

Never in my life had a woman ever had that kind of effect on
me, and after I'd shamefully indulged myself in the shower, leaving
me feeling dirtier than it did clean, I'd spent several minutes staring
in the mirror, berating my reflection for my inexcusable actions before convincing myself that I'd imagined Monroe to be more beautiful than she really was. I blamed the soft lighting of the ballroom,
along with the classical music and bold city skyline for creating an
atmosphere straight from the final scene of a romantic comedy.
Her tight, low cut, sparkly blue dress was like a beacon in a sea of
standard black, and with her smoky eyes and the way her hair was
up, revealing that long, creamy neck, I didn't have a chance. I mean,
even *I* had looked pretty debonair in my designer tux with my long
hair tamed into a low knot and my facial hair neatly-trimmed, and
I was often mistaken for being homeless in Chicago. *Okay, maybe it
wasn't that bad.*

I came up with all kinds of excuses for why she'd affected me
the way she did, and had I not seen her again afterward, I might've
gone on believing she wasn't nearly as impressive as I'd first made
her out to be in my mind. But as I stood there in front of her, for
the second time in as many days, in my slack-jawed, semi-aroused
motionless state, I knew I'd been wrong. In her modest turquoise
blouse, linen capris, and tan wedges, Monroe had left her hair
down, allowing the wavy, golden locks to cascade around her shoulders and frame her fresh, youthful face, somehow appearing even
more beautiful than I remembered. How that was possible, I hadn't a
clue, but there she was. The most exquisite sight I'd ever seen.

"Those aren't very good jazz hands, Sandy," Monroe's voice
broke through the awkward silence that seemed to last a lifetime. A
playful smirk teased the corners of her mouth as she glanced down
at my outstretched arm. "If you're gonna be in The Pink Ladies,
you've gotta nail the jazz hands and kick-ball-changes every time.
Otherwise, you may be too pure to be pink."

Then, like the altruistic idiot she seemed to bring out in me, I chose not to muster up any sense of dignity and self-preservation I had left, and instead did the exact opposite. In front of her, Allison, and anyone else around that cared to watch, I kick-ball-changed in place three times before my face split in two with the goofiest grin known to man. My mom, who was a dance teacher all of my life, would've been proud. "You makin' fun of me, Riz?"

"Northcutt, party of three, your table is now available," the hostess announced from behind the wooden stand where she waited with menus, saving me from the double pirouette I was about to execute. And what a shame that was.

Monroe and I turned to follow the young woman to our table, only to find Allison watching us with what could only be described as a what-the-fuck-is-wrong-with-you-people look etched across her features. Narrowed eyes. Crinkled forehead. Mouth slightly ajar. Disbelief everywhere.

I snickered as I gestured for the two women to go first. "Fear not, oh mighty leader Allison," I teased. "We promise the future of your organization is in safe hands . . . though perhaps not completely sane ones."

Directly behind the girl who led us to the back of the restaurant, Allison threw a roguish smirk over her shoulder, pausing briefly on Monroe then landing directly on me. "You've been adorably odd and outlandish since the day I met you, sweet Oliver. I just had no idea you'd rub off on Monroe so quickly. If we ever open up a fourth home, I'll be sure to ask the new director to brush up on his or her *Grease* trivia before introducing them to you two. I wouldn't want them to not feel like part of the group."

We all laughed as we postured through the trendy, open-concept bistro and bar. The distinctive smells of basil and tomato sauce drifted through the air as bubbling pizzas were displayed in the open hearth oven and chefs tossed steaming pastas in large bowls. I allowed the ladies to select their places first at the square four-top, hoping I'd have the option to not sit next to Monroe. My level of idiocy was apparently directly correlated with my closeness to her.

However, because they settled in seats across from each other, either chair I chose was nestled between the two of them. *Naturally.* Sighing as I lowered myself onto the cushion, I ordered a water from the server, secretly wishing I could get something a bit stiffer to help calm my nerves. *Chill the fuck out, Sax. Just try to act normal.*

Thankfully, for the first five minutes or so, Allison and I skimmed over the menu as Monroe rattled off a few of her favorite items. Lobster Combo. *She had good taste. Who didn't like lobster and bacon on the same plate?* Beef Short Rib Bahn Mi. *Showed she was adventurous and not scared to try new things.* Chopped Southwest Salad with Salmon. *Not my favorite, but . . . wait! Why did I care what she liked to eat?*

"What in the world is Sweet Italian Sausage Pizza on a Paddle?" Allison cackled as she peered at us over her menu. "It sounds like a kinky food fetish or something. I wonder if we can get the calamari on cuffs, too?"

My cheeks burned with embarrassment at her flippant remarks, even though I knew she was just being funny. I couldn't bear to make eye contact with Monroe to see if her reaction mimicked mine, so as my boss rambled on about how a BDSM-themed restaurant called Grey's would be wildly popular, I pushed my glasses up on the bridge of my nose and stared at the menu. Soon the words began to blur and move across the page, but I refused to look up. When Monroe eventually chimed in and words like *blindfolds* and *ball gags* floated off the tip of her tongue, I thought I was going to lose my damn mind. My cock demanded to be freed with such intensity I worried it was going to burst straight through my jeans. And I'm not sure if I would've been more relieved or embarrassed had it happened.

Escaping to the bathroom wasn't an option. Neither was joining the conversation. But much like the impeccable timing of the hostess earlier, the server returned with our drinks and took down our food order, unknowingly saving me from what was bound to end in yet another humiliating moment for me. As if I hadn't experienced enough in my life during the previous twenty-four hours.

Once he left the table, I brought the glass of ice-cold water up to my mouth for a long, much-needed drink. The lunch was not going anything like I'd thought it would. When Allison had invited me to meet her, dangling the bait of an unknown proposition in front of my face, I'd assumed it had to do with expanding the Chicago-based Mending Hearts house, or maybe choosing a location for another one in a different city. After all, her ultimate goal was to have homes spread out all across the country. But up until that point, the conversation had remained on a personal level, with no hint to any business-related topics.

However, as soon as Allison lowered her own glass back to the table after taking a sip of her iced tea, her expression changed from lighthearted to one with a more somber undertone. Instantly, all other thoughts vanished from my mind and my sole focus was on whatever she was about to tell us. She had yet to utter a word, but I knew something was wrong, and dread sat heavy, deep in my stomach.

"As much as I don't want to talk about this, I'm sure you're both wondering why it was I asked you to meet me here today," she said, nervously tucking her short dark hair behind her ears. "I've always been a fan of ripping a bandage off in one swift motion, so here it goes." All three of us inhaled a collective breath and held it as she blurted out, "Three weeks ago, I was diagnosed with Stage II breast cancer. I've since met with an oncologist, and because it was caught early, he's extremely optimistic that we can beat it with a combination of surgery and chemotherapy. My mastectomy is scheduled for next Friday, and I'll begin the chemo treatments once I recover."

Stopping to finally exhale, Allison shook her head at me as if she could hear the only question that was repeating over and over again in my head. *Are you going to die? Are you going to die? Are you going to die? Oh my God, please don't die.*

"Look, I know it's going to be hard," she continued, reaching out to touch my arm with one hand and Monroe's wrist with the other, "and there are going to be days where I wish I was dead, but the important thing is *I won't be.* The five-year survival rate for the type of cancer I have is over seventy percent. I'm an intelligent person, as I know both of you are, and I urge you to do your research online for what I'm up against. I'll even send you some links if you'd like. God knows, I've scoured every page on the internet with any information. This will be a serious test of my character and will, and I've got a great supporting cast around me, especially the two of you, to help me get through this."

She focused her attention primarily to a sniffling Monroe and offered a small smile. "Sweetie, this project is going to continue on schedule, okay? I've discussed my condition fully with the Board of Directors, and they know there is to be no setbacks because of this. I can still help you select the house before the surgery, and the only thing that will change is that I'll no longer be able to temporarily relocate here to help you hire your team and get things set up. Traveling is discouraged, especially until I know how my body will react to the chemo." Twisting her shoulders in my direction, her pleading eyes found mine and I swallowed hard, knowing what was coming. "That's where you come in, Oliver. Since plans have been in place for me to stay in Boston for some time now, we've already signed a lease for a furnished downtown apartment here in Boston that I'd like to offer you in exchange for assisting Monroe in getting the house up and running. You were an active part of the startup at the Chicago house, so you're just as qualified to do this as I am."

"I, uh, I-I dunno," I stammered, choking on the emotions. "I'm having trouble processing the first part of what you said to even try and think about the second."

Chuckling at my raw honestly, she nodded. "I know it's a lot to take in at once, but unfortunately, we don't have time on our side. These decisions need to be made today. After lunch, I'm scheduled to meet with the landlord of the apartment to get the keys and tour the building. If you're going to say yes, I want you to come with me. I understand you'll have things at home that need tending to, so I'd ask that you be back and ready to get started two weeks from tomorrow."

"What about the Chicago house? Who would be responsible

for my kids if I was here? When would I go back home?" The questions tumbled from my mouth as my mind swirled with confusion.

"Jeff and Tracie, as well as your other counselors, are more than capable to run the house for six months," she replied. "And it's not like you're more than a phone call away, or in the case of an emergency, a few hours on a plane."

The idea of helping set up a new home sounded fun and challenging, but I loved my kids and my employees in Chicago, and I couldn't imagine being away from them for that long. Even though I'd always wanted to live somewhere outside of Illinois, and this would be a great opportunity to try out a new place, *new* often meant daunting and intimidating. And then there was the whole having to work closely with Monroe on a daily basis thing, which scared the living shit out of me. Being around her made me a stumbling, bumbling fool who couldn't conjure up a single coherent thought, so how in the world could I be of any assistance to her?

I shifted my gaze from Allison to Monroe then back to Allison, both waiting with bated breath for my answer. I sucked at making decisions on the spot. I preferred to make lists, compare and contrast, and mull over things for much longer than necessary. However, as a woman at a nearby table stood up to leave, I noticed the pink scarf covering her bald head and all of the conflicting thoughts warring inside of me were silenced. Whether or not her hairstyle was by choice or the result of medical treatment, the only thing it made me think of was no matter how much the statistics were in her favor, Allison—a woman I respected and sincerely cared about—would soon be fighting for her life against a terrible, putrid disease. There was never a decision to be made.

"I'll do it."

chapter
five

"We build
castles
with our fears
and sleep
in them
like kings
and
queens"
–Christopher Poindexter

MONROE

IT WAS 7:14, and Effie was officially late . . . even by her standards. In the five years I'd known Seth's younger sister—Alexandria Sheffield Andrews, or Effie, as he and Colin had nicknamed her when they were kids—I couldn't remember a single time the girl had ever been on time, much less early, to anything. According to the guys, it was a trait she'd possessed from birth, forcing doctors to induce Mrs. Andrews nearly two weeks past her due date. Once I got to know her, that story didn't surprise me in the least.

"Have you tried calling her again?" I asked Seth while pacing the distressed hardwood floors of the living room, or *pah-lah* (parlor) according to my husband in his Bostonian accent. I tried my best to subdue the irritation in my voice, but making others wait over forty minutes without so much as a phone call or a text crossed the line of her usual 'running a little late' to 'rude and selfish.'

My mood was already shot, as I was still reeling from the news that my mentor had breast cancer. I was drowning in an overload of emotion from the news, and I couldn't even imagine what Allison must be going through . . . no matter how much she had tried to downplay the severity of it. It took every ounce of willpower I had to keep myself from breaking down and allowing the fear and sorrow to engulf me. I fought off the tears, because she didn't want me to be upset for her, and since I wasn't able to physically heal her, all I could do was respect her wishes, try to keep her spirits up, and support her through the treatment.

Then, once I'd gotten home, I didn't want to put a damper on the happiness Colin and Seth were sharing after the apparent reconciliation from their fight a few weeks ago, so I'd spent most of the afternoon reorganizing my closet for no other reason than it had kept my mind busy. And I was about ready to say to hell with the game and march my tooshie back upstairs, slip into my most comfortable sweats, and feed my sadness a tub of cookie dough ice cream.

"Yeah, I did a few minutes ago. It keeps going straight to voicemail," he replied from the couch, where he and Colin were watching ridiculous YouTube videos on the laptop to kill time. Glancing at his phone on the coffee table, he grimaced and tapped Colin's shoulder then shot up off the brown leather cushion. "Shit, brah, it's after seven. We gotta go. Effie can just meet us—"

The chime of the doorbell cut his thought short and I blew out a sigh of relief as I snatched my purse from the ottoman where I'd tossed it after I'd grown tired of holding it . . . over twenty minutes before. Shutting the computer off, Colin rose to his feet and swiftly stole a kiss from Seth's lips before taking his place by my side, looping his strong arm around my waist. I peered up at him and offered a compassionate smile as I knew he was already missing the closeness of the man he loved.

"You ready?" I asked, tenderly rubbing my hands up and down his biceps.

"As I'll ever be." The smile he wore on his mouth didn't reach his eyes, but he nodded just the same. "Do I look okay?"

My gaze traveled up and down his body, searching for anything out of place. Red Sox ballcap. Throwback Nomar Garciaparra jersey. Khaki shorts. Brown leather boat shoes. All systems go for a baseball game. "Wicked smaht," I teased in a terrible fake Boston accent, trying to cheer him up. Then with a feisty smirk, I rose up on my toes to kiss his smooth cheek.

"*Wicked* is so last century, Roe," Seth scolded me for at least the hundredth time since I'd moved there. I knew it always ruffled his feathers when I said the word known for its New England roots, so I indulged every chance I got. "If you want to stay in the locals' good graces, you gotta cut—"

The doorbell interrupted him again, but this time it was followed by a series of hard, persistent knocks on the door. Clearly irritated, Seth abandoned our conversation and stalked toward the front of the house, with me and Colin hot on his heels. Throwing the door open, he puffed his chest out and curled his hands into tight fists, ready to lay into his sister. However, the second he saw Effie standing on the front porch with mascara streaks staining her face and a bright pink nose, he forgot all about his anger and rushed to her side, wrapping an arm around her shoulders and huddling her safely inside.

Out of habit, Colin and I both scanned the area in the front of our house, checking the popular hiding spots for paparazzi. A couple of years before, Colin's second on the Pats and his first as the starting quarterback, things got a little crazy with reporters and photographers following us around. Though it didn't come close to comparing to what I'd witnessed in L.A. as a kid, it still wasn't much fun to have our every move documented and scrutinized. We loved interacting and doing interviews when they were scheduled, but some mornings we would have a camera greet us the moment we walked out the door. Thankfully, a little while after the team's loss in the second round of the playoffs, they moved their efforts onto others who were either more controversial, or whatever top athlete was making the nightly highlight reels.

Because the NFL regular season still wasn't set to kick off for another week, "Clutch Coverage," as we jokingly called it in our house, wasn't in full swing yet. However, we remained mindful and cautious, especially when we're around any situation that could be viewed as contentious outside the security of our home. One snapshot of Effie in tears on our doorstep could be tomorrow's top headline on a gossip site. "Trouble in Perfect Paradise: Star QB's Mistress Confronts Wife." Despite how ridiculously far off from the truth it would be, and regardless if people believed it or not, it could plant a seed of doubt, a sliver of distrust, and if something like that ever happened to Colin and me, support for the Mending Hearts home would be jeopardized.

And that wasn't part of the deal.

"I don't see anyone. Let's get inside and make sure she's okay," Colin announced, his tone more gruff than normal. I wasn't sure if he was more aggravated that his Funday Sunday with Seth was over, or because Effie had shown up not only late, but looking like an emotional wreck. My guess was an equal part combination of the two.

Hastily shutting the door, we rushed back to the living room, where Seth had taken Effie to get her away from the front windows. He was standing with his hands on his hips and a frown wrinkling his chin, staring expectantly at her while she used the large framed mirror on the wall to wipe the black smudges from her face. "Okay, we're all here now. Tell us what happened."

"Yeah, whose ass are we gonna have to kick on the way to the game? I told you to stay away from those Harvard punks," Colin chimed in before she even had a chance to speak.

I dramatically rolled my eyes at the over-the-top big brother act he always tried to pull with her, and when she cut her gaze from her own reflection over to where Colin stood with his brawny arms crossed over his chest and gave her most adoring smile, I wanted to roll them again. Though Effie was always as sweet as she could be to me, and I truly liked her for the most part, she could be a bit of an attention-seeker, especially when it came to Seth and Colin. I wasn't sure if they couldn't see it as clearly as I could, but anytime they became protective or possessive of her, her entire face would light up with happiness. I never faulted her for having that reaction, mainly because I understood how she felt. She loved the guys just like I did, and I knew what it was like for them to make you feel appreciated and cherished. The three of them having grown up together, I could only imagine the connection they shared, and it usually didn't bother me . . . but I was having a rotten ass day and not in the mood for her immature games.

"It's not a guy," she retorted as she spun around to face all of us, keeping her eyes steady on Colin. "I already told you when I got back from Paris last month that I'd sworn off dating."

"Yeah, and since then we've met Nolan, Lance, and some other schmuck whose name I can't remember," Seth laughed dryly.

"Nolan is just a friend, Lance was a horrible blind date, and there was *no other schmuck!*" Effie shouted at him with a stomp of her heeled foot. "And this isn't about a fucking guy. I didn't get the job I thought I was guaranteed, and now Mom and Dad are gonna be pissed, because I spent the summer gallivanting around Europe instead of coming up with a back-up plan in case this shit happened!"

Throwing his arms in the air, Seth blew out an exasperated sigh. "Effie, what the fuck? Why didn't you get the job? Wasn't this the one at the marketing firm with your friend Monica that you were supposed to start next month?"

She nodded as the momentarily forgotten tears welled up again. "Yes! One of their account managers is retiring at the end of September, and Monica assured me the job was mine, but—"

"Wait," Colin cut her off. "How did she know you were getting the job? Does this Monica chick do the hiring?"

Effie dropped her chin to her chest as she shook her head, her gaze locked on the floor. "No, she was the personal assistant for the CEO."

Seth snickered as the picture became clear to everyone. "And let me guess, she was assisting him with all kinds of *special* projects?"

"Yes, but he told her he loved her!" she contended. "She thought he was going to leave his wife at the end of the year *and* he promised her that I'd get the job, but his daughter walked in on them this weekend and demanded he fire her, or she was going to tell her mom and the rest of the family."

"So now you're up shit creek without a paddle, and once again, you need someone to bail your ass out," her brother admonished as he gave his best *disappointed father* look.

Clenching her jaw, she pinched her brows together and threw daggers at her only sibling. "Seth, I don't need a fucking lecture from you. I'm sure Mom and Dad will be happy to give me an earful when I'm forced to tell them I won't be able to start paying my own rent and car payment in a couple of months."

"There are other damn jobs you can apply for, Alexandria! Get on a fucking computer and—"

The ringtone to Colin's phone—some rap song I'd never heard before that fittingly kept saying "Excuse Me" over and over again— interrupted the conversation, and I had to bite my lip to keep the laughter from escaping. My husband picked up all kinds of music from his teammates that I'd never heard before, and usually I didn't care for most of it, but I made a mental note to look that one up.

He pulled his cell out of his pocket and glared at both Seth and Effie, silently warning them to keep their mouths closed. "Hey, Barry. What's up?"

Waiting to hear what his PR rep had to say, he glanced down at his watch and grimaced. "Yeah, we got held up a little bit, but we're on our way now. I didn't know I was supposed to go down on the field before the game."

Another pause. "Sure, no problem. I'll stay after to do auto-graphs and pictures. Just let their people know I'll have Monroe, Seth, and Effie with me, so they'll need field credentials too. We should be there in a half-hour, hopefully before first pitch."

He exchanged goodbyes then disconnected the call. "Sorry, Ef, but we're gonna have to deal with your problem later. Kids from the Make-a-Wish foundation are at the game and we need to get there ASAP. Are you still coming with us?"

Wiping away the wetness on her cheeks with the backs of her

hands, Effie rolled her shoulders back, straightened her posture, and curled her lips up in a charismatic smile. "Yeah, I'll be fine. Sorry you're late 'cause of me. I'll make it up to you, Colin. I promise."

"No need for all that." He replaced his grumpy expression with a grin of his own as he grabbed the keys to the Range Rover and ruffled her hair. "Now let's get going, brat. Maybe I can introduce you to a few of the guys I know on the team after the game and we can do something about your no-dating thing."

The two of them strode away together in the direction of the garage discussing who Colin did and didn't know on the Red Sox, neither having any problem forgetting about the conversation that had been taking place. After Seth and I exchanged a knowing *there's-nothing-we-can-do-about-it* look, we followed behind them without a word and got into the SUV.

THE BASEBALL GAME had been awesome, a pitching duel where the Sox and the Yankees had both struggled to produce any offense until Christian Garcia, Boston's rookie shortstop, hit a solo homerun over Fenway's Green Monster in the bottom of the eighth inning. After a slight scare when our closer walked the first two batters in the top of the ninth, he struck out the next three to seal the victory and clinch a playoff spot for the hometown team.

Needless to say, by the time we reached the field from the box suite we had watched the game from, everyone was in full-out celebration mode. Players, coaches, and front office personnel were surrounded by family and friends, fans, and members of the media, everyone wanting to share in the jubilant memories being made. Between the nail-biting game and then witnessing the heartfelt smiles and congratulatory remarks, I briefly escaped the melancholy that had settled in my soul throughout the afternoon and evening. Even though I couldn't completely stop thinking about Allison and the upcoming battle she was about to face, the game and festivities did finally lighten my mood some.

"There it is!" Colin exclaimed as he suddenly appeared in front of me and looped his arm around my waist, lifting me off the infield grass.

Squealing as my feet went airborne, I clung to his neck and grinned. "There what is?"

"Your smile, beautiful. I thought maybe you lost it somewhere when you went to lunch today because I hadn't seen it since you left." He pressed a sweet kiss to my lips while holding me up against him. "But I see you found it again, so I won't have to send out any search parties."

I laughed a deep belly laugh and rested my forehead to his. "Oh, Colin, I love when you get all soft on me. You're just like a life-sized stuffed animal."

"Just for you, Roe," he replied softly as he lowered me to the ground. His eyes darted over to where Seth was chatting with an attractive young woman, who, based on the way she was thrusting her abundant cleavage up in his face and rubbing her hand along his forearm, was looking to play her own game of long ball. Unable to conceal the aggravation in his voice, Colin grabbed my hand and dragged me in the opposite direction, muttering under his breath, "You and me to the end, baby girl."

For the second night in a row, we didn't make it home until the early morning hours, and after the roller coaster of emotions I'd experienced over the previous thirty-six hours, I was more than exhausted; I was drained, depleted, and mostly just done. After Effie jumped in her car and took off the minute we returned and I gave Seth a goodnight hug and kiss on the cheek, I left him and Colin downstairs to say their goodbyes privately as I trudged up to my master suite on the third floor and headed straight for the shower.

Unfortunately, the hot water pelting me in the face and all over my body did little to improve my mood, and I'd be lying if I didn't admit I was thrilled to see Colin waiting for me in my bed, dressed in a white t-shirt and plaid pajama pants, his short hair still damp from his own shower.

"Come on, beautiful," he coaxed with a warm smile, patting the mattress next to where he was sprawled out. "Come let me cuddle you while you tell me what's got you down. I may not be able to make it better, but I'll do whatever I can to make you happy."

Instantly, my eyes overflowed with a deluge of tears—appreciative ones for Colin for knowing I needed him without me saying a word, sad ones for Allison as she dealt with a life-threatening condition, and angry ones for cancer for ruining so many lives on a daily basis—all blending together in a waterfall of overwhelming emotional release. Stumbling toward the bed through my blurred vision, I crawled up next to my husband and allowed him to hold me tightly against his comforting body as I told him all about what had happened at lunch with Allison and Oliver. Sometimes you just needed a hard cry and a good snuggle to reset your balance in the world. And that's what Colin did time and time again—he was my rock. My life-sized rock stuffed animal.

chapter
six

"If you ever
want your soul
to dance in the clouds,
you will at some point
have to juggle lightning
and taste the
thunder."
–Christopher Poindexter

OLIVER

AS I LUMBERED toward my departure gate at O'Hare with a one-way ticket to Boston in my hand, I suddenly realized I had no fucking idea what I was getting myself into. The two weeks between Allison telling us she had cancer and me clearing airport security that Sunday afternoon had been a whirlwind of events that left me feeling like a chaotic mess. After preparing my kids and staff at the Mending Hearts house for my extended absence, arranging for my mail to be forwarded to my new address and my neighbor to take care of my plants, and packing up the majority of my wardrobe and my alto sax that I couldn't live without, I was forced to make the nine-hour roundtrip car ride to my small hometown so that my parents could 'foster' my cat, Coltrane, while I was gone. The furnished apartment that had been rented for Allison didn't allow animals, so as much as I hated parting with the bastard of a pet he was, I didn't have much of a choice.

Naturally, my mom and dad made a big deal when I came into town, inviting my two older sisters, Mallory and Emma, and their husbands and kids for a big family dinner where they served my favorite meal—chicken fried steak, mashed potatoes, and corn on the cob. I have to admit it was great to see them all at a time other than the usual Easter, Thanksgiving, and Christmas holidays that we always gathered for, but the empty chairs where my youngest sister Charlotte and my oldest niece Callie typically sat were definitely noticed. Because they lived down in Nashville, they couldn't pop on over for dinner last minute like the others could; however, I did promise Callie over a phone call that she could come stay with me for a weekend once I got settled in Boston. I knew my sister could probably use the break from her seventeen-year-old daughter as much as my niece could use the break from her mom, but my agreeing to the deal was proof-in-point that I was rapidly losing my mind.

With nearly two hours to kill before my flight, I located the nearest bar to my gate and found an open stool to get comfortable on, hoping I could toss back a couple of beers and relax while I waited. All I wanted was a small break from having to think about any of the shit that had kept me awake for the last fourteen nights. *Allison battling cancer. Something happening to one of my kids while I was gone. The pipes in my apartment bursting while no one was there. My mom stealing Coltrane and never giving him back. My whole family harping on me about not having a girlfriend or starting a family yet. My inability to stop picturing the same perfect face every time I closed my eyes . . . and every time I stroked my cock. Monroe-fucking-Ca—*

"CASSIDY'S GOT A MAN WIDE OPEN DOWN THE FIELD! THIS COULD BE THE GAME, FOLKS . . ."

My chin snapped up the second I heard her last name from the announcer's voice on the TV behind the bar, and my eyes focused on the big screen just in time for me to see Colin throw a touchdown pass to win the game. I may not have known much about football, but I was a grown man living in America in the twenty-first century. And unless I was around Monroe, I usually wasn't an idiot.

"HE DID IT! HE DID IT AGAIN! THE PATRIOTS REMAIN UNDEFEATED THROUGH WEEK TWO OF THE REGULAR SEASON, THANKS TO NONE OTHER THAN THEIR STAR QUARTERBACK, CLUTCH CASSIDY, WHO BROUGHT HIS TEAM FROM BEHIND WITH A HUGE DOUBLE-DIGIT FOURTH QUARTER COMEBACK!"

The camera panned around the field, first capturing the receiver's celebration dance in the end zone, and then locking in on Colin as he jogged to the sidelines, surrounded by people patting his helmet and slapping him on the ass. A few more seconds of following him while he was congratulated by teammates and coaches, and then . . . there she was.

Plastered across the giant screen in her navy number-three jersey, the smile on her face couldn't have been any bigger or brighter if she tried. She jumped up and down in place while triumphantly punching her fists in the air, and maybe it was just me, but it seemed like the cameraman lingered the focus on her chest as her boobs bounced around under the clingy fabric. My dick stirred to life in my jeans as I wondered for the ten-thousandth time what those round, perky breasts would feel like cupped in my palms.

"Hot damn, that is one fine ass woman," a random forty-something guy sitting next to me announced none-too-quietly. Glancing over at me, he cocked his eyebrow and chuckled crudely. "What a guy like one of us wouldn't do to tap a juicy piece like that . . . mmm hmmm. I bet she smells like sweet Georgia peaches, and man-oh-man, I'd wear her ass out until she couldn't sit for days. Then I'd have her wrap those pretty pink lips arou—"

"Dude, what the hell? Are you serious?" I exclaimed, slamming my beer onto the polished wooden surface while pinning the douchebag with my murderous glare. "Not only do I not know you, but you're talking about somebody's wife, who is a real person with feelings and shit. Plus," I paused to look around the crowded pub-style setting we were in, "there are women all around us. Work on the whole respect thing and you may find someone who'd be interested in letting you *wear her ass out* and whatever else you were going to say."

A fleeting wave of shame washed over the guy's face, but it was immediately replaced with rage and retaliation. Raising up to his full height, he snarled down at me, shouting directly in my face. *"Feelings and shit?! Are you a fucking faggot, man? Is that why you've got all this long hair and wear those tight, pussy-ass jeans, huh? 'Cause your boyfriend likes to treat you like the whiny little bitch you are when he's pumping you from behind?"*

I felt the color drain from my face as his tirade went on and on and as everyone around us stopped to witness the debacle. The more he yelled, the more embarrassed I became for him, but instead of trying to cut him off or to diffuse the altercation, I held my position, silent but steadfast, until he finished spewing his load of ignorance. But before I had a chance to say anything back, though I truly had no idea of how to even respond to such absurdity, two armed officers emerged from the crowd in the terminal and escorted the man away with minimal resistance.

Then, almost as if nothing ever happened, everyone around me went back to doing whatever it was they were doing, while I was left wondering what in the world had just transpired. Why had I said anything to begin with? From the time I was a kid, I'd always been the non-confrontational type, avoiding playground skirmishes and my sisters' daily quarrels at all costs. Conflict and hostility filled me with an overwhelming uneasiness that threatened to make me physically ill, and when that happened, my fight-or-flight reflex was firmly set in the *flight* position.

The fact I'd reacted to the foolishness coming out of that fuck-wad's mouth in the first place was extremely out of character for me, and it wasn't like it was the first time I'd heard a guy spout off a lewd comment about a chick. Shit, even some of my friends would occasionally be crude and vulgar when we hung out at a bar or club, and though I never talked like they did or agreed with it, I never chastised them over it either. Especially not by calling them out in public.

But when he said those things about Monroe, a switch went off inside and a surge of adrenaline coursed through me, demanding I defend her. Only one other time in my life had that happened before, and that was to protect my baby sister from a monster . . . but I barely knew Monroe, and she wasn't in imminent danger. The guy was an asshat, but basically harmless. Why hadn't I just minded my own damn business?

"Hey," the bartender interrupted my wayward thoughts as he set another beer in front of me, "those ladies at the opposite end of the bar ordered you another and picked up your tab. They wanted me to tell you, 'Thanks for being one of the good guys.'"

Jerking my head in the direction he pointed, I found two quite attractive women around my age smiling brightly at me, one offering a little wave while the other shyly twirled her hair around her finger. I grabbed the amber-filled glass and lifted it in the air, tilting it toward them as I politely mouthed, "Thank you."

The young bartender smirked and wagged his finger at me. "You keep up that chivalry act, dude, and you'll have 'em lined up waiting for you. Maybe I should give it a try."

"It's not an act, man, and you shouldn't have to try," I retorted after taking a sip. "Just don't be an asshole. It's that easy."

Too disgusted to continue talking to the clueless bartender, I stood up before he could reply. All I wanted was to get to my new place in Boston so I could convince myself that I was over-analyzing the way in which Monroe Cassidy affected me.

"HEY, MONROE, GREAT game yesterday, eh? I saw you on TV."

"Hey there, Monroe! The team's looking great! How've you been?"

"Monroe! It's so great to see you again. Looks like the Pats are on their way to a championship this year!"

Sighing at my reflection in the bathroom mirror, I tucked the unruly, dark curls behind my ears and groaned. I was ridiculously lame. Who in the hell over the age of eighteen practiced how they were going to greet someone? I mean, it was a hello for fuck's sake, not a marriage proposal. Forget that it had taken me nearly fifteen minutes to choose what I was going to wear, only to end up in the original light blue pinstriped shirt and gray slacks I'd first retrieved from the closet. Then, I'd spent another ten messing with my hair. Down or pulled back? Were man-buns too hipster? Would I appear to be unorganized and unprofessional if I left it hanging free? Maybe she thought ponytails on guys were stupid?

I literally wanted to punch myself in the face. I should never have agreed to fill in for Allison; failure was inevitable. Why didn't she ask Jason, the director from the Indianapolis house, to do it? Sure, his wife was like nine months pregnant and due to deliver at any time, but they had good hospitals in Boston, right? *God, I sound like a pussy. I need to man the fuck up.*

My phone chimed with a text from my mom—a selfie of her and Coltrane reminding me to brush my teeth and wishing me good luck on my first day, like I was thirteen instead of thirty-three. *And I wonder why I have issues* . . . However, like the good son that I was, I took a selfie of my own—with my eyes crossed and my lips puckered in a fish face—and shot a message back, assuring her I even remembered to wear deodorant and clean underwear. It was no secret I was her favorite—a momma's boy from the day I was born—but beginning the day Dad was sent away during my junior year of high school, I'd felt an overwhelming sense of responsibility to keep our relationship strong and do whatever I could to keep her happy while he was gone. I'd even stayed at home and pursued my undergrad degree at nearby Quincy University so I could help out in his absence. And even though my entire family had bonded together and supported each other during that difficult time, I would've given anything to prevent the events surrounding it.

"Please rise," the stout, bald-headed bailiff announced to the packed courtroom, and without hesitation, I—along with my mom and sisters—pushed up to our feet, anxiously awaiting the ruling.

Dressed in our Sunday best, we stood in the front row of the stuffy space that smelled like anguish and despair, directly behind my father and his team of attorneys. As the judge entered the room, Dad took a brief moment to turn around and give us an encouraging smile, mouthing the words, "Don't worry. I love you."

The elderly man in the black robe, Judge Edward Langford, picked up the gavel and banged it three times once he was settled at the bench, prompting the bailiff to call the court to order and instruct everyone to take a seat. A nervous buzz could be felt throughout the outdated courtroom, while reporters from both the local and national media, as well as most of the members of my small hometown of Kinderhook, IL, waited with bated breath to find out what the judge had decided on sentencing, as the jury had delivered their "Guilty of Second Degree Murder" verdict three days prior, a lesser conviction than he was originally charged for.

Thankfully, he wasted little time. "Mr. Saxon, please stand," he commanded with a grunt, removing his glasses and scrubbing his hands up and down his face. "In my thirty-plus years of sitting on the bench, serving the people of the state of Illinois and the United States judicial system, I can assure you that I've never had a case like this cross my desk. It's hard for many people—especially those who are parents—to view your circumstances without bias and emotion. However, as hard as it may be to do, it's my job. What I swore on oath to do. As a father myself, it pains me to have to sentence you, as I can't even pretend to know how I would've reacted had I been in your shoes. And I know many people undoubtedly feel your actions were justified, but bottom line is you went outside the law to do it, and as such, must be punished accordingly.

"After thorough reviewing all of the testimony and evidence, most glaringly the span of time that elapsed between you finding out about Mr. Hilton's relationship with your daughter and when you ultimately confronted him, I hereby sentence you to ten years in prison and a fine of five thousand dollars with your time served of six months applied to the term. You will be allowed a chance to visit with your family directly following this hearing, after which you will be transported to Western Illinois Correctional Center to begin serving your sentence." He paused and stared intensely at my father. "Do you understand everything that I've just stated, Mr. Saxon?"

"I do, your honor," Dad assured him.

The judge began to speak again, but the heartbreaking sob that escaped from thirteen-year-old Charlotte on my left drowned out everything else. I peered over at her as she held her swollen belly, shaking uncontrollably, and my entire world crumbled. I was devastated knowing that not only would my little niece not be able to meet her grandfather until she was an adolescent, but that all of us would be without the most important man in our lives for years to come. The man who taught us to tie our shoes and ride our bikes. The man who carved the turkey every Thanksgiving and personally cut down the Christmas tree every December. The man who instilled in us appreciation for music, the importance of laughter, the meaning of unconditional love, and ironically, the value of life. He was now the man who would be missing from a huge chunk of our lives . . . all because he defended one of his own children.

First, one tear escaped, and then another, and by the time Judge Langford finished his speech and banged the gavel to close the hearing, I was bawling like a baby. My mom, who was on my other side, slid her hand in mine and squeezed, smiling down at me with her own tears streaming down her cheeks. "We're all gonna be okay, Ollie. I promise we'll figure it out."

As the judge exited the bench, the courtroom erupted in mass chaos as people began screaming and shouting about injustice and unfairness. A second bailiff came and escorted us away from the pandemonium and into a small room where my father was waiting. Sprinting to him as a group, we nearly tackled him as we all began to talk at once, spewing our frustration and rage at the ruling.

Holding his hands up in the air to silence us, he offered an understanding smile and did his best to console us. "I know you all feel that you're going to explode with the anger and wrath you feel inside yourself right now, and you have every right to feel that way. Believe me, I was hoping for a less harsh outcome as well, but let me remind you of what happens when you allow your emotions to control your actions. That's how we got here in the first place. If nothing else, please learn from my mistakes." His voice was calm and collected, and I remembered thinking that even in what had to be the worst moments of his life, my dad put the needs of his wife and children first, because that's what he did and who he was. Always.

"Now, we don't have a whole lot of time here before I have to go," he continued, "but I want you all to promise me that you will stick together as a family no matter what while I'm away. Your mother is going to need support and help around the house, as she now has both the music shop and the dance studio to manage. Mallory and Emma, you two have grown into such beautiful young women, and I can't wait to hear about your successful journeys into adulthood. I love you both more than you can ever know, and I'm so very proud of you girls," he addressed my two older sisters before turning to Charlotte, who was still unable to gather her composure. "Baby girl, there are so many things I've wanted to say to you since that night, but simply haven't had the opportunity or the right words, so I promise the first thing I'll do once I get there will be to write you a letter and explain everything. I want you to know I love you from the deepest part of my heart, and all I've ever wanted was the best thing for you. Promise me you'll do the same for this baby growing inside of you. Promise me you'll love her and protect her with everything you have."

Charlotte nodded through her wails, and as our dad engulfed her in his strong arms, I saw even the bailiff wipe a tear from under his eyes. Once Dad released her, he stood and focused his attention on me. "Son, this is much earlier than I thought I'd have to say this, but I have full faith in you to take care of this family. You're the man of the house now, and until you leave for college," he raised his eyebrows at me and pinned me with a stern look, "and you will go to college, I need you to take care of your mother and your sisters. I know it was hard for you to say the things you said up on that stand, but I'm proud of you for telling the truth. No matter what happens from this point out, I can rest assured that I have raised four honorable and respectful children. My love for all of you has no limit."

A woman stuck her head inside the door to let us know we had five minutes left, and after he hugged each one of us kids again, he and Mom shared a few private words and several kisses in the corner. Another law enforcement agent then entered the room and my dad allowed them to cuff both his hands and feet before he was led away. That was the day my dad became my hero and I vowed to never disappoint him.

A lump formed in my throat as I replayed the events of that day almost eighteen years ago in my mind, and with a hard swallow, I forced it back where it came from. It was then that I looked down at my phone and noticed the time on the display. *8:52!* Monroe was due to pick me up in less than ten minutes and I still hadn't put a tie on, nor had I decided on a proper hello. I scrambled into my bedroom, which still felt odd to call *mine*, since it wasn't my furniture or my bed linens, and grabbed the first skinny tie I came across in the closet, looping it around my neck just as I heard my phone ding again.

"Sweet Jesus! What now, dear woman?" I muttered while stuffing my wallet into my back pocket before going to retrieve my phone from the bathroom counter. Expecting another off-the-wall message from my mom, I stilled with a sharp intake of breath when I saw the screen.

Monroe: I'm parked in front of the building. Blue Volvo SUV.

Lifting my gaze to my reflection for a final assessment, I swore to myself I wouldn't stare at her breasts, fantasize about her lips, or bring up how I defended them both to the jackass from the airport bar. Then, with a hard swallow, I turned around and headed downstairs to meet her. It was show time.

chapter
seven

"We are
the scientists,
trying to
make sense of
the stars
inside
of us."
–Christopher Poindexter

MONROE

"HE SAID HE thought I'd smell like a *peach*?" Wrinkling up my nose, I shook my head with amusement as I glanced over at Oliver in the passenger seat of my car. "What do they even smell like? Is that a good thing? Are peaches some sort of aphrodisiac I've never heard about?"

He choked back a laugh and nodded. "Well, I haven't gone around sniffing a lot of peaches in my life, especially not Georgia ones, but using the context of his remarks, I'm guessing he thought it was a *very* good thing. I still can't believe he actually said those things out loud or that you're not more upset about it. I was livid *for* you."

My heart fluttered softly at his words, knowing he tried to defend my honor to some stranger at an airport bar, even though he and I barely know each other. After our initial meeting a couple of weekends ago, he'd been busy preparing things in Chicago for his six-month stint away from home, while I'd spent most of that time in Detroit with Allison helping her during her surgery and recovery, so we hadn't had much time to talk other than sporadic texts as I updated him on her condition.

Thankfully, all had gone well with the double mastectomy, and after four days in the hospital, she was released to finish her recuperation in the comfort of her own home. Since Allison had never married and had lived at the MH house for most of her adult life, it was important for me to be there with her during those first few brutal days. I refused to allow the woman who was more of a mother to me than my own flesh-and-blood to face that alone, no matter how many times she insisted she was good and didn't need me fussing over her. Plus, since the regular season had officially kicked off the weekend after the gala, it wasn't like Colin would be at home longer than to sleep at night for the next five or so months. I did, however, return in time to support my husband and the rest of the team for the home opener, which was apparently when Oliver and this other guy saw me on TV.

"I learned long ago not to worry about that kind of stuff," I replied matter-of-factly. "As long as I know it's not anything I'm doing or the way I'm presenting myself publicly that is provoking people to make negative or derogatory comments, then it's on them, not me. I can't control their thoughts, words, or actions, and I usually choose to ignore it. Do you know how many times I've seen on social media women making catty comments about me not being good enough for Colin? Or that the only reason he married me was because I grew up with famous parents that would help advance his celebrity status? I'd spend my entire life responding to that nonsense if I did."

I paused briefly as I turned into the driveway of the second house we were touring as a possible location for the MH home, giving him a moment to think about what I'd said. After shifting the car into park and turning off the engine, I twisted to face him and offered a grateful smile. "But I really appreciate you sticking up for me. You didn't have to do that . . ." My voice trailed off, but before he had a chance to speak, I added in a breathy whisper, "Most people wouldn't have."

"I normally wouldn't have, but it was you," he blurted out while staring down at his fidgeting hands in his lap. His beard didn't hide the hard bob of his Adam's apple as his words hung heavy in the tight confines of my car, the silence stretching on until he added, "Even if you are rebellious, Rizzo, you don't deserve to be degraded like that."

Laughter danced in his honey-colored eyes as they lifted to meet mine from behind his glasses, and when I noticed the endearing pink flush surface across his cheeks, warmth blossomed inside my chest and my entire body relaxed. I'd been a little worried, because when I first picked him up at his apartment, he'd seemed incredibly uncomfortable and nervous in my presence. The two other times we'd been around each other, he'd definitely come off as a little quirky, possibly even a bit eccentric, but not straight-up stiff and a whole-lot anxious like the first couple of hours we'd spent together that morning. There was no way we were going to be able to work together with that kind of tension surrounding us all the time, but after I'd told him a few funny things that happened during my trip to Michigan and asked him about his flight and getting settled into his new place, he'd finally started to unwind a bit, which was what led us to the story of the Peach Man.

"Well next time, you can tell him that Rizzo doesn't smell like peaches. She doesn't even like to eat them," I joked as I tossed my keys into my purse and opened the car door, stepping out into the sunny, late-September morning. I thought I heard him mumble something about oranges and ice cream as I shut the door behind me, but when his head popped up on the other side of the sedan, he simply grinned and motioned for me to lead the way toward the front door.

"MAYBE IT WOULD help if I wrote out a list of the pros and cons of each house so that we can compare them side-by-side. This flipping back and forth between the listings on the screen is confusing me," I suggested to Oliver as I pushed the iPad aside and grabbed my planner and a pen from my purse.

Even in the age of technology that we lived in, where a tablet, phone or even a watch could do any and everything you could possibly need it to short of launching a shuttle into space, I enjoyed actually writing things down on paper. Lists, letters, reminders—all of it I handwrote instead of punching it into an electronic device, because, for whatever reason, it helped cement the information into my brain. I half expected him to tease me a little for my archaic practices, but when I peered across the restaurant table at him, he was too busy devouring the chocolate brownie surprise to care if I was making the list with carbon and papyrus. His *second* chocolate brownie surprise, I might add.

"Oliver!" I exclaimed, stifling a giggle when he looked up at me with a few chocolate crumbs straggling around his lip and in his facial hair. "Do they not have brownies in Illinois? My God, man. Come up for a breath every so often. We're supposed to make a final decision on the house by the end of the week, and I'm starting to think you're just going to vote for the one with the biggest kitchen. A lobster roll, cup of chowder, basket of fries, and two desserts? Where do you put all of it?"

"My mom used to call me a bottomless pit. She said I'd outeat all three of my sisters combined and never gain a pound," he divulged as he swiped at the remnants of the sweets with his napkin before tossing a playful grin in my direction. "And for the record, Miss Smarty Pants, they do have brownies in Illinois, but they don't have lobster rolls or chowder . . . at least not like this."

With a stifled giggle, I grabbed the napkin from my own lap and leaned across the table, brushing away the specks of food that he'd missed in his beard. "Well, I believe it. The bottomless pit part, that is." I dropped the cloth on the table once he was crumb-free. "But now it's time to work. I need your help analyzing all this info."

The same rosy color I'd seen on his cheeks earlier in my car returned as he tried to hide behind the curtain of his dark, wavy hair. I wasn't sure I'd ever seen a man blush before Oliver, and I liked it. Well, I liked when *he* did it, as it softened his sharp, masculine facial features and made him seem a little more warm, comfortable, and snug.

Kind of like a stuffed animal.

"I'm ready now," he announced after a drink of water, his lips still turned up in a coy smile, "but for future reference, if you bring a hungry man into a restaurant filled with all of these delicious smells, you shouldn't expect to get anything done until he's stuffed himself full. You're a married woman. You gotta know better than that."

Initially, his mention of my husband triggered a twinge of guilt that I didn't quite expect or understand. I wasn't doing anything wrong. Colin knew exactly where I was and who I was with, not that we had the kind of relationship where he would ever get jealous anyway. And Oliver and I had spent the day discussing floor plans, storage space, and square footage as we'd toured the two properties for Mending Hearts, only engaging in friendly conversation while we were in the car, which never came close to being inappropriate. Oliver wouldn't even tell me what the guy at the bar actually said about me other than the smelling like peaches thing, claiming the rest was too obscene and offensive to repeat in my company.

It clearly didn't make any sense that I should feel guilty for anything, so I chalked up the foreign emotion to my inexperience of spending one-on-one time with a man other than Colin or Seth. Before Oliver, I rarely found myself in a situation where I was alone with a guy who wasn't one of them for an extended period of time, and that was completely on purpose. Men in social settings, I could handle just fine; there were even some whose company and conversation I enjoyed quite a bit. But that was where my comfort level began to waver.

I'd known from the night at the gala that Oliver was different than most men, however. A combination of his closeness with Allison, which in and of itself spoke volumes, his devotion and dedication to helping abused children, and his sweet and tender dis-position immediately placed him in the safe zone in my mind, which was why I had no issues when I found out he'd be taking Allison's place working side-by-side with me. I'm not sure what I would've done if that hadn't been the case, but thankfully, I didn't have to worry about it. Now, I just needed to realize this was my new nor-mal. *He* was my new normal.

"Earth to Monroe. Come in, Monroe. Repeat, come in, Monroe. Please return to Boston, where your esteemed colleague is waiting on you." Oliver's pretend-robot voice sliced through my wandering thoughts and reeled me back to reality.

Shaking my head, an embarrassed smile crept across my face as I focused in on Oliver, who was waving his arms around in the air like he was trying to flag down someone on the other side of the street instead of the other side of the booth. "Sorry," I apologized lamely. "I was just making a mental note to not attempt any more working lunches with you."

"A note or a chapter?" he taunted with a mischievous smirk. "You were lost in thought for a good twenty minutes. I already chose the house and called the realtor with our offer."

Trying not to laugh, I rolled my eyes. "I checked out for *maybe* twenty seconds. So hush your mouth, Saxon."

"I think you're the first female who's ever called me by my last name, unless it had Mister or Doctor in front of it." His smirk grew into a mega-watt smile, showing his perfectly-straight, pearly whites. "I think I like it."

"Oh yeah?" I mused as I lifted my iced tea to my mouth for a sip, mainly to hide the face-splitting grin threatening to take over my mug. "What do the girls usually call you?"

He pushed his glasses up on the bridge of his nose and licked his lips nervously. "I'm just Oliver to everyone except for my family, who call me Ollie when they want to annoy me. But I guess that's what families are for, right?"

Jealousy licked cold under my skin at his words, as I secret-ly wished I'd grown up with a normal family who called me cute nicknames like Ollie. I was pretty sure "Disappointment," "Home Wrecker," and "Jealous Slut" weren't quite the same thing. My mom always did have a way with words.

Pushing aside the hurtful memories, I forced myself to match his smile and picked up the pen from the table. "Right," I lied before abruptly changing the subject. "Now, about this list . . ."

We then spent the next hour and a half comparing and contrasting the properties until we both agreed on which one would be perfect for the new MH home.

But in the back of my mind, I wondered what kind of nickname Oliver might come up with for me, if he had to choose one.

chapter eight

"The thing about
chaos, is that while
it disturbs us,
it too, forces
our hearts to roar
in a way we
secretly find
magnificent."
–Christopher Poindexter

OLIVER

I DIDN'T WANT the day to end. I know that sounds stupid, but it's the truth. My first day of 'work' with Monroe had gone five thousand times better than I'd expected, even despite the few times I'd gotten tongue-tied while talking to her or found myself eye-guzzling every inch of her flawless face and shapely body. Thankfully, she never caught me in perverted-creeper-mode—or at least, not that I was aware of—and by the time she dropped me off late in the afternoon, my confidence in not only myself, but also the rapport that had developed between us, had grown immensely. If I could only get past the way my heart soared in my chest every time she flashed me one of her million-dollar smiles, or the way my cock twitched with lust-driven hope each time we accidentally touched, then I'd have nothing to worry about for the next six months. If only . . .

"Same time tomorrow?" she asked as her car rolled to a stop in front of my apartment building. "We've got the appointment with the realtor at 9:30 to make the offer, and then after that, I thought I'd take you over to the Department of Children and Families so I can introduce you to everyone I've been working with there. They've all been so supportive of the MH house coming to the area, and they'll be happy to learn we've finally chosen a location."

Nodding my agreement, I blindly felt around for the door handle as I kept my eyes trained on her. I wanted to soak up every last second of her presence as I could before I went inside to my empty apartment for what was bound to be a lonely night with a sandwich from the deli downstairs and whatever was on TV. "Yeah, that sounds good. Do I need to wear a blazer for the trip to the DCF, or is something similar to what I have on today appropriate?"

Her lips curled up in an amused grin while she perused the length of my body. The weight of her stare caused me to shift nervously in the leather seat, and as I waited for her reply, the temperature inside the car skyrocketed from comfortable to surface-of-the-sun hot. If she didn't say something quick-like, I was going to be forced to open the door to allow some cool air in before I suffered from a heat stroke.

When her eyes returned to meet mine, she responded, "No jacket necessary, their office is pretty casual. Plus, you look great just the way you are." Then, as if her words hadn't already shocked the hell out of me, she reached across the middle console and lightly fingered the bottom of the thin argyle-print tie that suddenly tightened like a vise around my neck. "I like this look on you."

Holy. Fucking. Shit. Instantly, every drop of blood in my body flowed directly to the organ between my legs, triggering my shaft to swell and throb as it pressed against my zipper. There was no way she didn't notice the bulge in my lap as her gaze dropped back down to where she was still touching my tie, but gratefully, she didn't say anything or suddenly retract her hand.

"Um, yeah, uh . . ." I cleared my throat as I frantically searched my brain for a sensible response. "I've, uh, I've got lots of ties. No problem. I can wear one every day if you want me to. All the colors and patterns."

A stifled giggle escaped Monroe's mouth, and I could tell she was desperately trying to hold back more where it came from, though whether it was due to my untimely erection, the word-vomit spewing from my mouth, or a combination of the two, I wasn't sure. All I knew was I wanted nothing more than for a giant hole to magically appear and swallow me up, preventing me from saying or doing anything else ridiculous. I'd just gotten finished thinking about how well the day had gone, and yet there I was, as we were saying our goodbyes and setting plans for the next day, doing my best to ensure she thought I was a blathering idiot who couldn't control his raging hard-on before we parted ways for the evening.

"*All* colors?" she mocked playfully, finally allowing the silky fabric to fall from her fingers. "Even chartreuse?"

My face burned with embarrassment, and I prayed my dark beard helped disguise the flush I felt spread across my cheeks. "Okay, maybe not all colors."

"Well, whatever you have, I'm sure it'll look terrific. I'll text you when I get here in the morning," she smoothly changed the subject, mercifully saving me from further humiliation. "And if you have any questions or anything about the city, feel free to call or text me. I know you just got here yesterday, so I'm sure you'll want to get out and explore during your free time. I can help with good places to eat or shop or whatever you need."

Pulling on the silver handle, I pushed the door open and inhaled a deep, revitalizing breath of the fresh air that rushed inside. "Sounds good, and thank you. I think we made a great decision on the house today. I'll be ready to go in the morning."

As I swung my feet out onto the pavement, she said, "Bye, Oliver, have a good night."

"You too, Monroe," I murmured before closing the door behind me. Still frazzled, I stood there under the fading afternoon sun and watched until her car blended into the sea of brake lights. Still hard.

THAT NIGHT WAS spent much like I'd expected, though instead of the sandwich for dinner, I discovered a Chinese noodle house around the corner from my place that turned out to be quite good. After I Skyped with my parents for a little while, which mostly consisted of Mom showing me the sweaters she was knitting for Coltrane and Dad rolling his eyes behind her, I mindlessly surfed the web, reading articles and browsing images on one of those pop-culture websites.

When I randomly landed on a lifestyle piece where they interviewed a bunch of women about which famous female, young or old, they'd most want their daughters to have as a role model, my entire body tensed at the sight of Monroe's picture as the top response on the poll results, with a landslide seventy-eight percent of the vote. I shouldn't have been surprised to see her beautiful face staring back at me . . . but I was. I mean, not because she'd led the voting; I already knew the entire country had a love affair with her, and for just cause—she was truly an extraordinary person in every facet of life. No, the thing that struck a chord inside of me was the fact I knew her now. Like *knew her*, knew her. And then, all of a sudden there was this article listing off all these facts about her, just sharing her with everyone else like they knew her too.

She had just spent the entire day with *me*. She had driven to *my* apartment this morning. She had gone house-touring with *me*, where she'd asked for *my* opinion. She had eaten lunch with *me*. She had touched *my* tie and said she liked the way *I* looked. She was *mine*!

Whoa! Calm down there, Saxon. May want to slow your roll a bit with the caveman thing, considering she's someone else's wife and all.

Setting the laptop off to the side, I abruptly pushed to my feet and stalked to the bathroom, annoyed at the absurdity of my irrational reaction to seeing the story about her online. Even in a far-off fantasy universe where she wasn't married to Colin and actually had interest in me, I was never the jealous, possessive type. I hated when

I saw guys act like that, because ninety percent of the time, it was a coping mechanism to make up for their own shortcomings and insecurities. I *wasn't* that guy. Never had been.

I'd been in several semi-serious relationships before. Hell, I'd even lived with Lauren for almost a year and was very close to popping the question at one point, yet I still had never felt that way with her. Anytime we'd go swimming with friends or get dressed up for a night on the town, other guys would openly gawk at her in her bikini or in her mini-skirt and heels, and though I knew exactly the dirty, lascivious thoughts running through their heads, not once did I feel the need to be domineering or overprotective. I knew she was coming home with me, and that was all that mattered.

So why in the hell do I feel that way now? What the fuck is my problem? Why can't I just view Monroe like all of my other female friends and coworkers?

I stared expectantly at myself in the bathroom mirror for a few seconds and waited for the answers to come. They never did. Irritated, I shoved away from the counter and went to turn the shower on, hoping I could wash the ridiculousness away. After hastily removing my clothes and throwing them in the hamper, I stepped under the forceful spray and closed my eyes as the hot water pelted me in the face.

Unfortunately, as I squeezed my lids shut and tried to think about anything but Monroe and the effect she had on me, the more she consumed me. The way her striking green eyes lit up when she talked about the kids she worked with. How she rubbed her full lips together when she was deep in thought. The incredible view of her swaying hips when she walked in front of me. That damn perfume she wore that made me want to lick every inch of her fucking body. The soothing, melodic sound of her voice that I wanted to hear her beg me with before screaming my name in ecstasy.

I didn't even realize what I started doing, but when I finally opened my eyes and glanced down through my wet, spiky lashes, my fingers were wrapped firmly around my rock-hard cock, rapidly sliding up and down the length. *Fucking hell, it feels so good.* I envisioned what she'd look like in the shower with me—stark naked and on her knees, swallowing the swollen purple head of my steeled shaft as the water rained down around her. I'd let her suck me until I knew I was about to come, and then I'd lift her up to her feet, turn her around to face the back wall so that I could bend her over, and bury my full length inside her tight, sweet pussy. It would feel like nothing I'd ever experienced before, a sensual nirvana I didn't know existed.

My hand jerked my dick frantically as I imagined her peering at me over her shoulder, overwhelming lust pooling in her eyes while she urged me on. *Deeper . . . faster . . . more. Please, Oliver, I need more.* The sound of our wet bodies slapping against each other filled the bathroom, and the combination of the sweltering passion between us and the endless hot water blended together to create so much steam I couldn't see anything but her directly in front of me.

I couldn't have stopped if I wanted to. Monroe had hijacked my mind, controlling every thought and action. And when I visualized the look on her face as she found her euphoric release, her walls contracting wildly around my pulsating cock, I exploded violently in my hand with a thunderous roar I was sure people walking by on the street could hear. But I didn't have it in me to care. I had other, much more serious issues I needed to address . . . like losing my goddamn mind.

AFTER A NIGHT of endless tossing and turning, when the morning sunrays finally filtered in through the cream-colored curtains of my bedroom, I took it as a sign to get my ass out of bed. I still had over two hours before Monroe was to pick me up, but I desperately needed to release some of my pent-up energy and frustration, and apparently jacking off wasn't the answer. Unable to control my deviant, wayward thoughts the previous night after my lengthy shower, I'd ended up typing Monroe's name into a search engine online and stroking myself to climax two more times, thinking I could possibly work her out of my system. Clearly, I was wrong, because the only thing I was left with was a sore wrist and a metric ton of guilt and shame weighing heavily on my conscience.

Shuffling to the dresser, I grabbed a clean t-shirt from the middle drawer and pulled it over my head as I made my way toward the kitchen. I opened the refrigerator and sighed, momentarily forgetting I had yet to go to the grocery store. With a garbled string of curse words, I shut the door and snatched my wallet and keys from the bar, grateful the downstairs deli was open twenty-four seven.

Half an hour later, my belly was full, the caffeine from the coffee had started working its magic in my bloodstream, and I was ready to spend some one-on-one time with the best therapist I could ever ask for—'Leia', my Selmer-Paris Series II alto saxophone—before I had to get ready. Even though I hadn't played much in the last couple of weeks with preparing for the move and the impromptu trip to my parents', it was just like riding a bike and it didn't take long for me to get into the groove with her. I warmed up with a few chord progressions and some training riffs, and then, careful to keep the volume down for the sake of the other tenants in the building, I dove into the full forty-five minute set I was used to playing at Grooves, a Chicago blues bar I occasionally played at on the weekends. By the time I hit the last note of Robert Johnson's "Me and the Devil Blues," I felt a thousand times better and was grinning from ear to ear. Maybe I just needed to find a similar club in Boston where I could hum and blow my worries away. Literally.

Once I placed my instrument back in her case, I quickly showered then brushed my teeth and the unkempt mop on my head before tidying up my facial hair with the clippers. Then, moving to the walk-in closet, I changed into some black slacks, a pale green dress shirt, and an understated plaid tie, trying my best not to think about if Monroe would like it or not. Socks, shoes, and a belt later, I was ready to go. And when the text chimed in on my phone, alerting me that Monroe was downstairs, I refused to look at my reflection in the mirror one last time. *It doesn't matter what she thinks.*

Throughout the entire three minute journey from my apartment to her car, I gave myself a silent pep talk full of reminders about who she was, who she was married to, what our relationship was, and how I could play my little Leia to my heart's content as soon as I got home. But the moment I slid into the passenger seat and saw her toned legs sticking out from underneath a knee-length black pencil skirt and got an intoxicating whiff of oranges and cream, all sensibility escaped me.

The only thing I wanted to play was Monroe-fucking-Cassidy.

chapter nine

"Is it possible
to feel so much,
that you never really
know what kind of human
you are? If you are filled
with monsters or love or pain
or chaos?
I do not really know what
to make of who I am,
but I am waiting, nearly
bursting, for someone
who can."
–Christopher Poindexter

MONROE

WHEN I WOKE up on Tuesday morning, the nerves and hesitation from the previous morning had been replaced with an enthusiasm and anticipation I hadn't felt since I'd first found out I was awarded the Boston chapter of Mending Hearts. Confident that Oliver and I had established a friendly, working camaraderie during our first day together—soundly ignoring the way he made my stomach flutter more than any other person before him and the way I couldn't stop staring at his package in his pants while in my car—I was eager to learn as much as I could from him while he was staying in town. Strictly in the business sense, of course.

Hurriedly, I slipped into my workout clothes and threw my hair into a ponytail before bounding down the multi-levels of stairs from my master suite on the third floor to the gym in the basement. I couldn't wait to get a good ninety minutes of training in to start my day off on the right foot. Coincidentally, Colin emerged from the other master suite—which was identical to mine—at the exact moment I passed the second-floor landing.

"Morning, beautiful," he greeted me with a kiss on my fore-head then fell in step next to me as I continued my descent to the lower levels. "How was your day yesterday? Did everything go okay with Saxon? You still feel comfortable around him?"

I nodded and made a feeble attempt to hide the silly grin I could feel growing on my face as a result of hearing Oliver's name. "Good morning, and yeah, everything went great. We ended up choosing the house in Newton, right off Columbus Avenue, and we're meet-ing with the realtor this morning to put an offer in on it. Then I'm gonna take Oliver to the DCF and introduce him to everyone there."

"That's awesome, Roe. I was worried about you all day yester-day at practice, and you had already passed out when I got home last night before I could ask you about it."

We reached the ground floor and I stopped off at the kitchen to grab my morning granola bar and a bottle of water, handing him one of each as well. "No need to worry, babe. I promise. He seems like a really sweet guy, and Allison loves him and trusts him completely."

Colin cocked his head and shot me a peculiar, inquisitive look. "A really sweet guy, huh? How so?"

"Uh, I dunno . . ." A tingling warmth crept up my neck under his curious gaze and I dropped my eyes to the water bottle, where my fingers were fiddling with the plastic label. "I guess . . . umm, I mean he's a little dorky and kinda goofy. Really easygoing and friendly. I can see how kids would take to him easily."

"Hmph," was all Colin said in response, so I quickly seized the opportunity to change the subject.

"So this week's game is here at home against Denver, right?"

I asked as I lifted my chin to meet his stare once again, hoping he wouldn't comment on my awkward reply to him asking about Oliver. *I didn't even understand why his questioning had made me so uncomfortable, and I sure as hell wouldn't know how to explain the unfamiliar feeling to Colin.*

The expression on his face slowly morphed into a devious smirk as he nodded. "Yeah, it's early kickoff at one. And actually, that reminds me; Mom and Dad are out of town for their anniversary. Why don't you invite Oliver to join you, Seth, and Effie in the box? I'm sure he doesn't know anyone else here, so you can introduce him around, help the guy out a bit. Plus, maybe he and Effie will hit it off or something. With all of the jackholes she usually dates, she could use a *sweet* guy to show her how she should be treated."

My initial reaction was to scream, *"Not a chance in hell!"* but somehow I managed to hold back the outburst and think before I answered. *What in the world is my problem? First, yesterday, I felt guilty about having a working lunch with Oliver, when I was clearly doing nothing wrong. Now this?*

"I-I'm not sure that's such a good idea," I stammered. "He doesn—"

"Why wouldn't it be?" he cut in before I could finish my thought. "What American male doesn't want to go see an NFL game in a suite with the players' families? He'll love it, even if he's not a football fan."

I knew by the determination in his voice that Colin wasn't going to be convinced his idea wasn't a good one, and honestly, I didn't have a practical argument otherwise. So pushing aside my reluctance, I agreed to invite Oliver to join us while I silently prayed he'd decline. "Yeah, I'll ask him today and let you know what he says," I replied with a half-hearted smile.

"Good." Colin leaned down and kissed the top of my head before gathering his things to leave and heading out of the kitchen. "I love you, beautiful girl. I probably won't be home from practice until nine or ten. Don't wait up."

"I never do!" I called out after him.

I heard him chuckle before the door shut behind him, and then I dropped onto the nearest barstool, wondering what in the world I'd just gotten myself into.

YOU WOULD THINK that buying a six-million-dollar house with money that isn't yours would be fun, exciting even. But when Oliver and I walked out of the realtor's office that Tuesday morning, unsettled nerves churned in the pit of my stomach. Lots and lots of them. Even though we had thoroughly gone over everything from neighborhoods and school districts to bedroom layouts and outdoor living space, I hoped we had made the right decision for the kids, for Mending Hearts, and lastly, for myself. I'd be spending the majority of my time at the house once it was up and running, probably more than I was at my own home, and I wanted to create an environment that both the kids and the employees would love and thrive in.

"What's wrong?" Oliver asked once we were settled inside my car. "Are you worried they aren't going to accept the offer? Think we should've gone in a little higher?"

"No, nothing's wrong. I think we made a strong bid, and if they don't accept at first, that's what negotiations are for," I said while fumbling to put the key in the ignition.

Catching me completely off-guard, he reached over and rested his hand on my shaky fingers, stilling my actions with his touch. "I know something's got you worked up, Monroe. You've been licking and rubbing your lips together since the moment we sat down in there, so why don't you tell me what's going on before your mouth ends up cracked and bleeding?"

Will you kiss it and make it better?

As the errant thought flitted through my mind, I gasped aloud and my eyes widened in horror. With my hand still in his, I turned to look at him and found him staring back at me with a discerning gaze, probably wondering what my problem was. Then, I did what I did best when I felt cornered: I diverted and redirected.

"Do you want to go to the Pats' game with me on Sunday? A

couple of my friends are going too, and I thought maybe you'd like to get out, meet some people, and see more of the city," I prattled on without giving him a chance to respond. "I know you said you're not much of a sports guy, so if you don't want to, no worries, but Colin's parents are out of town this weekend, so we have the extra tickets, and I could pick you up and—"

"Monroe, calm down and take a breath," he interrupted, keeping his tone soft and gentle as his fingers tightened ever so slightly around mine. "I'd love to go to the game with you and your friends this weekend. Thank you for inviting me. But I know that's not what you were worrying yourself over earlier, so spill it, Peaches."

My jaw fell open. "Did you just call me *Peaches*? I thought you said I didn't smell like peaches? Do I stink?" Yanking my hand away from his, I brought my arm up to my nose and sniffed like a bloodhound from wrist to elbow, which in turn triggered Oliver to burst out in a fit of laughter.

"Oh, my God, your face right now is priceless," he cackled while shaking his head in disbelief.

I cut my eyes at him, daring him to say more.

After a few seconds, he caught his breath and straightened his posture as his expression became more thoughtful. "No, of course you don't stink . . . or smell like peaches, for that matter." His lips curled up into a lopsided grin as he ran his fingers through his thick brown hair. "You're just so tense right now, and I was trying to get you to lighten up. Smile. Be happy. If everything goes right, in a couple of months, you're gonna have a kick-ass house—that *you* chose for the kids—to start preparing for a group who needs the stability and support that it provides more than they need anything else."

Wow. He was right. I knew I'd done my full diligence in choosing the right place, with the kids' best interest as the primary driving factor throughout the entire decision-making process. It wasn't the time to second-guess myself. I needed to focus on the finish-line and what needed to be done next to get there.

"You're right," I admitted, relaxing my shoulders. "I've just been grilling myself all morning, wondering if I made the right choice, worrying about what would happen if I didn't. I don't want to mess this up. Failure isn't an option."

"The house is nothing but a structural building made up of brick, wood, and sheetrock, all held together by nails. The home is everything that happens inside the walls, made up of laughter, tears, and irreplaceable memories, all held together by love." Lifting his hand to my face, he softly cradled my chin between his thumb and forefinger and gazed so deep inside me I swore he could see the tarnished depths of my soul. "It didn't matter which house you picked. You and the love you have for the people inside that structure will be what makes it successful."

What happened next can only be described as one of those moments in life that one never forgets. Like the magical thing in fairytales where the prince and the princess first see each other and time stops while violins play, birds sing, fireworks explode in the background, angels get their wings, and a bunch of other enchanted shit happens. It was a total internal body shift as my axis was thrown completely off-center. I didn't understand it. It scared the shit out of me, but enthralled me even more. I couldn't have torn my eyes away from him if I had to. My body heated from the inside out. I didn't know if I was breathing or if my heart was beating. Nothing mattered but how much I *needed* him to kiss me right-fucking-then.

Our faces gradually grew closer together as his fingers slid around to cup my jaw. His eyes fell to my parted lips and instinctively I licked them, eliciting a gruff, rumbling moan from deep in his throat as he met my stare again. My inner thighs caught fire. I didn't care who I was, or where we were, or what this meant for everything in my life, or how long I'd known this guy, or how it would affect our working relationship, or any other goddamn thing except his mouth pressed against mine.

Thump! Thump! Thump!

The electrically-charged atmosphere shattered instantly as the sound of someone knocking on the driver's side window startled us so badly I jumped high enough in my seat to hit my head on the car's ceiling as Oliver simultaneously snatched his hand away from my face and banged his knuckles against the dashboard. *We don't look guilty or anything.* Twisting around to see who the culprit was that destroyed my *moment*, I saw Melissa Myers—the realtor whose office we were still parked in front of—standing there with a huge smile on her face while giving me the thumbs-up signal. *Seriously?*

A little annoyed and a lot flustered, I rolled the window down and put on the best innocent look I could muster, thanking God she couldn't get a pulse and blood pressure reading on me. I was pretty sure I was damn close to having either a stroke or a heart attack, but whether it was because I almost let a man who I'd only known for two seconds—and more importantly, a man who wasn't my husband—kiss me, or because we nearly got caught, I wasn't sure.

"You got it! You got the house!" she trilled excitedly. "They already accepted the offer, no counteroffer or anything. Once they execute the contract, we'll put everything into motion so that you can close on November fifteenth. Sorry if I scared you, I just saw your car still here out the window, so I thought I'd tell you the good news in person."

Learning we'd gotten the house temporarily made me forget about the near-kiss, and I threw open the door to jump out and hug Melissa. I'd been working with her for over six months, searching for the perfect place for the MH house, and during that time, we'd established a casual friendship.

"Thank you so much! This is incredible news! I thought we'd have to wait at least a couple of days to hear anything back," I said with unbridled enthusiasm as I released her from the embrace.

"I did too, but today must be your lucky day," she replied, briefly glancing into the car where Oliver still sat then back up at me. "You two should go celebrate. I'll call you when I have all the documents in and let you know what the next step is."

The guilt slammed into me like a runaway bullet train as I thought about what kind of *celebration* Oliver and I were getting ready to partake in before she'd interrupted us, but I did my best to maintain my composure. "Sounds good. I'll be looking forward to hearing from you."

With one last congratulatory smile, she spun around and returned to her office, leaving me alone with him again. Part of me wanted to take off running so I didn't have to face Oliver and address what almost happened, but another part of me wanted to crawl back in the car and pick up exactly where we'd left off. I pressed my lips together and closed my eyes, inhaling a deep breath through my nose.

"You're doing it again, Peaches," Oliver commented from inside the cab.

My eyelids flew open and I stooped down to glare at him. "Doing what? And stop calling me that!"

"The lip thing, and would you rather I go back to calling you Rizzo?" he mused, raising his eyebrows.

As I lowered myself onto the driver's seat, careful not to flash him my panties under my skirt in the process, I retorted, "I don't have a lip *thing*, and I'd like it if you just called me Monroe, like everybody else does." That was a damn lie. I knew it, and if the mischief twinkling in his eyes was anything to go by, he did too.

"Okay, Dr. Monroe Cassidy," he mocked, which riled me up even more, "but I don't want to hear any whining when your lips are all dry and chapped."

"Don't be an ass, and I don't whi—" I stopped abruptly when I realized I was indeed whining.

Erupting with laughter yet again, Oliver threw his head back against the seat and shook it from side to side, mussing his hair all up. *I wonder if that's what he looks like when he first wakes up.*

With an exasperated huff, which was directed mainly at myself and my inability to control my thoughts around him, I stuck the key in the ignition and cranked the engine, hoping Oliver thought I was irritated with him. Maybe that way he wouldn't try to kiss me again.

It didn't stop me from thinking about it the entire way to the DCF though.

chapter
ten

"She was strange
and beautiful
and those were human
qualities that I
had never seen weaved
together before.

She became terrifying
to me,
not because I feared
who she was,
but for the sake
of love,
I feared what
she could do to me."
—Christopher Poindexter

OLIVER

I COULDN'T BELIEVE I almost kissed her. My hand had caressed her face, my lips so close we breathed the same air. I wanted it more than I've ever wanted anything in my life, though I'm not sure I could've stopped once I started. The realtor knocking on the window was both the best and worst thing to happen in that moment, and when Monroe fled the car, I stole several seconds to regain my poise and self-control. It was day fucking two, and I was already putting the moves on my *married* coworker! And this was after I'd spent all night and morning swearing to myself I would stop with the preposterous fantasies I'd been having about her, which definitely meant *NO FUCKING KISSING HER.* She was turning me into someone I never thought I'd be.

When she got back in the car, I tried my best to play the situation off—to tease and harass her about the nicknames and her lips—in hopes it would help alleviate any awkwardness between us, and for the most part, it seemed to work. She pretended she was annoyed by my antics, huffing and rolling her eyes, but as she pulled out of the parking lot and onto the busy street, I saw the way her mouth tilted up in a hidden smile. And it made my day, even though I knew it shouldn't.

I am so screwed.

It took us about fifteen minutes to reach the DCF office, in which neither of us said a word. Some horrible pop shit was on the radio, but I was careful not to ruffle her feathers any more than I already had, so I kept my opinion on her music selection to myself and sat quietly, watching the city fly by. Once she shifted the transmission into park, Monroe hurriedly escaped the close quarters of the car and waited for me outside by the curb, making it clear she wasn't over what had almost happened any more than I was. I wasn't sure either of us trusted ourselves enough to ensure it wouldn't happen again, and that's what scared me the most. No matter how much I knew it was wrong, I couldn't just flip a switch and not want her, so if she instigated anything at all, there was no way in hell I'd be able to tell her no.

Joining her under the cloudless, late-morning sky, I fell into step next to her and offered a casual smile in hopes she'd relax a little. "So you have a good relationship with these people? The director is easy to work with?"

Monroe nodded, but kept her gaze straight out in front of her. "Yeah, they're a great group, and Dr. Prince is amazing. The Suffolk County Children's Home is right around the corner from here, so they're all very involved with the children, especially the older ones who have a hard time being placed in a foster home, let alone staying there."

"Can we stop by there when we leave here? I'd love to see the place and meet some of the kiddos." I stepped out in front of her when we reached the building to open the door for her and basically force her to look at me.

Her sharp glare softened when our eyes met and she nodded again as she stepped inside. "Yeah, of course. I wasn't sure if you'd want to."

"Are you kidding? I'm missing my crew back in Chicago like crazy," I admitted with a chuckle while following her to the bank of elevators in the lobby. "I haven't been away from them for more than two or three days in a row before this. Tracie and Jeff promised to send me weekly updates and photos, and I'm supposed to Skype with the group every Sunday morning, but I'm not sure I'll be able to wait that long." I stopped walking mid-stride and gently grabbed her arm, causing her to pull up too. Peering down into her expressive eyes, I needed her to understand the seriousness and sincerity of my next words. "It'd be obvious to a blind man that you're truly dedicated and determined to helping these kids, Monroe. The love you have for the cause radiates from you in everything you do. But please know that I feel just as strongly as you about what we do. Helping these kids who have been taken advantage of, who've never been given a fair shot in life, isn't just what I *want* to do; it's what I *have* to do. It's a part of who I am."

Finally, the mask cracked and the smile she blessed me with made my heart swell so big in my chest I was afraid it might explode. "I'd love to introduce you to the kids! They're gonna love you!" she exclaimed, lightly bouncing on the balls of her feet. "Four of them I know will definitely be transferred to our house in February when we open the doors, and there are another two or three that I'm hoping Mending Hearts will be awarded custody of, but the parents are still in the picture. So we'll probably have a fight in court over those, but I feel confident about our chances."

"Is that what you've been working on since graduation?" I

asked as we began moving toward the elevators again.

"Yep," she answered as her face flushed with enthusiasm. "I practically lived at the house from mid-May to mid-August as I got to know all of the kids, studied some of the specific cases that could qualify for MH, and basically just learned more about how the Massachusetts system works, especially here locally. Real-life application seems to be so different than all the crap they teach you in school."

She stopped talking long enough for us to get in one of the elevators and to press the button for the eighth floor then picked up where she left off. "I don't even know why they bother with textbooks in graduate social work classes anymore. The material is antiquated before it's ever published, and none of it can properly prepare you for the situations you're actually going to face . . . but I'm sure you know better about that than me."

"Absolutely," I agreed whole-heartedly. "I learned more in my first six months out of university than I ever did inside. Even in grad school, when I worked in one of the local children's shelters, I didn't fully comprehend the magnitude of responsibility I'd feel once I had my own cases, nor did I understand what a hindrance the legal system could be sometimes in keeping me from doing my job. I won't lie to you. There've been times I've been so fed up with protocols and laws and all that bullshit, that I just want to scream and bang my head on my desk, and even thought about walking away . . . but the frustration fades, and the reward of knowing I'm helping to keep abused kids safe, by far outweighs anything else."

The elevator dinged when we arrived at our destination, and as the stainless doors parted, I motioned for her to lead the way. "After you, m'lady."

As soon as we stepped out onto the floor, we were greeted by a smiling, grandma-looking receptionist who jumped up and scurried around her desk the second she saw Monroe, greeting her with a giant hug. "Well, would you look what the cat drug in?" she scolded in a motherly tone. "I thought maybe you forgot about us or something. I haven't seen your face in . . . what's it been? Two weeks?"

"Now, Miss Betty, I told you I was going to Detroit to be with Allison for her surgery," Monroe replied with a laugh.

"Yes, but I know you've been back in town. I saw you on TV at the game Sunday, so I at least expected you to drop by yesterday. And by the way, tell that husband of yours that I knew all along he was gonna bring us back. Ed was in his recliner, justa goin' on and on about how they needed to run the ball more, and I finally just told him to shut his damn mouth and watch our Colin get us the win." Miss Betty winked over at me. "And look who was right—me, of course. Young man, if you learn nothing else in this world, just learn to shut your mouth and listen to your woman when she tells you how things are gonna go down, 'cause chances are . . . she'll be right. By the way, who are you?"

Without giving me a chance to respond, she turned her attention back to Monroe and asked her, "Who's the Hottie McHotstuff you brought with you? It's too early for my Christmas present, and I'm not sure Ed's gonna approve if I bring one home with those bedroom eyes."

Monroe glanced over at me with a horrified look on her face, and the second our eyes met, we both erupted in laughter. Bent-over, struggling-to-breathe, tears-streaming-down-our-faces, holding-our-sides laughter. Between the stress of the house contract and the tension of what had almost transpired in the car, she and I had been strung up so tightly with emotions that once we started to unwind, we couldn't stop.

Miss Betty stood there with her arms crossed over her chest and watched us guffaw around like a pair of wild hyenas until we eventually caught our breath and were able to talk again. Her eyes twinkled with amusement, although she pretended to be annoyed, mumbling something about kids these days and how she never got good surprises.

Monroe spoke first, still struggling to keep a straight face. "Miss Betty, this is Dr. Oliver Saxon. He's the executive director at the Chicago chapter of Mending Hearts, and since Allison couldn't be here in Boston to train me and help me get things set up, he's taking her place. He's staying in Boston through the end of February."

They both fixed their attention on me, prompting me to stick my hand out in the direction of the petite, gray-haired woman. "So nice to meet you, Miss Betty," I said with my best charming smile. "I look forward to seeing you often while I'm here in town."

Ignoring my hand all together, she moved toward me and wrapped her arms around my waist, squeezing me in an embrace that resembled the jaws-of-life. "The pleasure's all mine, young man. It's about time we got some testosterone around here. All these damn women in this office drive me batty sometimes. Especially the week they're all cycling together." I cringed, but she didn't release her hold. "And a good-looking doctor, too. I guess that's all I can ask for if I don't get to take you home . . . although if you have any free time, I could use some training of my own and have a few things you could set up."

My head snapped over to Monroe and I silently pleaded with her to save me. Laughing quietly, she mouthed, *Peaches.*

I narrowed my eyes and shook my head at her, mouthing back, *You're gonna pay.*

But that only provoked her more.

When Miss Betty finally loosened her grip on my waist and I managed to discreetly step off to the side, Monroe smirked as she announced, "Dr. Saxon thinks the name Oliver sounds too uptight, so he prefers for everyone just to call him Ollie."

Oh, she's so going to get it later.

Miss Betty beamed up at me. "Ollie . . . I love that. I'm thrilled you're here and that my girl Monroe has someone to show her the ropes. We're all so proud of her."

With a smile I didn't have to fake, I nodded in agreement but didn't get a chance to say anything else before another female spoke up. "What's with all the ruckus out here? Is there a party I wasn't invited to? And who is this visitor we have?"

We all spun around in the direction the voice came from, and the introductions began all over again, this time with a little less talk about my looks and a little more on my experience and qualifications.

But still as Ollie.

Over an hour later, I'd personally met the entire staff of the DCF as we went around desk-by-desk so Monroe could introduce me to each of them, all of who were women except for one forty-something guy with his workspace tucked in the back corner of the office. I couldn't figure out if I should feel sorry for or be envious of him for always being surrounded by nothing but women.

Much like at the gala the first night I met Monroe, everyone clearly adored, respected, and appreciated her. It was obvious she had spent a substantial amount of time building meaningful relationships with those she'd be working with on a daily basis. In my first few months at the Chicago house, I'd learned very quickly that the people at the DCFS—which it was called in Illinois—could either be my best ally or my worst enemy. They not only controlled what kids were placed in my home, but they also had a voice in the local judges' ears, which went a long way in the few court placement battles I'd been involved in. I was extremely pleased to see that Monroe had everyone in her corner, though I really expected nothing else. We were all helpless against her magical charisma, drawn to her like moths to a flame.

By the time we'd made our way around and were leaving the office, it was almost noon, and the instant we stepped onto the elevator, my stomach growled loudly. Monroe snickered as her eyes cut over to me. "Are you always hungry, Ollie? I bet Miss Betty would love to feed you some of her home-cooking."

Luckily for her, the car stopped on the seventh floor and three other people—who were obviously leaving for lunch—joined us on our ride to the ground floor, preventing me from tugging on her ponytail until she begged for mercy like I wanted her to. I shot her a warning look as she giggled to herself in the back corner, and as soon as the other people exited the elevator, Monroe took off like a bat out of hell toward the doors, knowing damn well I was hot on her sexy heels.

I didn't catch up with her until we reached her car, and I'm not sure what came over me, but just as she went to extend her arm toward the door handle, I grabbed her wrist and twirled her around to face me, using my weight to loosely pin her up against the driver's side door. "You think you're so cute, don't you, my peachy little Rizzo?" I goaded her. "Purposely trying to ruffle my feathers . . ."

"What? You don't think I'm cute?" Exhilaration flickered in her green eyes, and when she pressed her lips together and rubbed them back and forth, a guttural growl rumbled in my chest.

"No, I don't," I rasped as I reached up with my free hand and used my thumb on her bottom lip to part it from the top one. She hissed in a swift stream of air as her pupils dilated, prompting my cock to spring to life. "I think you're fucking beautiful . . . more on the inside than the out, though I have no idea how that's even possible. You're so goddamn perfect it scares me."

"I'm far from perfect, Oliver," she answered softly, holding my intense gaze.

Leaning forward to rest my forehead on hers, I whispered, "Monroe, when God made perfect, he made you." Then, I did what I'd been dying to do since the moment I laid eyes on her.

I kissed her.

chapter
eleven

"We know
so perfectly
how to give birth
to the monsters
inside us,
but for reasons I
will never figure out,
we have not the slightest
clue of what to do
with all the
love."
–Christopher Poindexter

MONROE

HIS MOUTH CRASHED down onto mine and my world shattered around me. Everything I thought to be true was suddenly in question as his strong fingers skimmed along my jawline, slipping around to the back of my neck and anchoring my head as they tangled in the loose tendrils at my nape, all as he pressed his tender yet demanding lips against mine. My mouth opened for him instinctively and our tongues effortlessly stroked and curled around each other's with unbridled desire. It was passionate, reckless, and just plain stupid. But I never wanted him to stop. Not ever.

From the moment he'd kick-ball-changed into my life, I'd known there was something different about Oliver. My draw to him was undeniable, an electric charge that whirred through my body each time we touched. He made me want things I'd never before wanted. Physical things, like kisses and caresses and intimacy that used to make my skin crawl. Before him, Colin was the only person that I was okay with touching me, and even then, the affection I received from my husband never triggered a response in my body the way it did with Oliver. It petrified me, but at the same time, filled me with something I hadn't had in a long time . . . hope. Hope that I wasn't broken. Hope that there was more.

Drawing my lower lip between his teeth, he sucked and nipped at it like he couldn't get enough of me, and I was unable to resist the urge to rock my body against his. I whimpered into his mouth, and when I felt his hardening length press into me, the last ounce of sanity I was clinging onto dissipated. I needed this man more than I needed my next breath. He . . . me . . . *we*—it was inevitable.

"Monroe," he whispered as our mouths broke apart ever so slightly, "I'm sorry, but I can't. Not like this . . . not with Colin."

Reality slapped me square in the face at the sound of my husband's name, leaving a sting full of shame. Gasping, I shoved Oliver away and covered my guilty mouth as tears pooled in my eyes. *What in the hell am I doing? I just jeopardized everything I've worked so hard for over the last decade . . . all for a kiss with someone I barely know!*

"Oh my God, oh my God, oh my God," I chanted over and over into my palm, failing miserably to keep my composure as the waterworks began. "What have I done? I didn't mean . . . I can't . . . what's happening to me?"

"I'm so sorry. I never should've done that. Never should've put you in that position. Please don't cry. I swear it won't happen again. I'm not that kind of guy. It's just . . . when I'm with you, I do things that I wouldn't normally do." He moved back toward me, reaching out with his comforting arms to pull me into an embrace, but I sidestepped him and shook my head adamantly, afraid of what would happen if he touched me again.

"I know, Oliver. I get it, but you're right—we can't." I sniffled as I peered into his troubled eyes through my blurred vision, understanding exactly how he felt. "It's not all your fault. I wanted it to happen just as much as you did, if not more. I know we need to talk." Cutting my gaze over to the building and street, I shook my head. "But not here . . . or now."

Nervously running his fingers through his hair, he took several steps backward. "Yeah, you're right. I wasn't thinking. I keep fucking this all up. God, I'm so sorry."

I awkwardly diverted my gaze to the ground and kicked my pointed toe at a random pebble as I dried the tears from my cheeks. "Yeah, me too."

"Why don't we continue this conversation later, somewhere more private, after we've both had a chance to think about things?" he offered hesitantly. "I could use some food, and we had plans to go over to the children's home. I'm really looking forward to meeting the kiddos."

Nodding, I relaxed a little bit, his pacifying words exactly what I needed to hear. "That sounds good. I think I need a big, greasy cheeseburger to help calm me down."

He smiled cautiously, sticking his hands in his pockets. "Lead the way."

Temporarily putting the kiss behind us, we ventured out on foot to find a place where we could grab a bite to eat, careful to keep a substantial distance between us, and the conversation professional. Throughout the meal, Oliver went over the different employment positions we would need to fill to staff the house, including counselors, tutors, and an office manager, while I made lists. Hesitant to give up much control, I questioned the need for an actual office manager or assistant, thinking I could use a third-party company to handle most of the payroll and general administrative items. But, he insisted I would need someone who I could trust to handle a wide-range of tasks for when I'd struggle to find time to get everything taken care of. My mind immediately went to Effie as a prospect, but thought it was best to wait until I wasn't an emotional basket case to make any kind of decisions. Plus, I wanted to get Colin's opinion on it first before mentioning her.

I'm going to have a lot to talk to him about. Should make for an interesting night.

The tension between us dissolved a little bit with each passing minute, but a couple of times when I caught a glimpse of his mouth, or noticed him focused on mine, the swell of emotions from the kiss would flood through me, and I'd stare at my plate until the internal battle would subside. I was a fucking wreck.

After we finished eating and made our way toward the Suffolk County home, I eagerly filled him in with a bit of background on a few of the kids that would be transferred to the MH home, but hesitated before continuing on about the oldest of them, thirteen-year-old JoJo.

"So, that's Aaron, Alex, and Heather." He cocked his head and threw me an inquisitive look. "Didn't you say there were four definite transfers?"

"Yeah, JoJo is a tough case. She went from a bad home to a worse foster home," I explained, careful not to offer specifics, "and she's got a lot of anger and resentment toward the world built up inside her. I've managed to knock down a few bricks in the wall she's constructed around herself, but it takes a lot of persistence and a lot of weeding through her bitterness to get to the core. All of the kids in the county's house are homeschooled, but as you know with Mending Hearts, one of our main goals is getting them adapted to as normal of a life as possible, which means enrolling them in public school. She's at such an influential age right now that I'm really worried about her getting mixed up with the wrong people, or getting in so much trouble that she gets suspended or expelled. Any more rejection for her right now would be devastating."

Thankfully, we reached the building just before he could ask any more questions, and the minute we stepped inside, we were swallowed up by a group of rowdy kids excited to stop their schoolwork for a few minutes to greet us. It took a combination of me, Oliver, and their homeschool teacher, Ms. Lovell, to get the twenty of them settled back into their chairs, but once they were all seated and somewhat quiet, I was able to introduce Oliver to them.

"Guys and gals, this is Dr. Saxon, who is visiting us from Chicago. He's gonna be helping me set up the Mending Hearts house over the next few months, so I'm sure you'll be seeing quite a bit of him while he's in town," I announced with a bright smile, my personal worries no longer seeming important when I stared into the faces of those children who had much more serious issues to face.

As soon as I stopped speaking, the entire room broke out into chatter, several of the younger boys unable to stay in their seats. Everyone wanted to be the first to introduce themselves and talk to Oliver, but he knew exactly how to handle them all. Lifting his arms in the air, he held a one dollar bill and a five-dollar bill up in his hands and motioned for them all to pipe down as he wore the most adorable grin I'd ever seen on him, and wondrously, the entire room fell silent as everyone's eyes were glued to him.

"Anyone need an extra six bucks?" he asked, and the room erupted in cheers. "Okay, okay, settle down and I'll tell you how you can win it." Again, everyone instantly stopped talking. "I'm gonna do a magic trick with these two bills, and the first person who can tell me how I did it will get them. Sound good?"

A chorus of yeses followed, most of the little ones perched on the edge of their chairs, almost unable to contain their excitement. I gradually backed away from where Oliver was holding court, and joined Ms. Lovell by the wall.

"I'm sorry for disrupting class," I whispered my apology. "I wasn't thinking about what time it was."

"No worries, Monroe." She patted my shoulder soothingly. "You know you're welcome to stop in any time. The kids look forward to your visits, and it appears they're quite taken with your friend too. I enjoy seeing the smiles on their faces."

We both turned our attention to the front of the room, where Oliver called all of the kids up to circle around him, making sure everyone could see. He presented the bills up-close to them, front and back, until everyone was convinced they weren't tampered with. Next, he laid the bills on a table and began rolling them up, only to unroll them and discover they had changed places. Another wave of murmurs ensued as they all started talking amongst themselves, trying to figure out how he'd done it.

Abruptly, JoJo stood up in a chair and said, "Because of the way you laid out the money at the beginning, the one-dollar bill rolled up earlier than the five, which made it roll over first." She jumped down with a smug grin and marched over to the table, snatching the money up and shoving it in her pocket. "Thanks for the pack of cigarettes, jackass. I'm done with this bullshit today." Then she marched out of the room, and a few seconds later, we heard a door slam upstairs.

Oliver immediately swung his attention over to me and lifted his eyebrows, silently asking me if that was JoJo. With a sigh, I nodded and took off after her as he fished out another dollar bill from his wallet for another trick. Over an hour later, all I'd gotten out of her was that Oliver was 'fucking stupid, just like every other guy on the planet.' She refused to comment on the smoking reference, and when she finally got fed up with me talking, she used a few choice words, demanding I leave her alone, which I did . . . begrudgingly.

By the time I made it back downstairs, Oliver was sitting in between Alex and Aaron, helping them with a dinosaur jigsaw puzzle. They were my youngest—brothers, six and eight—who were taken from their aunt and uncle a little over a year ago for flagrant neglect. Once they were brought in for further examination, the bruises and burn marks were discovered, all purposely placed where no one could see them when they were dressed. Somehow, neither had lost their spirit, and even though they were both quite rambunctious little rascals, they were the sweetest little boys. Alex was held back after his first year of kindergarten due to his severe dyslexia but that summer, we'd made great progress with him, and he was doing much better this time around. Aaron was secretly a little cuddlebug when no one was looking, but he'd deny it if I said anything.

Almost as if he felt my presence, he looked up as soon as I entered the room and shot me a huge smile. I couldn't help but return one of my own as I saw the two boys stare up at him with adoring gazes, hanging onto his every word. Even though it wasn't the best of days with JoJo, it pleased me immensely to see the little ones so happy.

Once the T-Rex was fully put together, Oliver managed to escape their clingy hands, and we said goodbye to the rest of the group, promising we'd be back soon. Neither of us said a word during the walk back to my car, both completely lost in our own thoughts. Mine were swirling around so quickly that I began to feel dizzy and confused. The kiss . . . what it meant for me . . . how Colin was going to react . . . hiring Effie . . . JoJo and her outburst . . . the kiss.

The short ride to his apartment was more of the same, with only the radio to fill the suffocating silence. There were so many things I wanted to say to him, but I knew I had to talk to Colin before anything. When I pulled up in front of his building, every muscle in my body drew taught as the friction between us intensified.

"So, um, what's the schedule for tomorrow?" he asked nervously as he finally looked over at me.

I was struggling to get through the afternoon; my brain couldn't even process the next day. "I'm not sure. I guess we need to get a game plan together on visiting the social work school at Boston University and advertising for the job openings."

"We're going to need to set up a temporary office for the next six weeks or so until we get in the house," he reminded me from our earlier discussion over lunch. "I'm assuming you and Colin don't want to use your house for that, so we can set up on the kitchen table in my place. It's not like I'm cooking a lot of meals or using the dining room to entertain guests, and it's a pretty good size where we can both set up workstations."

The thought of being alone with him in his apartment set off all kinds of alarms in my head—and between my legs—but without a better alternative, I pushed away the guilty thoughts and nodded. "Okay, that sounds good. I'll be here around nine in the morning."

He opened the car door and climbed out, catching my gaze one last time before sending me on my way. "I know I already said it, but

I'm really sorry, Monroe. I didn't come here to cause you any issues. That's not my style."

Nodding, I gripped the steering wheel tighter and shifted my attention forward out the windshield. "We'll talk about it tomorrow. I just need some time to process everything."

"Yeah, me too . . ." He stalled for an extra second or two like he was going to say something else, but he didn't.

The door slammed shut and I took off, my tires squealing as I peeled out. The truth hammered in my chest.

The only thing I wanted him to be sorry about was kissing me just *once*.

chapter twelve

"I drank her
silence like
liquor and it destroyed
me the same,
but I fell for all of her,
hopelessly and endlessly.
My soul will always be lifted
when she walks into the room
and my blood will always dance
when her breath passes through me."
–Christopher Poindexter

OLIVER

THE MOMENT SHE sped away from my apartment, the eighteen-hour countdown began until she'd show up the next morning. I had eighteen hours to pull my head out of my ass, once and for all, and figure out how to get through the next six months of working alongside her until I could return home to Chicago. No matter what the connection was that she and I shared, it didn't matter. She was a married woman, and I had no interest in being 'the other man.'

But I'd never forget that kiss.

Not ever.

chapter
thirteen

"I hold a hope in me
that the reason
we all feel so heavy
is that we carry
a little piece of
each other
inside us."
–Christopher Poindexter

MONROE

TIME HAD NEVER moved as slowly as it did that night while I waited for Colin to get home from practice. Regardless of my attempts to keep busy by doing meaningless chores around the house, I played out at least ten different scenarios of how the conversation would go in my head, but to be quite honest, I had no idea how my husband was going to react when I told him that Oliver and I had kissed. It wasn't as though we had a traditional marriage by any stretch of the imagination. I mean, he *did* cheat on me with Seth for the first few years we dated, and then—with my approval, of course—continued their on-and-off-again relationship ever since, even after we got married. But nevertheless, I had a hunch he wasn't going to be thrilled with my news . . . and I despised confrontation, especially with the person I loved most in the world.

Unease gurgled in my stomach while dread pounded in my skull. I wished nothing more than for it to be the next day already, no matter what the outcome of the discussion would be; I just wanted it over. Emerging from the closet where I'd finished the annual autumn shift of my short-sleeved blouses and tanks to the back of the wardrobe while pushing the sweaters and cardigans forward, I looked over at the clock on the dresser. 10:17. *Ugh . . . where in the world is he?*

Trudging down the stairs to the kitchen for a hot chai latte and some graham crackers, I rubbed my temples with my fingertips as I quietly wished away the anxiety that throbbed insistently behind my eyes. When I reached the landing to the main level, I flipped on the light switch to illuminate the living room and dining area, and for the first time since we'd lived there, the house seemed empty and way too big. The space was decorated in rich, warm hues of burgundy and oak with oversized furniture that, at first glance, appeared to be homey and inviting, but other than waiting for Effie before the baseball game a few weeks prior, I couldn't remember the last time Colin and I had hung out in there at the same time.

During the off-season, we ate breakfast together in the kitchen, but then he'd be off giving motivational speeches, being interviewed for articles and news pieces, and filming commercials, while I was either up at the campus library working on my thesis or at the children's home, helping with the kids. We'd meet back in the kitchen for a quick dinner and a recap of our day before retreating to our separate master suites, only to start the entire process over the next day. Then, once training camp started, we became two ships passing in the night . . . or rather, in the early morning. Some days, I didn't see him at all and our only communication was via text messages. We never watched movies or listened to music with one another anymore. He never asked me to help him study his playbook like he used to do in college. My life completely revolved around Mending Hearts and the kids, while his primary focus was football and branding his name.

Not that any of this was exactly new to me. It had been that way since we'd gotten married and moved from Ann Arbor to Boston, both of us planting our roots in the community where we planned to make our mark. It was what we both wanted. It was part of our plan. So what I couldn't understand was why I suddenly felt so alone.

I drew in a deep breath and shook my head back and forth, jolting myself out of my melancholy thoughts. The roller coaster ride of emotions I'd been on throughout the day was taking its toll on me, physically and mentally, and I needed a relaxing bubble bath after my late-night snack. However, as soon as I turned my Keurig on to warm up for the tea, I heard the front door open and close, followed by heavy footsteps on the wood floor heading in my direction.

"Monroe? Are you down here?" Colin called out from the foyer just seconds before his bulky frame appeared under the archway leading into the kitchen. Pinning me with a concerned gaze, he surveyed me head-to-toe like he was searching for something wrong. "Why aren't you in bed, babe? It's late. Do you not feel well?"

"Hey, you." I threw him a small smile as I grabbed a ceramic mug from the cabinet. "I'm good . . . feeling fine. I was just waiting for you to get home so I could to talk to you about something."

Cocking his head with confusion, he dug his cell phone out of his pocket and glanced down at the screen. "Why didn't you call me? What's going on?"

"It isn't a conversation I wanted to have over the phone," I explained as I kept my eyes locked on the hot, frothy drink pouring out of the machine and into the cup, "but I didn't want to worry you or ask you to come home early from practice. It's really not that big a deal . . . just need to talk."

Swiftly closing the distance between us, he wrapped his burly arms around my shoulders, spinning me around into a bear hug. "Roe, baby, anytime you need me, you call. I don't care how important you think it is or what I'm doing." He pressed his lips to the top of my head then leaned back to peer down into my eyes. "You know better than that, sweetie. Now what is it you want to talk to me about? You've got my full attention."

I swallowed hard, hoping to find my voice behind the lump

of nerves lodged in the back of my throat. All of the ways I'd re-hearsed leading him into the story—explaining to him how I knew that Oliver was different from the first time we met at the gala and how comfortable and at ease I was around him, much like I was with Colin . . . it all flew straight out the window when I opened my mouth to speak.

"Oliver kissed me today in the parking lot of the DCF," I blurt-ed out in a single breath, then backed up a few steps and waited wide-eyed for his response.

So much for finesse.

For a few moments, he just stood there frozen and silent, not blinking or even breathing that I could tell. My heart pounded out the drum line of trepidation behind my ribcage as I waited for him to react, so violently that I was certain he could hear it. Nausea rose higher in my chest with each passing second, and right when I was about to open my mouth and start talking again, he stopped me by raising his hand in the air and shaking his head.

"Don't," he ground out through a clenched jaw. "Don't you even dare start making excuses for him, Monroe, so help me God . . ."

Spinning away from me, he began pacing the floor as he ran frustrated fingers through his short hair, mumbling something inco-herent to himself. I didn't know what to do—or to say, for that mat-ter—so I watched with every muscle in my body coiled as tightly as they could possibly get while he processed the information. Finally, after what seemed like forever, he stopped and jerked his chin in my direction.

"What's the address of his apartment?" he snapped, his eyes glowing red with rage.

"Wh-what? Wh-why?" I stammered.

He slammed his palm down on the marble countertop and roared, "Because I'm gonna go over there and make sure-and-fuck-ing-well that he never touches you again, Monroe! Who in the hell does he think he is, waltzing his skinny, four-eyed dorky ass into town and putting the moves on my fucking wife? That shit doesn't fly with me, and it sure-as-shit shouldn't fly with you. Not only is it disrespectful as hell to both of us, but doing it right out in the open, where anyone could see? He might as well have rented out a goddamn billboard at the next fucking home game that says 'I'm seducing the quarterback's wife!' It's unacceptable, and it's not going to happen again. I don't care if I have to call Allison myself and get his ass fired from Mending Hearts. He needs to know he's screwing with the wrong fucking dude!"

In the seven or so years I'd known Colin, I may have heard him say a handful of curse words, and it was always because he'd physically injured himself, never because he lost control of his temper. And though I didn't expect him to be overly joyous about the whole announcement, I definitely wasn't expecting his nasty response. I was completely taken aback, and unexpectedly, I felt the need to defend Oliver to my husband.

"It wasn't like that. It just happened . . . an in-the-moment kinda thing," I argued. "He wasn't trying to seduce me. Oliver isn't that kind of a guy."

"Not that kind of a guy?! Are you kidding me?" he sneered, throwing his arms up in the air with exasperation. "What kind of guy relocates to a new city, where he's supposed to be helping set up a home for kids who've been abused, for Christ sakes, and within five fucking minutes of being there, is sticking his tongue down the throat of his very *married* colleague? Who, in case you may have forgotten in *your moment*, is easily intimidated and unsettled around other men. I know you said that Allison swears he's a good guy, and that you feel comfortable around him or what-the-fuck-ever, but as a guy myself and as your *husband*, I'm telling you right now he took advantage of your meek, compliant personality, and only weasely pieces of shits do that kind of thing!"

I shook my head adamantly, frustrated he wasn't understanding. "No, Colin, he's not. I swear to you, Oliver's different. I like him, and I wanted the kiss just as much as he did."

And . . . gasoline, meet fire.

"What in the hell did you just say?! Do you even hear the shit coming out of your mouth?" His face turned beet red as the angry words exploded from his mouth, and instinctively, I retreated away from him. "Let's forget for a minute that I am the only person that you've ever kissed in your entire life—and that there's a pretty damn serious reason for that—and let's focus on what that kiss you claim you *wanted* could've cost you . . . and what it could've cost *us*.

"We've worked too damn hard over the last five years to build this life—this life that we *both* wanted," he admonished, his booming voice reverberating off the walls as he shook a livid finger at me, "to throw it all away for a fucking kiss or roll in the sheets with some yahoo from the Midwest that you know not a damn thing about! Best-case scenario, in six months, he'll return home and brag to all of his pencil-dick friends about how he hooked up with Clutch Cassidy's wife while he was here, making you look like a stupid whore and me a fucking schmuck. Worst-case, you get caught by some random person with a camera phone who's only interested in selling to the highest bidder, and the next day, everything we've busted our asses for is gone. *Gone!* Do you have any idea of the field day the media would have with that? Your life . . . my life . . . destroyed."

Angry tears began to cascade down my cheeks as he lectured me. I was mad at Colin for making me feel small and stupid, and even more incensed at myself for not pointing out what a hypocrite he was being. But I just continued to stand there and listen to him rant on, because ultimately, I knew he was right.

"If this is about being curious and having sexual urges, Monroe, just tell me." Both his voice and expression softened as he took a step toward me. "I didn't really expect you to be celibate your entire life, despite you insisting otherwise, but we can do something about that where there's no chance of getting caught or getting emotions involved. I've actually been thinking about this for a while, when I knew this day would come, and I think I have the perfect solution. You know Seth loves you and thinks the world of you, and I'm sure he'd be super gentle and take—"

"OH MY FUCKING GOD, STOP!" I burst out before he could finish his appalling suggestion, holding my arms out in front of me to keep him from getting any closer. Blood rushed through my ears as I flew into a rage. "You wanna talk about the words coming out of my mouth?! Were you really about to suggest that I allow your *boyfriend* to help me with my *sexual urges*? What fucking planet do you live on where that could ever sound like a good idea?!"

Abruptly, the tables turned in the argument and it became me stalking forward, and my husband backpedaling through the kitchen, my finger jabbing him in the chest. "Look, I know our arrangement is far from normal, and I also know I agreed to this life, but if anything were to ever happen again between Oliver and me, I'd be sure to make sure it was somewhere safe so *our*," I motioned back and forth between the two of us with my hand, "precious, perfect life wouldn't be put at risk.

"I'm not a fucking dumbass, Colin, but for you to propose that I fuck Seth to appease my goddamn curiosities, I'm starting to think that you are! What, were you planning on watching him with me? Would that turn you on? Or is it because you get jealous thinking about him being with women on nights he's not here?" Cruel, wounding words spewed from my mouth for no other reason than to make him hurt, but I couldn't control myself. The fight was no longer about my and Oliver's kiss. "Were you hoping if he started fucking me regularly that he wouldn't go out looking for other pussy and you could just keep him here all the time? That way, you could control both of us and keep us all to yourself. After all, that's what you really want, right? Control? You want to control the world. If both of us really play our cards right, we may be the fucking President and First Lady before it's all said and done, and Seth can be your own personal Monica Lewinsky!"

"Sorry, but I refuse to wear a blue dress," Seth's unexpected voice broke through my tirade, and both Colin and I swung our heads over to where he stood in the doorway. Throughout our screaming back and forth, neither of us had heard him let himself in, and I had no idea how long he'd been there, but based on the hard ticking of his jaw and the daggers flying from his stare, I assumed it was enough.

Colin moved toward him instantly, but Seth shook his head and warned, "Not another step."

My husband froze midstride, despair written all over his face. "Seth, please, baby, give me a chance to explain," he beseeched. "It's not how she made it seem."

A cynical smirk played on the corners of Seth's mouth as he crossed his arms over his chest and leaned back against the wall. "Funny, 'cause I'm pretty damn sure I just heard you propose to your wife that she use me for her sexual pleasure," he glanced over and shot me a sympathetic smile before turning his attention back to Colin, "and though it's true, I do love Monroe like a *sister*, and I'm admittedly adventurous in bed, incest isn't really my thing. Not to mention, having the person who supposedly loves me more than anyone else in the world offer me up like I'm a fucking possession doesn't really say a lot about that love."

"I wasn't treating you like a possession," Colin contended with a frustrated huff.

"The hell you weren't!" Seth shot back. "It's how you've always treated me. Our relationship only works when it's on your terms. I only get you when it's convenient for you. If you've had a bad day at practice or if you're not feeling well or if you're horny, you call and I'm supposed to appear on command . . . which I always do, because I'm so fucking in love with you I'll take you any way I can get you! I'm glad you get jealous when you see me with women, because now you know how I fucking feel all of the time I don't get to be with you. No one else would put up with this shit, but we do it, because we love you! It's not fair to Monroe, it's not fair to me, and if you'd pull your head out of your parents' and the public's ass far enough to see straight, you'd realize it's not fair to you either! I thought after our last break that things would be different, but they're not. And it's becoming more and more apparent to me that they never will be."

Stopping to take a deep breath, Seth scrubbed his hands up and down his face then dropped his arms to his sides with slumped shoulders. "Look, Colin, you know how I feel. I'll love you until the day I die, but I can't keep doing this to myself. I'm still your best friend and your biggest fan, and I still want to be a part of your life, but the rest is over. I'm tired of getting my hopes up for more, only for them to come crumbling down time and time again. You need to figure out what you really want out of this life, and I hope to God you realize what a gem of a wife you have to put up with this shit. 'Cause I can guaran-fucking-tee you that nobody else would."

And with that, Seth spun around and marched out of the house, the slamming door an exclamation mark on his visit.

I didn't dare move or speak, hoping Colin would stomp to his room without any more confrontation, but I couldn't be so lucky. He turned to me and glowered, his nostrils flared and his face flush. "I really hope that kiss was worth all of this."

Defiantly, I lifted my chin in the air and marched past him, pausing just before I escaped to my room. "I really hope *you* are."

chapter
fourteen

"Her eyes carried
a certain kind
of silence that
begged to be
understood and I
felt as if I was
a scientist,
staring with eager,
fervent eyes into
galaxies that have not
yet had the chance
to be named."
–Christopher Poindexter

OLIVER

MONROE KNOCKED ON the door at precisely nine o'clock, and although I'd been counting down the minutes for her to arrive ever since the moment she'd left, I suddenly wasn't ready to face her. I'd spent the entire night going back and forth between replaying that fucking kiss in my mind and beating myself up for acting so thoughtlessly. So selfishly. All I wanted was to pretend like it never happened, to erase the way her soft lips welcomed mine and how having her body pressed against me felt like the most natural thing in the world. But it was impossible. She'd hijacked my every thought.

Dark half-moons perched atop her cheeks were the first thing I noticed when I swung the door open. *At least I wasn't the only one who didn't sleep.* She forced a smile that didn't quite reach her usually bright eyes, and held out one of the steaming paper cups she was holding in my direction.

"I wasn't sure how you took it, but you strike me as a guy who likes his coffee black," she announced as she walked inside, careful that our fingers didn't touch when she passed the coffee off to me, "but if you don't like it, I can drink yours too. This stuff is like crack . . . or what I think crack would be like, because I mean, obviously, I've never done crack." She stopped in the middle of the living room and turned to face where I still stood, holding an open door. "Well, close the door, for Pete's sakes. Do you want your entire hall to listen to me ramble on like an idiot? It's bad enough I act like this in front of you, but I'd rather not share my foolish behavior with your neighbors too."

Immediately releasing my hold on the knob and giving the door a gentle shove, I began to move toward her cautiously. I wasn't sure what was going on, but she was clearly on edge and I didn't want to upset her more. "Thanks for the coffee," I said as I brought the piping hot drink to my mouth for a sip. "Black is perfect."

Another half-smile as she glanced down at her own cup that she was now clutching with both hands, followed by a nervous lick of her lips. Instinctively, my eyes followed the path of her tongue across the plump, delicate flesh, and I groaned internally as my pants abruptly grew snug in the crotch. *This woman is going to be the death of me. I can't fucking control myself around her.*

"Uh, yeah, no problem," she eventually replied, keeping her stare fixed on the green plastic lid as she shifted her weight from one leg to the other then back again. "I, uh . . . I had this whole speech planned out on my way over here. Stayed up most of the night thinking about what I wanted to say and how to properly express what I'm thinking and feeling, but now that I'm here, it all seems incredibly stupid. I mean, I don't even really know you . . . I don't know how what happened yesterday even happened. It doesn't make any sense at all. I pride myself on the control and restraint I have over my thoughts and my actions. As a public figure, I'm constantly judged on the things I say and do, and if I behave irresponsibly, not only will that reflect poorly on me and my morals and character, but it'll also affect Colin and Mending Hearts."

She stopped her rambling to gradually raise her chin, her troubled green eyes seeking out mine as she whispered, "Regardless of how out of control I feel when I'm around you, I can't afford to lose either of those things. They're my world. My everything."

I took a tentative step in her direction, but made sure to leave plenty of space between the two of us. I didn't want to think about why her control faltered when she was around me. Thinking about that would only lead to more questions that I'd never get answers to. For the preservation of both of our sanity, I had to do the right thing.

"Monroe, it's okay. I understand," I assured her softly, fighting the urge to reach out and touch her. "You don't need to explain anything. I told you yesterday that I don't do that kind of thing either. That's not who I am, nor is it who I want to be. I wish more than anything I could go back and undo that kiss so that things don't get awkward between us, but I can't. It's done. It's over. And all we can do is ensure it won't happen again."

Pausing for another swallow of the much-needed caffeine, I then continued on, unsure of where the sound and rational words were coming from, but thankful for them nonetheless. "We just need to move forward and focus on our common goal of getting this house ready to be the best it can be for the kids who are gonna live there. We've got a little less than six months of working closely together, and even after that, as long as we're both with Mending Hearts, we'll still see and talk to each other occasionally. I think we've established that whatever happened between us yesterday was a fluky thing. For whatever reason, we both acted impulsively and out of character. It was a one-time thing, and we're both professional and adult enough to carry on as friendly colleagues. Am I right?"

Monroe nodded and her body visibly relaxed, which in turn made mine do the same. It was as if someone had abruptly flipped the on-switch to an invisible vacuum and sucked nearly all of the tension out of the room in one broad sweep. And although I knew it'd be a constant struggle of my willpower not to think about how amazing that kiss had been every time I looked at her lips, I was relieved at the rapid shift in her demeanor. Her happy made me happy.

"Yeah, I guess you are, but don't get used to me admitting that kind of thing," she teased with a bashful grin before lifting the coffee to her mouth for a drink.

I was about to retort something equally as snarky, but it was then that I noticed what was scrawled in black marker across her white paper cup: Rizzo. Glancing down at my own beverage, I saw the name "Sandy D." staring back at me, and everything I'd just said flew swiftly out the window. What happened between us the day before wasn't a fluke at all. I was falling for a married woman.

chapter fifteen

"The truth about
romance is
this: We are
all novels;
our pages stained
with the fingerprints
of either our
lovers
or loneliness."
—Christopher Poindexter

MONROE

COLIN WAS WRONG. Oliver was a good guy. A little *too* good if you asked my wounded ego . . . because even though I knew it was the right thing for him to say for both of our sakes, when he admitted that he wished he could go back and undo the best kiss of my life, it was like being kicked in the gut. With a steel-toed boot. By an MMA fighter.

But, like I knew how to do so well, I pushed past the hurt, plastered a smile on my face, and pressed on.

Thankfully, it didn't take long after our serious—and incredibly awkward—conversation for Oliver to have me laughing and joking around while we set up the dining room table in his apartment as the temporary headquarters for Mending Hearts Boston . . . though the kiss was never far from my thoughts. I did my best to keep plenty of physical space between us by sitting across from him instead of next to him, and I was careful to never allow my gaze to drop to his mouth, afraid I wouldn't be able to tear my eyes away from his soft, tempting lips, now that I knew exactly how they felt pressed against mine.

Never before had I struggled with my willpower like I did that day, but by the time lunch rolled around, I'd managed to get my lecherous, immoral thoughts under control, and Oliver and I had developed an effective and efficient method of sorting through the advisor applications. "You about ready to stop for a bite to eat?" I asked, looking up from my laptop. "I'm pretty sure my stomach is planning a mutiny over here."

"Hold on, one minute. I'm almost done with this email."

The light of the screen warmed his amber eyes as he typed out the message, and I couldn't help but allow my gaze to linger on him for a few seconds longer than I should have. His long chocolate curls were tucked behind his ears, begging my fingers to twist in them, and his dark-framed glasses had fallen down on the bridge of his nose, in desperate need for me to reach out and adjust them. So to keep myself from doing either, I abruptly jumped up out of my chair and made a beeline to the kitchen. *For the love of God, Monroe, get ahold of yourself. He already told you that he regretted the kiss. Don't embarrass yourself anymore.*

"I can start getting something ready while you wrap up what you're working on," I offered as I opened the refrigerator to peruse our options. Only, when I swung open the door, a cold box of nothingness greeted me. Like absolutely nothing. Not even a beer or random to-go packet of ketchup.

Chuckling, I closed the fridge and turned to open the pantry, only to find it just as bare. "Umm . . . Oliver?"

"Yeah?" he asked absently, still pounding away on the keyboard.

"Why don't you have any food here?"

"Because cooking for one isn't much fun," he laughed and swiveled around to face me, crossing his arms over his chest. "Nor do I know where the grocery store is around here, so I've just been eating at the deli downstairs and a few of the close-by restaurants."

I scrunched my nose up with disapproval and shook my head. "But what if you get thirsty in the middle of the night? You don't even have anything to drink!"

"I'm not sure if you've heard of this cool thing called water? It's this really great liquid for hydrating. Plus, it's free with this swanky apartment." He smirked as he pushed to his feet, slowly swaggering toward where I stood. "And as for lunch, I assumed we'd be ordering delivery or grabbing some to-go food, but if you'd rather we eat here, I can stock up on some things. Just let me know what kind of stuff you like."

The temperature spiked the instant we were both inside the narrow, galley-style kitchen, and by the grace of God, he stopped a few feet in front of me and jokingly turned the faucet on, pointing at the stream of water with a lopsided grin. "See? Water."

Desperate to escape the close quarters, I used his bad joke as an excuse to roll my eyes and saunter past him, scooping up my purse and keys off of my makeshift desk. "Come on, funny guy," I called out over my shoulder, making my way to the door. "We're going grocery shopping."

"WHAT IS THAT?" Oliver scowled at the gallon of milk I'd just set in the shopping cart. "Does that stuff even come from a cow?"

Confused, I lifted the carton up in the air and skimmed over the label, thinking maybe I'd grabbed the wrong thing by mistake. Once I realized I hadn't, I cut my eyes over at him and gave him the what-in-the-world-are-you-talking-about look. "Of course it comes from a cow," I scoffed. "It's fat-free, organic milk. You said you need-ed some for your cereal, right?"

With a snicker, he shook his head and walked around the cart, taking the milk out of my hands and placing it back in the cooler. Then, shuffling farther down the dairy section a few feet, he reached down and pulled out a gigantic plastic jug of chocolate milk.

Donning a huge grin, he proudly placed the replacement milk in the cart and gave me a triumphant nod. "You can't ruin Peanut Butter Captain Crunch with that healthy crap you picked. Chocolate milk is the only way to go. Please tell me you've tried it before."

"Uhhh . . . no. I've never tried any kind of Captain Crunch, not with regular or chocolate milk," I laughed. "Actually, I've never had any kind of cereal, unless you count granola or oatmeal."

"What? No cereal?!" Oliver's eyes grew wide with astonishment. "Surely you ate some when you were a kid."

"Nope. Never." I shook my head emphatically.

Moving back to the rear of the cart so he could push it down the aisle, he continued to gape at me in disbelief. "Really? Not even like the gross stuff like Shredded Wheat or Raisin Bran?"

"I'm serious. Not even the gross stuff."

He stopped momentarily to add butter, sour cream, and cream cheese to the growing pile of food, and then resumed his skeptical questioning as we headed toward the bakery. "How is that even possible? I mean, even if your mom didn't keep it in the house for whatever reason, how did you not try it when you spent the night with friends or went on vacation? Cereal is like a staple of all kids' diets. It should probably be its own food group."

I shrugged nonchalantly, pretending to read the nutritional facts on the back of a package of pita bread crackers while strolling next to him. "I dunno. I didn't grow up like most kids. I didn't stay out over at friends' houses, and at home, we had a personal chef who did all of the shopping and cooking, so I ate what was put in front of me . . . which was always whatever my mom wanted. She was very strict and disciplined about her diet. We usually had egg whites with fresh fruit, or something similar. Then, when I went away to boarding school, I had a meal plan, so it was pretty much the same thing. I ate whatever the cafeteria was serving that day. And I can assure you, my ass is thankful it was never a bowl of sugary cereal with chocolate milk, or I'd have lived on the elliptical machine when I wasn't studying," I joked to hide the mixture of disappointment and embarrassment coursing through me.

Glancing up, I was surprised to find him staring so intently at me, and although I had a hard time placing the expression brewing in his fascinating eyes, there was no denying my body's physical response to his attention. Much like the first time I met him, and several occurrences since, goose bumps prickled over my skin as warmth arose in my core. He looked at me like no one had ever looked at me before, and it was equally as unnerving as it was exhilarating. I never wanted him to stop.

"What?" I questioned in a hushed voice once I realized we'd been standing in front of the baguette stand, staring at each other for who knew how long. "Is the cereal a deal-breaker on the friendly colleague thing?"

Oliver barked out a laugh, my words obviously breaking him free of whatever train of thought he'd been lost in. "No, Rizzo." He shook his head as he began moving forward again with the cart. "It's not a deal-breaker, but you are aware it's the first thing I'm making you eat when we get back to the apartment, right? I don't care how long you're gonna have to work out later. I promise every bite will be worth it."

Half an hour later, as I sat at his table slurping down the remnants of my first—but definitely not last—bowl of Peanut Butter Captain Crunch with chocolate milk, I could see the I-told-you-so smile dancing in the creases next to his eyes, and once again, he was right . . . it was *sooo* worth it. And I was starting to think he might be too.

chapter
sixteen

"It is ripping me
apart knowing
that I am loving
you with only
a broken version
of me.
I can only hope
that it is enough.
My god,
please be enough."
–Christopher Poindexter

MONROE

WHEN I LEFT Oliver's apartment late that afternoon, I wasn't quite ready to be alone with my thoughts or to face the emptiness of my house. I hadn't seen or talked to Colin since our argument the night before—not even as much as a simple text message either way. We had never fought before, and I hated it. He was the one person who was supposed to support and love me no matter what, and for him to react the way he had, I was not only disappointed, but I was hurt. He, of all people, should've known what a big deal it was for me to come to him with something like that, and how I most definitely wouldn't have taken it lightly. Part of me had expected him to call or text an apology at some point throughout the day, once he realized how insensitive and hypocritical he had been, but the message never came. And instead, I was left alone to deal with the onslaught of emotions I was feeling, not only about Oliver, but about Colin too.

Confusion.

Guilt.

Self-doubt.

Exhilaration.

Remorse.

Desire.

I was a damn mess.

It was the first time I wished I had a girlfriend to confide in, but honestly, Allison was the closest thing I had to that, and I wasn't about to burden her with my issues while she was preparing to start her chemotherapy treatments. Plus, I didn't want her to feel guilty about having Oliver taking her place in Boston, seeing that none of this probably would've happened had she been the one training me. *No, that definitely wasn't an option.* So, I went to the one place I knew would make me forget about all of my own issues and put a smile on my face: the Suffolk County Children's Home.

The moment I stepped inside the building, all of my personal worries and troubles were left with my coat at the door, and I was free to be whatever the kids needed me to be, whether it be a teacher, a counselor, a supporter, or even just a friend. And some nights, it was all of the above. I didn't mind at all. The one thing I knew, without a doubt, was that regardless of everything else, *they* were worth it.

"Monroe! Monroe! You're here again! Two days in a row!" six-year-old Alex shouted when he saw me appear inside the rec room, just after I'd checked in with the evening advisors on duty. Dropping his game controller, he sprinted over to me and threw himself around my leg, squeezing me with all his might.

Laughing, I pried him off my boot and lifted him up in my arms. "Hey, big guy! I'm happy to see you too!" I exclaimed, giving him a quick kiss on the cheek. "Are you already finished with all of your homework to be playing games?"

He nodded as I lowered his feet back to the ground, his mega-watt grin staying in place. "Yes'm. Miss Lovell says I'm the smartest boy in the whole wide world, and that one day I'm gonna be the Present of the Unitard States. They may even make money with me on it!"

"Money with you on it?!" I gave him my best I'm-so-impressed face as I hid my chuckle. "That's pretty remarkable, buddy. I hope it happens though. I know I'll vote for you."

"Do you think Dr. Saxon would do magic tricks with my money? That would be so cool, right? I bet he'll vote for me too so he can have my money!" I didn't think it was possible, but Alex's small freckled face lit up even more when he thought about the possibility of Oliver doing silly magic tricks with dollar bills that had his face on them. In just one afternoon with the kids, he'd already made a lasting impression.

"I'm sure he will," I agreed as I tapped my finger gently on the tip of his nose, pretending his mention of Oliver didn't completely knock me off-kilter. "You just need to keep doing so well in school, and Dr. Saxon and I will take care of all the votes. Deal?"

Holding his child-sized hand out in my direction, he waited for me to rest mine inside of his before shaking it and repeating, "Deal." Then, like a gust of autumn wind, he took off back toward the TV, plopped down with his controller, and resumed his game.

I smiled as I scanned the rest of the room, pleased to find Aaron playing checkers with one of the boys close to his age and Heather curled up in a beanbag chair with a book. Not surprisingly, JoJo wasn't with the rest of the group, so after I said hello to the others, I trudged up the stairs to her room, hoping she was in a better mood than the day before. However, just before I reached the top of the steps, my phone chimed inside my purse, alerting me of a new text. Stopping at the top of the landing, I fished it out of the bottom of my bag and glanced down at the screen.

Colin: Are you at home?

Sighing, I quickly typed out a reply. Usually when I got that text, it was because he needed me to bring him something up to the practice field, and though I normally didn't mind, I was still extremely irritated with him and didn't want to leave the house, especially since I'd just gotten there.

Me: No, I'm at the SC house. I was gonna eat dinner with the kids. Why? What's up?

Colin: Oh ok. No worries. I'll just talk to you when I get home tonight. I had a question about our insurance.

Our insurance?! Was he serious? As if the belittling and patronizing me wasn't bad enough, he'd offered up his boyfriend like he was loaning me his lawn mower or something . . . all without so much as an 'I'm sorry' afterward. And then he wanted to ask me a question about our fucking insurance?!

My blood boiled inside my veins as I thought of at least fifty different ways I wanted to tell him to go screw himself, but I refused to allow him to ruin my time with the kids. One of the best things I ever learned in my years of therapy is that I held the power to decide what kind of mood I wanted to be in. Other people only affected that mood if I let them, and right then, I wasn't giving Colin that privilege.

Me: Yeah, it'll have to wait. Or maybe you can call our agent yourself. His number is in your contacts.

I hit send and then turned my phone on silent-mode before tossing it back in my purse and making my way down the hall to JoJo's room. Grateful to discover the door open, I peeked my head inside and found her lying on the bed, thumbing through one of those ridiculously fictitious weekly tabloids you find in the checkout line of grocery stores. I bit my tongue as I refrained from commenting on her reading selection and knocked on the wooden frame with a warm smile. "You busy? Up for a little girl talk?"

For a fleeting second, I saw a speck of happiness in her big brown eyes when she peered up from the bound glossy pages and saw me, but it vanished as quickly as it had appeared. Shrugging her shoulders, she looked back down at the pictures in front of her and mumbled, "Not busy, but don't feel much like talking either."

That was about as much of an invitation as I was ever going to get, so I accepted it as just that and joined her atop the twin-sized mattress. For a couple of minutes, we sat together quietly, the crinkle of the pages when she turned them the only sound filling the room. I'd learned early on after JoJo had arrived at the house to move slowly with her in both conversation and actions; otherwise, she became cagey and defensive, like a trapped animal. After her lash-out the day before, the last thing I wanted was to set her off again.

"I'm not sure if you were downstairs yesterday when I announced that we'd signed the contract on the house," I said once I felt confident she was okay with my being there.

She nodded, but didn't look up. "Yeah, Heather told me last night. So I guess this means you really are gonna be stuck with me, huh?"

My chest constricted at her self-deprecating words, even though I knew most of why she said them was so I'd tell her how much they weren't true. The fact she needed me to reassure her that I didn't feel 'stuck' with her, and that I truly 'wanted' her was the problem at its core. For as much of a tough-girl act that JoJo put on most of the time, the truth was she was an insecure thirteen-year-old girl who'd never been made to feel appreciated or cherished.

Born to a heroin-junkie for a mother who would do anything for her next fix, including allowing men to take advantage of her young daughter, JoJo's lot in life didn't improve any when she entered the system and got placed in a home with a couple who was just looking to get the government money that came along with fostering kids. Their complete disregard of parenting and utter neglect to realize what was going on under their roof led to two of the older boys in the house sexually-assaulting JoJo on a daily basis. It wasn't until a case worker showed up on an unannounced visit one afternoon and witnessed the act herself that anyone ever found out about it. That was one day before her twelfth birthday.

There were some days—particularly those when she screamed in my face that there was no way I could ever understand what it was like to live her life—that I wanted so badly to tell her how wrong she was. I knew exactly what it was like to have a mother that was so addicted to something that she'd turn a blind-eye to the destruction and devastation of her only child in order to keep it. Only my mom's vice wasn't drugs; it was fame.

"Don't you mean you're gonna be stuck with me?" I teased, brushing my shoulder against hers. "How long until you're sick of hearing me singing Wilson Phillips off-key around the house all the time? And you don't even know what this face looks like without makeup on. Colin hides under the covers when I come out of the bathroom at night so he doesn't have to see this craziness. You may even try to take pictures and sell them to that tabloid you're reading there."

Finally, I got a small laugh out of her as she looked over and rolled her eyes at me. "Whatever . . . you're like the most naturally beautiful person on this planet. You probably look exactly the same with or without makeup, and I'm damn sure Colin's only hiding under the covers, because he wants you to meet him there for some action. You guys are so perfect it's sickening. There's nothing you two don't have—you're rich, you're famous, and you both look like models. So sorry if I don't feel bad for you if you can't sing," she playfully stuck her tongue out at me, "but I just may have to record one of your impromptu concerts and sell that to the magazines instead."

A chuckle escaped my throat as I briefly imagined a home video of me singing "Hold On" as it aired over national TV. My rockstar dad would probably roll over in his grave, second-guessing the validity of the paternity test that claimed I was his, and I'd definitely receive a phone call from Mommy Dearest asking me not to embarrass her again. *Yep, pretty perfect life.*

"Yeah, that would be pretty awful." I scrunched up my nose and shook my head. "But all joking aside, JoJo, no person or relationship is perfect. Anybody can put on a façade for the public, but it's what kind of person they are behind closed doors that matters most."

"So what kind of person are you behind closed doors, Monroe?" she challenged me, raising her eyebrows up into her forehead.

I knew she was just trying to be cute, not expecting a real, introspective answer from me, but with everything that had occurred over the prior couple of days with Colin and Oliver, it caused me to stop a moment and ponder the question. And for the first time in over a decade, I wasn't sure what the answer was.

"The kind who wants to sing terribly off-key while not wearing any makeup, if it makes my favorite teenager smile for a few minutes," I quickly replied, covering up for my momentary stall.

Thankfully, it worked. The edges of JoJo's mouth curled up in a big grin as her cheeks brightened a rosy color. "Good, 'cause I'll have my camera ready."

I ended up hanging out with JoJo until it was time for dinner, and then the two of us headed downstairs, where we ate spaghetti and listened to the room full of kids each take their turn telling what their favorite part of the day was. When it was time for JoJo to share, an activity I'd seen her not participate in countless times, she stole a sly glimpse over at me and said, "Finding out I'm getting a new home."

My heart was still soaring when I stepped outside into the chilly night air after I'd said my round of goodnights to all of the kids. However, as I tightened my coat around my chest and looked up at where my car was parked in the adjacent lot, everything came crashing down when I saw Colin standing out in front of my hood. My first thought was something bad had happened, either with his parents or that he'd gotten injured at practice, so I scampered over to him, forgetting about all of the animosity I'd been harboring toward him throughout the day.

"Colin? What's wrong? What are you doing out here? Why didn't you come inside to get me?" I called out question after question as I drew near, but his face remained stoic until I was less than a foot from him.

Then, in a move that completely blew my mind, he swung around the arm that had been hidden behind his back and held out an enormous bouquet of flowers as he stepped toward me. I stilled, caught off-guard and still confused by what was happening, and waited for him to speak.

"Monroe, baby girl, I'm so sorry about last night," he whispered as his troubled green eyes bored into me. "I messed up with both you and Seth. Big time. I know I acted like a massive selfish jerk and I said ugly things that really hurt you . . . and I never want to hurt you."

My vision swam as the sobs built in the back of my throat, but when I opened my mouth to respond, he held his hand up to stop me.

"Please let me finish, and then you can yell and scream at me all you want," he said with a nervous laugh before continuing. "You came to me with something that was weighing on you, and not only did I not value your feelings, but I completely demeaned and humiliated you. And I'm so damn sorry for that. I'm still worried if you get involved with this guy, everything could get really messy in our lives, I'm willing to listen to you and talk about it . . . if you still want to."

Once my first tear broke free, an ocean's worth followed, but as I grabbed the flowers from Colin's hand and threw my arms around his neck, I clung to him, feeling the most overwhelming sense of relief. I didn't think anything else would ever happen between me and Oliver, seeing as how he seemed pretty dead-set on forgetting the one kiss we had shared, but I knew that as long as I had Colin next to me, I'd be just fine.

"I love you, Monroe," he murmured into my hair.

"I love you too, Clutch." I smiled into his chest. "To the very end."

chapter
seventeen

"Her eyes
played
silence like
it was an
instrument the
world had never
known"
–Christopher Poindexter

OLIVER

OVER THE NEXT couple of days, Monroe and I fell into an easy routine, setting up interviews with graduate students from not only Boston College, but several others from nearby universities that had notable Social Work programs as well. Our individual working styles meshed so well together it seemed as if we'd been operating as a team for years instead of a measly week. If I'd had any lingering doubts about her running her own MH house before then, they all would've been eradicated after seeing the way she meticulously ran my dining room table like the point-of-command of an exhaustive military campaign. Of course I didn't have any reservations, as I was pretty sure the woman could've persuaded Satan himself to perform a Good Samaritan deed or two, so it was a moot point. But there was something about watching her work that made me fall even more in awe of her . . . and it wasn't just the way her blouse would dip down and give me a teasing glimpse of her cleavage when she'd reach across the table for a piece of paper or a pen.

Well, maybe it was a little bit of that.

Okay, it was a lot of that . . . but hey, I was a straight, thir-ty-three-year-old guy who had a serious fucking crush on his co-worker. Yes, she was married. And yes, I'd foolishly kissed her in a rash and reckless moment of weakness when I'd lost sight of who we both were, giving in to the overpowering need to feel her lips against mine. But ever since we talked the next day and cleared the air, I knew nothing was ever going to happen between us again, so it didn't hurt to look just a little. It was only for a few mental snapshots I could use late at night when I was alone. *God, I'm going straight to Hell for breaking no less than three of the Ten Commandments every time I'm around this woman. Do not pass go. Do not collect $200. Simply burn for the rest of eternity.*

Even despite the incessant thoughts of my impending spiritual doom, I couldn't help but stare at her ass when she stood up and strolled into the kitchen that first Friday afternoon we worked to-gether in my apartment. I'd never seen her dressed casually before then—as she was in an evening gown when I'd initially met her, and after that, always wore stylish but modest business attire—but holy shit, the way those fitted jeans cupped her round cheeks and showed off that tiny little gap between her legs . . .

I discreetly adjusted the growing bulge in my lap, wonder-ing if I should suggest that every day be Casual Friday. Unless, of course, we had appointments to meet with other people, and then I wanted her in the frumpiest thing she owned so they couldn't gawk at her too. She was *my* denim goddess to worship. *Make that four commandments.*

"Do you want something to drink?" Monroe asked as she glanced at me over her shoulder, catching me red-handed as I ogled her ass that was bent over at the refrigerator.

The tips of my ears burned with pure mortification, and I had no doubt that they—as well as my cheeks—were glowing the guilti-est shade of pink. Lowering my eyes to the laptop screen in front of me, I cleared my throat to cover up the nervous bubble of laughter that waited in the back of my throat. "I'm sorry. What did you say? I didn't hear you . . . I was really focused on this thing here on my computer," I lied with the most unconvincing voice possible.

Turning around to face me head-on, she playfully shook her head as she crossed her arms over her chest. "Drink, Oliver. I asked if you wanted something to drink. Like water or a soda? Maybe a coffee to help you wake up?"

"Oh, right." I gave her my best innocent look, which usually worked on my mom and sisters. "Do I, uh, have any fruit juice left in there? I can't remember if I drank it all."

With a mischievous smirk, she rolled her eyes at me then spun back around to look in the fridge, a muffled giggle escaping from her as she purposely cocked her hip in my direction. *What the . . . ? That little minx!*

"I don't see any in here. What kind did you think you had?" she called out as she moved a few things around to scan the items in the back, her glutes tensing as she shifted her weight from foot to foot.

I wasn't sure if the extra movement was for my benefit or not, but fuck if my dick cared what the underlying intention was. He sprang to life with visions of kinky kitchen sex dancing in his head, complete with spatula-spankings, whipped cream bikinis, and fruit-and-vegetable play. Go figure—the only channels I watched on TV were the Food Network and Penthouse. When I opened my mouth to answer her, it was as if Dick the Iron Chef had taken control of all my brain functions, because the only word that I could come up with was "Peach," which I promptly tried to catch with my hand and shove it back into my mouth. Unfortunately, it wasn't before she heard it loud and clear.

Then, by the grace of the dear mighty God above, who had apparently not given up on my sinning soul quite yet, my cell phone began to play the chorus to Billy Idol's "Caribbean Queen" at the loudest volume possible as it vibrated across the table. Knowing who it was by the ringtone, I snatched it up quickly and accepted the call, eager to talk to my niece, but even more thankful for the impeccably-timed interruption.

"Hi, Callie! I've been waiting to hear from you! How's it been going, baby girl?" I answered a little too enthusiastically as I gave Monroe an apologetic smile that wasn't even the tiniest bit genuine.

"Hey, Uncle Ollie," she chimed into the receiver. "Why do you sound so weird? Is this not a good time? I can call back later—"

My gaze remained locked and loaded on Monroe as she grabbed a couple bottles of water then sauntered back toward me with hips that swayed ever so slightly and an unreadable expression that I'd never seen on her before. "No, no! It's a fine time," I cut her off, trying my hardest to focus on the phone call and not the beautiful woman who was leaning over the table to set my drink in front of me, giving me clear access down the V-neck of her fuzzy black sweater to the matching black bra that covered her gorgeous fucking boobs. "I, uh, I was just, uh," I stammered around, frantically searching my brain for something logical to say, but I physically could not tear my eyes away from her cleavage, "just finishing up a little tit . . . I mean bit . . . a little bit of work I had left to call it a day."

My ears and cheeks flamed yet again at my own daftness, and this time, Monroe made no qualms about showing how much she enjoyed my discomfort with her impish grin spreading from ear to ear. I pinched my eyebrows together and gave her a stern warning with the shake of my head, but that only made her erupt in a fit of laughter.

"Holy shitballs! Are you banging a chick right now, Uncle Ollie?!" Callie shrieked so loudly it caused me to drop the phone, and somehow, when I tried to catch it, my finger must've hit the speakerphone button, because the next thing I knew, her high-pitched, seventeen-year-old voice was being broadcasted throughout the entire apartment. "Is she hot? Did you play Michael Bolton for her? I bet you totally played Michael Bolton for her. No matter how ugly he is, I'm sure he gets mad pussy because of that sax."

Dropping to my knees, I fumbled around trying to grab the damn thing, but it was like I'd suddenly sprouted six thumbs on each hand and then coated them in baby oil with the way it kept slipping out of my grasp. And all the while, she kept talking—without ever stopping for a breath. "I've always thought you probably scored a ton of chicks too. That's why you had to move away from Kinderhook and go to the big city, right? Because you'd probably tapped everything that was available around there by the time you graduated high school and needed some fresh meat. You know that whole man-bun thing you've been rocking forever is finally coming back into style, so you can totally play up the whole grungy-hipster-musician-who-wants-to-save-all-the-children-in-the-world angle. I bet that'd be like hitting the pussy lotter—"

"Enough! Good Lord, that is enough!" I screamed when I finally grabbed hold of the goddamn piece of life-ruining technology and stopped the speakerphone option, afraid my ears would start bleeding if I heard my niece say the word *pussy* one more time. What kind of parenting job was my sister doing? And what had happened to the sweet, innocent kid who'd helped me hide Easter eggs for the little ones just that Spring? "My God, child, do you kiss your mother with that same filthy mouth? How do you even know about this stuff? Where's Charlotte? Let me talk to my sister, so I can tell her that you spend entirely too much time watching stuff on TV and online that you have no business watching."

"So, she's hot, right? Nice tits? You totally mentioned her tits, so I bet they're really nice." It was like she hadn't registered one single thing I'd said. "Do I get to meet her when I come visit? I swear I won't mention that you banged the whole high school cheerleading squad back home."

"I DIDN'T BANG THE WHOLE HIGH SCHOOL CHEERLEADING SQUAD!" I shouted as I teetered on the brink of losing my cool, forgetting that Monroe was still bearing witness to the disastrous debacle. "I DIDN'T BANG ANY OF THE CHEERLEADERS! AS A MATTER OF FACT, I WASN'T BANGING ANYONE IN HIGH SCHOOL, NOR AM I BANGING ANYONE NOW. NOT THAT IT'S ANY OF YOUR GODDAMN BUSINESS!"

The absurdity of the entire scene had risen to Mach-5 level, and I realized that I had been sorely mistaken, for God had not forgiven me at all. The purpose of the phone call wasn't to save me from anything; it was punishment for my errant, immoral thoughts and for breaking a good chunk of his sacred rules. I mean, there were only ten of them, and in the five days I'd been around Monroe, I managed to cover coveting my neighbor's wife, adulterating (to a certain degree) with said wife, lying to the wife about my true thoughts, secretly idolizing the wife, and using God's name in vain on a pretty regular basis. While I was thinking about it, I'm pretty sure one of the first things my Dad taught me once I was old enough to know what he was talking about was, "Don't ever stick your finger in another man's honey, son." So by nature of the whole adulterating thing, I was also disobeying my parents in the process. Hey, at least I had no plans to bear false witness or murder anyone anytime soon, right?

"Dude, Uncle Ollie, chill out. I'm just messing with you, because I heard a girl laughing in the background earlier," Callie snickered. "Geez, maybe you do need to get laid though. You sound way uptight."

Squeezing my eyes shut, I pinched the bridge of my nose and shook my head. "No, I'm good, Cal. Thanks for caring about your good ol' uncle though," I gritted out. "Now, can we please get back to the reason you called in the first place?"

Totally unfazed by it all, she jumped right into telling me that PawPaw (my dad) had already booked her a flight from Nashville to Boston the Sunday before Thanksgiving, and that she'd stay with me until that Wednesday, when the two of us would fly together to St. Louis for our normal family holiday weekend. By that point, I didn't have it in me to bring up how I would've liked to be included in the planning before flights were actually booked, nor how I was actually supposed to be working the Monday and Tuesday she would be visiting, so I just told her it sounded great and that I couldn't wait to see her.

After disconnecting the call and tossing the phone off to the side, I plopped back down in my dining room chair and face-planted onto the table. I was done. Finished. Terminado. Finito. All of that shit. I just wanted the day over. But I couldn't be so lucky . . .

"Your niece . . . she seems like a nice girl." Monroe's voice broke through the buzz of static running between my ears, prompting me to lift my head and gaze over at her sincere, compassionate smile. "Yes, it sounded crazy, but you forget: I know teenagers. And I could really tell at the end of the call how much you love her. I'm sure you guys are gonna have a blast when she comes to visit."

Taken aback by both her understanding and perceptiveness, my body slackened in my chair as I blew out a huge breath of relief. "She's the reason I do this, ya know? The Mending Hearts stuff."

"Really?" Leaning back in her chair, her eyes grew wide with curiosity. "Is it something you mind talking about?"

I shrugged and grabbed the unopened water bottle from in front of me. I was thankful the sexual charge in the room had all but dissipated, but the story I had to tell was on the complete other end of the spectrum from the mood prior to and during Callie's phone call. "I don't mind. It's just not a very pretty story," I cautioned, pausing for a much-needed drink in my dry mouth. "But if you're interested, I'll give you the abridged version."

Monroe nodded, mirroring my actions with her own water bottle. "I'd love to know Callie's story."

Inhaling a deep breath for a small boost of confidence, I began telling her the story of my family's nightmare—a story I hadn't told in over a decade. "First, I'll give you a quick background of my family. I'm the third of four kids—the only boy—and all of us are exactly two years apart, just like my mom wanted it. We were raised in a tiny blip on the map in Western Illinois called Kinderhook, where my mom owned a dance studio in a nearby town, right down the street from where my dad owned a small music shop. It was one of the places where everybody knew everybody and no one locked their doors, not at night or during the day. Crime didn't exist in our world. It was unfathomable for our neighbors to worry about anyone doing anything to hurt anyone else, so all of us were just living our happy-go-lucky lives, when my younger sister Charlotte got pregnant at thirteen."

A long hiss passed through Monroe's lips as she realized quickly where the story was heading, and I used the moment to take another swig of my drink.

"Not to dwell on the absolute repulsive part of the story," I continued, my voice shaking slightly with the rage I still felt nearly twenty years later, "but it turned out that her best friend's father—and a close friend of our family for years—had been molesting her since she was ten, pretty much every time she spent the night at their house, threatening that he'd hurt our other two sisters if she told. When she first admitted the truth to my parents, he was out of town on a business trip for a couple of days, so there was nothing much they could do until he got back. They wanted to wait to file the police report, so that neither he nor anyone else in his family caught wind of it before he returned to town and came up with some sort of alibi. So, he got home late that Friday night and texted Charlotte to come spend the night with Tara, and lo and behold, my dad showed up instead."

"Oh shit."

"'Oh, shit' is right. Once my mom realized where Dad had taken off to without telling anyone, she had me—who only had my learner's permit at fifteen—follow him to make sure he didn't do anything stupid before she could get the cops there." Closing my eyes, I could see the entire bloody scene laid out before me like it was yesterday. "I don't think I'll ever forget seeing my first—and hopefully, only—dead person, nor will I ever forget the look of satisfaction that had settled in my father's eyes as he stood victorious over that sorry fucking excuse for a human being."

She probed further, her expression empathetic. "What happened then?"

"Dad was sentenced to ten years in prison, but he got out after seven. It sucked for me that he wasn't there for the end of my high school years, but I understood why he did what he did, and if you asked him today whether or not he'd do it again, his answer will be yes a hundred out of a hundred times. It sucked the worst for Charlotte, obviously. Not only did she not have her dad for all of her teenage life, but she had to grow up real quick when she became a mom. The options of abortion and adoption were discussed at great lengths, but it all boiled down to neither of my parents could place blame on a small, innocent baby, and they always believed everything happened for a reason. Thus, Callie entered our lives, and she's the light of all our lives . . ." I chuckled softly as I glanced down at the phone. "Well, before today she was."

"So dealing with all of that is what made you want to work with abused kids?"

"Yep, like I told you before, it is who I am." I nodded, surprised to feel much lighter after confiding in her with my defining-moment story.

I wasn't sure why I'd initially been hesitant to tell her. I guess I'd been afraid she'd pass judgement on my family, but after thinking about it, I realized that was silly. She was just as connected and devoted to helping abused kids as I was. Which led me to wonder . . .

"Now, your turn," I prompted, turning on my most charming smile. "What is it that made you want to do this?"

Lightning bolts of panic struck in her eyes the instant I asked the question, and immediately I knew the answer to my question, without her ever having to open her mouth. I also knew I wasn't going to get an honest answer.

White-hot rage boiled in my bloodstream, but when it came to this, there was nothing I could do. I wouldn't force her to tell me . . . shit, I wasn't even sure if I can handle hearing her talk about it. So when she quickly recovered and gave me the bullshit line she recited in all of her interviews of how she knew it was her calling from the time she was a little girl, I nodded and accepted her answer.

But that night when I went to sleep, I dreamed in vivid detail that I murdered the man who had preyed upon Monroe as a child, and when I woke up the next morning, remorse for the satisfaction I'd felt in my dream was nowhere to be found. Because a hundred out of a hundred times, I'd break that Commandment too.

Because she was worth it.

chapter eighteen

"what do you
want me to say?
love is safe?
i will not spit out
those plastic words.
sometimes
love is taking
the train
because you
are terrified
of planes
but the train
derails
and blood is
spilled
anyways."
—Christopher Poindexter

MONROE

AS I PULLED up in front of Oliver's apartment building Sunday morning, I still wasn't sure taking him to one of Colin's games was a very good idea . . . for numerous reasons.

Sure, Colin and I had made up after he'd shown up at the children's home and apologized, and once we'd gotten back home, we'd stayed up late talking about the enlivening yet terrifying feelings that were all so new to me. With a much more understanding attitude—and an even gentler tone—than the first time we'd discussed it, my husband expressed his valid concerns about the risks I'd be taking individually, and the ones we would face as a couple, if I pursued something with Oliver. And even though I promised him I wasn't interested in heading down that road once I'd had a chance to think about it, Colin urged me to become friends with Oliver, to get to know him better, without allowing the kiss to cause any awkwardness between us, and to see if the attraction continued to grow.

But I already knew Oliver regretted what happened, and though I was pretty sure he felt a similar connection to me, he wasn't interested in carrying around the burden of guilt in being 'the other man' any more than I wanted him to think of me as a cheating wife. And it wasn't like we could tell him the truth about our marriage . . . as much as I secretly wished we could. Colin and I had made vows to each other, and even though they weren't the traditional pledges that man and wife usually made, they were binding all the same. We'd keep each other's secrets safe and be there for each other . . . to the very end.

That led to the next problem—my 'secret' that Oliver had asked about Friday afternoon. Everything was going great, excellent really, especially during the comedic showcase he put on with my juice-hunting in the refrigerator, and then his niece's phone call. I'd felt like we were fully comfortable around each other again, when he had to go and not only share with me his family's heart-wrenching story of devastation and perseverance, triggering an explosion of emotions inside my chest that left me feeling vulnerable and exposed, but then ask me about the one thing I can't fathom talking about.

What was even worse was when I managed to gather my wits about me and give him my standard, not-completely-untrue answer, *I* knew that *he* knew. His amber eyes bore straight through my earthly body to the depths of my soul, where the repugnant stains of shame still remained, no matter how many years' worth of good deeds I'd tried to hide them behind. And although Oliver may have pretended to be satisfied with my response then, I knew without question that the conversation between us wasn't over. Not by a long shot.

As I typed out a text to let him know I was waiting for him downstairs in my car, I hoped and prayed he wouldn't be eager to bring it up again so soon. Then, I decided if he did try, I'd just kiss him again to shut him up. That would kill two birds with one stone—redirecting his attention away from my past, and fulfilling the perpetual desire I had to feel his lips pressed against mine once again. *Great plan, Monroe. That won't set off any red flags in his mind at all.*

I rolled my eyes at my own senselessness, but before I had time to derive another masterminded plan or to contemplate the other reasons us going to this game together was a terrible idea, Oliver emerged from the rustic brick building looking like he'd literally just stepped off the cover of *GQ* magazine. In a gray cashmere sweater over a plaid button-down and paired with khaki chinos, he appeared every bit the chick-magnet his niece had claimed he was. *Put a damn saxophone in his hands, and my God, he could Michael Bolton me all night long.*

My stomach flip-flopped as I watched him draw near, and to stave off the craving to bury my fingers in his dark, silky waves that glistened in the mid-morning sunlight the minute he got in the car, I white-knuckled the steering wheel until I was sure I had initiated the early stages of carpal tunnel syndrome. I really needed to get a grip on my out-of-control hormones before I completely lost my mind. I'd always thought that between the combination of my small bullet vibrator and my own fingers, I'd be able to keep my sexual needs sated, because before that point, it had been. Once or twice a month while reading one of my romance novels seemed to do the trick just fine, but I'd done it just the night before—two times in a matter of a few hours! And already, at the mere sight of Oliver, a tingling sensation surfaced between my legs and spread rapidly over my entire body, heating me from the inside out. *Maybe I need a bigger* vibrator.

"Good morning, Rizzo," he greeted me with a warm smile as he lowered himself into my car. "You coulda warned me that it was freezing outside today. I probably should've brought my jacket. Maybe you have a Pink Ladies' one in the back I can borrow?"

Returning the cheerful grin, I pointed at the two coffees nestled securely in the drink holder that I'd stopped to get on my way over. "Or you could be a big boy and look up the weather all by yourself," I teased back. "There's this new, really cool thing called the internet that provides all kinds of information, like the weather forecast in every city, including when cold fronts are blowing in. You should check it out sometime."

"I'll keep that in mind, smartass," he chuckled as he reached for the steaming cup labeled 'Sandy D.' "And thanks for the coffee. I wasn't sure if that was only a Monday through Friday perk of our friendship, or if I'd have to beg you to stop some place on the way there."

Once he'd taken a sip and buckled his seatbelt, I shifted the transmission into drive and took off into the relatively light traffic in the direction of the highway before replying, "Friends don't let friends go without caffeine. Plus, being such the rabid football fan you are and all, I figured you'd need something to help keep you awake."

"Hey, now," he retorted, pretending to be offended. "I'll have you know I stayed up late when I got home last night to do a little bit of research so I didn't completely embarrass you around your friends today. I know I may not be the coolest cat around, but it's not from a lack of trying."

His passing mention of having gone out the night before stung a little bit, though I wasn't quite sure why. It wasn't as if I expected him to never leave his apartment unless he was with me. The guy was going to be in town for half a year; he needed to get out and explore, make new friends, and meet women who didn't have baggage like gay husbands and fucked-up childhoods.

"So you went out last night? Have a good time?" The words

tumbled out of my mouth before I could stop them, the curiosity eating away at me.

Cutting his eyes over at me with a strange look on his face, he nodded hesitantly. "Yeah, I got out and walked around the neighborhood yesterday. I was mainly looking for some new places to eat, but I happened to stumble across this little jazz bar about three blocks over from me that was really chill. I went inside for a drink and to check it out, and ended up talking to the manager for a while. If he likes my stuff, I think I'm gonna get a weekly gig there on Thursday nights. The guy he had booked for that slot recently moved, so he's been scrambling to find someone to fill in. Even though he knows it would be temporary, it gives him some time to find someone else for after I leave."

"That's awesome!" I exclaimed with full sincerity, more than a little relieved to hear he hadn't been out trolling the local bars. Not that I had the right to feel any way at all, even if he had. "We didn't get a chance to talk about it the other day after your niece mentioned it, but why hadn't you told me before that you play the sax? I asked Allison about it when I talked to her yesterday, and she didn't know either! Are you like some musical savant you don't want any of us knowing about?"

He barked out a deep belly laugh as he threw his head back against the leather seat. "No, no, nothing like that. I assure you. My family tends to over-exaggerate my musical talent," he shook his head, still amused from my question, "but I guess that's what families usually do, right? Think you're a lot better than you are at whatever it is you do?"

I pressed my lips together and nodded, pretending I knew what he was talking about. My mom definitely didn't go out of her way to make me feel like I was good at anything but ruining her life, and according to her, I was amazing at that. "Yeah, but that's still cool that you know how to play an instrument well enough to perform in a bar. My dad was apparently a stingy asshole who didn't pass down any of his musical abilities to me," I joked half-heartedly, pausing to take a drink of coffee. "I'd love to hear you play sometime. Maybe I can come watch your first Boston show?"

His cheeks turned pink as his eyes fell to his lap, where his thumbs twiddled nervously. "If you want to, I'd like that," he mumbled softly. "Though it'll probably seem a bit underwhelming after seeing the seventy thousand that come to watch Colin play today."

"Don't do that," I admonished him with a sharp gaze. "Don't belittle or devalue yourself, especially when comparing it to what Colin does. Most of the people there today care about one thing and one thing only—the Patriots winning the Super Bowl. They really don't care who it is who takes them there. They are fans of the team, not any specific player, despite what they'll tell you today. If Colin were traded to the Jets tomorrow, all of those people who supposedly love him so much would suddenly view him as the enemy and be throwing darts at his face in a pool hall. The only ones who truly care about him will be the people you meet up in the box . . . plus his family, of course."

He offered an apologetic smile. "Sorry, I didn't mean for it to sound quite as disparaging as it did. So who is it that I'll be meeting today? Some close friends of you guys'?"

For the remainder of the drive to Foxborough, I told Oliver the story of Colin growing up next door to Seth and Effie and how, even after all three of them went away to college, they all ended up back in Boston, tight as ever—leaving out the obvious part about the guys falling in love and living in the closet for eight years. My stomach turned over—and not in a good way—when he asked a couple of extra questions about Effie, but I convinced myself it was only because I'd told him I was planning to ask her to be my office manager/personal assistant. *Though I'm not sure what her marital status has to do with that . . .*

I was thankful when we finally pulled into the special parking lot for the families of the players and got out of the car, so I could start showing him around the stadium and stop talking about the Andrews kids altogether. I knew Colin still hadn't heard from Seth since the Tuesday night blow-up, but when I'd texted him on Saturday to see if he'd be at the game the following day, he said he would, but nothing else. So with that source of tension, Effie's usual random dramatics, and the addition of a new person to the mix, the day had all the makings of a real doozy.

I GLANCED UP at the scoreboard and silently begged the time to speed up. Nine minutes left in the fourth quarter could lead to thirty in real life, and I wasn't sure I could make it that long without my ears starting to bleed. Seth had brought a date with him—no doubt a statement to Colin—who had whined non-stop from the moment they'd arrived. It started with her not being able to see the field, so after we'd all shuffled around to accommodate her, she then decided it was too cold and windy in the front row, forcing us all to move back. Then, her drink didn't taste good, she was a vegetarian and couldn't eat any of the food, and the latest was heights made her dizzy—an issue she didn't have for the first two and a half hours of the game!

When she finally excused herself to the back concourse to answer a phone call—another etiquette no-no—I whipped my head toward Seth and glared menacingly.

"What?" he laughed out, acting like he wasn't equally as annoyed with Whiny Wendy.

"*What?!* Really?!" I whisper-shouted back at him, looking around to make sure no one could hear us. "What in the hell are you doing? Are we supposed to believe that you really like her? If you're gonna try and make him jealous, at least make it believable."

He shook his head with a wicked smirk and continued to play along with his charade. "I don't know what you're talking about, Roe baby. I do really like Jessie. She's such a sweet girl. Don't you think so?"

Huffing, I rolled my eyes. "Whatever. I don't understand either of you, which is exactly why you deserve each other."

"It's over, Monroe. Let it be," he warned under his breath as he scooted closer to me. "I've been tired of it for a while, and he just made my decision easier this week. I love him. You know that more than anyone, but I just can't do it anymore. I've tried and tried, for so many years. And every time I think I'll be able to change his mind, to convince him that our love is strong enough, but the truth is, it's not. I deserve better than being his dirty little secret." Pausing, he turned and peered down at me. "And you deserve better too."

The truth in his words knotted in the back of my throat, and I swallowed hard, trying to make it disappear. But it didn't, so he kept on talking.

"It's Oliver, isn't it?" he asked, glancing back over his shoulder to where Effie and Oliver had been looking at a Boston coffee table book for most of the second half.

As I had anticipated, Oliver wasn't interested in the game much at all. He'd paid attention for a while, but when he'd discovered that book at halftime, he'd sat down on one of the sofas in the lounge area to flip through it. Thirty seconds later, Effie had sidled up next to him, pressing her thigh against his and occasionally brushing her breast across his arm when she'd point at something on one of the pages. I'd attempted to join the conversation, but Effie declared that she was showing him all of the places he needed to make sure to visit while he was in town. Then she offered up her own services to take him around town, so I took my cue and left them alone.

"Is *what* Oliver?" I answered his question with my own, knowing damn well how guilty it sounded.

"He's the one you guys were fighting about the other night, right?" Seth playfully bumped his shoulder into mine and waggled his eyebrows. "It's okay, Roe girl. You don't have to lie to me. It's written all over your face."

My jaw dropped. "It is?" I hissed.

Laughing, he ruffled my hair and made the *tsk-tsk* sound like I'd asked something silly. "Well, maybe not to everyone, but I know you pretty damn well. We've been roommates on-and-off for the last three years, ya know?"

"Yeah," was the only thing I could come up with as my mind swam with an overload of incongruent thoughts.

"It doesn't make you a bad person to have feelings for someone else," Seth stated matter-of-factly. "You know that, right? It was bound to happen. I've been telling Colin for a while now, but his stubborn ass refused to listen."

The game at this point was a complete after-thought, especially since the Patriots had taken an early lead and not let off the gas pedal. I hoped Colin wouldn't look up and see me so close to Seth; otherwise, I knew he'd grill me when we got home, but at the same time, I wanted Seth to keep talking.

"I honestly didn't think it would ever happen," I murmured while keeping my face angled toward the field. "I thought that part of me was broken forever, but then Oliver just popped into my life, and in less than a week, I'm starting to question everything about the last twelve years . . . about who I thought I was. I don't understand it, and it scares me shitless, Seth."

"People change, Monroe. It's just a fact of life. There's no way you can be the same person at twenty-five as you were at thirteen, and there's no way you'll be the same person at thirty-seven that you are at twenty-five. There's no way I can ever even pretend to understand what you went through when you were a kid, so I won't try to. And I really do understand why you married Colin, and I know in your heart-of-hearts that you believed his companionship would be all you needed for the rest of your life when you agreed to his deal, but I'll say it again—You. Deserve. More.

"Look, I know it's scary. And I also know it's risky as hell. Believe me . . . I know better than anyone." He chuckled, but there was no humor in his voice. "You ask yourself, 'Why would I give up this perfect life that I've worked so hard for? Why risk it all for something that could or couldn't amount to something worthwhile and significant? Why take that chance?' And I'll tell you why. Because you're worth it, Monroe. You deserve to know what it's like to be loved fully, on the inside *and* the out. You deserve to have someone who worships your body just as much as they adore your pure heart and wicked-smart mind. Don't settle. Don't short-change yourself from the life and love you deserve to have, all because of some fucking sick asshole from your childhood. All you're doing is allowing him to keep you as his victim. Why give him that power?"

By the time he finished, my eyes were pooling with unshed tears and I wasn't sure if I wanted to hug him or slap him. Everything he'd said was exactly what I needed to hear, yet everything I never wanted to. Unfortunately, I wasn't able to do either as Rude Ruth rejoined us, naturally complaining about the cellular service in the stadium. In desperate need of a few minutes alone, I excused myself to the ladies' room, where I splashed water on my face and stared intriguingly into the unfamiliar eyes that gazed back.

Colin had called me meek and compliant. Seth claimed I was settling and content at playing the role of a victim. And though I didn't know much about what was happening with me, I knew I didn't want to be any of that.

And I also knew who made me feel the exact opposite of all those things when I was with him.

My Sandra Dee.

chapter nineteen

"I sleep
with the wolves
in my head
and wake up in
my own blood

we love the
things that
kill us"
–Christopher Poindexter

OLIVER

THE NEXT SEVERAL weeks passed in the blink of an eye. When Monroe and I weren't conducting interviews for the dozen or so positions we needed to fill, we were meeting with Dr. Prince, the executive director at the DCF, and filling out all of the necessary legal documents for us to begin the placement proceedings for JoJo, Heather, Aaron, and Alex in the state courts. In addition to our working effortlessly together, a true friendship formed between us with natural ease.

Once I convinced Iron Chef Dick that he wasn't going to get dipped, dunked, or even drizzled, I managed to keep my lustful thoughts to a minimum and was able to focus on Monroe the Woman, instead of Monroe the Sex Goddess. Though I did still look forward to casual Fridays and the way those damn jeans clung to her perfect curves. And how on the days we'd have a bowl of Peanut Butter Captain Crunch with chocolate milk for lunch, she'd slurp down the sweetened milk off her spoon, causing my eyes to hone in on the way her sweet, pouty lips wrapped around the bulbous shape—okay, who was I kidding? I was so fucking gone for her it wasn't even funny, and getting to know all of her little quirks, likes, and dislikes only made me want her more. My one-way ticket to the fiery pits was punched.

Effie had accepted the office manager job Monroe offered, and although she wasn't officially supposed to start until we moved into the house at the beginning of December, she claimed she wanted to get a jumpstart on learning her responsibilities and how the system worked, so she began showing up at the apartment two to three days a week, which led to an extremely cramped working environment. One where I couldn't openly flirt with Monroe—nothing too outrageous, of course, just a little roguish teasing here and there—and instead, had to spend my time fighting off advances from the tiny blonde firecracker who had apparently never been told 'no' before. Naturally, Monroe thought this was hilarious and loved to give me hell about it anytime Effie wasn't around. *If she only knew . . .*

Before I knew it, the entire month of October was almost behind us, and one of my favorite holidays was fast approaching—Halloween. As much as I loved my family and the big holiday dinners and celebrations they had at Easter, Thanksgiving, and Christmas, it was Halloween that I had really grown to enjoy as an adult. When I was a kid, sure it was fun to dress up and go out trick-or-treating, but my mom usually threw away over half of the candy, claiming she'd have to pay for all my teeth to be filled and capped if I ate all of it. So when I went away to college and experienced my first Boos and Booze party at my fraternity, I was like a kid in a candy store—a store where I could eat as many pieces as I wanted. The word 'Boobs' definitely should've been added to the name, because I saw and touched more tits that night than I'd seen in eighteen years of living with a mom and three sisters. Even the dorky little freshman I was, with my Dracula costume on, I became someone else for the night, and I was offered plenty of necks to suck on. It was safe to say I was a big fan, and for the next three years, I was the chair for planning that party.

Even after university, I'd rent out a private room at a bar or club and throw a huge Halloween bash for me and my friends, viewing it as my one big party-like-a-rock-star night of the year. But with me being in Boston and only knowing a handful of people in the city, I was a little bummed out I wasn't going to be able to celebrate like I normally did. So when Danny—the owner of Riff's, the jazz bar I'd started playing at—asked me if I could help him put something together last-minute for a Friday night event, I jumped at the opportunity.

In less than a week, the hero-and-villain themed party was planned and being blasted all over the place with flyers and radio ads. Whenever my work day with Monroe (and sometimes Effie) ended, I'd hit the streets to either help promote the event or to practice with a few of the other musicians who played at the bar, as we were working on a few special collaboration pieces that we planned to debut at the big bash.

I never mentioned the party to Monroe, because I didn't want her to feel obligated to come. I knew she was taking the kids trick-or-treating early in the evening, and even though the thing at the bar didn't start until nine, I also knew she wasn't much of a partier or a night-owl. When she'd come to watch me play my first show at the club, she powered through until the very end, but the next morning while sitting across the table from me, she yawned continuously and even nodded off a couple of times. I'd felt terrible that she was so tired because of me, but at the same time, I was so fucking thrilled that she'd come to see me and truly seemed to love it.

I didn't bring up the party to Effie for obvious reasons. The last thing I needed was for her to get the wrong idea, and to be honest, I was kind of looking forward to a night where I could just let loose and channel a little of my still-young-at-heart Oliver, without worrying about having to act a certain way or be on my best behavior. I didn't have specific plans to bring anyone home with me that night, but if it happened, it was safe to say I wouldn't have minded. It had been a *long* time since I'd been with anyone but my own hand, and it was apparent that my feelings for Monroe weren't ever going to go anywhere but where they were—safely in the friend-zone. Which is exactly where they needed to stay.

"Hey, man, you 'bout ready to get this shindig going?" Danny asked as he joined me in the back office of the bar, where I was securing the last piece to my Batman costume—the black mask with bat ears. "We've actually got a line down the street waiting to get in."

I took one last glimpse in the mirror then turned around to face him in his Captain America suit, my smile uncontainable. "Absolutely! You unlock the doors and I'll get the guys up on stage. Let's do this."

Chuckling, he shook his head. "I still can't believe you got this all organized. What am I gonna do next year when you're gone?"

"No need to worry about that now, Capt'n. Your only concern should be to rid this city of evil," I grinned slyly as I exited the office, "and make sure you bring all the real naughty ones here."

He roared with laughter as he moved to open the front doors, and as promised, I rounded up the other guys and we grabbed our instruments, taking our places on stage. With the very first note of music that rang out, the party took off full-steam ahead, and within minutes, the place was jam-packed with people drinking, dancing, and having a ball. As costumes were required for entry, I thoroughly enjoyed scanning the room and seeing what everyone had on—particularly the scantily clad women dressed up as Catwoman, Wonder Woman, Supergirl, and a few others I didn't recognize, but would've been eager to investigate more closely.

The opening set lasted for nearly an hour, and by the time I set my sax down on its stand and went to join the crowd, I was hot, clammy, and in dire need of a cold adult beverage. Batman may have been one cool-ass superhero, but his get-up was not made for performing on a stage under a bunch of spotlights.

Slinking my way through a room full of writhing, sweaty, half-dressed bodies, I finally reached the bar, where Spiderwoman—a.k.a. Sheila the bartender—had a Crown-and-seven waiting for me. I thanked her and flashed one of my best smiles before turning around to peruse the crowd once again. I wasn't quite sure if I wanted to take my chance with an earth-saving heroine, or explore my wicked side with an impish villain.

Luckily, I didn't have time to make the hard decision for myself because before I could even make it halfway through my first drink, a busty brunette Batgirl approached and grabbed hold of my wrist. Lifting up on her tiptoes to talk to me over the noise, she pressed her overflowing cleavage against my bicep and winked. "You were awesome up there! You really know how to use your mouth and fingers, don't you?"

I forced a laugh at the unoriginal pick-up line, because . . . well, because I was pretty sure the top of her nipples were peeking out over the black leather cups of her outfit, and I'm a guy who likes nipples, especially on attractive twenty-something-year-olds. Sue me. "I may know my way around the body," I smirked smugly and took a drink then leaned down and whispered, "of a finely-tuned instrument."

As I figured, she giggled at my corny one-liner and batted her fake eyelashes. "I bet you do, Batman. Or would you prefer I call you Bruce Wayne?"

"I prefer Batman as long as I'm in the suit," I replied as I playfully flexed my muscles.

Scratching her black-tipped nails across my chest, she purred into my ear, "So I'll get to meet Bruce later?"

"That's a possibility," I laughed after downing the last of my cocktail. "You want something to drink?"

"Absolutely."

I twisted slightly to my left to catch Sheila's attention behind the bar, and when I did, I lifted my empty glass up in the air with one hand and two fingers up with the other. She nodded, indicating she saw my request, so I swung my focus back to my little crime-fighting sidekick, but in the process, my eyes caught on the ethereal vision that was walking through the door at that exact moment.

Amidst all of the commotion and throngs of people, there was no missing the woman who was dressed as Poison Ivy as she made her way into the bar. She was drop-dead gorgeous. Better than the real Poison Ivy. And seemingly, alone.

Long, fiery red curls cascaded wildly over her shoulders and down her back that I wanted to tangle my fingers in. Flawless porcelain-white skin poured out the top and bottom of the miniscule green dress she wore, the fabric decorated with leaves and sequins. Vines of ivy were wrapped around each of her toned arms and legs, as well as around the crown of her head, making her look like the angel of the forest, rather than the make-believe criminal she was supposed to be.

The glittery green mask she wore concealed a good portion of her face, leaving only her eyes to shine through the oval-shaped cut-outs and below her nose visible, but there was no hiding the fact she was stunning. I had no doubt that every gaze in the room was locked on her—those who wanted her, and those who wanted to be her—but I didn't dare tear my own eyes away to confirm.

Four steps. That's how many steps she took before she stopped and turned then began skimming over faces like she was looking for someone. *Of course, she's meeting someone here.* Whatever small amount of hope that had built up inside me that I might have a chance to talk to her dissipated . . . until I saw her nervously rub her lips together in the exact way someone else I knew did.

Monroe.

I gasped and clutched my chest as my lungs collapsed beneath my ribs, all of the air sucked straight from them at my sudden realization. *She came. How did she know? Does she want me to recognize her? She left her house in that outfit?*

"Is everything okay?" Batgirl's squeaky voice rang loud in my ears, snapping my attention back to her.

"Huh?"

She looked up at me with a worried expression then cut her

eyes down to where my hand was grabbing at my pec. "Your chest. Are you okay?"

Dropping my hand abruptly, my mind swirled with a million different thoughts—none of them having anything to do with the girl standing next to me. I freaked. I didn't know what to do, what to say. I needed to get rid of her. I needed a minute to collect myself, to figure out what in the hell I was going to do. So I said the first thing that came to my head. "Uh yeah, but I, uh, just remembered I forgot to call my wife tonight. I'm supposed to call her at a certain time each night, or she'll, uh, get really mad if I don't." I slowly inched away from her as I rambled on, thankful she wasn't holding a drink to throw at me. "So yeah, it was nice talking to you, Batgirl. Hope you find a good Bruce Wayne to take home tonight."

Then I spun around and made a beeline to the office, not sticking around to hear her response. I sucked at acting under pressure, and that was definitely one of my worst improvisations.

Thankfully, the office was empty when I exploded into it like a bat out of hell—quite literally. I rushed to the small bathroom off of the main space and pulled up just short of the mirror, stilling when I saw the frenzied passion whirling in my eyes behind the mask. My heart pounded and my pulse spiked as exhilaration buzzed through me.

"What is she doing here? Why would she not tell me she was coming? Why did she wear that? What the fuck is going on?" I asked Batman, as if my costumed-reflection knew the answers.

Sighing, I ripped the damn thing off my head and scrubbed my hands over my face. After sticking my head under the sink, dousing my hair and face with cold water, I dried off the best I could with the paper towels then pulled my wet hair up in a bun. Another deep stare into my own eyes in the mirror, and I answered my earlier questions.

"She's here because of you. She either wanted to surprise you, or she doesn't want you to know it's her. She's wearing it so you can see her wearing it. And I have no damn clue."

Now, the question was, what was I going to do about it? *Should*

I just see how it plays out? Confront her? Pretend I don't know? Do I have the willpower to stop something if things go too far? The only answer I knew for sure was the last one, and it was a resounding HELL NO.

I wanted that woman from the first moment I laid eyes on her, and that desire had only continued to grow as I'd gotten to know her. She laughed at my obnoxious jokes. She loved the kids at the home like they were her own flesh and blood. She ate bad things with me. She liked to make me listen to terrible pop radio. She was the most gorgeous person I'd ever seen. She liked to tease me, and liked it even more when I teased her back. She was my Rizzo, my Peaches. And she was there in that bar, dressed like Eve from the Garden of Eden . . . for me.

No better than Adam himself, I put my mask back on, turned around, and strode out into that bar, knowing full-well if she tempted me with her fruit, I had no plans to say no.

chapter
twenty

"have you ever experienced something
so astonishingly beautiful,
you wanted nothing more
than for that moment to be burned
and in your mind be born
fresh once more?

the greatest second you will
ever have on this earth is
the exact moment you fell
in love."

–Christopher Poindexter

MONROE

"YOU. DESERVE. MORE. You're worth it, Monroe," I muttered Seth's words under my breath so that only I could hear them as I swung open the heavy wooden door leading to Riff's Jazz Bar, a place I had no place being . . . which was exactly why I was there.

Because I *did* deserve more.

And I *was* worth it.

Now, it was time to find out if Oliver thought I was. Because he was to me.

Right or wrong, no matter the consequence, I checked the fears that lingered deep in the shadows of my past along with my knee-length, fur-lined coat at the door and stepped into that hazy, overcrowded room with one goal in mind: to seduce Oliver Saxon.

Over the previous six weeks, my friendship with Oliver only continued to grow. Spending eight to ten hours a day together, we soon learned everything there was to know about each other—well, *almost* everything—and the more I knew, the more I liked. He was one of the goofiest people I'd ever met, always breaking out into song and dance at the strangest times or blurting out random, useless facts to get my attention when the two of us would get lost in our work for a while and not talk. But he was also one of the most genuine, good-hearted people I'd ever crossed paths with, and being in the field of Social Work and charitable organizations, I'd met some pretty incredible, selfless individuals.

I'd tried my hardest to flirt with him any chance I got, but apparently, I sucked at it, because he never again tried to touch or kiss me after that first time in the parking lot. Sure, he'd joke back, never passing on an opportunity to embarrass me, and occasionally, I'd catch him stealing a glance at my breasts or my mouth, which would trigger that buzzing sensation between my legs and the fluttering in my lower belly I was really starting to love.

Days that Effie would show up and pretend to work were not my favorite. With the subtlety of a herd of elephants playing the drums with their trunks, she threw herself at Oliver relentlessly, doing everything but 'accidentally' tripping and falling on his lap. Legs spread. Without panties. At first I almost felt bad for her when he'd politely but firmly reject her advances, but I soon recognized it was only a game to her. She wanted him because she couldn't have him, and Effie Andrews had rarely in her life not gotten something she wanted. It actually made her a great assistant. If I sent her on a mission, she got it done, because she wouldn't accept no for an answer. "Everyone has a weakness," she told me once after I asked her how she managed to get me on the state Senator's calendar. "You just have to pinpoint it early, and play the hell out of it until they can't refuse you."

Evidently, she hadn't pinpointed Oliver's weakness quite yet.

I was praying it was Poison Ivy.

It didn't take long for my eyes to adjust to the dim lighting, but as I shuffled inside the cramped space, I soon realized my first hurdle. There were multiple men dressed up as Batman. I don't know why I hadn't bothered to think of that possibility, wrongly assuming after I'd seen the flyer for the party, along with the receipt for his costume rental on his bar, that he'd be easy to spot when I arrived. Clearly, my focus on the end prize of feeling his mouth on mine again—a memory that was forever tattooed on my mind—had clouded my ability to think out my plan thoroughly. *What am I going to do now? Seek out every man dressed up like an oversized flying rat with a gold-and-black oval emblem on his chest?*

I thought about going home. A big part of me wanted to hightail it out of there, with my dignity and pride still intact. No one but me and the woman I'd rented the costume from would be none-the-wiser. And the next week at work, I'd just pretend I had no idea about the party he hadn't invited me to.

But I didn't.

I stayed.

I stayed for hope that there was more. I stayed, because I finally believed I was worth it. And I stayed, because I wasn't going to allow that monster from my childhood to control another minute of my life.

I stayed for me.

Feeling comfortable that my own disguise adequately hid my true identity, I rolled my shoulders back and lifted my chin in the air as I strode forward, zigzagging my way through the dressed-up bodies and toward the bar. I'd purposely brought cash for my drinks so I wouldn't have a credit card with a name on it, and after I pushed my way up to the hand-carved wooden flat-top and ordered a glass of Moscato, I dipped my fingers into the bra cup of the green, foliage-covered corset dress to retrieve the bills I'd so carefully tucked in next to my boob.

"You won't be needing any of that," a familiar masculine voice rasped into my ear from behind me, his warm breath on my neck igniting a spark some place much lower.

Startled, my chin popped up and I stared straight ahead at the mirror that lined the back of the bar, fixing my gaze onto vibrant eyes shining through the cutout of the superhero's legendary black mask. Eyes that belonged to the man I was there to see.

I wished it would've taken him a little longer to discover it was me, even though I knew I wouldn't be able to fool him for too long. But instead of worrying about what was done, I chose to appreciate the time I saved in the hunt for my bat in carbon armor.

"Excuse me? And why should I listen to *you* telling me what I will or won't be needing? " I smarted, exposing a tone of sass I didn't know I had as I addressed his reflection. "Last time I checked, the two of us, Batboy, were sworn enemies."

A deep, thunderous chuckle rumbled in his chest as he drew closer, his front pressing flush against my back. "I'm all man, sweetheart, and don't you know what they say about keeping your friends close and your enemies closer?" he taunted, playing along like I hoped he would.

"Yeah? And?" I sneered, doing my best to keep up the feisty façade.

His two arms shot out on either side of me, grabbing hold of the bar and thus caging me in, and I gasped in response. With our eyes still locked and loaded in the mirror, he lowered his head so that his lips skimmed across the shell of my ear. "And you, my little Poison Ivy," he murmured lowly, "I think I need to keep *you* the closest. I'd hate to think what kind of trouble you'd cause if I let you out of my sight. Tell me, how did one of my enemies find out where I'd be tonight? Did she do some investigating of her own?"

"She has her ways, when the desire is there, it's amazing how easy it is to discover the information one needs. Batman should learn to be more careful of the evidence he leaves lying around his Batcave. He never knows who could be lurking around."

Heated desire bloomed inside of me and I struggled to keep my smug poise. Although I knew from the beginning that Oliver was physically attracted to me and had felt our initial spark, I'd been worried he was going to completely shut me down, holding firm on his insistence that he didn't want to involve himself with a married woman. Not that I would've blamed him . . . but damn it felt good knowing he was tired of ignoring whatever it was that was going on between us as well. I couldn't hide from it any longer. The farther I tried to run, the closer I found myself to him. And I was ready to know once and for all.

"Maybe it's the trouble I'll cause while right under your nose you should be most worried about." I smirked mischievously, proud of myself for conjuring up a witty remark in spite of the raging inferno that was now transforming my blood into liquid lust pulsing through my veins.

Spiderwoman the Bartender returned with my wine before he could reply, and I was grateful for the momentary break in the banter, as well as the cold, wet liquid to refresh my dry mouth. As I extended the twenty-dollar bill that was still in my hand out toward her, Oliver snatched it out of my grasp and shook his head. "All of Miss Ivy's drinks go on my tab, Sheila," he announced firmly before his tone turned playful. "Don't let her try to sweet talk you otherwise either. Remember, that's how she works—luring you into her trap with her breathtaking beauty and angelic voice—so you'll think she's sweet and innocent. But believe you me, she's nothing of the kind."

"Your wish is my command, Batman," Sheila laughed and rolled her eyes at Oliver then moved down the bar to help the next person waiting for a fresh drink.

I extended my arm out to take my twenty back from him, but came up empty as he moved it out of my reach with a *"tsk tsk tsk"* and a shake of his head. "Hey! Give me my money back!" I exclaimed, nabbing at it again. And again, coming up empty-handed. "I thought you were supposed to be one of the good guys, not some bully and bossy Batman who lies and steals from defenseless women."

Grabbing my shoulders, he gently but swiftly spun me around so that we were finally eye-to-eye, no longer allowing me to use the mirror as a buffer to the intensity that was radiating off of him. "Funny thing is, I always thought I was one of the good guys too." His full lips quirked up into a lopsided grin, drawing my attention down to his mouth, chin, and jaw, where I first noticed he'd shaved off all of his facial hair. More than anything, I wanted to raise my hand to feel the smoothness of his olive skin, but he continued talking, so I kept still and listened, hanging on his every word.

"And then you walk through the door and knock my world off its axis, making me question every damn thing I thought I knew about myself." He leaned down and rested his forehead to mine, mask-on-mask. "You make me want things I shouldn't want." He lifted the folded bill to my shoulder, softly dragging it across my collarbone and down my sternum until it dipped into the exposed cleavage. "You make me do things I shouldn't do." His voice was barely over a whisper, and even with the countless number of people surrounding us and the loud music, I heard every word. Sliding the money up over the swell of my left breast, he didn't blink a single time as his saxophone-calloused fingers dipped under the satiny fabric and tucked the twenty away with the others. "You make me ask things I shouldn't ask."

My pulse spiked under his tantalizing touch as the playful undertone to our exchange suddenly shifted to something much more sensual and serious. "What are you asking?" I pressed him.

His Adam's apple bobbed hard in his throat and I knew he was just as nervous as I was. But ultimately, the need and want outweighed the fears and doubts.

"Come home with me tonight?" he implored with a gaze filled with desperate desire that touched me deep in my core.

My heart stopped beating. There it was. The invitation I'd come for. Right there in front of me, mine for the taking. All I had to do was say yes.

One word that would change everything.

One word I couldn't take back.

One word I wanted to say again and again.

"Yes." The word fell from my lips on a ragged breath, and as a fiery blaze flickered inside Oliver's molten amber eyes, I clenched my thighs together and whimpered. I had no idea what was happening to me, but I couldn't control my body's carnal responses to him.

I didn't hear the noise with my ears, but I felt the vibrations of a deep growl in his chest, which was pressed against mine. "I need to go grab my things from the back and tell Danny I'm leaving. You stay right here and enjoy your glass of wine. I'll be back in a few minutes."

"Wait," I stopped him, grabbing his arm. "Aren't you supposed to be playing the sax tonight? If you need to stay, I don't mind waiting around or doing whatever your other groupies usually do until you're finished."

The fleeting look of fear that I'd changed my mind was promptly replaced with a smile that lit up his entire face, something I could tell even with his mask on. "Miss Ivy, I appreciate your concern for my responsibilities here at the club and for wanting to follow the expected protocol that my thousands of other groupies adhere to, but I think I can make an exception just this once." Surprising me, he bent down and feathered his soft lips over mine then winked. "But only for you."

Then, he was gone, snaking his way through the people toward a back hallway, and I was left standing there with the stupidest grin on my face and my fingertips touching my mouth, which was still tingling from his kiss. It was as if I was living in a dream-world, and not just because everyone around me was dressed up as legendary superheroes and infamous villains. Though it definitely added to the fairy-tale-type aura that hummed around me.

I couldn't believe it was really happening. And even less, I couldn't believe how confident I felt in my decision to allow it to happen. I knew Colin and I would be having a long conversation about guidelines and stipulations for mine and Oliver's relationship in the coming days. After my husband and I made up from our first fight, he promised he'd consent to my exploring something with Oliver if I still felt that way after a while of getting to know him better, and if I agreed to specific rules to protect all of us. At the time,

I told him that I appreciated his attempt to be open-minded on the matter, but that it didn't matter, because Oliver had made it clear he didn't want anything to happen between us.

However, the more time I spent with him, the more the desire grew and the deeper our connection entwined, but it was evident Oliver wasn't going to make the first move. So it was up to me, although I hadn't the first clue on how to go about letting someone know I was interested in having an affair with them. I mean, it wasn't like I could bust out at work one day, "Can you please pass me those reports? Oh, and hey, after that, would you like to make out?" *Uh . . . no.*

When I discovered the orange-and-black leaflet on the same day Colin had told me he'd be chaperoning a youth football overnight lock-in on Halloween night, I took it as a sign that it was time to act. And act I had, which was precisely what led me to that exact moment, where I stood in the middle of a bustling jazz bar, dressed in a miniscule dress with vines wrapped around my limbs and a glittery mask covering my face, waiting for a man who was not my husband to take me to his bed and show me how much *more* there was.

chapter

twenty-one

"I will love you,
not starting with
your skin or
your organs or
your bones:
I will love madly first,
your naked soul."
–Christopher Poindexter

OLIVER

NEITHER OF US said a single word during the short ten minute walk in the chilly October night from the club to my apartment building, though she clung to my hand through our interlaced fingers like she was afraid I'd change my mind before we got there. But that wasn't even close to the path my thoughts were headed down. No, I was all-fucking-in the second I realized she'd come to Riff's . . . for *me*. It said everything I needed to know about the way she felt, and integrity and morals be damned. I figured we'd deal with the other shit later. And by *shit*, I was well aware it was going to be a whole fuck-load of crazy-ass shit, but I could no longer deny myself the one thing I wanted more than anything else in my life. *Her*.

The overwhelming hunger inside me intensified with every step I took, suppressing my nerves and inhibitions, and by the time

I found my keys with trembling fingers and swung the door open, I was a man possessed. I couldn't wait another second to touch her, to feel her, and to please her until she screamed my name.

Two steps into the foyer, I had her coat off and her back against the textured sheetrock as my mouth crashed down on hers in a passionate, almost frantic kiss. I traced her lips with my tongue, and she responded immediately by parting them and granting me full access to explore her sweet, sweet mouth. I soon realized the memory of our first kiss that I'd jacked off to on countless occasions didn't hold a flame to the raw beauty of experiencing it firsthand. Like everything else Monroe Cassidy did, she was undeniably exceptional at kissing, making it seem like the way our tongues effortlessly stroked and caressed each other was a product of years and years of practice.

Our agitated fingers clawed at the fabric of our costumes as we stayed locked at the lips, neither of us wanting to break contact quite yet, despite the difficulty it made in stripping off our clothes. She found the zipper at the base of my neck and dragged it down my spine with lightning fast speed, helping me peel my chest and arms out of the bulky, neoprene-like bodysuit as I nipped gently along her swollen bottom lip. My hands skimmed up her ribcage and over the swell of her breasts, only tangling in the foliage sewn into and around her costume once—which I considered a feat in and of itself until I reached her smooth, milky white skin that was dusted in glitter. The combination of my feral rumbles and her tiny little moans and whimpers echoed off the tile floor in the small entryway, arousing my already over-stimulated senses even more than they were. My cock was harder than I'd ever thought possible, and I was quickly losing control.

"Damn, baby," I swore as I ripped my mouth from hers and took a step back, gasping for breath. It was too much at once. My body was a livewire ready to detonate. "Unless you want me to make a mess of this costume I rented and be forced to pay some outrageous dry cleaning bill, then I gotta take a minute to cool down. Plus, I want you in my bed, where I can take care of you the way you deserve, not like a heathen against a wall." Leaning in, I pressed my lips to the corner of her mouth and murmured, "Follow me to the Bat Cave, where all the Bat Magic happens."

"God, you're a goofball sometimes," she chuckled as she kissed me back and grabbed my hand, allowing me to lead the way.

My chest swelled with pure fucking happiness as I guided her through the apartment that she knew as well as I did to my bedroom, knowing that whatever happened afterward, whatever penance I had to pay for my wrongdoing, it would be worth every damn minute and more. Because I had not just fallen in love with Monroe's selfless heart, intelligent mind, and gorgeous face and body, I worshipped her soul—the very essence of her being. She was it for me. No one before and no one after would ever compare. And all I could do was treasure the time I was blessed with her, and whatever would happen in the future would happen. Good or bad, I'd deal with the consequences when I had to, but for that moment in time, I just said, "Fuck it," and took her as mine, because in my heart of hearts, I truly believed she was.

As soon as we were inside the spacious master bedroom, lit only by the street lamp outside the blinds, she began tugging at my jumpsuit again, trying to work it down over my hips, eager to pick up where we'd left off. Grabbing her hands, I moved them down to her sides and shook my head. With my hand under her chin, I lifted her gaze away from my half-dressed body and up to meet mine—though, I must admit I appreciated the way she was staring at my abs and licking her lips. But right then, there was something I needed to do before we went any further.

"You make the fucking sexiest Poison Ivy I've ever seen," I told her while my thumb stroked back and forth across her jawline. "I love the cute, little, pretending-to-be-appalled face you make when I call you Peaches," I continued as I bent down and softly kissed her lips. "And you'll always be my Rizzo," I confessed, lifting my fingers to the base of her mask. When she didn't say or do anything to stop me, I slid the mask over her face, tugging the wig off in the process and tossing them both on the floor. Then, removing my own headpiece, I chucked it on top of the pile, her eager emerald gaze never leaving mine. "But when we do this, I want it to be us. Monroe and Oliver. Not pretending to be anybody else except who we are. Naked to the core."

Cupping the sides of her face, I lowered my forehead to hers and gave her one last chance to back out. "You tell me now, Monroe, 'cause once I'm in, I'm in until you say I'm out. This isn't a game to me. I know we can't tell the future and we've got some major obstacles ahead of us, but I can't do this, and then the next time I see you, pretend it didn't happen. I understand there are discretions that will need to be made, and for you, I'm willing to make them, but once *you* and *I* become a *we*, whenever it's just the two of us together, we're most definitely gonna act like a *we*." My hands slid up the back of her neck into her hairline, sifting through her blonde tresses that had been tucked up under the wig, then anchoring the back of her head so that we were nose-to-nose. "You good with that?"

"Yeah," she agreed on an exhale, nodding her head so that her hair pulled taut in my grasp. "I'm good with that. But you're gonna have to be patient with me. I've never done anything like this before. I may suck at being a *we*."

Quickly deciding it wasn't the best time to bring up the fact she was indeed married, I pushed the thought out of my mind and smiled warmly down at her. "That's the great thing about us, Monroe. As long as you give me you and I give you me, the *we* just comes naturally."

Her eyes flashed with what looked like hope and exhilaration. "I'm all yours, Oliver," she whispered, lifting up on her tiptoes to press her lips to mine. "Just promise you'll be careful with me."

Her words pierced through my chest, triggering something inside me that I wasn't quite familiar with. Even though I didn't know the horrid details of what happened in her childhood, I knew enough to know that I wanted to take care of her and pleasure her in every way possible, replacing every bad memory she had with at least ten good ones. More than I wanted to take my next breath, I wanted to show her how she deserved to be worshipped like the goddess she was.

And she was giving me that chance.

"I promise you," I said then sealed my words with a kiss.

Then, with the most tender of touches and a string of reassuring words murmured against the delicate flesh of her neck and throat, I slowly removed her dress and unwound the vines from her arms and legs, my mouth sweeping over where the foliage had left her skin pink and irritated. Left only in a black strapless bra, a matching thong, and clover green heels that matched the exact shade of her wanton gaze, I scooped her up in my arms and carried her to the king-sized bed, laying her on her back in the middle of the mattress with her head propped up with several pillows. Hastily grabbing one of the few random condoms I'd thrown inside the drawer of the nightstand when I'd first moved in, I flung it onto the foot of the bed so it'd be easily accessible when I needed it later.

Sensing my need to control the situation so I didn't end up in the same wild frenzy I'd slipped into when we'd first arrived at the apartment, Monroe allowed me to move at a deliberate pace, never once getting impatient or questioning my tactics. I shed the rest of my costume then joined her on the bed in just my boxer briefs that were doing a poor job of containing my throbbing shaft.

"Holy shit!" she exclaimed, her eyes wide as saucers as she stared straight at my package. "That's, uh . . . wow. Really?"

With a low chuckle, I bent down and rewarded with her a sweet kiss for the direct boost to the ego. I'd never been sure how my dick compared to the average guy, but I liked to believe I was blessed in the hardware department. I'd definitely never had any complaints, though I'd never had quite the reaction Monroe had either. Again, even though Colin was the last thing I wanted to think about while I was about to make love to his wife, the obvious question of 'How large—or small, rather—was he?' ran through my mind. Not that I cared about what another guy's cock looked like . . . it was just that it made me feel good knowing I had *something* bigger than Mr. All-American himself. He may have had a bigger house, car, bank account, and 401K, but Iron Chef Dick reigned supreme in the

Bedroom Stadium.

"I'll make sure you're ready, beautiful girl. You just need to lie back and let me take care of you. I promised you I'd be careful, and I meant it," I reassured her while I ran the tip of my nose up and down her neck, inhaling the heady combination of citrus, vanilla, and a scent that was uniquely Monroe's.

"Okay, Ollie, I trust you," she agreed softly as she tugged on the elastic band in my hair, freeing the unruly locks for her fingers to tangle in. Then with the shyness that I expected from Monroe, she peered up at me with her big green eyes and slowly pushed down my boxers, springing my dick free of its confines. "Please make love to me. I want to be yours."

God, she had no idea how much I wanted that too. In every possible way.

I shifted my body so I was hovering over her without crushing her with my weight, and then began a synchronized exploration of her form using a combination of my mouth and hands, starting at her shoulders and gradually working my way lower. With open-mouthed kisses, sensual swipes of my tongue, and fingertip caresses meant to simultaneously soothe and stimulate, I reached the swell of her breast overflowing atop the sexy but unnecessary bra. My dexterous fingers made quick work of the three-pronged clasp at her spine, and as the delicate fabric fell away from her body, my lips set out to conquer one exposed dusty peak, while an eager hand claimed the other.

Monroe released a guttural moan and arched her back up off the mattress when I drew her hardened nipple in between my teeth, laving the sensitive bud with my tongue. Her fingers that had been leisurely sifting through my hair, curled and pulled as she held my head close to her chest. "Yes, that . . . that feels so good," she panted as I took turns sucking on and playing with her perfect tits.

Once I was sure I had memorized the taste and the feel of her chest, I resumed my trek downward, kissing my way down the center of her lean torso until I hit lacy material once again. With the tip of my tongue, I followed along the waistband of her thong, over to one hip, then across to the other before my mouth ended up back dead center, mere inches away from her sweet center that I yearned to touch and taste.

Hooking both thumbs inside the thin swatch of fabric, I stopped before I went any further and peered up at her to ensure she wanted me to keep going. Her glossed-over eyes met mine and the right corner of her mouth quirked up. "Don't stop now, silly. You were just getting to the good part," she teased.

I chuckled and shook my head, swooshing her panties down over her hips, knees, and feet, and then flung them onto the messy floor with our other clothes. "Oh, baby doll," I ran my tongue across my bottom lip as I settled myself between her legs, "you have no idea just how *good* it's gonna get."

Surprising me, she abruptly sat up and grabbed my head, pulling me to her as she stole my breath away with a demanding, feverish kiss. "Show me," she begged against my mouth, lightly sucking on my bottom lip. "Show me everything. I want to know what *more* is, Oliver. I want your more."

I was too far entrenched in the moment to understand what she was really saying, but all I knew was I wanted to give it to her. All of it. The good. The more. Whatever she wanted or needed. I'd make it happen.

"Lay down, beautiful, and I'll give you everything I've got and more." I gently coaxed her back to where she'd been, comfortably supported by the pillows so she could relax but still watch everything I was doing to her.

My eyes roamed over every inch of her stunning body splayed out before me on the bed before I gently gripped the inside of her knees and pushed them apart. Watching her legs spread open bit-by-bit directly in front of me may have been the most erotic thing I'd ever witnessed, and as I lowered myself onto my stomach and got my first glimpse at her pink glistening folds, I couldn't help but thrust my hips a few times against the mattress, my aching shaft desperate for friction.

With a feather-soft touch, I edged my fingers up the inseam

of her thigh until they were met with her slick arousal. Gliding my fingertips through the sweet stickiness, I parted her swollen lower lips and dipped my face down to her sizzling core, swiping my tongue from her tight slit up to the treasured bundle of nerves that I couldn't wait to torment.

"Oh my gawd," she slurred, bucking her hips up when I pulled my mouth away. "Do that again. That's much better than good."

I smiled victoriously to myself as I got ready to repeat the action, but with the second pass of my tongue over her clit, I latched my lips around the pebbled nub and sucked gently. Again, her hips lifted up off the bed, though this time, I allowed her to grind her smooth mound against my face, reveling in the intoxicating smell of her desire, the honeyed taste of her juices, and the sounds of her wanton whimpers.

As my mouth still methodically worked her button, my nimble fingers worked their Bat Magic over, around, and inside of her wet heat, prepping her. Within just a few minutes of my teasing and taunting, Monroe fisted the sheets in her closed hands and allowed her knees to fall completely open to the sides, fully surrendering to the euphoric sensations that threatened to claim her release. Her chest heaved as she inhaled and exhaled rapid, shallow breaths, and when I latched onto her clit one final time as I slipped two fingers knuckle-deep inside of her, she unraveled beneath me in a magnificent fashion.

"Oh my God, Oliver!" she shouted as her thin frame shamelessly writhed and wriggled in ecstasy. "Please don't stop! God, please don't ever stop!"

Watching her come undone nearly sent me over the edge along with her, and suddenly, I couldn't wait any longer. I had to know what it would feel like to be buried inside her, and I had to know right fucking then.

Hastily, I pushed myself up to an upright kneeling position, still situated between her legs, and reached for the small foil packet on the bed. The sound of the package ripping garnered her post-climactic attention, and as her heavy-lidded eyes focused in on me rolling the latex over my shaft, she twisted her lips with curiosity. "I'm still not sure it's gonna fit," she half-laughed as she slowly reached her hand out to wrap her fingers around me.

"Do you want to guide it in? That way you can control how fast we go," I offered with my focus fixed on her dainty fingers as they began moving up and down my steeled length. Though she hadn't confirmed it, I felt confident that she had some sort of abuse in her past, and I was careful not to push or intimidate her in any way.

She pressed her lips together and nodded then wasted no time tugging me toward her, rubbing my head all through her folds and over her clit, coating it with her essence. It took every ounce of will-power I had not to explode right then and there, but somehow I managed to restrain myself. After about a minute, her wrist stilled as she lined the tip of my cock up at her slick entrance. Then, ev-er-so-slowly, she worked my shaft inside the incredibly tight walls of her contracting pussy, connecting us in the most intimate way possible.

It took a while to allow her body to adjust to my thickness be-fore she was comfortable enough for me to start stroking in and out of her, but I didn't mind one bit as I covered her face and neck with encouraging and affectionate kisses. Too absorbed in the emotional bond we were imprinting onto each other's soul, I didn't consider how it should've seemed a bit odd for a woman who'd been mar-ried for over three years to still experience discomfort during sex, no matter what size her husband's junk was. But after I worshipped her body until the point I could no longer hold off my own release, I exploded with an intensity like I'd never before experienced, com-pletely surrounded in her cozy warmth. Her. Me. *Us*.

It wasn't until she peered up at me through her thick lashes, smiling a sleepy, sated smile as she whispered, "I'm glad it was you, Ollie. Thank you for giving me more," that the realization of what had just happened set in.

And it changed everything.

chapter

twenty-two

"Undress my soul
and may I lay
naked before your
eyes.
Discolor the sorrow
and melt the pain
like snow,
for in this world
it has only ever
been a disguise.

Take me as I am naked."
−Christopher Poindexter

MONROE

OLIVER COLLAPSED ONTO the bed next to me, both of us still struggling to catch our breath. The realization of the underlying meaning of my words registered on his face seconds after they fell from my tongue, and though I had no intention beforehand of telling him that he was my first, the moment just felt right. I wanted him to know the depth of my feelings for him, as new and unfamiliar to me as they still were. I needed him to understand the magnitude and the significance of what we had shared. Something I'd never shared with another human being.

Once our chests had calmed from the erratic series of in-hales and exhales, Oliver excused himself to the bathroom, where I assumed he was discarding the condom and washing his hands. Returning in less than a minute, he surprised me when he climbed on the bed with a warm, wet washcloth and began to gently clean between my legs.

"Ahh," I winced at the tenderness of the entire area, even though it was apparent he was trying to be as soft and soothing as possible.

He stilled instantly as his concerned gaze shot up to find mine. "You okay?"

"Yeah, go ahead." I nodded, slightly embarrassed. "Sorry, just a bit sensitive and I have a pretty low threshold for pain."

"Don't apologize. I'm gonna get you some ibuprofen and water too. You're probably going to be sore tomorrow," he said, resuming the soft pats against my overly sensitive skin.

Offering a faint smile, I reached out and lightly dragged my fin-gers across his firm stomach as I murmured, "Thank you for taking care of me."

He finished cleaning me then leaned down and kissed the tip of my nose. "Someone should've been taking care of you long ago, beautiful girl. Now, stay right here and I'll be back in a few minutes to do more of just that."

I did exactly as I was told, not moving an inch from the happy place I found myself in, grinning foolishly at the ceiling as I wait-ed for him. Everything seemed so surreal. Nothing like I'd dreamed it'd be . . . somehow, it was so incredibly better. I was worried the disturbing memories that often haunted my dreams might make an unwelcome appearance the first time he touched me in places only my hands had ventured the previous twelve years, but the only im-ages that appeared behind my clenched shut eyelids were colorful starbursts of awe—inspiring pleasure, more spectacular than the night sky on the Fourth of July. Then, the way he gave me the pow-er to control the actual penetration . . . it was like he knew exact-ly what I needed to feel completely comfortable without me ever saying a word.

I also had expected to experience an onslaught of conflicting emotions in the immediate aftermath, assuming that at least part of me would feel shame or degradation, due more to my reservations about sex than because of Colin. But shockingly, the negative never came. Instead, I relaxed into a tranquil sea of pale blue sheets, basking in the waves of security, serenity, and sexual satisfaction that I knew without a shadow of a doubt only Oliver could give me.

He was my more. He was what I deserved. Now, my only fear was what if what I had to offer him wouldn't be enough.

Before I had any time to dwell on the challenges in front of us, Oliver reappeared in the doorway with a warm smile carrying two glasses of water and a bottle of Advil. And he was still naked. Good God, the man had some abs to kill for. And a nice, tight ass too. Oh, and the cock of a porn star. Okay, okay . . . maybe it wasn't that big, but it'd sure felt like it twenty minutes ago.

"Here you go," he prompted as he settled on the mattress next to me, placing a water in one hand and shaking two of the pills out into the palm of the other.

I threw the medicine in the back of my mouth then swallowed the entire drink in a single gulp. Evidently, sex was dehydrating. After stowing the empty glass on the nightstand, I rolled onto my side to face Oliver, fully aware he was patiently waiting for me to be ready before he peppered me with the string of questions I knew he was dying to ask. Questions he deserved answers to. Answers I wanted him to have . . . only some weren't mine to give.

We lay silently for several minutes, mirror images of each other, with our bottom elbows bent and our heads propped up on our hands, lost in each other's eyes. I wished with all my might that I could somehow telepathically transport the stories of my past to him so I didn't have to actually speak the words, but no such luck. I guessed I had used up all of my superpowers for the night.

Unsure of what to say or how to start, I grew shy in my nakedness and moved to cover myself with the blanket. Oliver's arm darted out and caught mine, his long fingers wrapping around my petite wrist. I lifted my gaze to meet his again and he shook his head, his eyes overflowing with compassion and acceptance.

"Don't hide from me, Monroe. Not now. Not after what you just gave me. I want you to be naked with me, beautiful," he urged softly as he pulled my hand to his mouth and kissed the inside of my wrist. "All of you."

My stomach fluttered as I watched his lips press against the delicate, translucent skin and I melted into the bed, no longer worried about how exposed I was in front of him. "Sorry, I've never done this before," I confessed like it was something he didn't already know.

Releasing my arm back at my side, he flashed me a shit-eating grin. "Yeah," he chuckled, "that's the part we need to talk about. Wanna tell me why you didn't alert me of this beforehand?"

"Well, it's not something that usually comes up in everyday conversation," I replied with a shrug. "Not to mention, once you found out that I was a virgin, you would've had a million other questions I wasn't ready to answer . . . at least not then."

"Are you ready now?" he probed, scooting his body closer to mine. "Would it make it easier if I held you while you talked?"

I nodded as he drew me in against his chest, enveloping me in his arms and intertwining our legs. Then, once I was safely inside my Oliver cocoon, my senses surrounded by everything that was him, I gave him my more.

Only mine wasn't so pretty.

"Hey, Mom," I rapped my knuckles against the door of her home office as I called out to her, hoping I would catch her before she got on the phone, "can I talk to you for a minute? It's kind of important."

Her exasperated sigh was so loud I heard it like she was standing right in front of me, not in another room, through a wood door.

"Yes, I suppose, but make it fast! I've got a schedule to keep!" she shouted back, not even pretending to care more about something I deemed important in my life to her hot yoga class that started at five.

No, Vivian Taylor had lost interest in me, her only child, about the time I was old enough to tell her that I had no interest in following in her footsteps and being a childhood actress. She tried to convince me to change my mind for several months after I first broke the devastating news to her on my eleventh birthday by signing me up for audition after audition, but once she realized I purposely put forth no effort to try and win the roles she claimed "were written just for me," she flat out informed me that I was the biggest mistake of her life and basically pretended I didn't exist from that point forward. Any nurturing I did receive came from our housekeeper, Martha, but my mom kept her so busy with her daily list of ridiculous tasks that I did my best to just take care of myself and not burden anyone.

I pushed the door open and tiptoed in as my teeth chattered with nerves. I didn't know how in the world I was going to tell her what I needed to tell her without getting sick. The thought alone made bile shoot up the back of my throat.

"Well, what is it, Monroe?" she huffed, not even looking up at me. "You know I hate to be pestered with your petty kid stuff. I'm a busy woman who's working her ass off so you can have all of these nice things since you refuse to work. If your dad wasn't such a washed-up has-been, maybe he could help me out a little bit with all of your expenses."

Staring at her in disbelief, I wondered what planet she lived on. I couldn't recall the last time the two of us had a conversation, she hadn't had a job in over two years other than a few commercials and guest appearances here and there, and the royalties she made off my dad's albums from when they were married were the sole reason she had half of the things she had, none of which I cared about in the least—including our extravagant Hidden Hills home.

"Monroe!" Shouting at the top of her lungs, she clapped her hands in my face and snapped me out of my haze. "Are you on drugs? What the hell is your problem? Do I need to take you to rehab or something?"

"No, Mom." I shook my head and glanced down at the floor. "I'm not on any drugs and I don't need to go to rehab. I'm thirteen years old."

"Spit it out then. Make it snappy." She flitted around the room, doing a bunch of nothing that I could tell, but it was obvious she wanted me gone as quickly as possible. Had it been anything else in the world, I wouldn't have bothered her, but with this, I had no choice.

Taking a deep breath for courage, I started talking as fast as I could.

"Last Saturday night, after you went to sleep, Richard came into my room to see if I was still awake. I was up watching a movie in my bed, so he asked if he could join me, that he wasn't tired yet. So, I-uh, I . . ." As I stammered over the words, my vision blurred with moisture. *"I said okay, 'cause I didn't really have a choice, and—"*

"Monroe, seriously!" She threw her hands up in the air and glared at me, incensed. *"Did you really come in here to tell me you watched a movie with your stepfather? Do you really think I care?"*

I shook my head as the humiliating tears spilled over my cheeks. *"No, but I thought you'd care that he touched and kissed me in my private areas, even though I told him not to. And I thought you'd care that he made me touch and kiss his too."* I paused briefly to wipe my running nose and to see if she had any reaction at all, but when she just stared at me with her face void of all emotion, I continued talking. *"I told him no over and over again, that I didn't want to, but he told me that if I didn't do what he said, he'd leave you and make sure you never worked in Hollywood again. I didn't know what to do, Mom. I begged him to stop. I told him that I wasn't that kind of girl. But he just kept saying mean and nasty things while he forced me to do stuff."*

By this time, the sobs were wracking through my body with such force I could barely stand up straight. I had showered over ten times in the two days since Richard—a bigshot studio executive and my third stepfather— had visited me in my room, and yet I still felt filthy and slimy from head to toe, no matter how hard I'd scrubbed and scoured my skin. In addition, I hadn't been able to sleep whatsoever. Every time I got in bed, I'd stare at the doorknob, praying it wouldn't turn. The only positive thing that had happened was he hadn't come back. At least, not yet.

"What kind of things did he say to you?" she asked sharply as she began to move toward me.

I shuffled my feet backward and shrugged, really not wanting to repeat the words aloud that had played in a continuous loop through my head. *"I don't remember,"* I lied through my hiccup. *"It was just dirty, ugly things."*

"You're a shitty actress, Monroe," she seethed, closing the gap between us in a split-second. I had backed myself against a wall, and with her rapid approach, I had nowhere to go. *"Tell. Me. What. He. Said."*

Another wave of tears splashed down my face as my entire body trembled with fear. I honestly hadn't anticipated an overly affectionate display of concern from her, but I did at least think she'd try to console me in some way. After all, I was still her daughter, and what her husband did to me was not only disgusting and despicable, it was against the law.

"He said I needed to learn how to be a good cock-sucking whore like you if I ever wanted to amount to anything in life," I admitted as I wept uncontrollably. "And then he told me that he'd been thinking about the way my baby-girl . . . pussy would taste and feel since the first day he met me. That it was one of the perks of marrying you . . . getting two hot pieces of ass for the price of one."

Then, catching me completely off guard, my mom—the woman who gave birth to me, the one who was supposed to love me unconditionally and be my fiercest protector—slapped me across the face. Hard.

"You lying little slut!" she shrieked, grabbing me by my left ear and dragging me by it over to her desk, where she shoved me down into the oversized leather chair. "I don't know what your ultimate game is, little girl," she frothed, spit flying from her mouth, arms flailing wildly around, "but you are not going to steal this man from me. I don't know why you've never wanted me to be happy, but this time, you've gone too far. I can't believe you, my own fucking teenage daughter, trying to seduce my husband, all because you're so damn jealous that I'm finally getting back to my old self again."

"Mom, I'm not—" I cried.

Slamming her hand on the intricately carved wood desktop, she refused to let me talk. "No! Don't even try that 'Mom' bullshit with me. I'm through wasting my fucking time on you. Get online and find a boarding school that you can transfer to immediately. I don't care where it is. I don't care what it costs. All I want is you and your slutty little homewrecker ass out of this house . . . like yesterday!"

And with that, she charged out of the room in full dramatic fashion, leaving behind a crushed and broken young girl who would never properly recover.

Richard visited me again that night to give me a going-away present. "Your first pearl necklace, Monroe," he claimed with a revolting smirk as he held me down and released himself all over my neck and chest, "but definitely not your last." Pulling his underwear and pants back up over his hips, he strolled casually out of my room, looking back over his shoulder just before he left. "And don't let me find out about anybody else touching your pretty little pussy while you're gone. It belongs to me."

That was the last time I ever saw Richard. I left three days later without saying goodbye to anyone. And although I didn't go home that year for Christmas, by the time I was finally forced to return the following summer break, he'd already left my mom for someone else. She never mentioned that day to me, nor did she ever apologize.

Not even when he was arrested some years later for possession of child pornography with intent to distribute.

chapter twenty-three

"She buried
her ears
into the calm
of his heartbeat,
and in a matter of seconds:
fell terribly in love
with the way
her loneliness fell
softly and suddenly,
asleep,
in his chest."
–Christopher Poindexter

MONROE

OLIVER HELD ME securely against him, soothingly stroking my back while I wept into his bare chest after finishing the first part of my story—the ugly part. I had only relived that day aloud one other time in my life, and that was when I'd explained to Colin and Seth that I had no interest in being intimate with Colin, or anyone else for that matter, for the rest of my life. At the time, the mere thought of someone else touching me in a sexual manner made my skin crawl.

But that was before I met Oliver.

"I'm so sorry, Monroe," he whispered into my hair. "I hate that not only did you have to deal with something as vile and abhorrent as what that piece of shit put you through, but that you had to do it alone. No child should ever face that."

Sniffling, I leaned back slightly in his arms so I could look up into his face. I needed to feel the comfort I could only find in his vibrant eyes. "Before you, I thought I was broken," I confessed. "I couldn't get over the repulsive, sick feeling I'd get anytime I thought about being with someone else in that way. I mean, sure, I thought boys were cute and stuff while I was growing up, and I like romantic movies and books just as much as the next girl, but when it came down to it, I just couldn't. But then you changed everything."

With the pad of his thumb, he brushed away the streaks of tears from my cheeks and smiled softly at me. "You're not broken, Monroe. Far from it. When I see you, I see one of the most put-together people I've ever met. You're sharp and intelligent, selfless and kindhearted, and beautiful beyond words. People flock to you like they just can't get enough. They all want to be you."

"But it's all built on a façade," I contended. "They want to be who they think I am. No one wants to live with the demons I have. I wouldn't wish that upon the devil himself."

"I know you wouldn't, beautiful girl," he leaned down and kissed me softly, "because that's the part of you that's selfless and kindhearted. People may not know about the things that happened in your past that made you who you are today, but you, Monroe, your spirit and your soul are not a façade. You're one of the most genuine people I know."

My heart swelled with warmth—with love. No one had ever made me feel so cherished and treasured before. Not even Colin.

"Aren't you even a little curious about how my marriage plays into all this?" I squeaked, clinging to his chest like a life preserver.

Oliver chuckled softly as he squeezed me with his long, ropy arms. "I think it's safe to say I'm a lot curious, especially knowing what I know now. Though I think I've got a pretty good idea, I'd rather you tell me so I'm not making any assumptions here."

Pressing my lips to the hollow part of his throat where I could see his pulse beating, I breathed a peaceful sigh before I started talking again.

"I met Colin my first day on campus. I was running late to College Algebra, having not taken in account the geographic location of my classes when I'd set my schedule, so I rushed into the classroom just as the professor was taking roll, and naturally, there was only one open seat—in the very front row, right next to Colin." A faint smile tugged at the corners of my mouth at the memory. "When class was over, he struck up a conversation with me like we'd been friends for years. Just jabbering on and on about how excited he was to be at school and about how different Ann Arbor was from where he grew up in Massachusetts as we walked across campus to the food court for lunch. We ended up eating together that day, and he didn't shut up the whole time. I think I maybe said five words throughout the entire hour we were together. I just sat and listened and watched him eat the amount of food I normally consume in a week, and afterward, as if it was our norm, he ruffled my hair then told me he had to get to practice and that he'd see me on Wednesday. And on Wednesday, we did it all over again. Then, Friday too."

I tilted my head back and peered up at Oliver's relaxed face, his smile urging me on.

"Before long, Colin and I were inseparable. If we weren't in class or he wasn't at practice or me volunteering at the MH house, we were together. Soul mate best friends from the word go. And despite my reluctance to trust pretty much anyone, male or female, I knew immediately he would never hurt me. His heart is so kind and gentle, like a life-sized teddy bear. It was as if God knew he was exactly what I needed in my life at that time."

"So when did you guys start dating, or how did that work out?" he prompted.

"We never really dated in the sense that most people think of it," I explained carefully. "Like I said, we did everything together, so after a while, people just assumed we were a couple, and we went with it. I had no desire to really date anyone with my history, and he was focused on football and school, not the coeds looking to get knocked up so they could get a free ride when he got drafted in the pros. No one knew the kisses we exchanged in public were the extent of our physical relationship."

Pinching his brow together in confusion, Oliver cocked his head to the side. "Okay, I'm with you so far, but why get married? I guess I understand your reasoning, but not his."

I paused briefly to ponder how I could explain the next part without saying too much. The last thing I wanted to do was to lie to Oliver, but it wasn't my place to tell Colin's secret.

"Our marriage is a security blanket for both of us," I expanded. "Colin knows I love him for who he is and that I won't ever screw him over. I know Colin loves me equally and that he will provide for and protect me until the day he dies. We have fun together. We enjoy each other's company. So it works for us. After everything that happened when I was younger, I never had a desire to be close to men . . . in that way. What Colin could provide for me was exactly what I always thought I needed. He gives me love, support, friendship . . . everything a marriage is. Just for us, for our marriage, we don't have the sexual intimacy. Until now . . . I thought that's the only thing I needed."

"And sex? You don't expect me to believe that your husband is a celibate man, do you?" he asked, not bothering to even sniff the bush, much less beat around it.

I shook my head while nervously rolling my bottom lip between my teeth. "No, I don't," I murmured, "but I don't concern myself with Colin's sexual activities. Whatever he does, whoever he does it with . . . he keeps it extremely discreet. He's smart enough to not get caught. He knows the price he'd pay if something were to get out."

Oliver opened his mouth to say something then closed it, giving his head a light shake. I worried for a split-second he was going to ask me the one question I knew I couldn't answer, so when he hesitated, I started talking to get his mind off of Colin's sex life.

"And as for me, like I said earlier, when I agreed to get married, I truly believed I would never find anyone I wanted to be sexually intimate with, so it wasn't a concern of mine. I'm smart enough to realize the vast majority of humans are nothing like Richard was. Even though what happened to me still happens far too often to other victims, it's not the norm. He was sick and twisted. But in all of the men I've met in whatever capacity over the last twelve years, some of who I thought were very nice people, never once have I had any desire to explore a physical relationship with any of them. That's why I said I thought I was broken. Like my sex sensors didn't work or something," I laughed softly. Lifting up on my knees so I was eye-level with him, I cupped his jaw with my hands and rested my forehead on his. "Then, I met you."

With a mischievous grin, he palmed my bare butt and lifted me up so that I was straddling his waist and I could feel his cock between my legs. "And then what happened?"

"Then I realized I just needed the right person to make me work." I nipped at his bottom lip while sifting my fingers through his shoulder-length hair.

It was in that moment I decided Oliver had the best hair of anyone ever. Soft, thick, and silky, his chestnut waves were like something straight from a hair commercial. I could play with it for hours and be a happy camper. I had serious hair envy.

"Feels like you work perfectly to me," he mumbled against my mouth as his shaft twitched underneath my bottom.

My lips parted on a quick inhale at the strange but arousing sensation, and when it stirred a second time, I instinctively rolled my hips against him, releasing a breathy whimper. "Yeah," was all I could manage before he flipped me onto my back in a single sweeping motion.

As he hovered over me in all his naked glory, Oliver's heated gaze swept over my equally bare body and a growl rumbled deep in his chest. "Tell me what happens next, Monroe. Tell me how I get you back in my bed tomorrow night, and the night after that," he urged, his tone suddenly serious. "I promised you I'd be patient, and I know we need to take things slow, but fuck, babe . . . all I want to do is show you the countless ways I can take care of you."

"I-uh . . ." I squeezed my upper thighs together as desire pooled in my center, struggling to concentrate on the answer he was waiting for. "I'm gonna talk to Colin tomorrow about everything, and then we'll go from there. He already knows we kissed, and he's also aware I think the world of you, so it's not gonna come as that big of a shock to him."

"You told him I kissed you?" His eyes widened with horror. "The guy probably thinks I'm a fucking schmuck who just goes around kissing other dudes' wives."

"Noooo." I shook my head against the pillow, snickering under my breath. "Well, at least not anymore. Initially, he wanted to come over here and beat you up, but I convinced him that wasn't a good plan. So after a little bit of time to think on it, he told me if I wanted to pursue something with you, he was cool with it, but I needed to keep him updated, and obviously not do anything stupid where we could be caught. Luckily for you and me, if we're photographed just out and about together, it's easily explained, because we are working on this project together. We just can't have any physical contact unless we're here or at my house, where we know it's safe."

Carefully lowering his body to mine, his lips found my neck and he began working his magic all over again. "So we're safe right now?" he whispered into my delicate skin, working his way lower with each open-mouthed kiss.

"Mhmm," I moaned as my hands found his hair yet again.

"Good, 'cause I told you I wasn't finished taking care of you." He stopped his oral descent just before he reached the top of my mound and looked up at me, smirking roguishly. "If my beautiful girl is sore, I need to kiss her and make her feel better. Don't you agree?"

"Most definitely," I mumbled as my knees fell open for him. "Lots and lots of kisses."

And kiss me, he did.

Lots and lots of times.

Until I felt much, much better.

Twice.

Sometime in the wee hours of the morning, Oliver and I finally stopped talking and kissing, and we fell asleep with me snugly tucked up against him, my back to his chest. And it was in that same position I woke up just a few hours later to the sound of my cellphone ringing continuously. Looking down at the screen, I immediately knew something was very wrong.

chapter twenty-four

"It was rather
beautiful: the way he
put her insecurities to
sleep.
The way he dove into
her eyes and starved
all the fears
and tasted all the
dreams she kept
coiled beneath her
bones."
–Christopher Poindexter

MONROE

"HELLO? COLIN? IS everything okay?" The questions rushed from my mouth in a single breath as my heart pounded nervously against my ribcage. Phone calls at 4:40 in the morning weren't typically a good thing, often the result of someone being arrested, seriously hurt, or worse. "Colin? Can you hear me?"

"Hey, babe, yeah, it's me," the familiar, comforting voice of my husband replied, but instantly, I knew everything was *not* okay. My stomach constricted into a tight knot as I waited for him to continue. "Sorry to call at this hour, but I've had a little accident."

I sucked in a sharp breath. "An accident? What happened? Are you hurt?"

Two strong, corded arms circled my waist from behind as I stood naked in Oliver's living room, the farthest place I could get from his bedroom when I called Colin back, in an attempt to not wake him up. Apparently it hadn't worked. Leaning my head back onto his shoulder, I welcomed Oliver's supportive touch and rested my free hand over where his were clasped at my belly button to show my appreciation.

"I was playing basketball with some of the kids and the other chaperones, and there was just a fluke collision between me, another dude, and the wall," he gritted out, clearly in discomfort. "Ended up dislocating my throwing shoulder, and who knows what other damage. I'm on my way to Foxborough now. One of the guys is driving me. I just got off the phone with Dr. Turner, and he's meeting me up there to do an x-ray and an MRI. Guess we'll go from there, but I already know I'm looking at a month minimum."

"Maybe it's not really dislocated," I hoped aloud.

He barked out a painful laugh. "Baby girl, it's currently not in the socket. I'm pretty sure it's dislocated."

"Oh, Colin honey, I'm so sorry," I lamented into the receiver as Oliver squeezed me tighter and kissed the top of my head, sensing my distress. Although I was obviously relieved he wasn't in a life-threatening situation like a car wreck or something, I knew football was his life, and if he couldn't throw the ball with the precision and accuracy he needed, to him, it was a fatal blow. "What do you need for me to do? Just say the word."

"Since I haven't been to sleep yet—the kids refused to lay down at any point in the night—I think I'm gonna shower and maybe catch a nap up at the facility while we deal with all this. Once word gets out later today, it's going to be a media circus, and I'd rather be there with Dr. Turner and the coaching staff to answer everyone's questions. I was hoping you could bring me a change of clothes, something suitable for a press conference, as well as the black scouting notebook that's on my desk."

I nodded as if Colin could see me through the phone. "Yeah, no problem. Let me get up and dressed and I'll be on my way. If you think of anything else, just message me. Okay?"

"'Kay, babe. Love you."

"I love you too. See you soon."

Disconnecting the phone call, I spun around in Oliver's arms and peered up at him, soaking up his sexy, just-rolled-out-of-bed vibe. Even with the fresh sheet-crease line on his right temple, the man rocked the unkempt, rebellious look like nobody's business, and seeing the combination of his messy mop of brown curls and a jaw lined with dark stubble, the entire phone conversation with Colin disappeared from my mind for a brief moment as I thought about dragging him back to bed for a repeat of the previous night, damn the soreness between my legs.

"Colin's hurt? What's going on?" he prompted, lifting his eyebrow inquisitively.

Nodding again, I gave Oliver the rundown of what I knew about my husband's condition while we stood naked in his living room in each other's arms. As wrong and deceitful as that may have seemed to anyone else on the planet who could've seen us, I'd never experienced anything more right than when I was with him. And as soon as I got the chance, I'd let Colin know everything that was going on, but right then wasn't the time.

"Do you need me to drive you wherever you need to go in your SUV? I don't want you behind the wheel if you're too upset or too tired," he offered while tenderly stroking my cheek with the calloused pad of his thumb. Closing my eyes, I delighted in the roughness of his musician hands against the smoothness of my skin along with the selflessness of his words.

"I'll be all right. I promise," I assured him as my lids flitted open, my eyes searching for his. "I'm sorry our first night together is being cut short like this. I wanted to wake up in the morning with you and have our Peanut Butter Cap'n Crunch and chocolate milk in bed together while we watched *Grease* or something."

Oliver's face lit up like Boston Harbor on Independence Day, and without warning, his mouth collided with mine in a forceful, claiming kiss as his fingers skimmed up the back of my neck and sunk into my hair. I whimpered against his lips when we eventually broke apart for air and he grinned down at me, rubbing the tips of our noses together. *I really don't want to leave.*

"Don't apologize for things out of your control, Monroe." He smiled with a gentle shake of his head. "Go take care of what you need to do, and me and the rest of the Pink Ladies will be right here whenever you can come back. I'll even save you some cereal."

After another kiss—this one soft, sweet, and full of promise—we retreated to his bedroom for me to get ready to leave. When I turned on the overhead light and saw the Poison Ivy costume scattered across the floor, along with several twenty dollar bills that must've fallen out of my bra when Oliver had undressed me, sensual visions of the night before flashed in my mind. The urge to stay with him pinged in my chest again, but I knew that wasn't an option.

The costume also reminded me that I had nothing but the revealing green dress and my jacket to wear home. But Oliver—who'd slipped on some pajama pants at some point—was already a step ahead of me, digging out some sweatpants and a hoodie from his closet. They were a little big, as I had to roll the waist of the pants to keep them up, but it was a vast improvement from my other option, so I was appreciative. Unfortunately, the only shoes I had were the sparkly green heels, which I wasn't wearing under any circumstance, so he gave me two pairs of socks to help keep my feet warm in the cab ride from his place to my street. I wouldn't risk being dropped off in front of my house, in case it was being staked out for any reason. Being photographed getting out of a taxi pre-dawn with last night's makeup and hair, no shoes, and in another man's clothes would appear to be exactly what it was. And exactly what I had to avoid.

"You look sexy in my clothes," Oliver announced matter-of-factly once I was dressed and ready to go.

Glancing down at the oversized getup, I laughed. "Sexier than in the costume?"

He nodded as he sauntered toward me, a waggish smirk tugging up the corners of his eyes and mouth. "Absolutely."

"Sexier than my business suits?" I cocked an eyebrow, knowing how much he appreciated when I wore my fitted pencil skirts and the matching jackets.

"Without a doubt," he chuckled as our bodies made contact and I found myself encased in his affectionate arms.

I squeaked as he lifted me off the ground and buried his face in my neck. My arms and legs instinctively wrapped around him and I clung to the final minutes I had with him before I had to leave. "I'm not very good at this kind of thing," I confessed in a soft whisper. "Not sure what to say. I don't wanna leave you."

He smiled against my skin and the warmth from his breath tickled my ear, sending a trail of goose bumps down my back. "That's it, beautiful girl, what you said right there. Knowing you don't want to leave is all I need to know."

His lips grazed mine as he lowered my feet back to the ground, but before we were entirely untangled from each other's embrace, my phone buzzed inside my wristlet. Worried something else had happened, I hurriedly fished it out and glanced down at the screen.

Colin: Please call Seth and let him know. Tell him I'm sorry and I love him.

Shoving the device back into my small purse, I peered up at Oliver and knew immediately by his dumbfounded expression that he'd seen the text. My stomach sank to the basement of my gut where guilt, failure, and self-loathing sunk in.

"Look, I'm sorry—" I started to apologize, but he pressed two fingers to my lips and shook his head.

"You trusted me enough to give me what you gave me last night, right? All of *you*—inside and out?" he asked, not removing his hand.

I nodded, my hopeful gaze searching his.

"Then you can trust me with this. I promise you," he swore. "No matter what happens between the two of us, I swear to you, I will never do anything to hurt either of you. That's not who I am. You know that. You wouldn't be here if you thought I was."

Oliver's words provided some relief, as I felt confident he wouldn't ever take my and Colin's story public, but I was still irritated with myself for the way it had happened. That was Colin's story to tell, not mine.

"'Kay." I offered a faint smile. "I'll update you when I know more about what's going on. I'll come back as soon as I can."

"I'll be here."

Walking me to the front door, he held my face in his hands and looked intently into my eyes before he leaned down and kissed my forehead, the tip of my nose and, finally, my lips. His hands made a slow descent down my arms until they met my own. He released one hand and as I walked away, not wanting to let go, his outstretched arm held onto my hand for one more gentle squeeze of his fingers before I reluctantly left his place.

THE SATURDAY MORNING sun was just beginning to crest over the eastern horizon as I pulled out of my driveway a little after six AM. A canopy of autumn leaves in brilliant shades of gold and red veiled the cobblestone street I drove down, a reminder that November was upon us and the frosty, snow-ridden days of winter would follow soon after. For everything I loved about my adopted hometown of Boston, the one thing I could do without was the winters. Colin was always deep in the season, spending countless hours away prepping for each week's game. Night would fall before I'd make it home in the evening, leaving me wanting to go to bed before nine. Plus, I was reminded continuously of the family I didn't have to share holiday meals with. As nice and as welcomed as Colin's family always made me feel, I couldn't help but feel melancholy at the lack of my own parents who cared.

Pushing aside my own forlorn thoughts I could do nothing about, I hit the voice activation button on my steering wheel and focused my attention on the task at hand. "Call Sexy Seth Andrews on mobile." I enunciated the words clearly for the car's computer, snickering at the silly name Seth had entered into my contacts.

"Would you like to call Sexy Seth Andrews on mobile?" the digital voice replied, eliciting another giggle from me.

"Yes," I confirmed then waited for the call to connect.

After three rings, I grew nervous he wasn't going to answer, but before his voicemail picked up, I heard his groggy voice on the other end of the line. "Roe? You okay?"

"Hey, Seth," I greeted him a little too cheerfully, unsure of how he was going to react. "Sorry to call so early, but I'm calling because Colin's been in an accident."

Suddenly, he sounded wide awake and panicked. "An accident?! Where is he? What happened? Is it serious?"

"He's okay, he's okay. Don't freak," I assured him. "It's not life-threatening, but he thinks it's a pretty serious injury to his shoulder and arm."

I went on to explain to him what happened and how I was on my way to take him some clothes, when he cut me off. "Monroe, I don't mean to be rude, but I'm not sure why you're calling me right now. I feel really terrible this has happened, because I honestly want the absolute best for him, but something like this doesn't concern me anymore. I told you a while back at the game that I'm moving on. I can't continue to fall back into something I know is going nowhere, and that's exactly where Colin and I are headed as long as he wants to continue living a lie."

"But . . . but he's sorry," I argued, my heart breaking for both of them, "and you know he lov—"

"Did he ask me to come?" he interrupted. "Does he want me to be by his side to support him as his lover?

I sighed. "No, but—"

"But nothing, Roe. I'm tired of being his dirty secret. I deserve more, just like you do."

Swallowing hard, I resisted the desire to tell him about Oliver and the night before. If Colin found out I told Seth first, it would hurt his feelings, and with everything else going on, I didn't need to pile it on. So instead, I replied, "I understand. Sorry I woke you up."

"No need to apologize, baby girl." Seth's voice softened. "If *you* need me, call any time. You're still my number one girl."

"'Kay, I will."

"Bye Roe. I love you."

"I love you, too. Bye, Seth."

The remainder of the drive, I tried to not think about what Colin's reaction would be when I relayed Seth's message by losing myself in terribly off-key singing to Top 40 songs on the radio. But when I found him in the medical wing of the team's training facility and conveyed his ex-lover's message, I watched the giant of a man who I loved crumble in front of me, destroyed by physical and emotional pain. Wanting to comfort him in any way possible, I went to him and held him in my arms for a long while as he sobbed into my chest.

After he got out whatever it was he needed to get out, he pulled away from me, kissed my cheek, and then spoke. "Doc says I really did a number on the shoulder. In addition to the separation, I have a partial tear in one of the ligaments, and I'm gonna need surgery to reset, repair, and tighten the surrounding tendons, in hopes it'll prevent future instability. He says I'm looking at eight to twelve weeks normally, but is recommending this brand new rehab place down in Miami. He thinks with whatever cutting-edge treatments they're doing, I could maybe be back in five or six."

Disappointment washed over me, though I tried not to let it show. This decision wasn't about me.

"Is that what you're gonna do?" I asked.

He nodded hesitantly. "If you think you'll be okay here by yourself? You know you've got my parents, Seth and Effie, and now Oliver around if you need anything. Plus, I'm only a short plane ride away."

I forced a smile and ran my fingers through his short hair. "Don't worry about me, babe. All I want is for you to get fixed up the best way possible."

"I love you, Roe," he said with a sad smile.

"Love you too, big guy."

Later that day, Colin underwent successful surgery to repair his shoulder, and the next morning, he was on the team plane bound for Miami, Florida for a minimum of four weeks.

Four weeks I had alone.

With Oliver.

chapter twenty-five

"We laid in bed
and watched the clocks
around us dance
until time to us,
was only the rise
and fall of our
ruptured heartbeats.
We kissed and we kissed
until we knew no other taste
and we no longer understood
the pattern of a day as
we fell in love with the
colors and the world
between each other's
eyelids."
—Christopher Poindexter

OLIVER

"I'M REALLY GLAD you let the beard grow back out," Monroe quipped as she melted into the mountain of pillows beneath her head, eyes squeezing shut and chest heaving in her post-orgasmic state.

As I looked up at her naked body from my vantage point between her legs, a deep laugh rumbled up through my chest into the back of my throat. "Is that so?" I smirked, licking the sticky, sweet taste of her release that coated my lips.

"Mhmmm," she moaned while sifting her fingers through my hair. "And I'm glad you haven't cut this either. I like to pull on it when *it* happens." Her grip tightened near the roots as she said the words, triggering my dick to jump in response.

After over three straight weeks of spending almost every non-working moment in that bed with her, I knew damn well she liked to pull my hair when she came. And even more than that, I knew I fucking loved every single time she did it. Even from the beginning, when I was careful to move slowly with Monroe, wanting her to feel in control and not pressured, she would twist her fingers in my mop of waves and yank hard each time she climaxed, regardless if it was on my hand, my mouth, or my cock. Which was often. Really often.

With Colin being out of town for at least the entire month of November, and Monroe and me in the full swing of the honeymoon phase of our relationship, we rarely left my apartment. When we weren't working, we were in my bed, naked, either exploring each other's bodies or watching movies on Netflix. Occasionally, we ate, showered, and slept, and all of that we did together too. The only time we spent apart was on Thursday nights when I played at Riff's and she'd have dinner at the children's home. We didn't want to take a chance of someone associating her being there only on nights I performed, so she utilized those evenings for some quality time with the kids.

Effie had started showing up more frequently during the work week as we neared the December first closing date on the house, and even though I hated when she was there, because I couldn't touch or kiss or break for a quickie when I wanted with Monroe, she actually proved to be a pretty good employee, and I was happy Monroe had her working for her. Her persistent, unrelenting personality annoyed the shit out of me when she was coming on to me, but it paid off big in the business world. Plus, I kind of liked it when Monroe would get jealous while Effie flirted. On those days, she'd damn near attack me the moment the poor girl walked out the door and the lock was turned. Her carnal need to mark me inflated both my ego and my shaft, which usually led to some pretty off-the-fuck-ing-reservation,   oh-my-God-she's-the-thing-dreams-are-made-of sex. So yeah, maybe I didn't mind Effie all that much.

"Well, beautiful girl," I pushed up on my hands and knees, pausing to feather my lips over her sweet spot one last time before crawling up the length of her frame, "as much as I'd love for you to pull my hair again right now, we need to jump in the shower and get ready to head to the airport. I don't want to be late for Callie's flight to arrive."

"Ugh," she complained, scrunching up her nose in the cutest way. "I don't want to sleep without you for a week. This sucks."

Chuckling, I stole a kiss from her pouting lips and rolled off the mattress before I allowed myself to get lost in her again. "I'm not arguing that with you, but it is what it is. My niece will be here for three nights, and then I'll be at my parents' house for four. But I'll be back before you know it, and then I can show you how much I missed you."

Her lids fluttered open and she looked over at where I was standing next to the bed. "You're not getting tired of me yet?"

"Of course I'm not, weirdo," I scoffed, throwing her a don't-be-ridiculous look. "I think I've made it pretty damn clear how I feel about you. You've been in my bed every night for twenty-one straight nights, and it'll take another twenty-one hundred before I could even think of getting tired of."

The instant her forehead dipped into a low V, I knew I'd screwed up the math. "That's like six years," she confirmed my fuck-up.

"Well, I meant twenty-one thousand. I can't math when you're laying there all naked, looking warm and inviting in my sheets, and Iron Chef is controlling ninety-eight percent of my brain activity," I contended.

Monroe grinned impishly as she scooted her body toward the edge of the mattress and locked her ankles around my ass. "Are we at a hundred percent yet?"

"Almost," I grunted, unable to resist her.

Slightly tilting her hips, she rubbed her wet center up and down the length of my throbbing shaft. Her daring green eyes never left mine, and finding her inner vixen, she cupped her own breasts and began rolling her nipples between her fingers. "How 'bout now?"

With a feral growl emitting from my chest, I scooped her off the bed and carried her to the shower, where I gave her every damn percent I had in me before we washed up and got dressed. It was with ten minutes to spare that Monroe parked her blue Volvo in the VIP lot at the airport, and the two of us put our romance on a temporary hold as we walked inside to pick up Callie—together, but not together like I wished we could be.

"I STILL CAN'T believe you didn't tell me you know Monroe Cassidy!" my seventeen-year-old niece exclaimed for at least the fourth time that day as her gaze bounced back and forth between me and Monroe, who was sitting next to me in the corner booth at the Lobster House, where we were finishing up our early dinner. "And I still can't believe I've been hanging out with her all day!"

Callie glanced over at the younger teenage girl next to her as she shoved a French fry in her mouth. "And you're basically gonna live with her! How bad-ass is that?"

JoJo smiled wide and nodded. "It's really cool when she brings Clutch around too. They're both awesome."

"Oh, my God, he is sooo dreamy," Callie swooned. "Do you have anything signed by him?"

As the girls dove into a lengthy discussion filled with giggles and squeals about how amazing Colin Cassidy was, I glanced over at Monroe and smiled like an idiot, unable to contain my happiness over how well the day had gone so far. After we scooped Callie up from the airport, we drove to the Suffolk County home to pick up Heather and JoJo to join us on our day of sightseeing around the city, but unfortunately, Heather had come down with a nasty cold the night before and couldn't come.

So the four of us had ventured out into the crisp, sunny November Sunday afternoon, first taking the Boston Movie Mile Walking Tour, where a local actor guided us around by foot for a couple of hours, pointing out prominent landmarks and well-known neighborhoods that have been a part of major motion pictures and network TV shows. Monroe had quietly pointed out her house to me when we passed it during the portion of the tour that led us through the winding, tree-lined streets of the historic Beacon Hill neighborhood. I wasn't expecting the pang of jealousy that shot through me at the sight of the house she shared with Colin, but it was there nonetheless. Even if he didn't know her in the intimate sense that I did, he was still legally her spouse, and together they owned a house, cars, and who knew what else. Her heart and body may have belonged to me, but she was his wife.

That fleeting twinge of self-pity had been the only snafu in the entire day, and thankfully, no one but I knew anything about it. I'd known exactly who Monroe was and what I was signing up for when she and I began our relationship. Admittedly, I'd felt infinitely better about my sealing the deal with the whole adultery thing once I knew that Colin and Monroe weren't husband and wife in that sense of the word. Even if I wasn't aware of that fact until after I made the decision to take her as mine, I chose to ignore that minor detail. After all, it was just semantics. The important thing was that I was the only man on the planet who had experienced the heavenly sensation of being buried deep inside her, and if I had it my way, that's the way it would stay.

"Are you about ready to meet some ghosts?" I teased Monroe when the girls excused themselves to the restroom, alluding to the Haunted Boston Ghost Tour we were getting ready to leave the restaurant and head to.

Taking full advantage of the few minutes we had alone, I shifted my inside hand to the pleather bench seat we shared and 'accidentally' brushed my fingers against hers. With a sharp, sudden intake of breath, her gaze fell to where our skin touched, and after a couple of seconds, a devious grin began to spread across her gorgeous face.

"It depends," she smarted back as her hand inched toward my thigh, completely hidden by the table, "on whether or not you're gonna hold and comfort me if I do."

The instant her fingers made contact with my leg, even though it was through the rough denim of my jeans, my dick stirred to life and I groaned. I shot her a you're-the-devil look and tried to shift away from her, but she tightened her hold to a death-grasp and shook her head.

"Unh-unh, no running away," she laughed, the beautiful sound dancing in my ears. "Answer my question. Are you gonna take care of me afterward if I get all scared when I see a ghost?"

"You already know the answer," I murmured, dropping my stare to the table, suddenly feeling shy. "I always take care of you."

Relaxing her grip, Monroe patted my leg soothingly as she leaned in to whisper, "You're right. You do. And I don't ever want you to stop."

My nostrils flared and my pulse spiked as I utilized every last ounce of willpower I had inside me to refrain from kissing her stupid right there and then, not giving a single fuck who saw us. I'd been captivated by her since the first time I met her, and the fast and furious ride from pipedream crush to practically living together in the span of three months had led me right to that very moment. Sitting in a corner booth at the local Lobster House, as dusk fell outside the window over her shoulder, with her hidden hand on my thigh and her warm breath floating across my neck, it was then I knew I didn't ever want to stop taking care of her either. As in *never* ever.

I wanted to wake up to her morning breath and fall asleep to her faint snores. I wanted her to make fun of me when we had dance parties in the living room and laugh until she snorted like a pig as I tickled her relentlessly in bed. I wanted her to get mad at me when I forgot to take out the trash and I wanted to roll my eyes each time she forgot to put the chocolate milk back in the fridge. It was always easy to want the good with someone, but it was when

I realized I wanted the bad with her even more than I wanted the best of anyone else, that my brain confirmed what my heart already knew.

I loved her.

Mind, body, and spirit, I hopelessly adored her and wanted nothing more than to keep her as mine forever.

"Monroe," my breath hitched as our eyes locked, electricity crackling in the air between us, "promise me that you'll tell him as soon as he gets back. I don't ever want to stop taking care of you either. Please don't ask me to."

Pressing her soft, pink lips together, she nodded slightly. "I promise, Ollie."

chapter twenty-six

"If darkness
is really not
darkness at
all, but rather,
the absence of
light,
then my flaws
are not really
flaws at all,
but rather,
the absence
of you."
–Christopher Poindexter

MONROE

"KEEP STIRRING UNTIL all the liquid is absorbed. This may take anywhere from three to five minutes," the gorgeous Italian chef instructed with a smile as she mixed the rice mixture with ease, exerting just enough effort to make her amazing boobs squeeze together and peek out of the designer V-neck blouse she wore.

"Oh, go blow on a tailpipe, Giada," I growled at the iPad, irritated because I had been stirring the damn risotto for over ten minutes and all I had to show for it was a tired arm and a skillet full of chicken broth and flat rice.

Blowing out an exasperated breath, I dropped the wooden spoon and stepped away from the stove, ready to call for delivery. I knew better than to think I could cook Colin's favorite dinner, even if his mom had walked me step-by-step over the phone through the recipes for the chicken Marsala and the garlic parmesan risotto that afternoon. Cooking just wasn't my thing—never was, never would be. I could manage to prepare a few simple things without total destruction of myself, the house, or the food, but anything with more than like three or four ingredients just never turned out right. Not to mention, I was usually cooking for only myself, and that wasn't very much fun.

However, that Sunday night, four weeks to the day since Colin had left for treatment in Florida, he was finally coming home and had promised to join me for dinner so we could catch up. Having flown into the city earlier in the day, he'd headed straight to the stadium to watch the team take on the Steelers for an early afternoon kick-off. Much to my chagrin, the Pats had lost . . . *again*.

With Colin out due to his injury, the team had lost three of four, and suddenly, their playoff spot was in jeopardy. I was well aware that his mood wouldn't be the best when he arrived home, so I'd called his mom for help when I stopped off at the market on my way home from Oliver's, in hopes his favorite home-cooked meal would help him relax, as well as soften the blow when I told him about the whole boyfriend thing.

As luck would have it, Oliver returned to Boston from Thanksgiving with his family on the same day Colin came home, their flights landing within an hour of each other. And although I was ecstatic to see Colin after going a month with only text messages and a couple of Skype sessions, I wasn't all that devastated when he told me he wouldn't be home until later in the evening, once the game was over.

Oliver, on the other hand, I was dying to get a piece of the minute he stepped off the plane, though I was smart enough to wait for him at his apartment and not at the airport. With the key he'd given me before he left, I'd let myself in that morning and waited in his bed until he joined me shortly thereafter—both of us eager to show the other how much they were missed. Even though it sucked not being able to spend the night with him while Callie was staying at his apartment, we at least had a blast roaming around the city for those three days, goofing off like carefree teenagers and sneaking kisses and touches anytime we got a chance. But the four nights he was in Illinois, when I couldn't sleep soundly or snap out of my overall funk, were absolutely abysmal and seemed to drag on for an eternity. My Thanksgiving dinner with the kids was the only time I didn't think about how much I missed him and enjoyed myself.

I was neither too stubborn nor blind to recognize the impact his absence had on me and what it ultimately meant, but before I could drop that three-word-bomb on him, I needed to talk to Colin first. If I deserved more, he at least deserved that. For everything that we were. For the love and respect we had for each other.

Which brought me to the epic failure of a dinner that I was scraping into the trash receptacle, burying all of my hopes to butter him up under the heap of inedible food. *If this talk doesn't go well, it's all Giada's fault.*

A half an hour later, Chinese food was delivered to the front door, and not ten minutes after that, I heard Colin pull up and the engine turn off. My stomach rolled with nerves as I waited for him to come in, but the second I saw my husband's red-rimmed eyes and tear-stained cheeks as he came through the back door, all of the things I planned to say to him were pushed aside and replaced with his need for me to comfort him in whatever way necessary. I had only witnessed Colin cry a couple of times in all the years we'd been together, so I knew something or someone had seriously upset him.

"Colin, babe," I gasped, throwing the kitchen towel I was carrying down on the counter and rushing to him. "What happened? Why didn't you call me?"

We converged in the middle of the living room and immediately wrapped each other up in a tight embrace, my face smashed against his chest. After taking a little bit to soak in the therapeutic qualities of the hug, he pulled back far enough that we could look into each other's eyes.

"I don't know what happened," he finally replied, wiping the wetness away with the back of his hands. "I was fine one minute while driving home, and then the next, I was crying uncontrollably. It was like I'd suppressed all this sadness and disappointment I felt after everything that happened with Seth, and then it felt like you were trying to pull away when you told me that you felt a special connection with Oliver, and I got scared." *Oh God, please don't say it.* "It seemed like everyone I love was just trying to leave me." *Yep, he said it.*

"Then that stupid, freak accident at the lock-in . . ." He paused to shake his head in disbelief. "You, Seth, and football—that's all I want in life. It's all I need to be happy. And this last month has been hell without any of the three. The game today was just the tipping point. It nearly killed me watching my teammates out there, knowing I couldn't do anything to help them win. And I guess all the emotions finally just got the best of me . . . I snapped in the car." Ruffling my hair, his offered me a small smile. "But now that I'm home, here with you, I surprisingly feel a million times better. And I know that starting tomorrow morning, my life will be nothing but New England Patriots football for the rest of the season. I've got four weeks to lead this team back to the top of the division, and I don't care if I have to move in to the practice facility. I will make sure I'm mentally and physically prepared each and every week to do just that."

My muscles tensed with the guilt coursing through my body while apprehension held my tongue quiet; there was no way in Hell I could tell him about me and Oliver right then, not unless I wanted to further trample on his already bruised and battered heart. And I loved him too much for that.

I encouraged him with an affectionate pat on the arm, ignoring my own inner turmoil. "Whatever you need, babe, I'm here for you. Until the very end."

"Until the very end, baby girl," he repeated, his small smile widening into a full-out grin as he stared down at me from his massive height. "Now what's the big surprise you mentioned for dinner? I'm starving."

With a sheepish grin, a nervous chuckle escaped from me as I glanced over my shoulder to the kitchen. "Well, uh, you see," I hee-hawed around for a minute before blurting it all out in a single breath. "I tried to make your mom's chicken Marsala and risotto for you, because I knew you were going to be in a not-so-great mood, but that ended up a total disaster, so we're now having Chinese takeout."

He howled with laughter at my confession and demanded I tell him the full cooking fiasco as we sat on our stools at the kitchen island, stuffing our faces with Mongolian beef, fried rice, and eggrolls. We didn't talk about Seth. We didn't talk about Oliver. And for a little while, we were just Colin and Monroe like back in college. Best friends until the very end.

Only the end was coming faster than either of us knew.

"I'VE NARROWED IT down to these—Elephant's Breath, Skipping Rocks, and London Fog. What do you think?" I asked Oliver as he joined me in the upstairs bedroom, carrying the ladder I'd asked him to bring up.

As I backed away from the wall, my eyes bounced back and forth between the paint swatches I'd been staring at for over an hour. It was Wednesday, our second full day of working in the MH house after we'd signed the mountain of closing paperwork on Monday afternoon, and I'd been working on the kids' bedrooms, choosing paint, furniture, and décor. Well, it was almost noon, and I hadn't made it past the paint part yet.

Oliver leaned the bulky metal equipment against the opposite wall then sauntered up next to me, dramatically crossed his arms over his chest, and narrowed his stare on the three gray squares I'd taped to the sheetrock, pretending he was in deep, serious thought.

"I think whoever comes up with these names should stick to writing Hallmark cards, and if this is gonna be your room, you're forty-seven shades short," he announced before erupting in a fit of laughter.

Rolling my eyes, I lightly slapped his arm as my face heated with embarrassment. Ever since I'd admitted to him a couple of nights ago that I was intrigued by the thought of using a blindfold in bed, he'd been making *Fifty Shades* jokes every chance he got. Naturally, when we'd gone to the home improvement store the previous day for things we needed at the house, the abundance of rope, cable ties, and tape provided him an endless amount of opportunities.

Admittedly, most of it was pretty funny, especially since there was not a chance in this lifetime I'd allow him or anyone else to restrain my hands and/or feet. Oliver had opened both my mind and heart up to so many things that I never thought possible for me, but with my past, I didn't care how much I trusted him—it was a big N-O on the bondage. But the blindfold . . . the blindfold I would consider, because I could remove it myself if I started to get freaked. I needed that control.

"Keep making fun of me and we'll see who's laughing tonight when Iron Chef goes to sleep without dinner," I warned before sticking my tongue out at him.

Doing his best to wrangle in his amusement—but failing miserably—he scooped me up in his arms and kissed me long and hard. My limbs instinctively wrapped around him. "Rizzo, you know I'm just teasing you 'cause I like you," he said when we came up for air.

"Mhmm," I mumbled, pretending to be unconvinced. "'Cause you like me, huh?"

Oliver caught my lips with his again, this time softer and slower. I clung to him, giving as much as I took. The man could make me forget about the entire world when his mouth was working its Bat Magic, the coarseness of his facial hair mixed with the soft, silkiness of his lips creating the perfect, mind-blowing sensation.

"You know I do a lot more than just like you, right?" he whispered as he tenderly rubbed the tip of his nose in small circles against mine, our eyes locking on one another's.

My heart skipped a beat, maybe two, before it began thumping wildly in my chest. I couldn't speak, my tongue a dried up rag in the middle of the desert. "Yeah?" I breathed.

"Yeah, beautiful girl, don't act like you don't know." He grinned wolfishly while tugging on my hair. "But I'm not gonna tell you how much until we're in the clear. At least with him. I know we don't know what happens after that, in the future, but we face those hurdles as they arise. Just like in every relationship, there are risks we both have to take, and I'm willing to take every single one of them for you, Monroe, but Colin *has* to know."

I nodded my agreement. "I know. And I swear to you once the season is over, which could be as early as four weeks from now, I will tell him. I just couldn't Sunday with the way he was . . ." Furrowing my brow with annoyed confusion, I asked, "You said you understood?"

"I *do* understand, and I'm not upset with you. But I just want you to understand what's keeping me from crossing that next barrier. I've given you everything I have but that. It's all I have to hold on to until you can give me all of you too," he replied, kissing my forehead until I relaxed it. "There. That's better."

Even though I didn't like his reasoning, there wasn't much I could say, because in the end, he was right. All I needed to do was talk to Colin and it would be a non-issue. Plus, the longer I carried on with Oliver without telling my husband, the more hurt and upset Colin was going to be once I did. But I really didn't want to let him down, not when he needed the stability I offered more than ever.

If we could just make it until the season was over—somewhere between four and nine weeks depending on their playoff run—then we could all sit down together and talk about what's next. Hopefully, that would include me getting to be with Oliver on a permanent basis. I loved him enough to ask Colin for a divorce, but I couldn't just yet.

"Ollie, you know how I feel too," I gently nipped at his full bottom lip, "and I'm giving you my word. As soon as football is over, I'll tell him everyth—"

"Hello? Anybody home? I brought lunch for everyone!" Effie's voice filtered into the bedroom seconds before she appeared in the doorway.

Somehow, Oliver managed to lower me back to the floor and we both turned to face the paint swatches in just the nick of time. Well, I hoped it was in time. We must've been so absorbed in our own conversation that we didn't hear the alarm chime when she came in the front door, and it was only by sheer luck that she called out at all. I didn't want to think about if she hadn't.

"Hey, Effie!" I spun around to greet her, hoping she didn't hear the shakiness in my voice. "Oliver just came in to help me choose a paint color. I could use your opinion too. What do you think of these three?"

Distract and redirect. Distract and redirect. My training as a therapist kicked in immediately, and all I wanted to do was to make her think and talk about anything but discovering me and Oliver in the middle of a tense conversation.

"My choice is definitely the elephant one," Oliver announced matter-of-factly then turned to smile at Effie. "And yes, food! I knew I liked you, pixie girl. Let's go set it up downstairs in the kitchen. I'll help you."

Swooning at Oliver and giggling like a school-girl, Effie floated on Cloud Nine right out of the room. I may or may not have snarled in her direction.

"No need to channel your inner Poison Ivy, beautiful," Oliver chuckled, swiping his thumb across my cheek. "I only see you."

After he followed her downstairs to help with lunch, I was left alone, staring at those damn gray squares on the wall, and the only thing I could think about was where I could buy a blindfold.

chapter
twenty-seven

"She doesn't see what I see.
To her, she is imperfection.
She is dust on pages of torn
books and broken hands on clocks
that used to spin in lovers
homes. To me, she is perfection.
She is the sun the moment it is
washed by the sea
and the children's heartbeat
the moment
it explodes from the water
once more."
–Christopher Poindexter

OLIVER

"YOU KNOW, YOU might as well tell me now," my mom probed, taking a drag off a cigarette, even though she convinced my dad she'd stopped smoking ten years before. "I can wait out here as long as you want, but it's a helluva lot warmer inside the house."

As she exhaled, I watched the cloud of smoke dissipate into the frigid, late-night December air just past the porch we sat on. Bundled up like Eskimos with a space heater pointed directly on us, we looked like fools sitting outside watching the snow fall around us, but my mom didn't care. This was her thing—the porch swing in the backyard. She used it with her kids like a therapist uses a couch with his patients. We knew when we were summoned there, we were about to be grilled with tough questions, and after the interrogation, we'd receive a valuable piece of Mom-advice that we didn't usually want to hear, but always needed to hear.

Mom did not fuck around in the swing. If I was acting like a little shit, she had no problem slapping me upside the head and telling me I was acting like a little shit. And when I was about thirteen or fourteen, I spent way too many nights on the swing being told just that. Thankfully, at thirty-three, I'd grown out of the swing sessions . . . or so I'd thought until that night after Christmas dinner—once my older sisters had packed their families up and gone home, my dad had gone to bed, and Charlotte and Camille left for an impromptu late movie—when my mom knocked on the door of my childhood bedroom, where I was texting with Monroe, and told me to meet her outside in ten minutes. I knew then I was in trouble.

"There's nothing else to tell, Mom. I'm not sure what you want me to say," I played stupid again, hoping she'd miraculously drop the whole conversation.

"Oliver Bradley Saxon, you may make six figures, live in a swanky high-rise, and have some fancy string of letters behind your name, but I am still the woman who gave birth to you, and I can tell when my son is in love!" she roared, her eyes wide and full of intensity. "From the minute you got here a couple of days ago, you've been walking around in this fog with a stupid-ass grin on your face that only gets bigger when you check your phone every other minute. I thought you were acting a little funny at Thanksgiving, always disappearing at the most random times, but then I was worried the deviled eggs had upset your tummy, so I didn't want to say anything. But now . . . now you may as well be wearing a blinking neon that says, 'Idiot in love.'"

"Mother, I'm a grown-ass man," I retorted. "Grown-ass men have stomachs, not tummies. Grown-ass men also do not need to report the status of their love life to their parents until a relationship develops that warrants that discussion."

"So there is someone!" she screeches, clapping her hands together. "I knew it! I knew it! I knew it!"

Sighing, I dropped my face into my leather gloves and shook my head. Why did I even say anything?

"What's her name? Can you at least tell me that?" Scooting closer to me on the swing, she hooked our elbows and kissed my cheek. "You have no idea how happy this makes me, Ollie. When all of your friends started getting married and beginning their own families and you didn't show any interest, I worried that because you grew up with so many females in the house that you would never settle down, knowing how crazy we can all be. I mean, even your friend Danny, who I thought would be single forever, finally shacked up with that Mo girl who'd been busting his balls since you guys were kids."

She paused to take another drag from her cigarette then continued her rambling. "So tell me more. What does she do? Is she beautiful? Wait, don't answer that. Of course she's beautiful. You've always had a selective eye. How old is she? Does she live in Boston? I knew there was a reason you were supposed to go on this trip. Wh—"

"Mom, please stop!" I shouted, raising my hands in the air to surrender. "For the love of God, please stop with the fucking questions."

Hurt and disappointment washed over her face as she retreated from me, and instantly, I wanted the words back. *Where is that damn rewind button?* I didn't mean for my tone to sound so harsh; the last thing I ever wanted in my life was to upset my mom, especially after all she had done to keep our family together during some crazy-ass shit. And I had done just that, all because she was happy for me that I'd found someone. I was a dick.

"I'm sorry, Mom. I shouldn't have spoken to you like that," I apologized as I wrapped my arms around her shoulders and tugged her back close to me. "I'm just really uneasy about it right now, and I'm scared if I talk about it, something will happen to screw it all up."

Her forgiving gaze lifted to meet mine and she tenderly patted my cheek. "You really like her then, eh?"

"I love her with a love I didn't know my heart was capable of," I confessed in a whisper.

"Then what's the problem, son? I see the hesitation in your face. Are you not sure if she feels the same? Scared to tell her?"

I shrugged and cut my eyes out to the yard, where she could hopefully not read anything else I wasn't saying. "It's just really complicated. I feel confident she feels the same way about me, but there are a lot of outside factors at play, and unfortunately, I have to wait and see how it all works out."

"Will it all work out before you return to Chicago, or are you planning on staying in Boston when the six months are up?"

The questions she asked were the same ones I'd been asking myself for the better part of the last week. December was almost over, and I was supposed to return home to Chicago at the end of February. The Patriots had already clinched a playoff spot after Colin led the team to three straight wins when he came back from his injury, so even though the upcoming Sunday was the last week of the regular season, nothing regarding Monroe and me and him would be resolved yet.

Never before had I been so interested in a football team's schedule as I was that December. With Colin home from rehab in Miami, Monroe only spent the night at my apartment when he was out of town for an away game. After we'd spend our day working at the MH house—where we had to stop our flirting with a full-time Effie around and other people dropping by regularly to deliver furniture and other items for the home—Monroe would give me a 'ride' to my apartment, which ninety-nine percent of the time ended with one of us riding the other, both before and after we ate dinner. Then around nine-thirty or ten, when she'd start yawning incessantly, she'd go home to shower and sleep, and he was none-the-wiser, thinking she'd just been with the kids or working late.

It sucked. And even though I understood why she was waiting to tell him, I hated it. I wanted it over. I wanted to know what was going to happen with us. Where we went next.

"Honestly, I'm not sure," I finally answered my mom, who was patiently waiting for me to wade through my stream of thoughts. "I wasn't expecting this. She wasn't expecting this. And it's all happened so fast, I don't think either of us knows what to do. I adore my kids in Chicago. I've been at that house since the very beginning, and I'm close friends with my advisors. I don't want to give all that up, lose all those people who I care about deeply, only for things not to work out between us. And she—" I swallowed hard, emotions burning the back of my throat, "—she can't leave Boston. At least, not any time soon. She just got this new position at her job, and there are a lot of other things tying her down there."

I stood up abruptly, striding to the edge of the wood decking, staring blankly out into the yard as if the answers were hidden behind the frozen limbs of the trees and the snow-capped bushes. "I dunno," I continued on, the hard bite of the wind slapping me in the face when I leaned out too far. "When I talk about it aloud, when I really think about our situation objectively, it seems like there's more working against us than for us . . ."

"I feel a 'but' coming on," Mom commented as she sidled up next to me, bringing the portable heater with her.

Chuckling softly, I looked over at her and nodded. "But I'd risk it all for her if she asked me to."

"Then do it," she urged. "Lay it all out for her. Tell her what you want and what you'll do to have it. Don't move back to Chicago two months from now wondering *what if*. Know that if it doesn't work out, for whatever reason, that it wasn't from a lack of effort on your part. That's what love is, Oliver—vulnerability. Handing over your heart to someone, exposed and susceptible, and having the faith they won't stomp all over it or tear it to shreds."

I closed my eyes and inhaled a deep breath through my nose as I really thought about her words. Naturally, everything she said made perfect sense, which made me question my decision to not tell Monroe I loved her until after she talked to Colin. Why was I putting that restriction on my love for her? Would her telling Colin have any effect on my feelings for her? Would him knowing make me love her more? Why hadn't I told her I didn't want to live without her? That I would sacrifice whatever I needed to if it meant we could be together?

"You're right," I finally spoke. "I need to tell her as soon as I get back. I don't want her to be wondering either."

Her face lit up like only that of a proud mother. "Excellent! I hoped you'd say that."

"Whyyyy?" I questioned when her grin morphed into something a little more mischievous.

"Earlier today, I took the liberty of changing your flight back to Boston from Sunday to tomorrow morning," she admitted, not even bothering to look guilty. "I assumed our talk would end with you seeing things my way, and then I knew you'd be eager to get back to her but not want to hurt my feelings, so I made the decision easy for you. Oh, and before you see her, you may want to clean-up that whole Grizzly Adams thing you've got going on your face. I'm all for a well-manicured beard, but I'm pretty sure you've got rodents living inside that thing."

Throwing my arms around her, I lifted her feet off the ground in a massive bear hug, purposely rubbing my facial hair all over her cheek. "Thank you, Mom. And I don't care what my sisters say, you're not so bad after all."

Her open palm met the back of my head before I knew what happened and then she muttered, "Still the same little shit," as she stomped off into the house.

The swing session had officially ended.

AFTER A SIX-HOUR winter weather delay, my flight finally landed at Logan International Airport a little after seven-thirty that Friday night. My hopes to talk to Monroe earlier that afternoon before she needed to get ready for the annual Holiday with the Pats black-tie event she was scheduled to attend with Colin were shot, but I wasn't discouraged. I was a man on a mission.

Pulling the tux I'd worn to the Mending Hearts gala in August from the closet, I laid it across the bed and disappeared into the bathroom to quickly wash away the grime I always felt after traveling and to address the disheveled mountain man look I was rocking. Mom may have had a point there as well.

A half-hour later, I was ready to go—clean, combed, and clothed. I did a final check in the mirror, and though I really could've used a haircut too, it was as good as it was going to get. I just hoped it was good enough.

As I grabbed the invitation Monroe had given me off the bar, the vision of her disappointed face when I told her I'd be at my parents' for the week of Christmas and wouldn't be able to make it flashed in my mind. At the time, I'd asked her why she would want me at an event that was for Colin and his teammates, and without hesitation, she replied, "Because I always want you where I am." When she said it, of course it made me feel all good inside, 'cause everyone loves to feel wanted, but I didn't really stop to think about it much past that. Now, I wondered if her words meant more.

It was time to find out.

The taxi ride from my apartment to the New England Aquarium was short, thank God. It didn't give me a chance to talk myself out of what I was about to do. After I paid and tipped the driver, I stood on the curb and stared up at the modern cement and glass structure, praying the nerves in my stomach would calm the fuck down before I found her inside. Untimely vomiting would not help in delivering my message.

A small group of people mingled around outside, smoking and chatting under a canopied pavilion lined with gigantic propane patio heaters as I waited in the short line at the entrance with other latecomers. I purposely trained my gaze downward, not wanting to make eye-contact with anyone. It wasn't as if I'd met many people during my four months in Boston, but I'd heard Monroe mention to Effie she'd given a couple of the ladies from the DCF invites to the party. Plus, I knew Effie and her brother, Seth, whom I'd been introduced to at the football game, would be there as well, so I didn't want to take any chances. All I needed was to find Monroe first, say what I needed to say, and then go from there, depending on her reaction. I knew the time and place weren't ideal, but another thing I'd learned in a previous swing session with my mom is you're never guaranteed a tomorrow. If you got something that needs to be said or done, do it, because you may never get that chance again. This was my chance.

Dabbing my forehead with a handkerchief I brought, I realized I was sweating. A lot. While snow flurries fell around me. In single-digit temperatures. *Don't fucking fail me now, deodorant.*

The doorman accepted the invitation as I entered the underwater fantasy-land, filled with thousands of aquatic life species, both common and exotic, nearly five hundred of New England's most influential people, including the entire Patriot's organization, and the one woman who I loved more than anything—the one I couldn't live without. Striding into the crowded, dimly-lit main exhibit area where makeshift bars and tables dressed in white-linens surrounded a small dance floor, I moved toward the back wall, where I could scan the room and hopefully remain unnoticed.

The sheer number of people jammed into the place was overwhelming. I'd been amazed when Monroe told me the tickets—depending on sponsorship level—ranged from $10,000 to $25,000 a person, which included a four-course meal, where you were guaranteed to be seated with one of the players, and they'd sold out in less than fifteen minutes. Even though the Patriots' organization had selected Mending Hearts as their principal charity to sponsor that year, she'd explained the proceeds from this annual function always went to fund their in-house charitable foundation that supported a variety of smaller non-profits in the area. And evidently, based on the sheer demand for a chance to spend a night wining and dining with the local football team, they were thriving.

I skimmed the sea of black coats and sequined dresses for her and, after my first pass, came up empty. Cursing under my breath, I didn't even notice the provocatively-dressed cocktail waitress when she approached.

"Sir, would you like a drink?" she asked, extending her small round tray in my direction.

With a polite smile, I thanked her and accepted a glass of champagne, hoping it would help relax me. Downing the flute of bubbly, I set it back on her serving tray before she even had a chance to walk away, much to her surprise.

"Another, sir? Or I can get you something a bit stiffer from the bar," she giggled as she blatantly dropped her eyes to my crotch then looked back up at my face, "if you prefer the hard stuff."

Shaking my head, I grinned, embarrassed. "No, thanks, I just needed a little liquid courage. I'm good now."

"Yes, sir," she purred, batting her false eyelashes. "Well, if you need anything at all, just let me know. My name's Alexis."

Not a chance in hell, Alexis. "Thank you again. I'll let you know if I need anything."

She lingered a couple of extra seconds, waiting to see if I'd say anything else, and when I didn't, she thankfully flitted on to the next guest.

After another perusal of the area, where I still didn't spot Monroe, I began to work my way to the opposite corner of the room, in hopes I'd find her before she found me. I skirted around the various football-related silent auction items lining the outer edge of the room that drew a crowd as the fans attempted to win items signed by their heroes, keeping both my eyes and ears open. Her beautiful blonde hair and infectious voice usually stood out in a crowd, but there were just too many people.

Suddenly, the lights flickered then brightened to garner everyone's attention and I spotted Colin along with several other men, who I assumed were his teammates based on size alone, heading toward the stage. As a hush fell over the mass of attendees and everyone stilled, I slunk back into the shadows and waited.

"Good evening, everyone, and thank you all so much for coming out tonight," the star quarterback addressed the room, exuding the same confidence I remembered from the first time I met him. *Funny how I'm not nearly as envious of his life as I was then, knowing what I know now. A part of me actually feels a little bad for the guy, living a lie, because he's afraid of what people would say and think if they knew the truth.*

Too wrapped up in my own thoughts, I missed most of what he said, and before long, everyone was clapping and cheering as the lights dimmed and the music resumed. Once the applause died down, conversations picked up where they left off and the crowd dispersed, leaving Monroe—dead-center of the dance floor, chatting with a small group of people—straight in my line of sight. Dressed in a long, sparkly, jade green gown with her blonde hair piled high on her head, I could only see her from behind, but even that made my pulse race and my dick twitch.

The conversation appeared to dwindle after several minutes, and with her typical poise and grace, Monroe smiled and excused herself from the group. Moving from my left to right, she approached the edge of the room, near one of the hallways that led to another exhibit, and stood on her tiptoes, scanning the area for Colin, I assumed.

"Don't back down now, Saxon," I mumbled to myself as I took off in her direction at a clipped pace.

I hugged the outer perimeter of the room as my gaze remained locked on her, hoping she didn't notice me before I made it to her. Taking a deep breath and a few seconds to pump myself up, I crept up behind her and grabbed both her hands, turning her to face me.

"Oliver?!" she gasped, her green eyes wide and full of disbelief. "What are you—"

With a firm tug, I spun around and headed down the mostly empty hallway, pulling her right behind me. Unsure of exactly where we were going, just seeking a little privacy, my hand shot out and turned the knob of a closed door off to the left, and—*bingo!*—it opened with ease.

"Come on, trust me," I implored when I felt her hesitate to follow me.

Thankfully, she didn't balk and slipped inside the dark room, lit only by a small round window on the back wall. As my eyes quickly adjusted to the lack of light, I realized it was a storage room of sorts, lined with shelves of cleaning supplies, toilet paper, and paper towels. Perfect.

"What's going on? Why did you come back early? Is everything okay with your family?" she whispered, concern heavy in her voice, once the door was shut and we were facing each other.

Smiling so big I was afraid my face would crack, I cradled her jaw in my trembling hands and lowered my mouth to hers, claiming her like a man possessed. "I love you, Monroe," I murmured against her lips mid-kiss. "I love you so fucking much. I'm sorry I didn't tell you before, but I didn't want you to go another minute without knowing for sure."

A soft laugh bubbled up from her as she leaned back slightly to peer up into my eyes. "You flew back two days early just so you could tell me you love me?"

"And to tell you that I don't want to be without you." I nodded and stole another kiss. "Ever." Another kiss. "I know it's gonna take some time to figure things out, but whatever we have to do, I'm willing. I want us to be a *we* forever."

Throwing her arms around my neck, she rubbed her nose back and forth against mine. "I love you too, Ollie. So damn much. I can't promise it'll be easy, especially at first, but as long as I get you in the end, it will be worth it. *We are* worth it."

My hands fell to her waist as I buried my face in her neck, pressing my lips to her delicate skin and inhaling her fresh, citrusy scent. "God, I've missed you, beautiful girl. When can you come over so I can properly show you how much?"

Pressing her body against mine, Monroe moaned while threading her fingers through my hair. "Tomorrow," she breathed, "but I'm not sure I can wait that long."

"Don't tempt me, Rizzo," I growled in a low voice. "I only have so much self-control when I'm around you."

Another little whimper escaped as she drew my earlobe in between her teeth and flicked her tongue across the sensitive flesh, and my resolve snapped. Whirling her around to face one of the metal shelves, I placed her hands up on the ledge and made fast work of lifting her dress up around her waist from behind. Hastily, I freed my cock, throbbing and desperate, from the burden of my black dress pants, and as I pushed her soaked silky panties to the side, I slid through the wetness until I was buried deep inside her.

Arching her back like a cat in heat, she looked over her shoulder at me with pleading eyes and purred, "Please, Ollie. I need you to show me."

"Fuuuuuck," I groaned, the overwhelming pleasure spreading throughout my entire body. Taking her like this in a storage closet had not been my initial goal when I'd shown up, but I sure as hell wasn't going to tell her no.

What happened next can only be described as frenzied and feverish, reckless and rash, and the single most arousing experience of my life. We came together minutes after we began, a firework-producing explosion where we panted I love yous until our bodies sagged with exhaustion. Once we could both breathe normally and our hearts had returned to normal activity, I cleaned her up with one of the handy paper towels nearby, which led to us both cracking up over what we'd just done. For two people with doctorate degrees, it probably wasn't our smartest decision, but gratefully, we hadn't gotten caught.

"I'll see you tomorrow morning. And in case you forget before then, I love you, Monroe," I said, giving her one last kiss and swatting her ass as she sauntered toward the door.

"I love you too, Ollie," she replied before exiting back into the party, looking more beautiful than ever bathed in the moonlight with her entire face glowing. "See you then."

I waited a few minutes after she left, just in case anyone was loitering around the hallway and had seen her emerge from the room. When I felt the coast was clear, I straightened my jacket and finger-combed my hair down then swung the door open and stepped into the hall. Only to find myself face-to-face with Effie.

THE PETITE BLONDE'S interest was piqued the moment she'd noticed him enter the aquarium. Positive he wasn't supposed to return to Boston for another two days since she'd made the flight reservations herself, she not only wondered why he was back, but why he was there. If she'd learned nothing else over the last couple of months, she knew that Oliver Saxon was not a fan of football, nor was he one to care about mixing and mingling with high society, which only made his appearance at the gala even more perplexing. Unless her suspicions all this time had been right . . .

Moving swiftly, she followed him around the main exhibit area undetected, watching as he scanned the crowd, obviously looking for someone. He kept close to the wall, as if he too wanted to remain hidden while slinking around the perimeter of the room. When the lights flickered and Colin Cassidy took the stage with a couple of his teammates, Oliver stilled, causing her to do the same to keep a marginable distance between them.

Impatiently waiting for the standard thank-you-for-coming-out-to-support-us speech to end, the attractive young woman attempted to follow his line of sight, but due to the sheer number of people, she couldn't. Frustrated, she tiptoed closer, hoping to get a better vantage point; however, just as she did, a hand shot out from behind her and caught her elbow.

"There you are, honey. Your dad and I have been looking everywhere for you," her mother greeted her with a refined smile and an air kiss to each cheek. "Have you seen your brother yet? I heard he brought a date with him. Let's hope it's not that same girl he brought to the Silverstein's Christmas party."

"Hello, Mother," she replied politely as she returned her sophisticated welcome, knowing she'd never hear the end of it if she didn't act in the polished, cultured manner she'd been raised. "I did see him earlier, but that's been an hour ago or so. And the date's name is Miranda, not the same one from the party. She seems very lovely. I'm sure you'll approve."

The older woman nodded, but remained unconvinced. "I won't hold my breath," she murmured before waving at someone else she knew. "Oh look, there's Patty Powell. I'm going to go say hi before she's mobbed again. If I don't run into you again tonight, I'll see you at the game on Sunday."

Fighting the urge to roll her eyes at her irritating mother, the young blonde hastily turned back to where Oliver had been standing, only to find the space empty. *Shit! Shit! Shit!* Frantically skimming the hundreds of heads in the room, she searched for his distinguishable long, dark locks, but came up empty. Back on the move in her four-inch, red-soled stilettos, her gaze landed across the room on the gorgeous, built-like-a-God quarterback who'd starred in her dreams long before he did on the football field. She paused briefly as their eyes met, and just like it did every time he flashed her that panty-melting grin, she felt like she was on top of the world.

He *is why this is important*, she reminded herself. If what she speculated to be true for some time now was actually happening, then all she would need to do is to provide him with the proof, and then Colin Cassidy would be all hers for the taking.

Focused on the end goal, she tossed her long hair over her shoulder and set off to find wherever Oliver Saxon had disappeared to.

And who he was with.

chapter twenty-eight

"as we made love,
you forgot my lips were
a loaded gun that would
destroy you
and my tongue,
the gun powder residue
leftover on your hips.

I walk down your body
in a sweat of destruction
and it's all I can do to
sift through the rubble
of every previous fuck
that couldn't handle
a barrel to the head."
–Christopher Poindexter & Marisa B. Crane

MONROE

"I WISH YOU didn't have to go," Oliver complained from my bed, where he lounged in only his boxers intently watching me pack my overnight bag.

It was a little after eight in the morning on Sunday, and I was getting ready for my eleven-thirty flight to Denver to watch Colin play later that evening in the AFC Championship game. Thankfully, the two previous playoff games had been at home, so I hadn't had to travel before then, and even though it was only for one night, neither Oliver nor I were very happy about my going. He'd kept me up into the wee hours of the morning, using his mouth and hands in all kinds of pleasurable ways to try to convince me to stay, but ultimately, he knew I had no choice.

Sighing, I dropped the travel-sized toiletries I was carrying from the bathroom into the bag then crawled up onto the mattress next to him, resting my head on his bare chest as he held me flush against him. "I wish I didn't either, but tomorrow afternoon, I'll be back in your arms, and it'll be like I was never gone."

He grunted while playfully swatting my butt. "I know you won't say it, but God I hope they finally lose today. I'm ready for this all to be over with so we can finally just be us."

I pressed my lips to his left pec and reveled in the sensation of his heart beating against my mouth, almost as if I could taste his love. "Soon, Ollie," I promised in a hushed murmur. "It'll all end soon."

Truth be told, I was cheering for the Patriots to win for a couple of reasons. First, I truly wanted Colin to be able to live out one of his lifelong dreams of playing in a Super Bowl, and hopefully, coming out victorious. It was something he'd talked about since we first met—getting the opportunity to play the game he loved on the biggest possible stage—and I knew how much a chance like that would mean to him. Regardless of my feelings for Oliver, I still loved Colin and wanted the absolute best for him always.

The second reason was a little more selfish than the first. Aware of the high Colin would be riding if his team happened to bring home the prized Vince Lombardi trophy, I thought the much-needed sit-down I was planning with my husband would go over a little smoother if he'd just won, softening the blow of my confession. Colin would no doubt be hurt that I'd been involved with Oliver for over two months without telling him, but since we talked about him before, I didn't think he'd be all that shocked. It was the whole asking for a divorce thing I knew wasn't going to go over well. We had sworn to each other "to the very end," and I still had every intention of keeping that promise as his best friend, confidant, and support system, but I wanted a real relationship with Oliver, and I couldn't have that being legally married to someone else.

"I know, beautiful girl," he assured me, kissing the top of my head, "but if you plan on making your flight in time, I'd suggest you get off this bed before I strip off all those clothes you just put on, tie you to the headboard, and keep you here forever."

"In your wildest dr—"

Before I could get the words out, his fingers descended upon my ribcage and an all-out tickling war ensued. After five minutes of me squealing, squirming, and struggling under the mercy of his relentless fingers, I surrendered and collapsed into a fit of giggles. Another five and I was finally able to breathe normally, and just as I leaned over to kiss the man I loved more than I ever thought possible, my phone buzzed atop the nightstand where it sat on the charger.

Stretching across the mattress, I glanced at the number on the screen as I grabbed it, and instantly, my heart dropped. The only reason someone would be calling me from Suffolk County Children's Home this early on a Sunday morning would be because something bad had happened to one of my four. Before I ever answered the call, I knew which one it was.

"Hello, this is Monroe," I said around the thick knot of dread in the back of my throat, my eyes trained on Oliver's face.

"Monroe, it's Dr. Prince," the familiar voice greeted me, her tone solemn. "Sorry to bother you so early. I wasn't even sure if you were in town or not, but I knew you'd want to know as soon as possible with something this serious."

I choked back a sob, unconsciously grabbing Oliver's hand and squeezing. "Know what? How serious? Who?"

"Heather found JoJo unconscious in her bed around seven this morning, and once the morning advisor was notified, she discovered any empty bottle of Tylenol PM in her nightstand, as well as a Ziploc baggie with some other pills in it too," she explained. "I hate to speculate, but it appears to be a suicide attempt. She was rushed to Boston Children's Hospital, which is where I am with her now, and after they performed a quick evaluation in the ER, they're moving her to ICU. It's not looking good."

An onslaught of emotions surged through me, and unfortunately, anger surfaced first. "Why in the hell am I just now finding out about this, Jessica? I should've been contacted as soon as the 911 call ended. She's my fucking kid, and you're telling me you didn't think to let me know until the point they admitted her to Intensive Care?!"

"Monroe, I know you're upset—"

"Hell yes, I'm upset!" I screamed, jumping off the bed with Oliver hot on my heels. "But I don't have time to list all the ways right now, because I needed to be on my way to the hospital *a fucking hour ago!*"

I didn't even bother ending the call as I slung the phone across the room and watched it shatter into hundreds of pieces against the wall. Spinning around, I found Oliver already dressed in the jeans and thermal he'd worn over the night before and putting his shoes on, acting before I said a word to him.

"Grab your keys and boots, baby. Let's go," he announced with a stern expression. "I'm driving your car, and you can catch me up with what's going on as you give me directions to the hospital."

"But—" I tried to argue, but he was having nothing of it.

Framing my face with his hands, he lowered his forehead to mine and pinned me with his arresting gaze. "There's no way I'm letting you get behind a wheel in the state you're in, so don't even think about fighting me on this. Not to mention, I love you too damn much to allow you to face this alone. Remember . . . you and me? We're a *we.*"

IN RECORD TIME from my house to the hospital, the second the transmission shifted to park, Oliver and I fled the car and sprinted inside to the ICU floor. Words were scarce once I'd filled him in with what had happened with JoJo, though the steady stream of tears hadn't stopped since I'd gotten the call. So many questions raced through my mind. *Why would she do this? What happened since I'd seen her just the day before at lunch and she seemed so happy? Had the progress I thought I was making with her all been a farce? Did someone hurt her?*

But unfortunately, I had no answers.

A large U-shaped nurse's station awaited us when we exited the elevators onto the seventh floor, and without hesitation, I marched straight up to the first woman in scrubs I saw.

"Hi, I'm Monroe Cassidy, here for JoJo Merritt. Can you tell me where she is? Is she okay?" I blurted out, my good manners gone by the wayside.

As if she had all the time in the world, as if kids weren't fighting for their lives just beyond the locked double doors behind her, she smiled and nodded then glanced down at the computer screen in front of her. "Good morning, Ms. Cassidy. I see you have been included on the list of authorized visitors for Miss Merritt, so I'm just going to need to make a copy of your ID and then I can buzz you through."

Reaching down to grab my wallet from my purse, I gasped and stumbled backward when I realized I didn't have it with me.

"What is it? What's wrong?" Oliver asked from behind me.

"My purse!" I cried, my eyes wide with horror. "I forgot my purse at home in our rush to leave. I need my ID."

"Okay, okay, just calm down," he soothed, placing his warm, strong hand at the small of my back. "Let's ask if they can make an exception just this once. Surely someone in this place knows who you are and can vouch for you."

I nodded mindlessly as my chest began to painfully constrict, but said nothing. Oliver approached the nurse and explained the situation to her, and even though she kept the smile plastered across her face, she shook her head and said, "I'm sorry, but it's hospital policy. No one is allowed into the ICU area unless we have a copy of their identification in the patient's chart."

"But she's Monroe Cassidy! Her husband is Colin Cassidy for

chrissakes. You have to know she is who she says she is," he contended, firmly pounding his fist on the counter with annoyance.

"I'm sorry, sir, but I don't care if she's the First Lady. These rules are non-negotiable for the safety of our patients. Once Ms. Cassidy has her ID, I'll be happy to escort her back and alert Miss Merritt's charge nurse of her arrival."

Defeated at the finality of her words, I clung to Oliver's arm and bawled into his chest, my ability to think straight shot.

"Shh, baby," he whispered while leading me over to the deserted waiting room. "Don't worry; we'll get you back there shortly. You stay here in case Dr. Prince or anyone else comes out, and I'll run to your house to get your purse. Do you know where it is?"

I cried harder. "I don't want you to go. Please don't leave me here by myself. What if she dies? What if they come out and say she's gone? I need you here with me."

Oliver held me close to his side as he dug his phone out of his pocket. "What about Effie? Didn't you mention she or Seth had a key to your place?"

"Seth does, but I don't know his number off the top of my head. It was programmed in the phone that I destroyed."

He thought for a minute, then said, "Okay, well let me call Effie and see if she can get ahold of him or get the key. Where's your purse at when they get inside?"

"In my closet, hanging on the hook in the closet," I blubbered, not even thinking about specifying Seth needed to be the one to go in my closet.

Absentmindedly kissing the top of my head, he squeezed my hand for support and then made the call. Less than thirty minutes later, with no more information than we had before, Effie and Seth emerged from the elevators, looking like they'd both freshly rolled out of bed, but most importantly, she was carrying my purse.

"Oh, my God, Monroe, I'm so sorry! I can't believe this. Tell me what I can do to help!" she exclaimed as she handed me the small black cross-body then glanced inquisitively over at Oliver.

Seth spoke with his actions first, wrapping me in a big bear hug and kissing the top of my head. "Please, Roe girl, talk to us. How can we help?" he urged after releasing me.

"I uh," I sniffled and wiped my wet cheeks with the back of my hand, "I haven't called Colin yet. I threw my phone and it broke, and I just haven't thought about it. Plus, he doesn't need this today. I don't want him to worry about anything but the game."

"Your flight to Denver was scheduled for eleven-thirty, right?" Effie asked as she grabbed her phone and started typing on the screen. "Let me get that cancelled for you and then we can decide what to do about Colin. He'll be just as worried if you don't show, so I think you need to let him know something."

Nodding, I stepped back and rummaged through my purse for my wallet. "Okay, I'm gonna go back there now and see what I can find out. Do you guys mind waiting here for a little bit? I'd rather wait to call him once I know more about her condition."

The three of them all agreed, and after I provided my license and signed the visitor log, I made my way back to where JoJo was, praying the entire way. Dr. Prince was the only one in the room with her when I quietly opened the door and let myself in. Gratefully, it appeared as if she'd already forgiven me for my outburst on the phone earlier as she rushed to greet me.

"Monroe, you're here! Thank God! I've been trying to call you!" she whisper-shouted as she enfolded her arms around me. "I'm so sorry about everything this morning. It was all so chaotic. I should've called you first."

Waving off her apology, I shook my head. "Don't worry about it. I shouldn't have spoken to you that way. I just freaked out and my phone took the brunt of it. Now tell me what you know so far."

For the next several minutes, she rattled off a bunch of medical terminology and explained what all of the machines, wires, and tubes were for as I stared down at the frail, lost, comatose young girl who I'd grown to love like my own child over the past few years, all boiling down to the fact that JoJo had purposely swallowed a toxic amount of acetaminophen and a handful of Xanax, from what the toxicology report showed, in a blatant attempt to end her own life. And though she'd been unsuccessful at her ultimate goal for the time being, she'd managed to seriously mess up all kinds of things internally, most importantly her liver and kidneys, which were failing.

Devastated doesn't even begin to describe the anguish and sorrow I felt that morning. I was so angry, so hurt, so confused. How could she do this? Why did she feel that was the only answer? Had I not done enough?

"Don't blame yourself for this, Monroe," she whispered as if she could read my thoughts. "It's the natural reaction we all have, but her decision to do this was hers, and it had nothing to do with what you did or didn't do. The doctor will be back soon with more information on what the next step is as they try to detoxify her body and what we can expect. I need to step outside to make a few phone calls, and I'm sure you'd like a few minutes alone."

As promised, Dr. Prince left the room for about ten minutes, leaving me alone with JoJo, and the entire time, I wept uncontrollably. Seeing her like that, lifeless in the hospital bed with all of those needles stuck in her arms, a tube down her throat, and a respirator helping her breathe, simply proved to be too much for me. I couldn't bear the thought of losing her. Not like this.

Once the director of the DCF returned, I excused myself to go back out to the waiting room, where Oliver and Seth were huddled up talking and Effie stood off to the side on her phone. As soon as Oliver saw me turn the corner, he jumped up and came straight to me, wrapping me in his strong arms, offering me comfort the only way he knew how. I repeated to them the information I'd been given and my plan to stay at the hospital for the foreseeable future, and as much as I knew he didn't want to make the call, Seth dialed up Colin and explained to him what had happened, in which he then asked to talk to me.

"I'm so sorry, Monroe. I wish I could be there for you right now, sweetheart. I love you so much," he said as soon as I got on the phone, triggering another round of waterworks as I not only thought about JoJo's critical state, but also about the guilt that weighed on me for keeping Oliver a secret from him.

For a long time, Colin was what made my life worth living. He was my happy place, my shining star. Colin loved me when I didn't know how to let someone love me and had never let me down. I never set out to hurt him, but at this point, it seemed inevitable.

"I'll be okay," I assured him once the tears let up. "Please don't worry about me. You need to concentrate on the game today. I'll be here when you get back tomorrow. Just say a little prayer for JoJo."

After we talked a little longer and said our goodbyes, the phone call ended and I thanked Seth and Effie for everything, letting them know they didn't need to hang around the hospital. In typical Seth-fashion, he hugged and kissed my cheek, insisting if I needed anything else to let him know, but strangely, before he stepped away, Seth smiled at Oliver and reiterated, "If she needs anything at all, no matter how small, you call me. You've got my number now. She's not to be alone, like we talked about."

Oliver tipped his chin in agreement and extended his arm in Seth's direction. "You have my word, man. Thanks again for saving us with the purse, and I'll make sure she gets home safely tonight."

My already-frazzled mind couldn't quite comprehend what that was all about, and before I could shoot either of them a questioning look, Effie appeared in front of me, looping her arm around my neck and pulling me into a hug. A very un-Effie-like thing to do.

"Me too, Monroe. Whatever you or Oliver needs," she repeated her brother's sentiments. Moving as if she was about to leave, she stopped and turned around then smiled hesitantly. "Oh hey, I saw your ticket for the game today sitting on your bar when I grabbed your purse earlier. Do I need to do anything with it? Contact the Pat's front office or anything?"

"No." I shook my head, having not even thought about anything as miniscule as that with the severity of everything else going on. "I don't think there's anything they can do, unless you know someone who's going to be in Denver tonight."

Her eyes flickered with hope. "Actually, I was toying with the idea of catching a last-minute flight out there. I just checked online and there are seats available on the flight you were scheduled for. That is, if you don't need me for anything around here today or tomorrow."

"Yes, of course, you can use it. I'm sure Colin would appreciate having at least one of us there to support him," I replied with a faint smile. "Just get Seth's house key and let yourself in to get it then return it to him later. I've got several extra jerseys hanging in my closet if you want to borrow one of those too."

"Thank you so much!" The hope in her eyes transformed into giddiness. "You have no idea what this means."

chapter
twenty-nine

"love is many things and
sometimes we are never
really sure if it even
exists, but all I know
is that if you were to
show me her soul
in a photograph
I wouldn't even ask
to see the other"
–Christopher Poindexter

OLIVER

I KEPT MY promise to Seth and didn't leave Monroe's side the entire day. Over fourteen straight hours at the hospital—a roller coaster of ups and downs as JoJo's body continued to fight through the drug poisoning—we were both drained and depleted by the time I shifted the car into park inside her garage a little before midnight. Walking from her car to the door was like a trip through quicksand wearing combat boots, and as my mind began fantasizing the pillow-top mattress waiting in her room, my stomach roared to life, reminding me that I still needed to eat something.

"Got it. First stop, food," she teased as she unlocked the door and stepped inside. "Though I hate to tell you I don't have any of that junk food you like in the house."

"I'm so hungry I probably won't even taste whatever it is I eat.

I just need to nourish my body enough that it allows me to sleep at least eight hours," I replied as I fell in step behind her down the tiled hallway that led to the main area of the home.

Only the second time I'd been to her house, the night before being the first, I was still a little in awe of the place as we traipsed through the living room and breakfast area to the gourmet kitchen. I couldn't believe when she'd told me that Colin had designed and decorated the majority of the rooms, because like most people—or what I assumed most people thought—I didn't visualize a big, macho NFL player dabbling in the world of interior design during the off-season, but apparently I needed to stop judging books by their covers.

"BLT good with you?" Monroe asked as she unloaded an assortment of ingredients from the fridge to the countertop. "I probably won't be working my ass out anytime in the near future, so I might as well eat some bacon to really make it fun."

"Absolutely," I agreed, strolling up behind her and palming her butt cheeks. "Plus, I plan to work this ass out plenty in the near future, so no worries, beautiful girl. You should make it double bacon."

With a soft chuckle, she rolled her eyes. "You're so silly, Ollie."

The sound of her laughter, as light as it was, swelled in my chest after having watched her cry on and off throughout the day, and I couldn't resist the urge to scoop her up in my arms and kiss her senseless. It had killed me to watch her so distraught and unable to do anything to fix it, and then on top of that, because we were in public all day, I had to limit the amount of physical comforting and affection I could show her in case someone was watching.

After the close call with Effie at both the MH house and at the holiday party, Monroe and I had made an extra effort to appear as platonic as possible while in public—though the more in love we fell with each other, the harder it became. Effie never mentioned anything about either of the occurrences, as I'd managed to make up a story on the spot about why I'd returned to Boston early when I'd ran into her at the aquarium that night, but afterward, there were times when Monroe and I would be talking about work stuff and I'd notice her eavesdropping from another room or eyeing us suspiciously. I never said anything to Monroe, because I didn't want to cause a rift between her and her assistant. Besides, once everything was worked out with Colin, Effie would find out eventually.

We just needed to hold out for two more weeks . . . because, of course, the Patriot's had won in Denver earlier that night. It was as if the more I rooted for them to lose, the better they became, and my negative energy had propelled them straight to the Super Bowl. *I knew there was a reason I didn't like sports before all this.*

Once I'd pressed my lips to every square inch of her face and neck, I finally lowered her back to the ground to let her resume the sandwich-making, which I assisted with by slicing tomatoes and washing lettuce. We ate without much talking, the weight of the unknown with JoJo still hanging heavily over our heads, and after the mess was cleaned up, Monroe decided to boil some water for a nighttime herbal tea she claimed would help us rest better. I had no doubt the second my head hit the pillow, I'd be out like a light, but if she wanted one and thought it would help, I was more than happy to appease her and drink some of it.

"Come here, love. Let me try to massage some of that tension out while we wait." I motioned for her to follow me into the living room where I plopped down on the oversized couch and she subsequently sat cross-legged on the floor in front of me.

She melted into my firm touch while I kneaded deep circles in the taut muscles around her neck, shoulders, and back. The small moans escaping her barely-parted lips involuntarily prompted a rise behind the zipper of my jeans, and by the time my fingers inched their way up into her hair, working her scalp and behind her ears, my dick was rock-hard and throbbing.

Leaning back into the pressure, her head rested right up against my crotch, and although my initial intentions were solely focused on helping her relax, my shaft twitched at her closeness. I groaned and shifted my legs in an attempt to reposition her, but instead of moving away from my erection, she turned around to face me, pushing up on her knees so that her mouth hovered directly over my cock.

"Looks like you need some stress relief too," she murmured, allowing her lips to graze across the raised denim, her emerald eyes heavy with a mixture of exhaustion and arousal.

I hissed in response, my self-control no match for the breath-taking sight she was, kneeling in front of me, bathed in the irides-cent moonlight streaming in from the glass patio doors. "Fuck, Monroe," I rasped as I clung to the last few threads of resolve I had left. "You're so goddamn beautiful. You have no idea what you do to me."

"Then show me," she whispered while her mouth traced the outline of my bulge, our gazes locked on each other's the entire time. "Help me forget today. Even if it's just for a little while. Make love to me, Ollie."

An equal-part combination of love and lust stormed through me and I snapped, succumbing to my carnal needs and the irresist-ible desire to please her. Whatever my Rizzo wanted, I gave her.

We lunged at each other, colliding in a feverish, frenzied kiss, complete with tangling tongues and gnashing teeth. The over-whelming fatigue I'd felt only minutes prior was replaced with sensual adrenaline jetting through my veins. Our impatient hands tugged, yanked, and jerked at our clothes until we were both fully undressed and left with no barriers to explore each other's body.

Scooting back on the sofa, I pulled her down on top of me so that she was straddling my lap and her slick warmth was nestled snug against my cock. The shrill whistle of the kettle pierced the air as I drew one of her nipples into my mouth, sucking hard and flicking the rosy bud with my tongue, but neither of us cared a damn thing about the tea any longer. Monroe closed her eyes and whimpered, knotting her fingers in my hair while grinding against my length.

"Yes . . . yes . . . yes," she mumbled over and over, losing herself in our connection. "That's it. Feels so good."

As I switched the attention of my mouth to her other nipple, I grabbed hold of her hips and lifted her up so that I could lower her down onto my shaft. Watching her ride me while I played with her tits had to be in the top three of my most favorite things to do ever, but just as my tip glided through her slippery folds and found the heat of her core, the neighbor's dog began barking and growling out back, loudly and persistently. I tried to ignore it at first, focusing on the exquisite woman in front of me and all of the ways I could make her feel incredible, but after a couple of minutes of the high-pitched yapping, I stilled and shook my head with a frustrated chuckle.

We both peered outside the glass doors to see if we saw anything unusual, and I asked, "Any chance he'll stop anytime soon?"

"Doubtful. All the people out celebrating the win probably have him all riled up." She smiled and pressed a soft kiss to the corner of my mouth. "But we shouldn't be able to hear him in my room. Let's go upstairs."

"What about the tea?" I questioned, glancing toward the kitchen.

With a wicked smirk, she wiggled her ass and whispered, "Screw the tea. You're all I need to put me to sleep."

Pushing to my feet with her wrapped securely around me, I didn't need to be told twice. I stopped briefly to turn the stovetop off, and then less than a minute later, I was flat on my back in her bed, gazing up as she bounced up and down on my shaft and rolled her hips in perfect little circles. The only noises to be heard were the moans, grunts, and pleadings from the two of us as we chased our release and climaxed together, breathlessly and magnificently. Afterward, I cleaned us both up and ran downstairs to grab our clothes strewn about the living room then crawled back into her bed and snuggled her as close to me as humanly possible, reminding her of how much I loved her.

We fell asleep shortly thereafter, only to be awakened a handful of hours later to the sound of someone pounding relentlessly on the door downstairs.

chapter
thirty

"i wanted what we had together to
burst into a display of iridescent
shooting stars, but we all know
how piercing the battle of wants
and happenings can be.

in the rubble i became,
i thought;

'love is just as much
of a poison as it is
a victory.'"
–Christopher Poindexter

MONROE

"WHAT IN THE world are you doing here so early? And why are
you at the backdoor?" I grumbled as I opened the French doors to
let a distraught-looking Seth inside.

Having only thrown on a silky robe in my haste to discover
who in the hell had been banging on the door at the early morning
hour, I wrapped my arms tightly around my chest to conceal myself as best as possible while I waited for him to explain his unannounced visit.

"Effie still has my key or I would've let myself in, and it's time to wake up. We have a problem," he replied tersely, glancing in the direction of the stairs then back at me. His eyes burned something fierce. "Where is Oliver? Is he still here?"

Confused and concerned, I cocked my head to the side and narrowed my gaze on him. "W-what?" I sputtered. "What are you talking about, Seth? What's going on? What problem?"

Unzipping his coat, he retrieved a handful of daily tabloids he had stuffed inside it and threw them down on the coffee table, a deep scowl etched into his face. "That's what I'm talking about, Monroe," he gritted out through clenched teeth, pointing down at the picture on the front page of all of them. "That's the fucking problem!"

My entire body began to shake and I fell to my knees as a blown-up photograph of me and Oliver from the night before, naked and intimate on the couch, in crystal-clear focus, stared back up at me. With my attention directed straight at the camera, there was no doubt it was me in the picture, and Oliver, who had my breast captured in his hands and his mouth on my neck, wasn't facing the lens, but his eyes were cut in the direction of the hidden photographer as well. After reading the first two headlines, "Sundance Wife Celebrates Pat's Win Without Clutch" and "Cassidy Wins on Field, Loses in Life," my vision blurred with a surge of tears spilling over my bottom lid and down my face.

Seth dropped down next to me and circled his arms around my shoulders, pulling me into his chest. "Baby girl, I know you're upset, but I need you to gather yourself right now. We've got a shitload of damage control to do right now. I take it you haven't heard from Colin?"

I pulled away slightly to answer him, but I was unable to stop my body from shivering, even though my face and stomach both felt like they were on fire. I couldn't believe it. After the shitty hand I'd been dealt when I was a kid, to persevere and finally find love and be comfortable with my sexuality, all to be violated once again . . . intimate photos of me, moments only meant to be shared with one person, viewed by millions. It had to be a terrible nightmare. The humiliation alone threatened to suffocate me.

"Monroe, stay with me." He waved his hand in front of my face to get my attention. "Colin hasn't tried to call that you know of?"

"No, I was going to get a new phone this morning. We were at the hospital all day yesterday, so I didn't get a chance to replace the one I broke."

"Where's Oliver? Still here?"

"I'm right here." Oliver's agitated voice cut across the living room as he emerged from the staircase in his rumpled t-shirt and jeans, clipping at a fast pace toward me on his bare feet. "What in the hell's going on? Why is she hysteric—" He stopped dead in his tracks the moment he saw the magazines, his unbelieving eyes swinging from the photos to me, then back to the photos. "Holy shit."

Seth stood and allowed Oliver to take his place next to me, cradling my body against his. "Holy shit is right. I went for a run first thing this morning and saw those outside the first newsstand I passed. When you check your phone, you'll see I tried calling you, but I figured you guys were passed out cold after yesterday, so I sprinted straight back home and headed over here."

Oliver and I remained speechless. It was if my brain refused to believe the black-and-white evidence lying right in front of me. I didn't know what to say or do. My world was crumbling down around me and I couldn't move.

"Okay, guys, we've got three separate issues we need to deal with," Seth continued, thankfully taking the lead. "I'm assuming you haven't told Colin?"

"Hold on, man. I know we've got a lot to talk about, but give us a minute or two to catch our breath," Oliver clipped.

Whispering sweet sentiments about how much he loved me and how we'd get through everything together, Oliver rocked me back and forth in his arms until I was able to somewhat get my shit together.

"I was waiting until the end of the season so I didn't add to the stress of everything else he had going on with you guys and then the injury," I eventually answered Seth's question as I looked up at him. "After he came back from Miami, he practically moved into the team facility, and now they just keep winning, prolonging it."

"You don't need to explain anything to me, Roe," he assured me, holding his hands up in surrender. "I get why you haven't, and you also know how I feel about the whole situation. I just needed to know what level of pissed-offness we're gonna be dealing with when he gets home . . . which is at what time exactly?"

"I think the team plane is scheduled to land early this afternoon, around one or two," I replied.

Seth began pacing the floor, scrubbing his hands over his face. "Right, okay then. So back to the three issues. First is dealing with an enraged, completely irrational, ready-to-turn-into-the-Incredible-Hulk Colin when he gets home. Second, we need to figure out how someone was able to get that picture from your backyard. We can call the security monitoring service and get the video feed from last night. If you know about what time this was taken, that'll help. It can't undo the damage that's been done, but if you can identify who took it and have evidence he was trespassing, you can press charges."

"What's the third?" I asked.

He looked over at Oliver and frowned. "Figuring out how to get him out of here with the media already camped out in the front," he said solemnly.

"In the front?!" I shouted at the same time Oliver exclaimed, "I'm not going anywhere!"

The pacing stopped and Seth glowered at both of us. "Yes, out front," he answered me first. "What did you expect? Your face is plastered on the front page of every daily in print and on every news channel you turn to, locally and nationally."

"But—" I tried to interject, but was immediately shot down.

"No *but* anything! This is a huge fucking story, Monroe. Your husband is the starting quarterback for one of the teams in the up-coming Super Bowl, and last night, while he was off busy winning the city an AFC Championship, you were banging your coworker in your house, using a sick kid as an excuse to stay here with your lover. The whole story is right here." He picked up one of the papers and hit it with his other hand. "Somehow, they knew all of it . . . about JoJo and everything. They're going to massacre both of you, your families. Mending Hearts is going to be called into question. I know you're in shock right now, but I need you to realize how serious this is."

Turning his attention to Oliver, he shook his head. "I know you want to stay with her. I can see that you love her and you don't want her to face this shit alone, but you can't help her here. She's gotta do this with Colin, however they decide to approach it. You need to alert your family of what's about to happen, because now that they have your name, it won't take them long to start staking out your place too. Take them on a vacation or something, the farther away the better, and do it fast. "

"I appreciate the advice, and I'm sure you know a lot more about this stuff than I do, but I'm not leaving her," Oliver contended, squeezing my hand the entire time he spoke. "I'll tell my family to leave, fine, but I'm not going anywhere. I knew the risks before I fell in love with her."

Seth stalked over to the couch and sat down, lowering his eye level to ours where we knelt on the floor. "Listen to me, Oliver, man. Please," he implored. "I'm not sure what all you know about her and Colin's relationship, but obviously you know it's not a marriage in the normal sense, 'cause you'd be a real fucking asshole if you thought it was and you were sleeping with some guy's wife. And I'm pretty sure you're not a real fucking asshole, because Monroe wouldn't like you if you were, and I have a pretty good inkling she loves you as much as you love her. So with all that being said, I'm interested in keeping you alive for my girl Monroe's sake here, but I can promise you, if you are in this house when Colin gets home, he will kill you. He may not mean to. He probably just wants to hurt you really, *really* bad, but he's a strong motherfucker, and if he gets his hands on you, you're a dead man. And then, I'm gonna have four issues to worry about instead of just three, and I really don't feel like adding murder to the list today. So for the sake of every-one involved, please allow me to somehow sneak you out of this house and then get your ass on a plane to Mexico, or Puerto Rico, or where-the-fuck-ever as quickly as possible. It's the only way any of this has any chance of working out. Please trust me."

Oliver twisted toward me, cupping my face in his hands and resting his forehead on mine. "Monroe, what do you want me to do? I don't want to leave your side, but I'll do whatever you want."

The hope swimming in his eyes gutted me. He wanted me to tell him to stay, and I wanted nothing more than to be able to say those words to him. But I couldn't. And it fucking killed me to hurt him.

"I'm so sorry, Ollie, but Seth's right," I rasped, my voice crack-ing. "I need to talk to Colin one-on-one. He deserves that from me."

"That's fine. Talk to him without me, but don't ask me to leave the city. I need to be here for you," he beseeched.

Placing a gentle kiss on his mouth, I smiled sadly. "I want you here; you know I do. But me asking you to stay is selfish, and I can't do that. I won't."

"Don't do *this*!" he hissed. "We knew this wasn't gonna be easy, and the first roadblock we hit, you just want to send me packing? I thought we were in this together?"

"We are! And I'm not sending you packing! At least not per-manently!" I scooted back, frustration setting in as hot tears stung my eyes and splashed on my lap. "Please, Oliver, I'm begging you not to make this harder than it already is. Setting aside the incom-prehensible level of mortification I feel, and focus on the fact that the entire world currently thinks I used a little girl—who is still ly-ing in a hospital bed fighting for her life—as a pretext to stay home and be a cheating slut behind my husband's back. That doesn't even take into account the fallout Allison and Mending Hearts is going to have because of this, and don't forget about your staff and kids at the Chicago house. I'm sure it won't be long before they hear you referred to as a home-wrecker, among a slew of other nasty things, on TV or see it on social media. And when they start talking bad about you, I'm gonna lose it . . ." I paused, reaching out to tenderly touch his cheek. "This isn't just a roadblock, baby. There's a mountain range sitting in front of us, and right now, we need to focus on meeting on the other side."

Defeat washed over his handsome face as he stood up. "All right, if that's what you want, I'll go." Turning to Seth, he nodded grudgingly. "Let me get my shoes and stuff from upstairs. Just tell me what to do."

Twenty minutes later, Seth had devised a plan to sneak Oliver out undetected, and after a single kiss and one last "I love you," the love of my life was gone. And I had no idea when I'd see or talk to him again.

chapter thirty-one

"nothing brings
to life
again
a forgotten
memory
like fragrance"
–Christopher Poindexter

OLIVER

"WHEN YOU TOLD me she had things tying her to Boston, I didn't think you meant *a husband!*" my mom shouted through the phone before even saying hello, clearly having either seen or heard the news.

Wincing at her ear-piercing scream, I huddled farther into the corner of the airport where I was waiting for the next standby seat available to St. Louis. "Hi, Mom," I replied in a low voice, careful no one around could hear me. "Sorry I couldn't return your fourteen phone calls until now. I've had a rather busy morning."

"Oliver Bradley, I am in no mood for your smart mouth today," she snipped, and without even seeing her, I knew she had her left hand cocked on her hip. "You better start talking fast, son, because if I have to tell one person who calls that I don't know what the hell is going on, I may permanently remove your penis so you can never stick it inside any woman—married or not—again."

"Mom, please listen to me. I promise I can explain everything, but not over the phone." I paused, shuffling out of the way as several people passed by to the gate waiting area. "Look, I'm at the airport now, waiting for a flight so I can come there for a while, until everything dies down. Once I'm home, I'll tell you everything, but I just wanted to check on you guys and let you know I'm on my way. When I have a definite flight, I'll text you the info."

She relayed what I said to my dad then got back on the phone. "What do you want me to say to the news-people who keep calling and asking for an interview? It's crazy, Oliver. We can't turn the TV on without seeing your face. What's gonna happen with your job? Are you gonna move back home? What if her husband tries to kill you?"

"Stop with the dramatics, Ma. Come on. Just don't answer the phone if you don't know who it is, and don't answer the door until I get there. I honestly have no idea what's gonna happen with anything—her, my job—it's all up in the air, but whatever happens, I'll get through it. One day at a time. Just like we did with Dad. For right now, though, I need you to trust me and support me on this. Okay?"

"Okay, Ollie," her voice softened. "I'm just worried about you. I get all Momma Bear when people talk bad about my kids, and I didn't know what was going on, which made me freak out a little. But I do know you love her after the way you talked about her at Christmas, so you do whatever you think is the right thing. Your dad, your sisters, and I always have your back."

Exhaling a sigh of relief, I whispered, "Thanks, Mom. I love you. I'll text you soon."

"Love you too."

I disconnected the call and scanned the waiting area, searching for a place to sit where no one would pay much attention to me. The place was rather full, leaving only a handful of empty chairs for me to choose from. With my baseball cap pulled low over my eyes, I moved toward the one farthest from the main walkway and on the end of a row. The seat next to it was occupied by a little girl, maybe five or six years old, traveling with whom I assumed was her mom, both seemingly engrossed in their tablets. Figuring the child would probably pay me little mind, I sat down, offered a polite smile in their general direction without making eye contact, and then twisted my body away from them. With my legs angled toward the window, I kept my gaze focused low as I pretended to read a random book I'd snagged at the gift shop. The last thing I wanted was to be recognized as the guy who had destroyed Clutch Cassidy's marriage, and if the Patriots ended up losing the Super Bowl, the guy who cost the city of Boston their championship. Especially while I was still *in* Boston, where they might've considered reinstating public flogging just for me.

Blankly staring down at the first page, I zoned out as I ran through the checklist in my mind of everything I needed to do, trying my best to keep the emotions at bay. The whirlwind of unexpected events that morning had turned my world upside down. From Seth's wake-up visit, to sneaking out of Monroe's house, then hastily throwing a bunch of clothes in a duffel bag and getting dropped off at the departure area, my brain was on autopilot, performing the necessary actions, but remaining emotionally numb throughout the process. I couldn't allow myself to feel, because that most likely would've led to a meltdown of epic proportions, and that helped no one.

"I want ice cream, Mommy. Can we go get it now?" I heard the little girl say, but didn't pay much attention as my phone vibrated in my pocket, alerting me of an incoming text. Hopeful it would be from Monroe, now that I knew she had gotten a replacement phone, I hastily fished it out and read the message.

> *Allison: I just spoke with Monroe, so I'm up to speed on everything. I'm flying out to Boston ASAP to see how I can help. You take care of yourself right now, and we'll talk later.*

Unsure how to interpret her tone, I started to type out a reply, but my phone buzzed again.

Allison: And in case you're stressing, I'm not upset with either of you, nor am I really surprised, but Mending Hearts has to remain my top priority, and right now, it's a mess. I've got nearly fifty kids depending on me to act in their best interest. I'm praying it works out for all of us.

A small portion of me relaxed after reading her second message, finding some comfort in knowing that my boss and mentor didn't completely hate my guts for jeopardizing everything she'd worked her entire adult life for. I must admit I wasn't so sure I would've been as understanding as she was, but I was thankful nonetheless.

Me: Thank you. I'll keep you updated with where I am and anything of note as this plays out. At airport now, headed to my parents.

Dropping my phone back in my pocket, I returned my gaze to the book and stared at the words *Chapter One* for I don't know how long, lost in thought about how Monroe was holding up, wishing I was there with her. As much as I'd grown to like and respect Seth in the short amount of time we'd spent together, I couldn't help but think it should've been me there comforting her through that tumultuous day, not to mention I felt a little bit like a pussy not manning up and confronting Colin myself.

A sudden gasp followed by an icy cold sensation on my thigh startled me from my thoughts, and instinctively, my eyes snapped over to my leg to see what had happened. Before my brain could make sense of the frozen orange blob sitting atop my jeans, I got a whiff of the intoxicating citrus scent that made my heart swell and my stomach flip. The scent that I wanted to smell on her skin every night when I fell asleep and the same one I wanted to wake up to each morning when I rolled over and buried my face in her pillow, trying to drown out her terrible singing while she dressed.

Cutting my attention over to the small child with big broken-hearted tears rolling down her cheeks and an empty orange cream-sicle container in her hands, I smiled for the first time all day. A real, true, honest-to-God smile.

The one thing I had been praying for all day was a sign, some sort of direction on what the right thing to do was. For her. For me. For *us*.

And the answer had literally just fallen into my lap.

"I'm sorry, Sir. I didn't mean to," she sniffled.

"No worries, princess. Nothing that can't be fixed," I said softly as I grabbed my wallet, pulled out a five-dollar bill, and handed it to her. It was the least I could do, since God had sacrificed her treat to show me my path. "Luckily, I've got a change of clothes in my bag here, and you can take that to go get another ice cream, if your mom says it's okay."

As she twisted around to ask her mom's permission, I stood up and grabbed my duffel, not caring in the least that I had an amoeba-shaped wet spot on my pants. The girl and her mother both thanked me and apologized, and again, without meeting either of their gazes, I told them it was no big deal and excused myself to change. And eventually, I did . . . once I was safely back in my apartment that gratefully still hadn't been discovered by the outside world, a mystery I could only assume was because the lease was in Allison's name and not mine.

After calling my mom back to tell her about the change of plans, I decided not to alert Monroe or Seth right away about my decision to stay. I wasn't quite sure what my plan was yet, but I knew I needed to be in Boston for whenever it was revealed to me. So while I waited, I made myself a bowl of Captain Crunch and chocolate milk and watched Grease for the 28,517th time, confident my Rizzo would be next to me for the 28,518th.

chapter
thirty-two

"I thought
as the sun
lifted once
more from
the sea,
of how truly
heartbreaking
it is that we
all feel so heavy,
and yet,
somehow,
so damn
empty."
–Christopher Poindexter

MONROE

I COULDN'T STOP staring at the clock on the microwave, the numbers displaying a countdown on a ticking time bomb. Colin was due to walk through the door at any minute, and I was a fucking wreck. I had no idea what to expect, what he was going to say. When Seth had called and woken him up with the news of everything, preparing him for what awaited him once he left his hotel room, Colin had refused to speak to me, telling Seth it was best if he had some time to cool down and work through his anger first. Although it stung, I couldn't blame him much. He'd been blindsided by the entire thing and was probably in a state of shock.

"You still haven't heard back from the security company?" Seth asked, glancing over his shoulder at me from where he stood at the stove, cooking tomato soup and grilled cheese sandwiches for us. I'd told him repeatedly I wasn't hungry, knowing if I tried to put anything in my mouth, it would only come right back up. But he wouldn't take no for an answer, and I didn't have the energy to argue with him.

I looked down to the kitchen island at the replacement phone Seth had picked up for me when he'd snuck Oliver out earlier, ensuring I hadn't missed a call, then shook my head. "No, not yet."

The representative had said it would take some time for them to review the feed, but I thought we'd have definitely heard something after almost four hours and have at least something positive to tell Colin when he arrived. Unfortunately, that wasn't the case.

"What about Oliver? Any update from him?" he probed.

Sighing, I pulled up the text history. "The last message he sent was that he was at the airport on standby for the next flight to St. Louis to go talk to his parents. He said the security officer did a double-take when he checked his ID, but he wasn't sure if it was because he recognized his name, or how different he looks without a beard and with his hair pulled up in a hat. Other than that, he hasn't been recognized."

"Good," Seth nodded, "though I'm sure it won't take the vultures long to find him, if they're not waiting on him already."

I shuddered at the thought of the paparazzi stalking Oliver and his family. He didn't deserve this. They didn't deserve this. I never meant for anyone to get hurt; I just fell in love and became blind to everything else. I acted selfishly, and now others were paying the price.

"I can't believe this is happening," I whispered for at least the hundredth time that morning, rubbing my fingers in tiny circles against my throbbing temples. "What have I done?"

Shooting me a warning glare, Seth plated the food, carried it over to the island, and plopped down on the barstool next to me.

"You gotta stop with the blame thing, Roe," he scolded in a fatherly tone. "What's done is done. There's no changing it. Plus, you didn't do anything wrong, nothing that Colin hasn't done. You were inside your own home. Now, we need to focus on what we can do to move forward."

"There's nothing we can do!" I exclaimed, growing exasperated with his stay-positive attitude. "I'm a prisoner inside this house. There are now over ten uniformed police officers staked out around the property to keep the thousands of reporters and photographers from nearly sieging the place. I'm scared to death to turn on the television or get online to see what other pictures are floating around out there. Whoever took these didn't just get one shot while they were there. And Lord knows they're all ready to burn me at the stake with a scarlet A around my neck. At least not until Colin comes home or we hear something from the surveillance people. And meanwhile, I just have to sit here and worry if Oliver and his family are safe. Oh, and let's not forget there's a thirteen-year-old girl lying in a coma, fighting for her life at Boston Children's, who needs me more than anything right now!"

Before he had a chance to respond, the sound of a disturbance outside caught our attention and we simultaneously stood up and moved to the living room, where we'd closed all of the shutters and drapes, to hear better through the walls. The chorus of muffled shouts and ruckus grew louder and louder until the front door flew open and Colin stepped inside the house. And he was pissed.

Slamming the door, he glowered at both me and Seth, nostrils flaring. "Do you have any idea what I just went through to get home?" he roared, dropping his duffel bag on the tile then stalking toward us. "A police escort! I've had a police escort from the moment I left my hotel room this morning because of all of this. This is insanity. My phone has rang nonstop since I woke up, and they're not calling to congratulate me about the game yesterday. My parents are freaking out, and the team . . ." He stopped right in front of me, pinning me with his furious gaze, and crossed his arms over his chest. "I've finally reached my ultimate goal of being a starting quarterback in a Super Bowl, and now, instead of being able to enjoy any of it, I'm gonna spend the next two weeks fielding questions about you sleeping around behind my back. Do you have any idea what you've done?"

My legs wobbled and my eyes filled with tears, but I held my ground, refusing to back away. Colin would never physically hurt me, and there was nothing he could say that could make me feel any worse than I already did. I'd already hit rock bottom.

"Look, I know you're mad—" I started.

"*Mad?!*" he shouted, cutting me off. "Monroe, *mad* is only the tip of the iceberg of what I'm feeling right now. If I was just *mad* about something, I'd yell about it for a few minutes, we'd make up, and then we'd go on about our normal lives. But this . . . what you've done . . . it's devastating in the most literal sense of the word. Not only did you lie to me for who knows how long about Oliver, but with your carelessness and irresponsible behavior, you've ruined everything we've worked for. It's all gone! Poof! Just like that! And for what? Some guy who is going back to Chicago next month?"

"I did it because I love him!" I yelled back, curling my hands into angry fists at my sides. "I tried to tell you, but you got hurt and went to Miami, and then everything got crazy when you came back. But dammit, I love him so much, and he loves me!"

"*Love?!* Are you serious?" Dramatically twisting to look all around the main level of the house, he threw his hands up in the air when he came up empty on his search. "If he loves you so much, then where is he now? Let me guess—he loved you enough to get you naked and take you to bed, but not to stick around when the shit hit the fan, huh?"

"Colin, that's enough," Seth—who had stayed surprisingly silent until then—calmly cautioned him.

My husband's eyes blazed red as he turned to his ex. "This has absolutely nothing to do with you! It's between me and Monroe. You made the decision to not be a part of this when you stormed out of here a few months ago and wrote me off like I meant nothing."

"Are you delusional?! Do you even hear the words coming out

of your mouth?" Seth took a step forward, and Colin defensively bowed out his chest, but the smaller man was not intimidated nor deterred in his verbal assault. "Since the minute you walked through the door, the entire conversation has revolved around how this fiasco affects *you*. How awful *your* morning has been. How *your* parents are reacting. How it's ruined *your* goals. That's always the problem with you, Colin. It's always about you first and everyone else second. Years and years of being told you're the best thing since sliced bread has warped your mind, and I don't even think you realize what a selfish prick you've become."

"I am *not* a selfish prick," Colin gritted through a clenched jaw.

Unfazed, Seth pointed his finger in Colin's chest and kept talking. "Have you stopped even once to think about what Monroe must be going through right now? People are saying terrible, nasty things about her, calling her demeaning names and ridiculing her. Doesn't knowing she's not any of those horrible things make you want to defend her honor? This could just as easily have been you and me! Those pictures were taken right here in this house. She wasn't out in public, taking unnecessary chances with your marriage. She was doing the same thing you and I did for years! And then, knowing her past, knowing how big of a deal being intimate with someone must have been for her in the first place, for that private moment she shared with the one person she's fallen in love with to be broadcasted to the entire world? Do you have any fucking idea how humiliated and violated she must feel again? I'm guessing not, because if you had, when you walked through the door, you would've set your own shit aside for at least half a second and checked on her mental wellbeing."

Colin's gaze cut to me and he opened his mouth to say something, but I held my hand up in the air and shook my head. "Not now. Not after you were shamed into it. Plus, we need to focus on what happens next. Has Barry put out a press release yet? Allison is waiting for direction from me on what Mending Hearts' is going to say, and at some point, I need to make sure Oliver has safely made it to his parents' and check on JoJo. Have you—"

A phone ringing in the kitchen interrupted my thought and Seth took off to grab it, leaving Colin and me alone briefly. For the first time since we'd met, thick tension filled the air between us as we stood in uncomfortable silence. And I hated every second of it.

Thankfully, Seth reappeared after only a minute or so with a small glimmer of hope in his eye. "That was the security firm. They found footage of someone in the backyard earlier in the day yesterday, kneeling down at the back line of shrubbery and apparently cutting out a small opening, which they're assuming was for the camera lens to stick through. They're emailing the clips to us now so we can review them and see if we can identify who it was."

Momentarily forgetting the harsh words that had just been exchanged, we all hurried to the office on the second floor and waited for Colin to start up his computer and open the email. Finding out who was responsible for the nightmare I'd woken up in wouldn't do anything to make it all disappear, or even help figure out the best way to move forward, but I still wanted to know who had set me up. And I wanted to know how they knew about me and Oliver to begin with, as well as where we would be the previous night.

The video feed they sent was a little over five minutes long, but it was within the first five seconds, when the petite blonde wearing *my* number-three Cassidy jersey walked out of the house and toward the bushes, that all my questions were answered.

chapter thirty-three

"And I don't
want your Jesus.
I just want to
smoke my cigarettes
and drink my whiskey
and for you to love
me for the monster
I am."
—Christopher Poindexter

COLIN

"WHY?! WHY WOULD you do this to me? To my family?" I bellowed, running frustrated fingers through my short hair as I paced the parlor floor.

A nervous, defensive Effie was perched on the edge of the couch, her shifty eyes following my every move. "I thought I was helping you. Excuse me for thinking you'd want to know that your wife was cheating on you," she contended, keeping the attitude she'd had ever since realizing I'd called her over to confront her about what she'd done, and not because I wanted her sympathy and support.

"Helping?! Are you kidding me? How could you have possibly thought what is going on out there," I scowled and pointed toward the front door to where a reporter from every news station, magazine, and newspaper waited for a comment, "would be helpful for me in any way? I should be preparing for the biggest game of my life right now, but instead, it's the furthest thing from my mind, because I've got the mother of all shitstorms positioned right over my head, and it's all your doing. Singlehandedly, you've managed to ruin every aspect of my life, not to mention what you've done to Monroe and her career!"

"Fuck Monroe!" she spat, leaping to her feet as angry tears spilled down her cheeks. "Fuck her and her lying, cheating ass! She's the one who did this, not me! You may not realize it yet, but I did you and the rest of the world a favor by showing everyone what kind of awful, deceitful person she really is!"

I stilled as rage burned inside of me. "Careful, Effie," I warned ominously. "She's still my wife, and you will not disrespect her in our house."

"No!" she shouted, marching up to me and beating her fists on my chest. "I won't be careful! This shit needs to be said. She pretends to be Mother Fucking Teresa, helping all the unfortunate kids and putting on this fake-ass act so everybody thinks she's so wonderful, when the truth is she's a user and a fame-hungry whore, just like her mother was! How can you sit here and defend her after seeing those pictures? What other evidence do you need, Colin? Your marriage is a sham! I know the timing may be shitty, but you deserved to know the truth so you don't waste another minute on that bitch and you can move on with someone who truly loves you. Someone like me!"

Grabbing her hands so she couldn't hit me again, I gently pushed her away from me, exercising every bit of self-control I owned not to explode and say things I couldn't take back. Her declaration of love wasn't a big surprise to me; I'd known since we were kids that she always wanted more from our relationship, but never once had I given her any reason to think there would be a chance for that. We were friends, always just friends, and I thought when she finally found someone, she'd realize it had always just been a silly little crush. I never in a million years thought it would come to this.

"Effie, I'm going to say this one time, and one time only, so listen closely," I stated, my voice eerily calm. "I do not love you like that. I will never love you like that. Before all of this, I valued your friendship very much, and I would've been first in line to help or support you. But now . . ." I paused, glancing over at the staircase where I knew Monroe and Seth were eavesdropping from the second floor, and then returned my attention to her. " . . . now the only thing I feel toward you is disgust and disappointment. In time, I'm sure I'll find it in my heart to forgive you, but I will never forget the pain you have caused both me and Monroe, nor the destruction your actions have resulted in. If your true goal was to help free me from this 'sham of a marriage' as you call it, you should've come straight to me and told me what was going on. Instead, not only have you humiliated me and my wife on a global level, but your selfish, thoughtless, inexcusable actions are negatively affecting hundreds of others, including Oliver and his family, the entire Patriots organization, and most importantly, all of the Mending Hearts kids who may no longer have a home to go to."

Deciding to take a different approach, she reached out to touch my arm and pouted her bottom lip out like a child. "But Colin—"

"No!" I moved away from her, shaking my head emphatically. "We're through here, Effie. I want you to leave now, and I don't ever want to discuss this again. Whatever friendship we had is gone, and there is zero percent chance of it ever returning. My parents will know the part you played in this entire debacle, so it's doubtful you'll ever be welcomed at my family's functions again. You can choose how you want to explain that to your own parents. I really don't care. I think it goes without saying you no longer have a job, and if I were you, I'd probably consider relocating to another city. When this all blows over with me and Monroe, and it *will* blow over, I don't imagine you're gonna have a whole lot of people standing in your corner."

"You asshole!" she spat, staring at me as if she could honestly not believe the words coming out of my mouth. "How could you choose her over me? She's nothing but a—"

"Leave now!" I shouted at the top of my lungs, not caring who heard.

The sound of her hand cracking across my cheek echoed through the room moments before the front door opened and slammed shut, but I only felt relief. At least a little bit. The hardest part was still to come.

LATER THAT AFTERNOON, once Effie had left and I'd eaten and showered, I found myself alone in my bedroom while Monroe and Seth holed themselves up in hers, neither of them my biggest fan at the moment. The chaos of the day seemed to finally be winding down a little—at least within the confines of the house, as I knew that wasn't the case if I stepped outside, or turned on the TV or internet, but at least inside, a temporary reprieve from the pandemonium had settled in.

It was there, in the quiet solitude, I was forced to face the man in the mirror. And to be quite honest, I wasn't sure I liked what I saw.

Thinking back on what Seth had said to me—not only earlier that day, but in the last argument we'd had that ultimately ended things between us—I focused on words like *controlling, jealous,* and *selfish.* I never considered myself to be any of those things; after all, I was one of the few good guys left. *Right?*

I didn't drink alcohol, do drugs, gamble, or get in trouble with the law. I didn't party or involve myself in anything that would tarnish my name or reputation. Whether I was at practice or playing in a game, I gave 110% effort and always supported my teammates. During my off-time, I spent hours upon hours volunteering myself for various charities and children's organizations, and I did it not because I thought it made me look good, but because it brought me real happiness to help people who weren't as blessed as I was. Even though I didn't attend mass as regularly as I had when I was a kid, I continued to have a strong spiritual relationship with God through daily prayer. So how was it Seth, someone who claimed to love me, could say such negative things about my character?

My thoughts turned to the separate relationships I had with him and Monroe, and it was there I began to stumble. There was no question my love for them both was unconditional—different for each, but without qualification nonetheless. The depth of feelings I had for them superseded that of all others, my parents included, which was what made it so hard for me at first to understand why they—Seth and Monroe—were the ones upset and disappointed in me, especially when it wasn't anything I had done to cause the upheaval.

But as the minutes ticked by and I delved deeper into the dynamic of our threesome, the rose-colored haze started to clear and I was left staring at a seriously dysfunctional picture that centered around me. For years and years, Seth had deprived himself of a serious relationship with either another man or a woman because of his love for me, hanging on to the thread of hope I'd extend each time I felt him slipping away. I wasn't willing to publicly claim my love for him—even though he'd insisted numerous times that for me, he'd take that leap of faith—and yet, despite my reluctance to give him all of me, I didn't want him to find a more fulfilling, all-encompassing love with someone else either.

Then, with Monroe, I'd always taken for granted that because of her vile, unspeakable past, she'd always be completely dedicated to me, and me alone. Instead of encouraging her to seek treatment that would help her heal and work through her issues with intimacy like I should've done, I was content to keep her broken and vulnerable, so she would be dependent on me and stay by my side. The time she first told me about kissing Oliver, my knee-jerk reaction to make her feel ashamed was solely because I felt threatened she'd find in him what I couldn't give her. And earlier, when she claimed she loved him, all I could think about was how that affected me and my life, so I mocked her feelings and purposely casted doubt if he really loved her too.

They were right. I was controlling, jealous, and more than anything, a selfish prick. And that wasn't even taking into account the high-handed, narcissistic way I'd behaved that day with the entire picture-leak disaster. For as much as I claimed to love my wife, not once had I bothered to consider how devastated and violated she must've felt as the entire world witnessed a private, intimate moment with someone she loves and then shredded her apart for doing the same thing I had done with Seth hundreds of times. I hadn't come to her defense. I hadn't tried to comfort her. All I had done was tear her down even more, because I couldn't see past how the entire situation screwed with the perfect life I'd created.

Wow. For as much time as I spent being a selfless role model to everyone else around me, I was a complete asshole to the people I cared about the most. The ones who had always sacrificed their own happiness for mine.

Scorching heat surged through my body, my chest tightening and my head pounding, as the overwhelming realizations stormed down on me. A thick knot formed in the back of my throat, woven with fibers of guilt and self-loathing, as beads of sweat dotted my brow. Bile burned as it shot up my chest and, afraid I was going to be sick, I stood up from my bed to head toward the bathroom, but as I did, the strangest thing happened. For whatever reason, I glanced downward, and the old, ragged, black leather Bible I'd kept on my nightstand for as long as I could remember caught my eye, almost as if it was calling out to me.

Reaching out to grab it, I lowered myself back on the mattress and suddenly my stomach settled as I began to cool down. When I set the worn book on the bed in front of me, it automatically opened to where the spine had been creased from the countless number of times I had read the highlighted scripture in the eighth book of John, a series of verses I could recite in my sleep.

"So Jesus said to the Jews who had believed Him, 'If you abide in my word, you are truly my disciples, and you will know the truth, and the truth will set you free.'"

I couldn't begin to tell you how many times in high school and college I'd stayed up late into the night scouring my Bible for verses that would help me understand why I was having the feelings and urges I was having for Seth. All my life, I'd been taught that homosexuality was wrong, one of the dirtiest of sins, so when I began to fall in love with my best friend in a way I'd been told was against God's will, I naturally panicked, freaked out, and then tried to find an explanation for it other than I was evil. And I always came back to that verse. God's truth would set me free.

The gender of the person who I loved had no bearing on whether or not I believed Jesus Christ was the Son of God. Sleeping with Seth didn't mean I lacked faith that he died on the cross for our sins and resurrected three days later, promising to return one day to take His people home. And lastly, wanting to share my life with Seth, both publicly and privately, had no effect on me being a kind, respectable, productive member of society, who spread love and the word of God to others.

Yes, I was also well aware of the passages in the Bible that discussed homosexuality, referring to it as an abomination that deserves the death penalty. That same Old Testament Law Code also included eating pork or shellfish and charging interests on loans as acts punishable by death, which is why in Hebrews it says the old law is obsolete and aging. So what was God's truth? Did He judge my love for another man differently than He judged people who ate bacon or lobster and those who used credit cards? Would He prefer I live a lie for the rest of my life, pretending to be someone I wasn't? Because last time I checked, that was a sin too. Or would He prefer I live a life full of love and happiness, spreading His word to those who did not yet believe?

I didn't know the answers, but the bottom line was I believed the final judgement of what I did on Earth would be between me and my maker when I died, but for my life until that point I hadn't lived my truth because I was too afraid of what everyone else would think. I thrived on acceptance—from my parents, from coaches and teammates, and from the public—and it was the fear of their rejection that had led me to taking advantage of and hurting the ones I loved, even if it wasn't my intention.

I've always heard of people talking about defining moments in your life, and how you either define the moment or let the moment define you. I'd always thought that the times I was on the football field, making a big play or winning a game for my team, were my defining moments. They showed how well I reacted under pressure; it was how I earned the nickname "Clutch." But as I sat there on my bed, reading and rereading John 8:31–32, it became clear *this* was my defining moment.

And for once in my life, I was going to come through in the clutch for the two people who deserved it most. And the truth of our marriage was going to set Monroe and Seth free.

chapter
thirty-four

"I closed my
eyes
softly and fell
in love with the
way I
remembered you:
body, soul,
and all."
–Christopher Poindexter

MONROE

DRESSED IN A gray turtleneck sweater and black wool slacks that matched the dark circles under my eyes, I lumbered down the two flights of stairs from my bedroom to the living room, where Colin, Seth, Barry, and Allison waited for me to go over the details of the press conference that was scheduled to start in twenty minutes. It had been a little over twenty-four hours since the shit hit the fan, and though the last thing I wanted to do was step outside my house in front of millions of people watching online or on TV to judge me even more than they already had, I agreed to do it, because Colin had begged me to be by his side so we could appear as a united front.

We still had yet to talk about what would happen next, regarding our marriage and my relationship with Oliver, but Seth had advised me to give it a few days, until everything calmed down a bit before tackling that hurdle. I missed Oliver incredibly and hated that he couldn't be with me as I dealt with everything, but I understood why, and for his safety, I didn't ask him to come back. Though I picked up my phone to do just that at least a dozen times.

"Hey, honey, you look beautiful," Allison said as she greeted me with a warm embrace.

Seeing her wear a beanie over her bald head made me smile a sad smile, and I hated that my and Oliver's actions forced her to have to deal with such negative publicity for Mending Hearts. She and I had talked at length the night before when she'd arrived in Boston, and leaving out the Colin-and-Seth portion of the story, I'd told her everything about my and Oliver's relationship, from the initial connection we'd felt at the MH gala in August, up until the morning before, when Seth had awoken us with the tabloids. Like a good friend, she didn't pretend to have the answers or guarantee me everything would work out perfectly the way I wanted, but what she did do was truly listen and ensure me that it would all work out the way it was supposed to, and we'd all move forward regardless.

"Morning, Allie," I replied, attempting a weak smile.

The three men moved toward me simultaneously, each one hugging me good morning. I feebly returned the gesture; my heart really wasn't into much of anything.

"Do you want a granola bar or something before we get started?" Colin asked, cocking his head in the direction of the kitchen. "I'll grab whatever you want."

I shook my head and shifted over next to Seth, who looped his arm around my shoulder. "No, thank you. I'm not very hungry."

"Okay, Roe. Just let me know if you need anything," he replied, his harsh tone from yesterday having been replaced by the gentle Colin I remembered.

Barry cleared his throat and stepped toward the center of the room, garnering all of our attention. "All right, I just want to run down what's going to happen with everyone really quick before we go out there," he began, quickly glancing at each of us. "There is a small podium with a microphone set up out front. Police officers

are stationed around the perimeter of the podium to prevent anyone who decides today is the day to act like a crazy asshole. Colin
and Monroe will follow me up to the microphone, and Seth and
Allison will stand off to the side, where Mr. and Mrs. Cassidy are already waiting. I will explain to the small city of media that this press
conference is basically a statement from Colin and that he will not
be taking questions. When Colin finishes speaking, you will all be
ushered back inside the house, and the police department will see to
it that the area is cleared in a timely manner. Does anyone have any
questions?"

We all shook our heads and murmured a cohesive, "No."

My pulse raced and my palms were clammy. I didn't know how
I could face these people after what they'd seen of me. Suddenly, my
turtleneck and long pants didn't cover enough. I needed a scarf too.

"Excellent." He smiled and looked over at Colin. "I know you
wanted a few minutes alone with Monroe before we start, so I'm
going to go ahead and walk Seth and Allison out. I'll be waiting just
outside the front door for whenever you're ready."

My husband nodded and thanked him, and then once they were
all gone and it was just me and him inside, Colin coiled his arms
around my shoulders and crushed me up against his body, making
me forget about the scarf. "Oh, baby girl," he whispered into my
hair. "I love you so much, and I'm so sorry for everything. There's
no excuse for the way I've taken you for granted or how selfish I've
been in this relationship, but I want you to know I plan on making
up for it, and I hope one day you'll be able to forgive me."

Leaning back slightly, but still holding onto my arms, his glassy
eyes met mine and he treated me to one of his most endearing, boyish grins. "I don't know how I got so lucky that day in Algebra to
end up sitting next to you, but I want you to know not another day
will go by that I don't thank my lucky stars for having you in my
life. I can't even pretend to understand how this entire disaster has
affected you, and I'm sorry I wasn't more focused on you yesterday,
but I'm gonna do my best to make it all better now."

Confused about what he meant exactly, I opened my mouth to

ask, but he placed a quick kiss to my forehead, grabbed my hand, and dragged me to the front door before I could get a word out. As he opened the door, the bright sun reflected against the fresh layer of powdered snow on the ground, momentarily blinding me as I shuffled my feet outside. Keeping my gaze downward, I focused on where our fingers intertwined, praying for the strength to get through the next half-hour.

I had no idea what Colin was planning on saying, but I assumed it was going to be along the lines of asking for privacy while our family worked through this difficult situation. It wouldn't stop the speculative reports, but it would get rid of most of those who'd been camped outside overnight. And then we could figure out our next step. I didn't have a whole lot of time to process his heartfelt apology at the door before being thrust into the spotlight, other than it gave me a brief glimpse of the Colin I always knew and loved.

Leading me over to the podium Barry had mentioned, Colin squeezed my hand when we stopped just behind the Patriot's PR Director and waited for him to say his part. I didn't look up at him. I couldn't. Not yet. I didn't want them to see me.

A minute or so later, he tugged on my arm, alerting me it was time to move again. I scuffled forward with him until there we were front-and-center, the focal point of a sea of people. All who had seen me naked.

Colin stepped up to the microphone to make his statement, releasing my hand in the process, and nausea rolled threw me. Closing my eyes, I inhaled a deep breath through my nose, counted to five, and blew it out. Then, I heard Colin's voice. And I focused on his words.

"I have to be honest with you guys. Doing something like this is even harder than it looks," he began with a light chuckle, nervously fidgeting with his collar as he flashed a charming smile toward the crowd. "Last night, I stayed up late working on what I was going to say today, writing and rewriting draft after draft, not happy with how any of them sounded. So I decided, against the strong recommendation of my public relations director," he tossed a sly smirk over at Barry, "to come out here and speak from my heart, without a script. I'm gonna ask you to bear with me if I ramble a little."

He paused to take a drink of water from the bottle sitting on the podium before continuing. "You know, sometimes life throws you a curve ball that completely blindsides you and knocks you on your butt, and when it happens, you think the effects are going to be devastating. Earth-shattering. That you'll never recover. Everything you've worked so hard for vanishes . . . all of it just gone in the blink of an eye. That's how I felt when I woke up yesterday morning. It was as if I'd just been run over by an eighteen-wheeler, who then stopped, put the rig in reverse, and plowed over me again. I thought all hope was lost, and I had no idea what I was going to do.

"But what I didn't realize at the time was that curveball was part of God's plan for me. He knew I needed to get knocked down, to remind me not only to be appreciative of the things I have, but also that He was in control and not me. Now, I know I've always been very open about my faith and my spirituality, and when I mention God's name, I take the risk of losing some of you because you think, 'Oh man, here he goes again with that stuff,' but stay with me until I finish this time. I promise it'll be worth it."

Glancing over at me, he winked then turned back to the microphone. I had no idea what he was doing, or what he was getting at, and I wasn't brave enough to make eye-contact with any of the reporters to see if they appeared to be equally confused.

"So after everything happened yesterday and I was back at home, I found myself with quite a bit of time alone to do some much-needed soul-searching and to really evaluate what my purpose was in this life. Through reading scripture and extensive prayer, I came to realize I wasn't anything like the person who I pretend to be, the person you guys see when I'm out on the field or volunteering at the neighborhood soup kitchen. Don't get me wrong; I'm not saying that playing football isn't my passion or that I don't find immense joy helping others in need, because I do, and they're both a huge part of who I am. But just like every single one of you, when I come home each day, the minute I step through that door and inside my house," he pointed behind him, "I'm free to just be me, without anyone watching what I'm doing or passing judgement . . . or so I had fooled myself into believing."

The smile on his face faded as he narrowed his brow. A chill ran down my spine.

"You see, what I lost sight of somewhere along the way is I believe the only one whose judgement ultimately matters is God's, and He can see me all the time. There's no hiding from Him. The person I am behind closed doors is just as much a part of my character as the football player and the volunteer is, and if my peers choose to judge me for who I am and what I believe, then that's on them and not me. All I can do is try each and every day to be the best Christian I can be, and when my time comes, hope that I did enough to pass His judgement."

He stopped and took a deep breath, priming himself for whatever he was about to say. My own body stiffened in preparation for the blow.

"Last night, after I made the realization that I've been so caught up in what other people think about me and the pretense of this perfect life I live, I also realized that while doing this, I've been hurting and taking advantage of the people I love the most. And that's not who I want to be." Shaking his head with disappointment, he sighed softly.

"So now you're all probably wondering how any of this ties into leaked intimate photos of my wife with another man, and I'll tell you." He looked over at me and smiled my favorite smile, then pulled me next to him. "Monroe Cassidy is my closest friend in the entire world and I love her more than she will ever know, but what no one else knows until now is that we are husband and wife in name alone . . . because I'm gay."

I gasped as my hands flew to my face and tears instantly started spilling down my cheeks. *He did it. Oh, my God, he really did it.*

When tapping the microphone in an attempt to get the attention of the frantic media didn't work, Colin raised his hand in the air, and surprisingly, everyone quieted down.

"I understand there are many questions you all have, but as Mr. Maxwell indicated at the beginning of the press conference, we will not be answering any today. However, there are a few more things I'd like to address before I wrap this up and leave you all to have a field day seeing who can come up with the wittiest headline for my coming out speech," he joked lightheartedly.

"First, please take down and stop running all of the photos of Monroe and the man who she loves dearly, out of respect for their privacy and because they were taken illegally. Also, if you or your publication were one of those who called into question the working environment that Mending Hearts harbors, the not-for-profit they both dedicate their lives to, I'm requesting that you print a retraction. Mending Hearts is highly dependent on donations and sponsorships, and without these houses, many of the abused children who live there will be forced back into the system. And finally, with Super Bowl coming up in less than two weeks, it is my hope that during that time I can focus my attention on preparing to defeat a tough Seattle team and bringing a championship back to the city of Boston. Once that has passed, a Q&A-style press conference will be set up, probably at the team's facility, in which I will further expound on the details of my private life and how I view my sexuality in the context of my spiritual beliefs. But until then, I'd appreciate if we can keep the questions centered around football and the upcoming game."

Barry approached the podium and nodded his head at Colin, giving him the signal that he would take over from there. Pivoting on his heel, Colin grabbed my hand and tugged gently, leading me in the direction of our house. I stumbled over my own feet, still too in shock to move, but quickly recovered without falling. As soon as we walked inside, he picked me up, cradling me in his arms, and spun us around the living room with a gigantic smile plastered on his face.

"What are you doing?" I squealed, looking up at him in bewilderment. "And what in the world did you just do? Your parents are going to kill you."

"I told the truth, so I could set you free, Roe," he replied as he lowered me to the ground, cupping my face in his gigantic hands and kissing both of my cheeks. "It was something I should've done a long time ago so we both can live and love without hiding. And don't worry about my parents. I called them last night and told them what I was going to do. I still need to have a long sit-down with them, but all in due time. They ensured me last night they love me unconditionally, no matter what they thought about the decisions I make in my life."

"And Seth? Did he know you were gonna do that?"

Colin shook his head and looked down at the floor sheepishly. "No. I know I've put him through a lot over the years, and I'm not sure if it's gonna be too little too late or if he'll be interested in trying again. For real this time."

My heart overflowed with joy and hope for the two of them. I had faith they'd find their way back to each other.

"Hey, aren't you gonna call Oliver to make sure he was watching?" he asked, giving me a curious look. "I figured that'd be the first thing you wanted to do when you got inside."

Nodding, I lifted up on my tiptoes and kissed the dimple on his chin. "I'm about to go do that, but I just wanted to tell you how proud I am of you and how much I love you. Just because we're not married or don't live together doesn't mean I won't be here for you."

He grinned. "To the very end?"

"To the very end."

As I bounced up the stairs to my bedroom, eager to call Oliver and find out how quickly he could get to me or I could get to him, I heard the front door open and shut, followed by a chorus of voices I assumed to be Barry, Allison, and possibly Seth. Even though I wanted to talk to all of them about what happened, Oliver was my first priority.

Slipping into my room, I grabbed my phone off my dresser, hurriedly found his name in my contacts, and connected the call. I paced the floor next to my bed as it rang and rang, but it eventually went to his voicemail. Irritated, I waited about thirty seconds then tried again. Same result.

How was he not waiting on my call? He knew the first thing I'd do once the press conference was over would be to call him, especially with what it meant for the two of us. But he still didn't answer.

Nearly ten minutes and twelve unanswered calls later, I was on the brink of tears. I didn't understand why he wasn't picking up, and with each passing minute he didn't call back, a pocket of self-doubt began to form inside of me.

A knock on the door startled me, and though I didn't want to be rude, I needed a few more minutes alone. "I'll be downstairs in just a little bit," I called out, hoping whoever it was would take the hint.

I picked up my phone to try him one last time before giving up for a while, but before I made the call, the person knocked again.

"Just a minute! I'm on a phone call and I'll be out shortly!" I yelled as I pressed Oliver's name on the screen with my shaky finger.

This time, when I heard the phone ring, it sounded like an echo effect. Like it was ringing inside my phone and outside of my door at the same time.

Confused, I rushed over to the door and threw it open, not knowing exactly what—or who—I expected to be there. But when my eyes landed on Oliver and all that dark, messy hair that I loved to pull, standing there holding a brown grocery sack, I gaped at him incredulously.

"What . . . how . . . when did you get here?" I finally managed to get one of my questions out.

His mouth curled up in a wicked grin. "I never left, Rizzo. I just couldn't, not when I knew you might need me," he replied.

"B-but you said you were at your parents," I contended.

"I know, and I'm sorry I lied." His smile disappeared. "I promise you right now that I won't ever do it again. I felt like such crap afterward, even though I knew I was doing it for you."

"So how did you know to be here? And what's in the bag?"

"Colin called me last night and told me what he was going

to do today so he asked me to be here for you," he answered matter-of-factly. "If you'll invite me in, I'll be happy to let you look inside, and if you're lucky, I might even let you kiss me too."

Laughing, I shook my head, still in utter disbelief he was there, and motioned for him to come inside my room where he sat down on my bed and waited for me. I hopped up on the mattress next to him, giddy to the point of ridiculousness, and began to go through what he brought.

"Peanut Butter Captain Crunch," I announced as I removed the orange box from the sack then continued to do the same for the rest of the stuff. "Chocolate milk. Popcorn. *Grease* DVD. And what's this?" I questioned, pulling a shiny metal key out of the very bottom and holding it up between us.

His amber eyes sparkled when I peered over at him expectantly. "It's a key."

"Yeah, I got that, Einstein," I joked nervously, wondering if I was reading too much into the object. "A key for what?"

"For the apartment I signed a year lease on first thing this morning."

My heart slammed against my chest as butterflies fluttered in my belly. "You're staying in Boston?"

Shaking his head, Oliver scooped me up and pulled me into his lap, crushing my lips with his in a kiss that left me little doubt to what his answer was. When we finally broke apart for air, he rubbed the end of his nose against mine and murmured, "And you got it wrong, silly girl. I'm not staying in Boston . . . *we* are."

epilogue

"in the end,
when our eyelids
find their
infinite darkness,
you will know
that our bodies
were tiny
universes,
and that I
loved you
with a thousand
seas."
—Christopher Poindexter

Seven Months Later
MONROE

"HAVE I MENTIONED how much I hate wearing heels?" I complained, peering down at my feet inside the pretty, sparkly blue torture devices that matched my evening gown.

Oliver, who looked downright delectable in his tux, chuckled as he stepped into the closet behind me and circled his arms around my waist, open-mouth kissing the side of my neck. "Only every time you put them on, Peaches."

Rolling my eyes at the absurd nickname, I twisted around in his embrace so I could see his handsome face and straighten his bow tie. "Next year, let's have this thing at the zoo or something, where we can wear shorts and tennis shoes."

"The zoo?" he asked, trying to keep a straight face. "Because nothing says 'Please donate money' quite like hairy, stinky elephant ass or monkeys flinging their shit at you. Maybe if we're really lucky, it'll be mating season for the giraffes, and we can all see what a four-foot erection looks like in action."

I swatted at his arm and shook my head. "Is that all you took away from that show the other night? The size of their penis?" I asked, referring to *Babies of the Serengeti- Giraffes*, an Animal Planet special we'd watched in bed a few nights before. Well, *I* had been watching the show, while Oliver played some game on his tablet. He hadn't been too impressed with the part about the males tasting the females' urine to determine if they were ovulating, so he'd tuned it out . . . or so I thought.

Humor danced in his eyes as he nodded. "Baby, a man hears the words *four-foot penis* and he takes note. That's some serious competition."

"Well, maybe you should've also taken note on the part where they said that up to 94% of giraffe sexual encounters are between two males," I mused, tapping the end of his nose with my finger. "So chances are, if you ever got to see one of those four-footers in action, you'd probably get to see two at the same time. I texted Colin and told him he should come back as a giraffe in his next life, but he told me he wasn't a fan of sleeping while standing."

He threw his head back with laughter then grabbed my shoulders and steered me out of the closet and into our bedroom. "As fascinating as I find this conversation about giraffes' genitalia and their progressive sexual behaviors, I'm nixing the zoo idea now. And if you don't stop talking about next year's gala, we're never gonna make it to *this* year's," he playfully slapped my ass, "so grab your purse, beautiful, and let's go. The driver just texted and he's downstairs."

I did a final check of my makeup and hair in the mirror before snatching my beaded clutch off the dresser, making sure I had everything I needed in it. "Okay, I'm ready," I announced with a smirk, "but for the record, I'm not giving up on the zoo thing. I think it has real potential."

Oliver grinned but said nothing. Holding out his arm toward me, I slipped my hand in his and allowed him to lead me out of our apartment and down to where a car awaited to take us to the Second Annual New England Mending Hearts Gala. During the short elevator ride to the first floor, I silently went over my speech in my head for at least the hundredth time that day. Even though I had grown accustomed to talking in front of groups of people over the previous year, it still made me a little nervous to have all those eyes trained directly on me. I'd mostly gotten over the fact that the vast majority of the world had seen me topless, and I rarely thought about it any longer on a day-to-day basis, but there were still times— particularly when speaking at a large event such as this one—when the self-doubt and insecurities would creep up and wrap themselves around my throat, cutting off my air supply.

"Come on, Slowpoke McGoke," Oliver prodded, gently tugging on my hand as we stepped off the elevator and into the lobby. "I've got a surprise for you."

"A surprise?" I parroted excitedly as fell in step next to him, forgetting about the building nerves in my stomach. "What kind of surprise?"

Ignoring my questions, he smiled roguishly while ushering me into the glass revolving door that led outside. As soon as my heels met the sidewalk in front of our building, I froze, slack-jawed and wide-eyed, staring in disbelief at the car parked at the curb directly in front of me.

"Oh, my God," I whispered, my vision blurring with the happy tears I couldn't stop. "How in the world . . ."

"You like it?" Pulling me toward the street, he beamed with pride as we approached the iconic vehicle. "It's the real Greased Lightning they used in the movie. Colin helped me locate it and get everything worked out, but I thought since this is the first anniversary of Rizzo and Sandy D. meeting, we should celebrate in style."

Unable to contain the overwhelming happiness bubbling up inside me, I threw my arms around his neck and peppered kisses all over his face. "You are the craziest, quirkiest, sweetest person I have ever met, and I thank God every day that you're mine. I love you so much, Ollie!" I exclaimed.

Laughter rumbled deep in his chest as he lifted me off the ground and twirled me in the air. "I love you too, beautiful girl. But it's still a no to the zoo."

OLIVER

THE TOP FLOOR of the Sixty State Street building was even more impressive than I'd remembered it from the year before. Crystal chandeliers, white twinkling lights, and the floor-to-ceiling wall of windows created the perfect ambiance for the perfect night with the perfect woman by my side. The car surprise had gone over better than I expected, as she didn't mention the wind from the convertible messing her hair up once on the drive over, and I only hoped the rest of my plan would follow suit.

"Hey, man, you ready for this?" Colin asked under his breath, sidling up next to me as I sat back and watched Monroe and Allison greet the guests.

Taking a sip of my cocktail, I nodded and glanced over at him. "As ready as I'll ever be. Is she here?"

"She's here, and everything's all set up," he assured me with a pat on the back. "Once you're in place, Seth will draw Monroe away from the party, saying he needs to speak to her privately about Effie's trial, and bring her to you."

I cringed, but didn't argue. Effie's trial wasn't something I liked to think about, especially not on a night that was supposed to be so positive, but I was happy that Monroe had agreed to press charges against the psychotic woman. Unfortunately, after the press conference where Colin had come clean to the world about his sexuality, Effie hadn't taken it so well and ended up taking out her frustrations with a golf club on the inside of the Mending Hearts house, which she still had a key to. When she had finished her handiwork, there wasn't a piece of furniture left intact or a wall that didn't have a hole in it. Over two months of work we'd put into setting the home up was demolished in less than two hours, but thankfully, when the word got out about what happened, volunteers from all over the area had shown up and pitched in to get the house cleaned up and refurnished just in time for Heather, Alex, and Aaron to move in on March first.

"Sounds good. As soon as she finishes her speech, I'll head that way and get ready," I told him, pushing aside the bad memory.

"Perfect."

An hour and a half later, I was outside on the rooftop deck, hiding in the shadows up against the building, when I heard Monroe and Seth's voices approaching. They walked out to the center of the small space, presumably talking about the trial, and on cue, Seth's phone rang and he excused himself to answer it, leaving her alone under the pale moonlight. Not wasting any time, fearful she might venture back inside and not wait for him, I made my move.

With my saxophone in hand, I began to play the opening chords of "When A Man Loves A Woman" as I strolled out toward her, reveling in the surprised expression on her face when she spun around and saw me. I continued playing as I approached her, and like the goofball she was, she began dancing around me wearing the biggest smile I'd ever seen. My heart was pounding so hard, so loud, that I honestly feared my chest my split right open.

The song came to an end and she stilled, her expectant gaze locked on me as she waited to see what I was going to do next. Carefully lying the instrument down next to me, I reached inside my pocket and fished out the small black velvet box then dropped to a knee in front of her, beaming up at her breathtaking face.

"Monroe, I know your divorce has only been final a little over a week, but I didn't want to take any chances that some other ya-hoo might flash his jazz hands in your direction tonight and steal you away before I could put a ring on it," I teased. "I've pulled out the stops tonight—the over-the-top car, the tuxedo, and even a little Michael Bolton in case you were on the fence about me. So I'm begging you, please do me the honor of making me the happiest man in the universe by saying you'll marry me."

Dropping to her knees next to me, fancy dress and all, she cupped my jaw in her petite hands and brushed her thumbs over my beard. "Only if you promise me that you'll never shave this off again or cut your hair short," she choked out through her tears.

"Promise!" I exclaimed as I engulfed her in my arms and claimed her mouth with mine.

The sound of someone clapping broke through our kiss and startled her, causing her to pull back to see who it was. I kept my eyes on Monroe's face as I watched her expression morph from confusion, to skepticism, to all-out exhilaration. Jumping up to her feet, she took off running in her heels to the young girl who was doing the same. The same young girl who was holding her court-signed papers that granted Mending Hearts' full custody of her, effective immediately.

JoJo was finally all Monroe's.

And Monroe was finally all mine.

about the author

ERIN NOELLE IS a Texas native, where she lives with her husband and two young daughters. While earning her degree in History, she rediscovered her love for reading that was first instilled by her grand-mother when she was a young child. A lover of happily-ever-afters, both historical and current, Erin is an avid reader of all romance novels. Most nights you can find her cuddled up in bed with her husband, her Kindle in hand and a sporting event of some sorts on television.

www.erinnoelleauthor.com

You can also connect with Erin on:
Facebook, Goodreads and Twitter.

books by
Erin Noelle

BOOK BOYFRIEND SERIES

Metamorphosis (Book Boyfriend Series 1)

Ambrosia (Book Boyfriend Series 2)

Euphoria (Book Boyfriend Series 3)

Timeless (Book Boyfriend Series 4)

LUMINOUS SERIES

Translucent (Luminous Book 1)

Transparent (Luminous Book 2)

DUSK TIL DAWN SERIES

When the Sun Goes Down (Dusk Til Dawn Book 1)

As the Dawn Breaks (Dusk Til Dawn Book 2)

A FIRE ON THE MOUNTAIN SERIES

Spark (A Fire on the Mountain Series 1)

Flame (A Fire on the Mountain Series 2)

STANDALONES

Surviving Us

MILF: Wrong Kind of Love

CO-WRITTEN

Conspire

acknowledgements

EACH OF THE books that I write is like one of my children and these people are the village that helps me raise them. Thank you all so much for everything you do and all of your support.

My kick-ass family

Jill Sava ~ the best assistant and friend in the whole wide world

Stacy Kestwick ~ my incredible CP and bestie

Chelle Northcutt ~ for your amazing insight and talking me off the ledge repeatedly

Hang Le ~ I still can't stop staring at this amazing cover

My betas ~ for keeping me on track and entertained with your shenanigans

Jammy Jean Lovers ~ 'Cause y'all are just fucking awesome

Kayla Robichaux ~ My awesome editor and Twinnie. I owe you big time.

Jenn Van Wyk ~ I still don't know how we did it, but thank you so much!

Jessica Prince ~ I'm the worst work-wife ever and yet, you still love me.

CM Foss ~ You're the best lap-dancer I know.

Natasha ~ how many books is this now?

Ever Afters ~ the most amazing reader group ever

Bloggers ~ The hardest working people in the business that get little credit and no pay. I greatly appreciate the time you spend reading, reviewing, and/or promoting the books we authors pour our heart and soul into. We couldn't do it without you.

Readers ~ I have the most fantastic readers imaginable. You're the main reason I continue doing this! Love you all!

Giraffes ~ because . . . *four-foot penises*